Meeting Mr. Anderson
Elle Nicoll

Rose Hope Publishing

Copyright © 2021 By Elle Nicoll

All rights reserved.

Visit my website at: https://www.ellenicollauthor.com

Cover Design: Abi at Pink Elephant Designs

Editing: Kimberly Dawn Editing

No part of this book may be reproduced or transmitted in any form or by any means, electronical or mechanical, including photocopying, recording, or by any information storage and retrieval system without the written permission of the author, except for the use of brief quotations in a book review.

This book is a work of fiction. Names, characters, places, and incidents are either products of the author's imagination or are used fictitiously. Any resemblance to actual persons, living or dead, events, or locales is entirely coincidental.

Contents

		VII
1.	Chapter 1	1
2.	Chapter 2	17
3.	Chapter 3	29
4.	Chapter 4	39
5.	Chapter 5	53
6.	Chapter 6	63
7.	Chapter 7	77
8.	Chapter 8	95
9.	Chapter 9	109
10.	Chapter 10	123
11.	Chapter 11	143
12.	Chapter 12	165
13.	Chapter 13	179
14.	Chapter 14	193
15.	Chapter 15	207

16.	Chapter 16	221
17.	Chapter 17	243
18.	Chapter 18	263
19.	Chapter 19	275
20.	Chapter 20	285
21.	Chapter 21	305
22.	Chapter 22	317
23.	Jay 10 years Earlier	337
24.	Holly Present Day	343
25.	Chapter 25	361
26.	Chapter 26	371
27.	Chapter 27	389

Epilogue 6 Months Later	407
Extended Honeymoon Epilogue	423
Chapter 1 Jay - Now	425
Chapter 2 Jay - Then	429
Chapter 3 Holly - Now	433

Chapter 4	439
Holly	
Chapter 5	451
Jay	
Elle's Books	455
About the Author	457
Acknowledgements	459

To Dan,
Thank you,
Now, Always and Forever.

Chapter 1

"Last call for Atlantic Airways Flight 77 to Los Angeles, boarding at Gate 22."

I speed up as the announcement screeches in my ears. *Can't be late, can't be late.* The aircraft is at a gate on the other side of the terminal. *Typical.* I need to make this flight; otherwise, it's back to being stuck at home on standby. I shudder at the thought. I don't know a single flight attendant who enjoys standby duty—sitting at home for hours on end in full uniform—just in case they need you to operate a flight. Then having to rush to the airport, sometimes only making the flight with minutes to spare.

My foot slips out of my shoe and I almost go head over heels onto the shiny tile floor. Whoever thought up the red high heels for the uniform has obviously never been on standby. Trainers would be more practical right now.

Finally, I reach the top of the jet bridge and get to the door of the Boeing 747.

"Holly Havers," I pant, lifting the lanyard around my neck to show the ground agent my airline ID.

He ticks my name off a list on his clipboard and I pass him to board the plane. I head straight to the upper-class galley where my best friend Matt, the flight service manager, is completing his pre-flight paperwork. I love Matt. He lives near me and my other best friend and housemate, Rachel. Matt's gorgeous, tall with olive skin and short dark wavy hair. Totally gay, though. I've seen many disappointed girls' faces when they realize.

"I'm so glad I made it," I puff. "I couldn't believe it when I got called for your flight." I smile at Matt.

"Boy, am I glad to see you too, Holls. We are full, full, full; it's going to be a busy one!" Matt kisses me on both cheeks. "I've got you working in position CM2. Here's your passenger manifest for your section," he says, handing me a paper printout.

"Thanks." I take the list of passengers' names, fold it, and put it in my pocket, before changing into my flat cabin shoes and stowing my crew bag in an overhead locker.

"Safe flight, guys," calls the ground agent as he pushes the aircraft door from the outside. I made it just in time.

"Thanks very much!" Matt calls back as he pulls the plane door shut and closes it using the giant operating handle. Then he picks up the intercom phone from between the two jump seats next to him.

"Cabin crew, doors to automatic and cross-check," sounds over the PA system.

I arm the door I am responsible for and switch sides with Matt to double-check his.

"Cross-checked," we report in unison.

"Manual demo, Hun," Matt says with a regretful shrug of his shoulders. Usually, we show a video, but sometimes Head Office requires us to perform a manual one. It's unpopular with the crew. During the video is our last chance to have a drink before takeoff. Sometimes it's hours before we have the chance again, particularly on full flights.

I grab the gray demo kit bag from behind my jump seat and make my way up to the front of upper class. Putting my kit on the floor, I check to make sure I have everything—seat belt, oxygen mask, life jacket, safety card. I'm all set. Matt reads the safety briefing over the PA and I stand, ready to start. I'm being watched by the passenger in seat 4A—a few rows away, his piercing blue eyes examining me. My breath hitches under the intensity of his gaze. He should pay attention, so he knows what to do in an emergency, but God, he is *staring*.

When the demo ends, I start to prepare the cabin for takeoff, checking that seat belts are fastened and bags stowed. I pause at 4A's seat and take a proper look at him. He has an American jock look—dark-blond tousled hair, square jawline, designer stubble. *I wonder how it would feel underneath my fingers.* His black jeans hug his thighs and the sleeves of his gray T-shirt stretch over muscular biceps. Someone like him must live in the gym.

Masculinity oozes from him. I gulp down the lump in my throat.

"Sir, do you have your seat belt fastened?"

"Yes," he replies in a smooth, deep voice and lifts his T-shirt so I can see. The sight of his tanned, rock-hard abs fills my eyes before I snap them away.

"Thank you," I squeak before moving on.

Holy crap.

I've got to serve him all flight and can't melt into a puddle at his feet or blush whenever he talks. This is going to be a nightmare. He must have noticed the effect he had on me. Professional, that's what I must be. It's not like I haven't served celebrities and high-profile passengers before. None have had this effect on me, though. What the hell's gotten into me? Deep breaths, I can do this.

"Excuse me, dear," a sweet elderly lady sitting close by says. "Could I please have a glass of water to take a pill?"

Smiling back at her, I answer, "Of course. I'll just be a minute."

When I return, I kneel next to her seat and hand her the glass.

"Oh, thank you, dear." She smiles at me as she picks up a packet of pills. Her smile turns to a frown as she fumbles to press them out of the foil.

"Here, let me." I place my hands over her shaking ones. They're cold as ice. Her skin, which looks as delicate as tissue paper, is laced with pale-purple veins. I press two tablets out into her palm. "I'll fetch you a blanket after takeoff; it can get cold."

"Oh, you're a love. I never enjoyed flying much." She sighs, leaning toward me. She smells of lavender and sugar. "I always get a headache now that my George isn't with me. He'd tell me not to worry, safer than driving a car." She chuckles to herself as she swallows the pills.

I place my palm over hers again. "Your George is right; it is safer than traveling by car. He sounds like a clever man."

"He was, dear." Her eyes stare off into the distance. "He was the love of my life, passed two years ago."

"I'm so sorry to hear that," I say, squeezing her hand.

"Are you in love, dear?" Her gaze turns to me.

"Oh." I hesitate, taken aback by her directness. Maybe when you're older, you learn not to waste time when it comes to talking about the important things in life, like love. "Er, no, I'm not." I offer her a small smile.

"He'll be a lucky man, whoever wins your heart. You're a treasure." She grins at me, patting my hand.

"Thank you." I smile, picking up her empty glass as she lets my hand go. "You just tell me if I can do anything for you today, okay? My name's Holly."

"I will do, Holly. I'm Vera."

"It's a pleasure to meet you, Vera," I say as I stand up.

Her eyes light up as she looks past me, and as I turn to leave, I understand what's captured her attention. Mr. Blue Eyes is listening to our conversation, a thoughtful, distant expression on his face. I chew my lip to hold my giggle in. Even mature ladies like Vera aren't immune to his charms.

As I sit down on my jump seat, ready for takeoff, Matt walks past doing his final cabin secure checks.

"Lucky bitch!" he whispers. "You've got Jay Anderson to look after, that man is a sex god! The rest of the crew are green with envy that you are the one who gets to serve him." He lifts his eyebrows at me.

"Who?"

Matt tuts, rolling his eyes. "For God's sake, Holls, have you been living under a rock? He's been in loads of films and now he's the lead in that US FBI series; what's it called?" He clicks his fingers in the air. His eyebrows draw together as he tries to remember. "Oh, you know the one I mean!"

I shrug my shoulders at Matt with a slight smile. I don't know. I prefer to read or do yoga when I'm away on stopovers. I don't watch a lot of the American TV. Matt's eyes widen at me and I realize he's still talking about Jake Anderson or whatever his name is.

"Get this, once he was photographed getting undressed by a pap who snuck on set, and the picture crashed Instagram when it was uploaded!" Matt fans himself with the paperwork he's holding and places a hand up to his forehead, feigning feeling faint. "He's rumored to be the next superhero in that new film trilogy that's coming out. He's single and straight. Give me a chance though; I could turn him." Matt's eyes have a naughty glint.

"Ha, I bet you'd like to try." I smirk.

Matt's always great fun, believing that the guy of his dreams is just around the corner, ready to sweep him off his feet, or onto his knees maybe.

"Jay Anderson." Matt sighs with a dreamy expression on his face as he continues on past me.

I lean my head back against the seat as I fasten my harness. So, the hot man in seat 4A with a deep voice that makes dormant areas of me flutter, is Jay Anderson, successful Hollywood star and sex god. And I am stuck serving him for the next eleven and a half hours. This is just fantastic. I hope I don't do or say anything dumb. He must see women tongue-tied over him all the time. If I can make it through this flight, I will never see him again, so at least there's that.

Matt takes his seat and straps himself in, using the interphone to call the captain and confirm the cabin is secure for takeoff. Then the engines roar as we speed down the runway, taking off for LA.

I sit in my jump seat and wait for the chime from the pilots, indicating we've reached ten thousand feet and the crew can move around the cabin. As soon as they give it, I jump up from my seat and grab a blanket to take to Vera. Her eyes light up as she sees me approaching.

"Oh, you are kind love, thank you." She beams.

She's such a sweet lady. I smile at her as I take the blanket out of its bag and lay it across her lap. "You're very welcome, Vera. That's what I'm here for, to make you as comfortable as possible."

"I don't know how you do it, Holly."

I look at her, puzzled.

"Fly like you do. All the time." She chuckles.

"I like it, and I get to meet some lovely people."

She chuckles again before casting her eyes over my shoulder. "Yes, I can see."

My eyes widen and she shakes her head. "I may be old, but I'm not dead yet. Although, I think if I were, then the kiss of life from someone like him would soon sort me out," she whispers.

Oh my God.

Her eyes are lit up with mischief as the giggle I'm holding back spills out. She grabs my hand as we lean our heads in and chuckle like a couple of naughty children that just got away with sneaking extra cookies out of the jar.

"So, what are you doing when you get to LA?" I ask.

"I'm visiting my granddaughter." Vera beams. She's clearly very proud of her and tells me all about how she has her own business and built it from nothing.

"Still hasn't found love yet though." Vera sighs. "I've told her. When you find the one, you just know. I did with my George. Knew the moment I laid eyes on him. It was a kind of magic. It happens like that for some of us. The really lucky ones." Her eyes twinkle.

"George was a very lucky man to have found you too."

"I know, dear." Vera pats my hand. "I reminded him of it every day." She chuckles to herself as I stand up and tell her I will come and chat again later.

She's such a livewire. I hope I have that much zest for life when I'm her age. I'm grinning as I turn away from her seat.

Vibrant blue eyes grab my attention, their owner smiling at me. My stomach dances in my throat. *This is ridiculous.* I need to get a grip; otherwise, the next eleven hours will be torture. I take a deep breath.

"Mr. Anderson?"

The brows above those beautiful eyes rise as I address him.

"May I offer you a blanket too, sir?" Before I can stop myself, my eyes have dropped down to his lap, lingering for a second too long on where the fabric strains over his groin. "For your legs," I add brightly, whipping my eyes back up.

He narrows his eyes at me, but his smile remains.

Busted. He totally saw me check out his crotch. Now he must assume I'm thinking about his cock—crap! I am thinking about his cock!

I bite my lip as I wait for a response.

"I'm fine. thank you...Holly," he says, drawing his gaze back up from my chest and name badge. He looks straight into my eyes, this time with a twinkle in his.

"Okay. Please let me know if there's anything you need," I say, making sure to keep my eyes on his face, before I head off, back toward the galley.

Halfway into the flight and the drink and meal service is over. I've spent a lot of time at Vera's seat chatting with her. She's such a character. Passengers like her make this job so worthwhile. Mr. Anderson has been polite. Smiling at me and making my stomach flutter with those eyes every time I've spoken to him. But most of the time he's had his head buried in some paperwork, so our exchanges have been brief. Suits me, at least the chances of me making a fool of myself reduce that way.

I peek up the aisle at him from the galley. He's drinking what looks like a protein shake, the solid muscles visible in his broad neck as he tips back his head. Vera gets out of her seat and opens the overhead locker. I'm about to go to her when Mr. Anderson rises out of his seat, lifting her bag down for her. She beams at him and pats him on the arm before he sits and starts reading again. Probably the lines for his show or a movie script or something. What's it like being an actor in LA? A different world to the two-bedroom house I share near Heathrow Airport with Rachel, no doubt.

As I'm staring, he looks straight up at me.

Shit.

He's caught me gawking at him. I drop my eyes to the floor. He's going to think I have the hots for him, or that I'm unprofessional and nosy. I curse myself and raise my eyes. He's still looking at me. God, he is gorgeous; there's no denying it. He keeps his eyes glued to me as he reaches down next to his seat. The next second, the call light illuminates above his seat. Crap. Now I have to go up there. What if he demands to know why the hell I'm standing here watching him? I glance around, hoping one of the other crew will answer his call light, but they're all busy.

Oh God, here goes.

I make my way up the aisle to his seat.

"Can I help you, Mr. Anderson?" I ask, trying my best not to reveal how mortified I am that he saw me gazing at him.

"Yes," he says, his smooth, deep voice and American accent making my stomach swirl. "I wanted to know what you recommend."

"Recommend?" I say, puzzled.

"I can't decide what to watch." He gestures toward the TV screen at his seat. "I'm considering a documentary." His sharp blue eyes roam across my face and rest on my lips.

"Oh, I see. Well, *Blue Planet* is incredible. I love how clever nature is, and funny too." The words spill out before I can stop them. "Did you know there's a male bird that clears a patch of the jungle floor and spends ages selecting the perfect stick before inserting it upright in the ground and dancing around it like a pole to attract a mate?" I blurt.

Jay raises an eyebrow as the corners of his mouth curl.

"The female birds all watch and decide if they like the show or not," I continue.

Shut up, Holly! Stop talking, you idiot. I'm telling him about a pole-dancing bird, for goodness' sake.

"That does sound amusing," he says, smiling at me, and I'm rewarded by a flash of his perfect, straight white teeth.

I grin back like an idiot. *What is he doing to me?*

"I will leave you to it then." My cheeks burn and I press my lips together, not trusting myself to say anything else. As I turn to leave, Vera catches my eye and gives me a wink. I can't believe she just witnessed that total humiliation and is winking at me as though I just pulled off the best flirtation in history. I smile back at her. I will take her a cup of tea in a minute, but right now I need to get back to the galley so my face can return to its normal shade.

The rest of the flight goes by with little excitement. There's a steady stream of crew members needing to come up to upper class to get something. Matt and I know they're all really craving a glimpse of Jay Anderson. I look up as the galley curtain flies open and one of the crew named Megan from the economy cabin comes in.

"Guys," she whispers. "Come see this." She's holding a magazine open at an interview with Jay Anderson. There are a few pictures of him looking moody and thoughtful. One of him standing on a beach draws my eyes. The sea is behind him, and he's laughing, his face angled up at the sun. It's a perfect shot.

"Let me see, let me see!" Matt squeals, sliding next to Megan so they're both squeezed together, poring over the pages. "It says here he's single, but was rumored to be dating the model Anya Katiss, after they were pictured together on a friend's yacht." Matt reads out loud. "Oh, and he likes photography, capturing the beauty in nature," quotes Matt. "He's deep too, Holly! Not just a so-handsome-it-should-be-illegal face." He swoons as Megan laughs.

They keep devouring the magazine while I tidy the galley, trying to tune out as they flip between making "ooh and ah" sounds as they read. I don't fancy hearing all about Mr. Anderson's dating life.

"You're so lucky, Holly." Megan sighs, closing the magazine and tucking it under her arm. "I wish I was working in upper class today. I bet the moment crewing called you off standby, you never dreamed you'd be meeting Jay Anderson today. You should be thanking whoever made the decision to call you out."

I glance at her, but she's got a dreamy expression on her face and isn't expecting an answer. We carry on chatting about what we are all planning to do in LA. We've got two nights in a hotel before we operate the return flight home. Megan says she and two of the crew are doing the Walk of Fame to see all the stars on the path. I've done that a few times, so I say I'm going to skip it.

"What are you thinking, Matt?" I ask him after Megan heads back to the economy cabin. I pull out a metal storage canister from its stowage in the galley and turn it on its end to sit on top of.

"Well, I was thinking of doing some shopping, run at the beach, have a few drinks, dinner. Nothing too wild this time, babe. I'm still recovering from the Hong Kong flight I just did. Man, that was a wild one!"

I laugh. Some brilliant nights happen when we get a layover in Hong Kong.

"Sounds good, mind if I join you?" I ask as I take a sip of the peppermint tea I made.

"As if I would have it any other way!" He pretends to be outraged that I would even consider not spending the trip with him. "Always love having time with you, Holls. You can fill me in on what's been happening in Holly's world," he says with a wink.

"A fat lot of nothing, as you know. I'm so glad this is my last block of standby, and then I'll be back on a normal roster again," I say with relief.

"You haven't bumped into Simon at all, have you?" he asks, looking worried.

"No, thank God, but I'm sure it'll happen at some point." The image of my ex, Simon, a pilot, pops into my head. We dated for a bit until things ended badly nine months ago. I'm still piecing back together my self-confidence which he shredded.

"Been on any dates I don't already know about?" Matt asks, changing the subject.

"No, no, no." I shake my head. "I've given up for a while. I keep meeting weirdos. Remember the last guy I went out on a date with? He flirted with the waitress all evening." I grimace as I remember. "I'm looking for something more. I want to connect with someone, and them looking at *me* on a date would be a good start."

"You and me both, babe," says Matt. "Maybe we will both get a visit from our fairy gay-mother soon to whip up our Prince Charmings," he says, giving me an elbow in the ribs.

"Ha, maybe you're right."

The sound of someone clearing their throat makes me look up—straight into the eyes of Mr. Anderson. They are the brightest blue. My stomach flips. *How long has he been standing there? How much did he hear?*

Matt shoots up off his galley box seat like there's a rocket up his ass.

"Hello, Mr. Anderson. What can we do for you, sir?"

As I stand up, the corners of Mr. Anderson's eyes crinkle as he smiles at me and Matt. I can see them properly now that he's standing close. There's kindness in them, perhaps a touch of sadness too? But I shove that thought away. What do I know? I know nothing about him.

"I just wanted to say thank you. I've had a great flight. You've both looked after us so well." He glances from Matt and back to me.

I'm pretty sure by us, he's referring to him and Vera. Every time I spoke to her, I got the impression he was listening. He always had an amused smile on his face whenever I left her seat. I'm not surprised though, after some of the things she talked about. I've certainly learned a thing or two I didn't know before. She gave me a list of books she said I must read, insisting they had the best 'book boyfriends.'

"I thought you may like a couple of tickets I have for the *After Hours* show tonight? As a way of saying thanks," Jay continues.

Matt's eyes widen like a child's at Christmas. The *After Hours* show is the hottest talk show in America. They have different celebrity guests with a live audience, and it seems like such a fun show.

"Wow! That sounds amazing! Doesn't it, Holly?" Matt says as he turns to me.

"Oh, er, yes, absolutely!" I manage, still looking at Mr. Anderson, who hasn't broken eye contact with me.

"Great." He smiles. "I will leave them at the door of the studio for you. Tell them I put them aside for you."

"That's so kind of you! Thank you!" gushes Matt.

I eye him sideways. This is like a fantasy for him. I can tell he's barely keeping it together. Mr. Anderson is about to leave but halts suddenly, leaning closer to me. My neck tingles and all the tiny hairs stand up as his breath tickles the side of my face. He smells incredible—a fresh earthy smell combined with citrus. *What the hell is that?*

"That guy you went on a date with was a jerk, Holly," he whispers.

He draws back as heat fires between my legs. I try to think of something to say in response, but he's already gone, his unique scent lingering. I turn to Matt, who is doing some weird, excited dance.

"Oh my God, Holly! Jay Anderson invited us to the *After Hours* show! It's going to be amazing!" He squeals with delight.

Chapter 2

"Coming," I call as I walk to my hotel room door to answer it.

We landed a few hours ago, and a bus transported the entire crew to our hotel for the next two nights. I grabbed a quick power nap before getting ready for tonight.

I open my door to reveal Matt dressed in tight-fitting black jeans, a black shirt, and a blazer.

"You look great, Matt," I say as I let him in.

"Says you, Holly!" He looks me up and down with a wolf whistle. "You look divine! If only I were straight!" He wiggles his eyebrows at me, and I laugh.

I turn and look at myself in the mirror. I've got a figure-hugging strappy gold dress on that shows off my curves and nude peep-toe heels. My last trip was to Barbados, and I caught a bit of a tan. The sun has drawn out more of the golden highlights in my hair, which I've styled in loose waves and swept round to one side with a vintage hair clip. I've done my eye makeup sultry and smoky and kept my lips nude. I'm so glad I packed an emergency going out outfit in my suitcase. Hopefully it's not too much, but people dress up in LA. It's not like I'm making the extra effort in case I talk to Jay Anderson again. I spray one last spritz of my perfume, the one I save for nights out. It's heady and rich. I always feel sexy when I wear it.

"Shall we?" I take my nude clutch and key card off the bedside table and turn to Matt.

"Ladies first," he says, and we head out.

After a couple of preshow drinks in the hotel bar, we find ourselves a little tipsy as we take our seats in the *After Hours* film studio.

"This is awesome!" Matt whispers to me.

It's almost full now with everyone in their seats, and there's an excited hum of chatter all around us. The audience members are predominantly women. A dark-haired girl sitting next to me turns and talks, her voice high with excitement.

"Hi, I'm Macy. I'm so thrilled to be here! Can you believe that Jay Anderson is a guest on tonight's show? I've come from New York with my girlfriends just to see him." She gestures at the three buzzing women next to her who all smile back as I raise a hand in greeting. "He's such a private person; he doesn't give much away about his personal life in interviews like this. I think it's so sexy that he's mysterious, you know? Like, for the right woman he would open up and bare his soul. So romantic." Macy sighs with a hand on her chest.

"He's certainly got something," I say to her. "I'm Holly by the way, and this is my friend Matt." I gesture to my left. He raises a hand to say hi.

"Oh, you're English!" says Macy in delight. "I love your accent!"

"Thanks." I laugh.

Our conversation is cut short by a loud cheer, and a guy appears at the front of the stage, introducing himself as Jimmy, the warm-up guy. He explains how he will hold up different boards with instructions on them, such as the applause board signaling when we should clap. He has us all practice a few times and tells some jokes and the entire audience is laughing, whooping, and whistling. The atmosphere is electric and energetic. I look around the studio where the show will soon start. There are cameras on tracks, enormous lights, and lots of people with headsets on. The stage itself looks like a trendy apartment with bookshelves in the background and a large window with lights from the city twinkling in the distance. There are two plush leather sofas in a deep brown and a table between them with a jug of iced water and glasses.

The audience hushes as Jimmy holds up a countdown timer signaling that the show is going live in *3,2,1*. The familiar theme tune plays and the audience stand up from their seats, erupting into applause as the show's host, Patrick Howard, appears on stage. He's wearing a gray pinstripe suit and a white shirt. He's maybe sixty years old, with wavy gray hair and a warm, friendly face. The sort of person you perhaps feel you can tell your secrets to. No wonder he's so successful as the show's host, a job he's had for years. He's never short of famous guests willing to come and sit on his couch and be interviewed.

"Thank you, thank you," he says. "Wow, what a night we have for you, ladies and gentlemen," he begins. "We've got Victoria's Secret model, Anya Katiss here, country music band, The Rush, playing their new single from their platinum album, and ladies," Patrick pauses, "and men of course." He smiles. "You are in for a treat tonight!"

Someone in the audience shouts out, "Yes!" and the rest of the audience laughs.

Patrick continues. "Tonight, for your visual and audio—and every-other-sense-you-want-to-invoke pleasure—we have the incredible star of the US FBI show *Steel Force*, Jay Anderson!" The audience goes wild, bolting up from their seats, screaming and cheering. I even see what looks like a thong being flung toward the stage. I turn to Matt. He saw it too, and we both burst out laughing.

"This is crazy!" I whisper to him as the roar dies down.

"I know, right." He looks at me, slightly glassy-eyed from our earlier drinks. His excitement is undeniable. "I feel like an obsessive eater at an all-you-can-eat buffet! I don't know what you did on the flight, Holly. You obviously made an impression on Mr. Anderson for him to invite us like this."

"No, I just did my job" I say. But a brief flicker of something stirs deep down in my stomach. I quickly extinguish it. The thought is ridiculous. I'm a girl from a small town in England. He's a Hollywood actor. "He was just being kind, that's all."

"Oh, Holly Darling, you need to give yourself some credit we are here because Jay Anderson wants in your panties! I'm telling you, if you get the chance to let your hair down with a man like that, even if it's just for one night, grab it by the balls—literally!" he says, giving me an exaggerated wink.

"Matt!" I gasp. "That is not it."

"If you insist, Holls, if you insist," he says, deciding to believe his far-fetched version of reality instead. "One day you'll realize just how amazing you are, and you'll find someone who almost deserves you. Then I'm coming to your wedding to have first dibs on the hot, single guys."

We sit on the edge of our seats as we watch the rest of the show. There are some light news segments and funny clips played that viewers have sent in. Patrick interviews Anya Katiss, the Victoria's Secret model. I swear I have never seen such long, perfect legs in my life. It makes me think of a video online I saw of a woman in hot pants and stilettos performing a high kick to close the trunk of a car while holding a baby in one arm. How genetics even engineer legs like hers is a mystery to me. She looks like an exotic goddess, her long raven hair poker straight, long eyelashes fanning over her high cheekbones as she blinks, her mouth a perfect dark rosebud. She's talking about a new perfume called Capture that she's launching, and free samples are being handed out to the audience. The bottle is made of frosted glass in a heart shape with red and silver metallic streaks through it. It's stunning, and the perfume smells like an enchanted orchard in moonlight.

"This is some good shit," Matt says, taking a sniff.

"You have such a way with words," I joke. But I must agree with him. Anya Katiss and her perfume are otherworldly.

I draw my eyes back to the stage as a hush of anticipation falls across the studio. The host, Patrick, seems to enjoy the building suspense.

"I'm afraid that's all we've got time for tonight," he says, shaking his head.

A gasp runs through the audience and someone wails "No!" Patrick looks up guiltily.

"I'm just messing with you! Hell, I want to make it home tonight in one piece," he jokes as he pretends to look worried.

There's a relieved murmur around the audience as Patrick throws his arms wide.

"Ladies and gentlemen, please welcome our next guest, the one and only, Jay Anderson!"

My eardrums might explode. The noise the audience makes is insane. I glance around and they're whooping and whistling. Macy, the girl next to me, is jumping up and down in excitement. Matt grabs my hand and squeezes it. I'm worried he's going to break a finger and am about to yank my arm back when he lets go, his eyes glued to the stage. I look over and there he is.

Jay Anderson.

He looks even better than I remember. He's wearing smart dark-gray trousers, brown shoes and belt, and a white shirt, open at the neck with the sleeves rolled up his forearms. An expensive-looking watch glints under the studio lights on his wrist. He's waving to the audience and smiling, his perfect white teeth dazzling us. His dark-sandy hair is just the perfect length. It looks effortlessly styled, like he just wakes up like that. He shakes Patrick's hand, and they have a man hug, patting each other on the back like old friends before he sits down next to Anya Katiss, kissing her hello on the cheek. She seems to slide ever so slightly closer to Jay as he sits down. Or maybe I'm imagining it.

"Thank you for coming, Jay. I think it's safe to say we've got some fans of yours in the audience tonight," says Patrick.

A woman calls out, "I love you, Jay!" and holds up a sign, with what I presume is her phone number written on it.

He smiles and his eyes crinkle at the corners. "Thank you for having me, Patrick."

There's that deep, dreamy voice again. I swallow as I sit glued to my seat, watching him.

"Now let's start with your show, *Steel Force*," says Patrick. "You've been the lead character on the show for two seasons now and it's just been renewed for a third."

"Yes, that's right. We've got a couple of months break from filming now, before we're back at it."

"So, what have you got planned for the next two months?" asks Patrick.

"I want to take some time to see my family, and I've got some projects I'm working on."

"Any special friends in the picture?" Patrick asks with a cheeky smile. "Come on, you can tell your friend, Patrick," he jokes.

Jay smiles and looks down at his shoes. "I will know her when I meet her," he says, his voice soft.

Anya Katiss uncrosses and recrosses her legs on the sofa. She must feel it too, his undeniable sex appeal. Sitting that close to him and not being able to jump into his lap must be torture.

Patrick continues the interview, and they talk about upcoming movie roles and the superhero trilogy rumor. Jay is charming but gives nothing away. Then Patrick gets up and takes a handheld microphone from one of the stage assistants.

"Okay, ladies and gentlemen, it's now time for you, the audience, to ask the questions." He bounds up the stairs in between the seats and looks around at the eager hands which have flown up into the air. He holds his microphone out to the lady wearing the 'I love Jay' T-shirt, who grabs it in both hands.

"My question is for Jay," she says. "How would you describe your perfect woman?"

Jay looks up at her. "Well, I like someone to be honest and upfront," he says, gesturing to her T-shirt. The audience chuckles. "Someone who can make me laugh and challenge me to look at things differently. A best friend, I guess," he says with what I detect is a hint of sadness.

I'm still pondering this when Matt elbows me hard in the ribs.

"Ow, what did you do that for?" I say as I turn to him, but my annoyance turns to sheer terror when I see Patrick Howard grinning at me with his microphone thrust under my chin.

"Your name, my darling?" he says, amused at my reaction.

"Er, Holly." I gulp.

"Well, lovely Holly, do you have a question for Jay?" he asks.

There is silence as the whole studio waits to see what I am going to say.

"Um," I squeak.

Shit, I need to think of a clever question and fast. My face is getting hot and I'm pretty sure if my heart beats any harder I could start a band.

"Do you have any pets?" I blurt out.

There's a disgruntled mumble from some members of the audience, disappointed that I didn't use my chance to ask him more about his ideal woman or even what he likes in bed. Jay, however, looks happy at the change in subject.

"Holly," he says in his beautiful, deep voice that makes my insides melt. "No, I don't have any pets. However, I find animals fascinating. I saw an interesting program recently on rainforest birds." His eyes hold mine and an amused smile plays on his lips as he runs his hand over his jaw.

"Lovely," I manage, wishing aliens would abduct me now so I could escape the mortification of my lame question. Patrick moves on and I take a deep breath. Jay is still watching me with the same amused expression. He must think I'm such a loser.

Matt and I watch the rest of the show before the country band plays their latest song release, a catchy number about drinking whiskey under the stars. It's been incredible being part of the live audience and watching the show being filmed. We've had a blast. We say goodbye to Macy and her friends and make our way to the exit when a guy with a clipboard and earpiece approaches us.

"Hi, Holly, Matt, I'm Stefan." He holds out his hand and we both take turns shaking it.

He's dressed in skinny jeans and a checked shirt. Thick-framed glasses outline his dark hazelnut eyes, and he has a dark quiff. He's rocking the trendy nerd vibe, and I can tell out of the corner of my eye that Matt is checking him out.

"I'm Jay's manager," he says. "He asked me to look out for you guys. Listen, there are a few of us going out to a club nearby now that filming has finished. You guys are welcome to join us."

I look over at Matt, who widens his eyes at me. I can tell he's into Stefan and would kill me if I cut tonight short.

"Sure, sounds like fun," I hear myself say.

I mean, what's wrong with another opportunity to humiliate myself in front of Jay Anderson?

Chapter 3

WE TAKE A CAB to the club Stefan gave us the name for. It's tucked away down a side alley off the Main Street. I look up at the neon sign that says 'Geode'.

"Hmmm, looks interesting," says Matt, frowning.

"Are you sure we've got the right place?"

"It's where Stefan said they'd be." I look around in confusion.

We would have missed Geode if we hadn't had directions from Stefan. There are no windows, just a big dark-gray metal door and the small neon name sign above it.

"There! Look," I say to Matt, pointing to a small, illuminated button on the wall.

He presses it and after what feels like ages, the huge door opens outward to reveal a security guard. He assesses Matt and me, looking us up and down.

"Names?"

Matt straightens his back and pushes his chest out. "Matt and Holly, we are friends of Jay's."

I bite my lip at his blatant exaggeration, but the security guard doesn't seem to query it. He says something into the cuff of his jacket before nodding at us and standing aside so we can enter.

"Have a fun evening," he says as we pass him.

In front of us is a dimly lit stone staircase; the sound of sexy club music drifts up from below. We walk down the stairs and at the bottom it opens up into the bar.

I'm not sure what I was expecting, but it wasn't this. The main room has a long lit-up glass bar running down the length of it, leading out onto a dance floor. Around it are what looks like individual caves with booth seating for around ten people inside each one. The walls of them are made of stone and glisten like there are crystals embedded into them.

"Wow!" says Matt.

"Wow indeed," I say as I gaze around.

Now I can see why it's called Geode. I feel like we are in an enchanted underground cave, one that plays sexy music. It's full of men and women talking, drinking, dancing, and by the looks of it, having a great time. Some I recognize from the studio team, like Jimmy, the warm-up guy.

"There you guys are. You found it okay then?" We turn at the sound of Stefan's voice.

He comes over and gives us both a kiss on each cheek. "Sorry if you thought you'd gotten the wrong place. The paparazzi haven't discovered it yet, hence why we love it so much." He chuckles. "Anyway, I'm so glad you could both make it. Jay said you'd looked after him so well on the flight over, he will be really pleased to see you. He's around here somewhere." He waves a hand in the air. "Come and get a drink," he says as he leads us over to the bar. "This place does the most amazing cocktails; you've got to try one, or four." He laughs.

Matt laughs too. I can see his eyes light up as he studies Stefan in closer detail, and if I'm not mistaken, Stefan's eyes are drinking Matt in too.

"Holly?" Matt asks.

"Oh yes, please, can you order for me? I'm just going to go to the ladies' room."

"Sure thing, gorge," Matt says to me, his eyes still on Stefan.

I smile to myself. I doubt he's going to miss me while I'm gone.

Stefan points me in the direction of the restrooms, which are at the back of the club. I make my way down past the bar and follow the sign around the corner, passing some more stone alcoves with seating. I find the ladies' room, which is decorated in the same crystal and stone walls. I check my hair and makeup before leaving.

As I walk past the stone alcoves on my way back to the main bar, an unmistakable voice calls my name.

"Holly?" I turn around and am face-to-face with Jay Anderson.

He looks even more edible up close than he did on stage earlier and I can smell his scent again, the same intoxicating one as on the plane.

"Hello, Mr. Anderson." My cheeks feel like they're on fire. I'm glad the lighting is dark in here.

"Hi," he says, with a twinkle in his eyes. "But I'd really rather you call me Jay. Mr. Anderson is my dad, and besides, it makes me feel ancient."

"Oh, er...sorry...okay...Jay." I smile as I look at him, my hands gripping on to my clutch bag for something to do. "This place is quite something," I say, looking about, anything to stop myself from being drawn into the intense gaze from his incredible eyes. "Thanks again for inviting me and Matt to the show. It was fun," I continue babbling.

"It was," he says, studying me. I look at him and notice he looks amused again. He must think I'm a total clown. "I'm glad you came." I wait for him to elaborate, but he doesn't. He just keeps studying my face. I stand there, staring back at him when Matt bounds over, almost spilling his drink.

"Hi, Jay!" He beams as though they're now best pals. Clearly the cocktail's effects are already kicking in.

Before Jay can answer, he's speaking again. "Holly! Stefan was right! These cocktails are to die for! This is my third already. You have to try this one I got for you." He thrusts it into my hand. I take a sip, conscious that Jay's eyes are on my lips as I raise the glass to them and sip the honey-colored liquid.

"Oh! Yum." I lick the sweet, intense flavor from my lips. "You're not wrong. These are delicious," I say as I take another, much larger mouthful. I could do with the Dutch courage.

I sneak a glance up at Jay over the rim of the glass. Matt's already disappeared, back to find Stefan probably. Damn. Now we're alone and I need to think of something to say. Luckily, he speaks first.

"So how long have you been flying, Holly?"

"Oh, um, eight years now. It's an amazing job. I get to travel and be paid for it, come to places like LA."

"You like LA?" His eyebrows lift and he sounds pleased.

"I do," I say, feeling braver from the cocktail. "I love the feel of it here, like anything is possible. The people are welcoming." I look up at him and he's listening intently, completely focused on me. "You've got the beaches, the hills, Big Bear mountain for skiing not far away," I continue.

"You like skiing?"

"Well, actually, I probably look like Bambi on ice. I should stick to yoga," I say before willing myself to shut up. I say such stupid things! But Jay's smiling and it reaches his eyes. Oh God, they're such beautiful, kind eyes. "How about you? What's it like living in LA?" I say, dropping my eyes down so I don't combust under his gaze. It doesn't help though. Now his perfect teeth and full, soft-looking lips are in my eyeline.

Jay pauses before he speaks, thank God. I would have missed whatever he is about to say otherwise.

"It's good, I mean I'm lucky." He hesitates and takes a breath and I watch his Adam's apple as he swallows. I never realized how arousing a neck could be. I wonder what it would be like to kiss… "I get to do what I love," he continues, "but there's a lot of fake people here, Holly. People that want something from you. You hold your real friends close as they're hard to find. I'm just a guy who wound up with a job in the spotlight." He rubs his hand over the stubble on his chin in thought as he looks at me.

"Yeah, I guess it is just a job. Although I bet you don't have to collect bags of other people's vomit," I say, before throwing a hand across my mouth, mortified that once again I've just said something ridiculous out loud.

Jay looks at me, his eyes lighting up as he laughs. It's possibly the best sound I've ever heard. It's a kind laugh. He's not laughing at me; in fact, he looks relaxed and happy. The photograph in the magazine article looking free and happy at the beach, face up to the sun, comes to mind. I drop my arm by my side and find myself laughing with him. He shakes his head. "That's what I like about you, Holly; you're real, you're not trying to be someone else. You've got your own way of looking at things," he says. "It's refreshing. You remind me that there's a real world outside this weird LA fishbowl."

"Some days I think it might be more fun to change and be someone else," I murmur while I process his words. *"That's what I like about you Holly."* Did I just imagine him saying that?

"Please don't change, Holly," Jay says softly, drawing me out of my thoughts.

When I look up into his eyes, there's a vulnerability hiding there that I can't put my finger on. He's a wealthy, successful actor with probably a million women ready to drop their panties for him, yet he seems, I don't know—normal. As though he's got his own insecurities and regrets. I let out a deep breath. He's actually easy to talk to. He seems genuine and down-to-earth. I mean, he is smoking hot. I'm not sure I've ever seen a guy that looks like him in the small town I grew up in back in England. Physically, he would stand out like a sore thumb. But who he is as a person maybe isn't so far removed from the rest of the world.

"Do people comment on your eyes?" he asks, studying them.

"Sorry?" I'm too busy calming the somersaults my stomach is doing to process what he just said.

"Your eyes? They're such a deep green."

"Oh." I place my drink down and my fingers reach up and touch the skin on my cheek.

His eyebrows knit together, as though he's trying to make a decision. Then he reaches out his hand and rests it on top of mine on the side of my face, his thumb dusting across my lips. I freeze; surely he's not going to? My thoughts are cut short as he leans in toward me and his lips find mine. I'm stunned, but then the warmth of his lips against mine brings me back to the present. The scent of earthy citrus invades my senses and takes control of my body. He kisses me gently at first, slowly, his lips brushing against mine and parting them.

"Mmm." I sigh, remembering to breathe.

He must take this as an invitation, as he pulls me in deeper, his tongue parting my lips further to seek out mine. He's an incredible kisser. The sound of my own heartbeat pounds in my ears, and my pulse throbs out a rhythm deep between my legs. *What is he doing to me?* His arms move down around my waist and pull me up against his hard, muscular body. I reach up, running my free hand over his broad chest and slide my other hand free, snaking them both around the back of his neck.

Something about this feels so right.

I reach one hand up higher and run it through his hair, tugging some between my fingers. He groans into my mouth and draws me tighter against him, his kiss getting hungrier, more urgent, his tongue really exploring mine now. I am pressed up against him and there's no denying he has a rock-hard erection.

I swallow as a wave of arousal flows through me. I don't do this. I'm not that girl who kisses hot guys she barely knows. Yet, I never want it to end.

"Holly," he says as he pulls back, his eyes burning into mine. He looks like he's battling with something in his head; a small frown passes over his lips, gone as soon as it appears.

I stand there stunned, silenced by his kiss and the intensity in which he's studying me. He looks like he's going to say something else, but instead leans in close and presses a gentle kiss to my tingling lips.

"Do you want to dance?"

All I can manage to do is nod. He's going to need to hold me up; my legs are about to give way. That was one hell of a kiss. I have never been kissed like that before in my life, with so much desire. It was like we were the only two people in the world at that moment. If I could orgasm from a kiss alone, then that would have done it. I glance around. The club is busy, but no one seems to have noticed what just happened, yet to me it feels like a mass of fireworks have just gone off.

Jay takes my hand. It seems small and delicate inside his long, strong fingers. He leads us over to the dance floor. It's packed, so we are pushed up close to one another.

We dance together to song after song. Jay's eyes never leave mine as I sway and move my body against his in time to the music. The way he's looking at me, I'm pretty sure there could be an earthquake and he would keep dancing, his hands resting on my hips, his eyes delving into mine.

The music changes to something more sensual and he smiles at me as he spins me around so my back is resting against his chest. I lean back against him, happy to let him take control. His breath tickles my neck, making the hairs stand on end as a shiver runs from my head to my toes.

I feel like a stranger in my own body. I don't dance like this. I'm not a sexy dancer like my friend Rachel. I'm the one who closes my eyes and gets lost in a good song, arms waving in the air. Jay seems to like it though, judging by the erection pressing into me.

Just for one night, suppose I can be someone else? I can be the girl who has a fun night with an almost stranger. It's not as though I'm likely to see him again. Matt's words at the show about grabbing opportunities echo around my head. It's time I stopped letting the old wounds Simon inflicted on my self-confidence control me. I need to find me again. Maybe a hot distraction like Jay Anderson is just what I need tonight.

His hands tighten on my hips. It feels so good to be desired again. So what if he does this all the time with women he's just met? Surely I can get something out of it too?

I slow my hips down and rock them side to side, dragging my body over his again and again. Who knew I could be such a tease? Although am I only a tease if I don't go any further? I don't have long to consider the thought before Jay brings his mouth down to my ear and nips it with his teeth. I shudder as a small gasp escapes my lips.

"Holly," he growls. "You're coming home with me, now!"

Chapter 4

JAY PULLS ME TOWARD the stone staircase and exit, his hand gripping mine.

"Wait, I just need to tell Matt."

I look around but can't see him anywhere. I pull my cell phone out of my clutch bag and send him a quick text.

Me: I'm heading off Matt, will share a lift with Jay. Catch you tomorrow?

Three dots show up to signal he's texting back.

Matt: Okay, babe, don't do anything I wouldn't do!

That doesn't leave much then, does it. I smile at his cheekiness as I put my phone away.

"Ready?" asks Jay.

I can't help thinking that this is a loaded question. What the hell am I doing going home with a man like Jay Anderson, whom I barely know? This is so unlike me. A voice in my head screams, *'Shut up and enjoy it while it lasts, Holly. This guy is a sex god, and you haven't had sex in forever! Take what you get and fucking love it!'* It sounds like Matt has taken over my head.

"Yes." I smile at Jay. "I'm so ready."

He grins back at me and we climb up the stairs and out into the warm California night.

The cab journey to Jay's house doesn't take long, but it feels like ages with the anticipation of what might happen after our earlier kiss. We don't talk, but his hand hasn't let go of mine since we left the club. His thumb alternates between tracing circles over the back of my hand and stroking across my knuckles. I look out the window at all the lights as we drive, but every now and again I can see Jay out of the corner of my eye watching me.

The cab drives up a winding hill. Finally, it stops outside a building, but I can't see much as it's too dark. Jay pays the driver from a wad of cash and I notice he gives him a generous tip, then we thank him as we climb out.

I look up at the building, which is behind tall security railings that run all the way around it as far as I can make out in the darkness. Jay puts the thumb of his spare hand—he's still holding my hand with his other—onto a screen held on a metal post to the side of the railing. There's a gentle whir as the gates slide open. The security lights come on so we can see our way. I look up at the building. It's two levels high, large, white, and modern. It's built into the side of the hill and has a large driveway across the front of it and a large detached garage off to the left-hand side. It must be apartments. I bet the view is beautiful from the back, looking down at the city.

Jay leads me up to the main door at the front. It's huge and black with a giant handle running down its length. He puts his thumb on another keypad and the door clicks open. Inside Jay presses some buttons on an alarm pad and there's a double beep as it deactivates. He presses a button and lights come on.

My breath draws in sharply. I was so wrong. This isn't an apartment block. This is all one house. The true extent of Jay's success and wealth sinks in as I gaze around.

"Would you like a tour?" Jay asks me.

"Yes, please." I draw in a breath. It will give me time to get my head around just how unexpectedly this night is turning out. "This is incredible!"

"Perk of the job." He shrugs, seeming embarrassed.

The open double height entryway we are standing in has two staircases, one on each side leading upstairs, with a large modern chandelier hanging down the center. It's all very neutral and modern—white walls, chrome switches, and a large glass table with a giant exotic-looking flower arrangement on it, its heady scent noticeable as we walk past.

"My housekeeper likes flowers," he explains as he sees me admiring them.

"You have a housekeeper?"

"Yeah, Maggie looks after the house for me, makes sure things are kept in order."

We walk into an open-plan lounge and kitchen area. The floor is a kind of polished concrete. One entire wall is glass windows that look out over the city. The lights of LA twinkle below us like tiny stars. There's a giant U-shaped dark-gray sofa around a marble coffee table, facing a giant TV screen up on the wall. A long dining table with more chairs than I can count with one glance is over to one side. The kitchen is white with dark marble counters and a large breakfast bar with four stools stretches out, dividing the room from the lounge area. There is another door, which I assume is the laundry room and a corridor on one side of the space, which Jay leads me down, and I can see that one room is a huge home gym with every piece of equipment I can think of.

So that's how he stays so fit and muscular.

"This is my office," he says, opening another door.

The room has an enormous desk and chair set up with a computer and lots of pictures on the walls. They look like a mix of stills from films and modeling shots. One is of a younger-looking Jay wearing just a pair of jeans pulled down low, with his tanned muscular torso on display, his hair a bit longer and scruffier on top, and the best 'come fuck me' look on his face I've ever seen.

"That's from one of my first modeling jobs. I was eighteen. I hate it but Stefan insists on having it up there to remind him of the early days, and he uses the office just as much as me when he's here," Jay explains.

"Stefan's been working with you a long time?"

"Yeah, since my first job after I got scouted by a modeling agency. Can't get rid of him," he jokes. "Seriously though, he's a great friend now. I trust him, which, like we were talking about earlier, is hard to come by here," Jay says with a small sigh. "This house is too big for just me, but it goes with the territory. It's what people expect and it's near work. Plus, it's nice to have the space when I have family and friends stay. Let me show you the view." He leads me back out to the main living area.

He presses some controls on the wall and the entire glass wall of windows slides open, revealing a deck area with seating and sun loungers and an infinity pool. The way it's been designed and built into the hillside means it's private and not overlooked. I search for something to say but come up with nothing. It's like something I've seen in the stars' homes sections of magazines, but then that's where I am, in Jay Anderson's home and he is a big Hollywood star.

This suddenly feels rather surreal.

"Let me get you a drink," he says as he sees my expression.

"That would be great, please,"

He disappears into the kitchen, then comes back and hands me a glass of champagne, clinking his glass to mine before taking a sip.

"To rainforest birds," he toasts with a straight face. "May those poor fellas always find the best stick and bust the best moves to win the girls." His eyes crinkle at the corners as he laughs out loud.

I can't help it; I throw my head back and laugh too.

"I really said that," I say, rolling my eyes.

"You sure did. It's when I decided there was more to you I had to know, Holly," he says, his eyes meeting mine.

My heart races and I drink my champagne a little too fast, feeling warmth rush to my head.

"Let me show you the rest of the house," Jay says, taking my hand again and leading me back inside.

We go back to the main hallway and climb up one flight of stairs. I'm barely paying attention as he points out luxury bedrooms and bathrooms. Five so far? I've lost count. All I can think about is that his bedroom must be last. *What's going to happen when we get there?* My stomach twists into a nervous knot.

Finally, we reach a set of double doors.

"This is my room," he says as he presses down on the handles and the doors swing open.

I look around at the room. It's modern, like the rest of the house. The walls are painted in a soft cream and there is a huge bed with thick, sumptuous-looking white bedding on it. The walls have giant framed prints of coastal photography, incredible images of waves crashing and stretches of perfect white sand. To one side of the room there is a walk-in wardrobe that I can glimpse lots of neatly arranged clothes and shoes in. I like this room. It has a different feel than the rest of the house. It's still modern, but more inviting and homey. I slip off my shoes and my feet sink into the cream carpet as I walk in ahead of Jay. I turn to look at him. His eyes are roaming up and down my body, taking in the curves of my hips and the way the gold dress plunges at my neckline, showing off my cleavage. He brings them up to meet mine and they're dark with desire.

"I just need to use the—" I gesture toward the master en suite bathroom, slipping inside and closing the door behind me.

I let out my breath once I'm inside. I'm really here, doing this. I can feel my heart racing. I look up, distracted for a moment. Even the bathroom is luxurious, like a hotel spa. There's a vast walk-in rainfall shower off to one side, double sinks set into a marble countertop, and a huge free-standing bathtub set in front of the floor-to-ceiling windows which, like the living area downstairs, look out over the incredible view. I take a deep breath and look at my reflection in the mirror above the sinks. The edge of the marble counter feels cool underneath my grip.

This is crazy. What am I even doing here in Jay Anderson's bathroom, of all places?

My green eyes stare back at me, my pupils dilated from a mix of champagne and arousal. The small voice inside my head pipes up, *'Being a lucky bitch, that's what you're doing here. Now get out there and enjoy one night off from being just Holly Havers.'* I won't ever see him again. I can let loose and be whoever I want to be tonight.

A mischievous glint grows in my eyes; I'm really doing this. I open the door and walk back into the bedroom where Jay is waiting for me.

His gorgeous blue eyes look dark as they roam over my body. "Come here, Holly." His voice sounds strained as though he's finding it hard to hold back and not stride across the room and grab me.

I walk over to him. I don't know what it is, but this feels different to every other time I've been with someone; maybe it's because it's my first one-night stand. Something deep inside me starts to awaken, and something about Jay makes me feel like I can do anything. Perhaps it's the way he looks at me, the intensity in his eyes, knowing I am his sole focus, or how he's so openly showing that he wants me. I glance down to where his cock is straining against his trousers.

I can be whoever I want to be tonight. I stop in front of him and look at him from under my lashes. He swallows and sucks in his breath before putting his hands either side of my face and pulling me toward him, his mouth finding mine in a heavenly rush of heat and pressure. I rise on my toes and deepen our kiss, our tongues hungry against each other.

I want more, so much more. I can't pull him in close enough before he draws away and starts tracing a line of kisses along my jawline and down my neck, sweeping my hair back over my shoulder. I lean my head to the other side and expose more of my neck to him.

"You are so beautiful, Holly," he whispers in my ear, his hands now on my ass, digging his fingers into my skin so he can pull me against him. His erection pushes against my stomach. "The things you make me want to do to you," he says, his lips finding mine again.

"Show me," I whisper against them.

He doesn't need any more encouragement. He reaches up with one hand and unzips my dress, sliding each strap off my shoulders so it drops to the floor in a pile around my feet. Then he unfastens my strapless bra, and it too falls away.

"Fuck," he hisses, taking in the sight of my breasts rising and falling with each breath I'm trying to catch. He cups them in his hands, squeezing and rolling my hard nipples between his skilled fingers.

"That feels so good," I moan, throwing my head back and arching my breasts up toward him.

He leans down and takes one nipple in his mouth, sucking it hard and stretching it out. A rush of arousal soaks my panties and I reach out to feel him through his trousers.

"I'm so wet for you, Jay," I hear myself say in a voice that doesn't sound like me at all. "I can't wait to feel your big cock filling me up." My words make him lift his eyes from my breasts. but he soon recovers as he sees the dark arousal in mine.

There's no going back now.

"Fucking hell, Holly," he groans as his eyes search my face.

I can tell that I've surprised him. I've surprised myself, too.

I give him a small smile as I part my legs a little wider. His eyes drop to between my legs.

"I need to taste you now!" he says, dropping to his knees in front of me and sliding my lace panties down, both hands lingering on my legs.

He scrunches my panties in his fist and lifts them to his nose, inhaling deeply, closing his eyes in pleasure. It is the hottest thing I have ever seen in my life. He puts them into the pocket of his trousers and then lifts one of my legs and puts it over his shoulder, his eyes locked back on mine.

His kisses trail up the inside of my thigh as I moan in anticipation. I reach down and grab his hair in my fists, pulling his head further into me. It seems to ignite something in him as then he's all over me with his tongue, licking and sucking, his stubble rough against my skin. His mouth finds my clitoris and I roll my eyes back in my head as another rush of wetness meets him and he laps it up hungrily.

"You've got such a beautiful body, Holly," he says as he draws back to look up at me, his face glistening with my arousal.

He's still fully dressed and I'm here, ready and open for him. I can't believe I'm here, doing this with him. It's almost more than I can take.

"I need to feel you, Jay," I gasp urgently.

He places my leg back down on the floor and rises to his feet, kissing up my body on the way, sucking each nipple hard. I grab his face and pull him into a kiss, my tongue eager to find his and share the taste of myself that is all over him. As we kiss, I unbutton his shirt and slide it down his biceps, his skin hot under my touch. His heady scent almost renders me unable to think. My hands find his belt and I unfasten it.

"I can't wait to see your cock," I pant against his mouth.

A deep groan escapes his lips, and he grabs my hand to hurry it up. Together we pull down his trousers and boxer shorts and his cock springs free. I look down; it's large and smooth and has a bead of pre-cum on the tip. I want to taste it, but before I can do anything else Jay walks me backwards toward the bed and pushes me down gently onto it.

"You look incredible lying there on my bed, Holly." His eyes roam over my body.

I love the way he looks at me. I feel like a goddess, powerful and strong, my inhibitions set free.

I take my hand and slowly put two of my fingers into my mouth and suck them. I have Jay's full attention and he's watching me with growing intensity in his eyes. I put my hand between my legs and touch myself, rubbing little circles over my clitoris.

"Does that feel good?" Jay asks, his eyes burning into me.

"Oh," I moan. "It feels so good," I say, and then I slide my two fingers deep inside myself and watch his eyes widen and his breathing quicken. He has his cock in his hand and is stroking it as he watches me. "I need you now. I want to feel you inside me."

He jumps up and grabs something from his bedside drawer. When I look down, he is rolling a condom onto his now angry-looking cock. I smile at the effect I'm having on him.

"Fucking hell, Holly," he says as he lies down over me and kisses me deeply.

"Mmm," I moan as I wriggle underneath him.

He reaches one of his hands down and his fingers swipe across my dripping wet skin, hot and ready for him. He plunges two of his warm, thick fingers deep inside me and I gasp, my back arching up from the bed. He catches my mouth with his again and kisses me, sucking my bottom lip. I can't take much more of this; I've never wanted anyone like this before.

"Fuck me, Jay," I demand. "Now!"

His eyes flash and he lifts one of my legs up and wraps it around his waist, holding himself up with his elbows on either side of my head. I hold his gaze as he slowly slides into me, inch by gloriously thick inch. I lose my breath for a moment and he pauses while I get used to his size, then he slides in farther until he's as deep inside me as he can be.

I let out a soft moan. "More."

He pulls backwards and then pushes forward again. It feels so good. He pulls out and pushes back in, finding a rhythm, his thrusts growing harder each time. I cry out and hear a deep growl as he says my name, then he straightens his arms, putting them underneath my legs so they're held up over his shoulders.

Then he lets me have it.

He plunges into me harder and faster while I grip on to his biceps. They're solid and tense under my fingers as they hold him up. The bed bangs against the wall, and

I cry "Yes!" over and over again, lost in the sensation of his body taking mine.

"That's it, baby," Jay growls. "Come for me; I want to feel you."

I feel my orgasm building deep inside of me as Jay pounds into me. I can hardly breathe as it builds and builds.

"I'm going to come, Jay!" I scream, throwing my head back, as suddenly waves crash over me.

I've lost all control over my body and completely surrender to him. I'm shuddering uncontrollably as my orgasm continues, my body squeezing Jay's cock as my muscles ripple around him.

"Fuck, Holly!" He lets out a guttural moan and screws his face up as his cock pulsates and he comes. As he empties himself, his thrusts slow, until he's still, holding himself inside me.

We're panting, sweat running down our bodies. Jay rolls to the side of me, holding my leg as he does so our bodies stay connected. We look into each other's eyes. I'm now painfully aware of how well our bodies fit together, and how good it could be under different circumstances.

Jay Anderson allows me to be a different woman—free and uninhibited. Too bad she's only visiting for one night.

"You are something else, Holly," Jay says softly as he rubs his thumb across my bottom lip, before leaning in to kiss me again.

I kiss him back, trying not to let myself get carried away by how close I feel to him at this precise moment. I can't deny there's something about him, something magnetic pulling me closer.

But this is just one magical night and he's wrong.

I'm not the special one.

He is.

Chapter 5

"You keep surprising me, Holly," Jay says as he studies my face.

"A good surprise?"

I feel more sober and self-conscious about the fact that I'm naked with his body in mine.

What if he thinks I act like that with everyone I've just met?

I move my leg back so we separate. Jay takes the condom off, ties a knot in it, and drops it on the floor next to the bed before turning back to face me. He wraps a warm arm around my waist and pulls me to his chest.

"An exceptional surprise." His eyes twinkle. "Like eating your favorite cereal and hunting for the toy in the box, only to discover you've got the entire frigging set in there!" he says before breaking into a smile and looking like a schoolboy who's met his superhero. "It's always the quiet ones," he says in mock disbelief, watching for my reaction.

I can't help but giggle and his eyes crinkle at the sides as he smiles at me, seeming pleased that he's made me laugh.

"Seriously though, Holly"—he runs a finger up and down the curve of my hip—"please tell me if I'm overstepping the mark here, but you don't seem to realize how great you are."

I look at him, his face full of sincerity and concern. I want to open up to him. My gut tells me I can trust him, and anyway, I may never see him again.

"My ex," I begin, moving back from Jay and looking down at the bed. "He, um, he told me I was..." I stop talking, my hand fiddling with the edge of the pillow.

"He told you what?" Jay's gentle voice coaxes.

"He told me I was boring in bed, you know, frigid," I say as I feel heat rise in my cheeks.

"He what?" Jay whips straight up into a sitting position.

"That's not all." I take a deep breath to steady my nerves over what I'm about to say. Even though it's been nine months, talking about it still brings back all the feelings of shame I felt when it first happened. "He filmed us together and showed it around to some of his friends."

I swallow back tears, my cheeks burning at the humiliation and complete betrayal of trust. I vomited in shock when I first found out.

MEETING MR. ANDERSON

Jay's eyes are on fire, his expression murderous. A vein in his neck pulses and his hands are in tight fists by his sides. I shouldn't have told him; he looks so angry.

"It was a long time ago," I say, sitting up and reaching for his hand. "It doesn't matter."

"It matters to me," Jay says, taking my hand in his. His anger is obvious, but I can tell he's trying to rein it in. "The thought of some asshole doing that to you. Doing that to anyone. God, I want to snap his neck!" He spits. He looks at me, his beautiful eyes holding mine. "He doesn't know a thing, Holly. He didn't deserve you." He takes a couple of deep breaths and his shoulders loosen ever so slightly. He reaches out and takes my other hand. "Come with me."

Jay leads me into the bathroom and turns on the shower. Steam fills the room. He pulls me in under the warm water with him, and as it runs over our bodies, he takes my face in his hands, staring into my eyes.

"Only listen to me from now on, Holly. My voice," he says as he presses my body back against the cool tile wall.

He lowers his lips to my ear and his warm breath sends goosebumps up my arms.

I'm transfixed as his deep voice whispers into my ear. "You are incredible." He kisses behind my ear as he places one hand between my legs, parting them gently. His hand strokes, slowly caressing me. My legs feel like jelly, weak from the incredible orgasm I just had. He has to use his other arm around my waist to hold me up and support me. I wrap my arms around his neck and run my hands through his hair.

"You are so sexy," he whispers, continuing to stroke me, his lips grazing against my collarbone as he sucks, nibbles, and kisses up and down my neck. "You amaze me," he says as his arm tightens around my waist and he pulls me even closer. His other hand keeps moving between my legs, his strokes slow and purposeful, his fingers skilled.

I moan out loud, his name escaping my lips as my arousal grows. He slides two thick fingers through my wet lips and deep inside me. My body clenches around them, sucking him in.

"Holly, beautiful Holly," he murmurs into my ear and I shudder at the intense pleasure as his thumb finds my clitoris and circles it. He's gentle at first, taking his time, building up the pressure and speed.

I tilt my head back against the hard tiles as my orgasm builds. It's going to take every last ounce of energy my body has. The pressure builds, my entire body tensing, before I shatter in his arms and come. This time with his words and touches of adoration filling my senses.

We stay like this for a long time. His strong arms supporting me, my head resting against his chest.

He holds me, letting the water just wash down over us. What he's just given to me is incredible. I glimpsed who he is, how big his heart is. He's a beautiful person to want to heal the pain from my past in such a tender way. *How can this be a one-night stand?* It may be my first, but this can't be normal? Don't his actions prove it's more to him?

He loosens his grip on my waist, steadying me on my feet before letting go. My skin burns at the loss of his touch. He reaches over to a recessed shelf built into the tile wall and picks up a white shower puff and bottle, then squeezes some shower gel onto it. Then he places the puff against my skin, tenderly rubbing it across my body. He washes my neck, breasts, stomach, hips, and then my back, before bending down to his knees and washing up and down each leg. When he stands, he places the puff against my pussy, still throbbing from his earlier touch.

His eyes hold mine as he washes me there.

"My turn," I say quietly.

Jay hands me the puff and watches as I put more gel onto it. I swirl it across his chest, admiring his toned muscles and strong, broad shoulders.

He really is an intense example of the male sex.

I wash across his washboard abs, admiring the perfect *V* shape his muscles make down from his hips, so masculine and virile, I can't help smiling. I gently wash between his legs and his cock twitches at my touch.

"Turn around, pretty boy." I smirk at him.

He pretends to look outraged and splashes some water toward my face. "Don't get cheeky now, my juicy little berry."

"Berry! Who are you calling a berry?" I squeal as I splash him back.

He tries to hide his smirk before speaking. "Holly, I know you have such a juicy, tasty little berry." He pretends to sound seductive. "So I shall call you my juicy little berry," he says firmly as he turns around.

What the?

I try not to laugh as I don't want him to think he's funny, even though he can probably tell I'm trying to hold back a giggle.

His juicy berry? As if.

I wash his legs and then his bum. It's the first time I've really seen it. It's toned and muscular, smooth, and perfect. I fight back the urge to bend down and bite it, instead choosing to run my hands over it while it's slick with soap.

This night has turned out so unexpectedly. Twenty-four hours ago, I was running to catch what I thought was just going to be another regular flight and now I'm here, in Jay Anderson's shower, washing his incredible ass. I bite my lip to stop myself from breaking into a goofy grin, afraid that if I let it appear it will never leave my face.

As I wash Jay's back with the puff, I notice he has a small tattoo on his right shoulder, the initials '*RC*', in a beautiful, black, spiraled script.

"Who's RC?"

The muscles in his back immediately tighten. He doesn't answer straightaway.

"RC was my best friend," he says, his voice not much more than a whisper. "Rob died when we were twenty-one."

I freeze for a moment. The only sound is the shower water falling around us.

I slowly start washing his back again. "I'm so sorry... Do you want to talk about it?"

He lets out a big sigh, his shoulders slumping, like he has the weight of the world on them. "Not right now, Holly, not tonight. Thank you, though."

"Okay," I say, wrapping my arms around his back and holding on to his chest.

I press my lips tenderly against his back and kiss it.

After the shower, I'm standing at the sink to take my makeup off with a hot washcloth and some soap. Jay is watching me, fascinated.

"What?" I eye him in the mirror.

"I'm just waiting to see if I still recognize you," he jokes.

I turn and throw the washcloth at him, aiming for his chest, but he lifts a hand and catches it with ease as he grins at me.

He comes up and wraps his arms around me from behind, moving my hair away from one shoulder so he can press a kiss to it. "You look beautiful. Your hair's like a ray of sunshine around you."

"I didn't know you were a poet." I grin.

I look at our reflection in the mirror. Him, tall, strong, and muscular, with his sandy hair all tousled, and his intense blue eyes. Me, smaller, my long gold-blond hair kissed by the sun, making my green eyes look brighter and alert.

Could this work?

I feel so connected to him somehow. Being with him, I forget how different our lives are. But then, this must happen all the time for him. Bringing a girl home. Only…I cast my mind back to the tender orgasm he gave me in the shower. The way he whispered all those words to me while he worshipped my body. I'm sure there was more to it, something deeper.

"Come on, Berry." He smiles. "You look shattered."

"That's because some sex god took me back to his house to have his way with me for hours," I shoot back, raising an eyebrow at him.

"A sex god, hmm? The way I remember it, a sweet girl named Holly came home to see the view from my window, and a dirty-talking sex kitten emerged and had her way with me." His voice sounds innocent. "I was powerless to her charms, didn't stand a chance," he teases.

"Whatever." I roll my eyes at him, grinning like an idiot inside.

We go back into his bedroom and get into the bed together.

I sink into the plush bedding that has Jay's scent on it. He lies on his back and pulls me up against his side so my head rests on his chest.

I say nothing. I just listen to the sound of his breath going in and out of his body as I fall into a deep, peaceful sleep.

Chapter 6

THE SUN PEEKING THROUGH the window drapes wakes me up. For a moment I wonder where I am and then the events of last night come flooding back to me.

I sneak a look over at Jay, who is still fast asleep on his back, the sheets wrapped around his long tanned legs. His chest is uncovered, rising and falling with each breath he takes.

Sliding out of bed, I tiptoe into the bathroom, shutting the door behind me. I go to the sink and splash some water on my face.

Despite the late night and alcohol, by some miracle I look bright-eyed and fresh. Luckily, I left my clutch bag in here last night. I always carry emergency items in here—one quirk of being airline crew, you never know when you may need to quickly freshen up. I comb my hair and brush my teeth. *I could apply some makeup. No. Way too obvious.*

I creep back into the bedroom and slide back into bed next to Jay. He stretches and murmurs, but his eyes stay shut, his long eyelashes resting on his cheeks. My eyes linger over his face, his strong jawline covered in stubble, his soft, kissable lips. He is so handsome. How many other girls have been lucky enough to wake up to this view?

My eyes roam down his torso and to the sheets barely covering him. They're low on his stomach, the top of his strong V-shaped muscles visible. *I'll just peek. It would be a terrible waste not to.*

I slide the sheets down and expose his cock. It's smooth and perfect, resting up against his stomach. I wriggle down the bed and reach over with one hand and cup his balls. They tighten with my touch. Holding the base of him with my other hand, I lean over and take him inside my mouth. He's big, and it's good to finally taste him. I suck and swirl my tongue over his tip. His body rewards me with a small bead of wetness. He tastes so good.

His breathing changes and I realize I'm being watched.

I look up and Jay's bright-blue eyes are fixed on where my lips wrap around him. He reaches down with one hand and plays with my hair, stroking it back off my face and running it through his fingers. I gaze up at him as I slowly sink down, taking all of him deep into my mouth and throat. He's so big I'm worried I might gag, but I manage not to. I rise again, swirling my tongue around him. I find a rhythm, up and down, moaning with my appreciation of his beautiful body. It's so good having him here in my mouth. I tug on his balls with my hand and he sucks in a breath.

"Ah, Holly." His eyes blaze into mine as he says my name.

My lips smile around him. I love hearing him say my name like that.

"Come here, Berry," he says, and I slowly release him from my mouth, kissing his tip and crawling back up the bed.

He sits up, resting his back against the fabric headboard, and pulls me onto his lap so I'm straddling him. His warm hands drop to either side of my hips. I roll them around so I'm rubbing myself over his rock-hard cock, back and forth, back and forth. He groans and closes his eyes, lost in the sensation.

Reaching over to his bedside table, I take a condom out of the box he used last night. Tearing the packet open, I take it out and roll it down onto him. Jay opens his eyes and watches what I'm doing. He reaches up to cup the side of my face, rubbing his thumb along my bottom lip. I place my hand on top of his and turn my head, drawing his thumb in between my lips, sucking it. His eyes glitter as he leans forward and pulls me into a deep kiss. His strong tongue finds mine, sucking and stroking.

I could get lost in his kiss, lose hours in it, and still never feel like I'd had enough.

I raise my hips up and hold the base of him as I lower myself down onto his waiting cock. I roll my hips side to side to get used to his size. Jay groans and he pushes deeper into my mouth with his tongue. His hands go back to my hips as he lifts me up and back down onto him, the sound of my wetness against his body getting louder. He stops kissing me, resting his forehead against mine as we watch our bodies meeting together with each thrust.

"You feel so good, Holly, so damn good."

I move faster as Jay digs his fingers into my hips. My hands glide up his chest and over his shoulders, up into his hair. I grab it in both hands and tug his head back so he's looking up into my face. The dark look in his eyes sends heat racing through my core.

"That's it, baby," he growls. "Look at me while you ride my cock."

I see the glint in his eyes, a silent dare to see if I will take the bait.

"I'm going to ride your cock so hard," I hear myself say, accepting his challenge to let my desires flow from my lips.

I don't know what it is, but I can do this with him. I can let my inhibitions go.

"Do you like being deep inside me? Feeling me wrapped around you?" I sigh as I continue sliding up and down.

He smiles at me as he grips my hips harder and raises his, slamming into me.

I just got my answer.

"I can't get enough of it," he says, sounding pleased that I played the game.

"Then give it to me hard, big boy." I smile back at him, trying not to giggle.

He smirks up at me as he slams me up and down, over and over. Each time he slams me down, he circles his hips, and a delicious friction rubs against my clitoris, causing the inside of my thighs to shake. The familiar pressure grows inside me as I tip my head back and let out a deep moan.

"That's it, baby," Jay says. "Come for me, let me feel you."

His deep voice pushes me over the edge, and I can't hold it any longer. I throw my head back and open my mouth, screaming his name as a huge orgasm rushes through me.

"Oh yeah, Holly, that's my girl." I hear Jay moan, but it sounds as though he's far away as I'm lost in my own waves of ecstasy. "I'm going to come," he groans, his voice pulling me back to him.

He drives into me one last time and I feel his cock swell as he comes long and hard. His body is shuddering, sweat running down his chest. I put my hand there and his heart is pounding while he holds himself deep inside me, riding out the last waves of his orgasm.

"I can't get enough of your dirty mouth, Holly. It's such a fucking turn-on that you feel free enough to let it out with me." He looks at me while he catches his breath.

I smile at him. I love this new side of me too. I hope she gets the chance to come out more.

I gaze down at Jay's content face.

A lot more.

I take a shower as Jay goes down to his office to call Stefan about work things. He's given me one of his white T-shirts to wear over my gold dress. At least now if I tie it in a knot around my waist, it looks like a skirt and top combo and less like I've hooked up and spent the entire night in someone else's bed.

I pull my hair up into a messy bun on top of my head and look at myself in the bathroom mirror. I've put some mascara and lip gloss on that I had in my bag from last night, and I look quite awake. It's not obvious I've been up half the night having the best sex of my life.

I make my way downstairs and into the big open-plan living area. Something smells delicious and my stomach growls. Jay is barefoot at the stove in the kitchen with his back to me. He's wearing faded blue jeans and a white T-shirt. My eyes run up and down his body, resting on his perfect ass. He hears me and turns.

"There she is," he says as he spoons some poached eggs out of the pan he's holding onto two plates of brown toast and wilted spinach. "Come, sit," he gestures to the breakfast bar, where there's fresh juice poured into two glasses and some napkins and cutlery laid out. I perch myself up on a stool and take a sip of the juice as Jay sits down next to me.

"Mmm, yummy." I lick my lips. "What is that?"

"Only the best for you, little Berry. That is a mix of mango, orange, and guava, squeezed by yours truly this morning," he says, puffing out his chest.

"Really?"

"Yes, I squeezed each fruit between my thighs while you were in the shower," he says with a smirk.

"You idiot." I laugh, swatting him with my napkin.

"Oh sorry, I forgot. It was you squeezing my fruit between your thighs, wasn't it?" he teases. "And idiot sounds so terribly English, Holly," he says in a fake posh English accent.

"Oh, I'm sorry if my accent and terminology offends you Mr. Big Shot Actor," I throw back.

"Not at all." He smiles, taking a bite of his breakfast, chewing thoughtfully before swallowing. "I take delight in the words that escape your lips, Holly." He winks at me and I smile down at my plate.

As we eat our breakfast, I look around the room, my eyes resting on a framed photograph on the side. It's of Jay with an older couple and another guy with darker hair and more stubble. The other guy is wearing a brown T-shirt and combat trousers, and is incredibly good-looking, in a rugged way. They're all smiling at the camera with their arms around each other.

"Who's that?" I ask, pointing toward the photo with my fork.

"That's my parents and brother Blake." He smiles.

"You look like your dad," I say as I take in the older man. He's got salt-and-pepper hair and a strong defined jawline, but it's his bright-blue eyes that hold the most resemblance; they're full of warmth. The lady next to him is delicate and beautiful, her smile wide and her light-blond hair cut into a stylish layered cut that just skims her shoulders.

"Yeah, I get told that a lot," Jay says, taking a swig of his drink. "I'm hoping to get up and see them while we have a break from filming the show."

"That sounds lovely. Are they far?"

"Not really, around an hour and a half on a good run. It's just been so crazy with work recently that I haven't made it back for a few weeks," Jay says, looking at the photo.

"Much-needed then." I smile.

"Definitely," he agrees.

We eat the rest of our breakfast in companionable silence before Jay speaks again.

"So, I've got some meetings to go to today, but I should be finished by late afternoon. Can I take you out for dinner tonight?" he asks casually.

I almost choke on the mouthful of food as I swallow. "Oh yeah, sure, sounds good."

He wants to see me again tonight? Maybe this isn't just a one-off thing to him.

"Great." Jay smiles. "I'll drop you back at your hotel on my way to my meeting and can come back to pick you up tonight."

Ten minutes later I've gathered my things and am sitting in the passenger seat of Jay's Ferrari. I should have known. I had rolled my eyes when I saw it, much to Jay's amusement. I can't believe I thought the garages belonged to apartments when in reality they all belong to Jay.

He drives me back to my hotel, one hand on the steering wheel and the other resting on my thigh. We pull up outside the main doors and the valet guy does a double take from his desk near the entrance. I'm not sure if it's recognizing Jay or checking out the car, but either Jay doesn't notice or is so used to it he isn't bothered. He gets out of the car and comes around to open my door for me. I climb out and he catches me around the waist, pulling me in for a deep kiss that is over far too quickly.

"See you tonight," he calls as he gets back into the car, and after giving me one last smile, he drives away.

Then he's gone, leaving my lips tingling.

I put my fingers to them.

Yes, see you later, Jay Anderson.

Back in my hotel room, I flop myself backwards onto the bed, my body sinking into the mattress. I kick my shoes off my feet and stare at the ceiling.

Maybe I dreamed the last twenty-four hours? I pinch my arm hard. Ouch! Nope, not a dream.

I sit up and look around the hotel room, my suitcase open on the floor, my uniform hanging up. This is my life. It's a world away from Jay's Hollywood existence. The last twenty-four hours have been amazing, but when I fly home, that's it. It'll be over. He won't even remember my name. Just another girl that couldn't deny her attraction to him. Yet, deep down, I can't let myself believe that. There's a connection between us. I can feel it, I swear, or maybe I'm delusional?

"Oh, Holly, what have you got yourself into?" I groan, dragging my hands down my face.

The phone beside my bed rings, making me jump. I reach over and grab the handset.

"Hello?"

"Holly! You naughty little minx! I've been trying to call you for hours!" Matt shouts through the phone. I can't help smiling at his tone despite my mood just moments ago. "I need all the details, you know! You aren't getting away with it! Did you at least give the man a rest at some point last night?" Matt asks.

I bite my lip. He's got me. He always cheers me up; his bubbly personality is infectious.

"Should I be asking you the same thing?" I tease.

"Oh, Holly, I'm in love!" he gushes. "I just need Stefan to realize that I am the answer to all his prayers!"

"He would be the lucky one," I say to Matt, and I mean it. He has a heart of gold. Although Stefan doesn't stand a chance. Once Matt wants something, he goes for it.

"So, what's the plan for the rest of today then? Assuming you can still walk, that is?" Matt chuckles, amused at his own joke.

"So, Jay wants to take me out to dinner tonight," I say nervously.

"So, you and me need to go shopping right now!" Matt fires back.

"Okay, okay." I laugh, giving in to him. "Give me ten minutes to get changed and I will meet you in the lobby."

We hang up and I grab my cell phone, tapping out a quick text to my other best friend, Rachel. I already texted her yesterday and told her we were off to the show. There's no way she will expect what I'm about to send, though.

Me: You'll never guess what happened last night. I only spent the night at Jay Anderson's house!

I grin as my phone beeps with a text straight back from her.

Rachel: Holly! OMG! You so deserved a night of hot sex… Please tell me the sex was HOT!

Me: Scorching…

Rachel: YES! Lucky bitch! I need to know EVERYTHING!

Me: Lol, okay. I'm just about to meet Matt. Will call you ASAP.

Rachel: Can't wait, speak to you soon.

Three hours later we have been in what must be nearly every shop in the mall. Matt has had me trying on outfit after outfit for the perfect thing to wear tonight.

"I don't even know where we're going," I huff as I collapse onto a bench outside Victoria's Secret. "I might not need to dress up at all. What's wrong with my black jeans and that silky blouse?" I suggest, thinking of the only other smart outfit I have packed for the trip.

"You can't wear jeans!" Matt cries in outrage. "Not for dinner, Holly. What if lover boy wants to caress your leg under the table?" He raises his eyebrows at me.

I should think up a witty comeback for feminist rights, but the thought of Jay putting his hands anywhere on my body is so appealing that I jump up off the bench with a newfound enthusiasm.

"Well, what are you waiting for then?" I bark at Matt. "Let's continue the search in there." I point as I march off toward the doors of Victoria's Secret.

An hour later we are in Starbucks, sipping on chai lattes, feeling pleased with ourselves, the evidence of our success scattered around our feet in various shopping bags.

I bought a sexy strapless lingerie set in a gorgeous cream lace with gold flecks and the most beautiful strapless copper-colored dress that cinches in at the waist and then drapes down over the curves of my hips to just below my knee. It shimmers as I walk, and I feel like a fifties starlet in it. Matt even persuaded me to get a pair of gorgeous strappy sandals in the same color. Well, he grabbed my card when I wasn't looking and ran off to the till, but I'm glad he did as they are stunning.

"So, tell me more about Stefan," I say to Matt, leaning across the table with my chin on top of my hands.

"Holly, he's great, really great," gushes Matt. "Nothing happened last night; we just talked for hours. He's so smart. You know, he studied business and then got a job as an intern at a top PR firm. He worked his way up, and then that's when he met Jay. Jay was his first client." Matt's eyes look dreamy as he talks. "They hit it off so well as friends that when Jay's career took off, Stefan left the agency to work with him full time."

"It sounds like they're close."

"Yeah, they must be. There must be times when they disagree over things, though. Imagine working with your friend and seeing them all the time," Matt says.

"Yeah, imagine that. Having to work with a friend for hours at a time and he works you like a slave driver, nowhere to escape to as you're stuck in a metal tube in the sky," I joke.

"Yeah." Matt sighs. "Hey! What?" he says, sitting up straight as he realizes what I said.

"You know I love you really, Matt." I wink at him.

He narrows his eyes at me. "Yes, Holly, you're lucky that I do know that. Otherwise, you'd have sole responsibility for cleaning the toilets every flight."

I shudder at the thought.

"Right, drink up!" Matt orders, signaling to my still half-full mug.

"What? Why?"

"Duh." He rolls his eyes. "We need to get you ready."

I glance at my watch. "Matt, it's only four o'clock."

"Then we're already late!" He slaps his palms flat on the table, making the people at the nearby table look over.

I do as I'm told and down my drink, looking at the determined focus his eyes have taken on. Compliance might be my best option here and besides, the quicker I get ready, the sooner tonight will be here.

The sooner I can see *him* again.

Chapter 7

IT'S SEVEN P.M. AND I'm ready to go.

Matt really went to town on me. I had a salon manicure and pedicure; my nails are now a beautiful shimmery nude. Then he suggested we visit the makeup counters in Macy's, and one salesgirl did an incredible free makeover on me. My eyes are smoky and lined with a hint of copper to match my dress. The mascara she used makes my eyelashes almost look false; they're long, full, and soft. I bought two of them to take home. One for me and one for Rachel. She worked magic on my cheekbones too; they look high and sculpted, and my lips are a gorgeous barely there nude. I tied my hair up in a loose bun and am hoping it looks effortlessly sexy, and not just effortless. Matt wolf-whistled when he saw me and told me to have an incredible night. Then he got a text from Stefan asking what he was up to, so he danced off to his room to call him in private.

I take a last look at myself in the mirror and spray some of my perfume on, my hand shaking.

There's a knock at the door and my stomach leaps into my throat.

He's here.

I can see Jay waiting through the peephole. He's wearing smart dark-blue trousers and a crisp white shirt, open at the neck. His hair is screaming at me to run my fingers through it.

Here goes.

I take a deep breath and open the door. His eyes drop down my body and back up again as a shiver runs down my spine.

How can him just looking at me make me feel like I might combust?

"You look incredible, Holly," he says, still drinking in my body as he reaches up to run his hand across his jaw.

"Not so bad yourself." I smile back.

His eyes light up, like a fire that's been fed more oxygen.

He takes a large stride into the room, closing the gap between us, kicking the door closed behind him. His hands grab either side of my face and he kisses me, his lips pushing against mine with the perfect pressure, his tongue dancing with mine.

"I've been wanting to do that all day," he says, his eyes twinkling. "Now let's go before I rip that dress off you and bend you over the desk with those heels on," he says darkly, looking down my legs at my new shoes.

"Such a gentleman," I reply, picturing the hot scene.

Maybe I don't need to eat after all, and we could stay here.

"Come on, Berry." He smiles cheekily. My shoulders relax with the use of his special name for me.

I take the hand he's holding out toward me and we leave my room and catch the elevator down to the lobby. As we come out, Megan from the flight is by the other side of the lobby. She smiles when she sees me, and then her eyes widen as she notices Jay next to me, my hand in his. I give her a small smile and wave with my free hand and for a minute she looks too shocked to respond, but then her eyebrows raise, and she grins back at me before we disappear out of the main hotel doors.

The valet guy from this morning brings Jay's car round, and Jay thanks him and hands him a tip.

"I should tip you, Mr. Anderson. Wait until I tell my brother I drove a Ferrari!" he exclaims in undisguised excitement.

"Your brother likes cars?" Jay asks.

"Oh, man. My little bro Eric can't get enough! He's a mechanic, but he's never got his hands on a Ferrari before. He will be so jealous, man!"

Jay laughs. "It is a beauty."

They exchange a few more car comments, while I look up at the sky. It's a warm California evening. I can smell the bougainvillea that spills from the hotel's flower beds. It's sweet and feminine. I'm not sure I will smell it again without thinking of tonight.

"Nice talking to you, Cooper," Jay says as he shakes the valet guy's hand before leading me around to the passenger side and opening the door for me.

I slide into the low seat, careful to keep my ankles together as I swing my legs in. Jay shuts the door and walks around the car to the driver's side before slipping into the seat next to me.

"Do you like Thai?" he asks.

"It's my new favorite."

His eyes are bright as he smiles at me in understanding—anywhere with him is my new favorite.

Twenty minutes later, we pull up and park opposite the restaurant. We spent the car journey chatting about work, places I've flown, and places he's traveled to for filming.

Jay opens the door for me, and I take his hand to climb out of the car. All the cars parked nearby are expensive sports cars and there's even a limo. A few journalists are set up on the pavement outside the restaurant as we cross the road.

"Don't worry, they don't bite," Jay jokes when he sees me looking worried. "This place has the best Thai in LA; a lot of people visit here. Those guys are here every night looking for a story."

I am blinded by some bright flashes as cameras go off.

"Jay!" calls one of the paparazzi. "Any storyline hints you can give us for season three of your show?"

"Now, that would ruin all the fun." Jay smiles.

"Who's your lovely date, Jay?" another with dark-brown shaggy hair calls, but Jay is already steering me past them.

"That was so weird," I whisper.

"Most of them aren't too bad." He shrugs. "You hear about the ruthless ones who will do anything to get a good story, but most of them have families at home and they're just doing their job."

"You're right. I never thought about it like that. Just heard the bad things, you know?"

"Don't judge a book by its cover, Berry," he scolds, dipping his mouth to my ear, "or I may have to spank you later for unacceptable behavior."

I know I'm blushing, but now I'm tempted, just to see if he means it.

I look up at the tall building in front of us. It's all black glass, sleek and commanding. The main entrance is two giant black doors with oversized intricate gold handles. They remind me of a temple I visited once. Two staff members dressed in black suits and ties open the doors for us.

My breath catches in my throat as we walk in. It's incredible. The décor has this kind of earthy, tropical vibe to it. There's a long bar running along one side and a mix of tables and booths in a dark wood with deep-green velvet chairs. There are large, lush tropical plants everywhere you look, and the lighting is low and sexy. Each table has a small lantern on it and hanging from the ceiling are dimly lit wicker pendants of varying sizes. There's a real buzz of energy. All the tables are occupied. This place is popular, just like Jay said.

"This is gorgeous." I look back over at Jay. His eyes are on my face.

"Yes, it certainly is," he says, looking down at my lips.

"Good evening, Mr. Anderson, and good evening, miss. Welcome to Fusion," a server greets us. "My name is Jack; may I show you to your table? We've seated you on the terrace this evening. I hope this is suitable?"

"Great, thanks," says Jay, and we follow Jack out a door at the side of the room and onto the terrace.

It has the same feel as inside with the large plants and lanterns on the tables. Above them is a wooden veranda covered in vines and scattered with fairy lights. Dotted between the tables are small potted trees covered in lights, giving each table a sense of privacy. Jack shows us to our table, and we order drinks before he leaves us to look at our menus.

"I'm glad you came tonight, Holly," Jay says, looking across at me. "I swear I listened to nothing in my meetings today. I just kept thinking back to last night." A flirtatious smile plays on his lips. "It's a good thing Stefan was there paying attention; otherwise, I have no idea what I might have signed myself up for."

Jay has been thinking about me all day?

"I'm sure Stefan has it all under control. He seems very capable."

Jay raises an eyebrow. "Don't go getting a crush on my friend now, Berry. I want all your attention on me."

I fight back a giggle as Jack reappears with our drinks. "Here you are," he says, placing two tall glasses of the house cocktail on the table. He takes our food order before disappearing.

"You two are close then?" I ask Jay, taking our conversation back to his relationship with Stefan.

"Yeah, he's one of my closest friends. We've known each other a long time. After Rob died, I found it hard. Stefan just seemed to get it. He understood somehow." Jay looks down at his drink at the mention of Rob.

"I'm sorry, Jay. That must have been so tough." I reach across the table to take his hand.

"It was, still is, some days. But Rob wouldn't have wanted me moping about. So, tell me about your family," Jay says, changing the subject.

"Well, my mum and dad live by the coast in Cornwall, where I grew up. My mum loves baking; I swear she's tried making every cake known to man." I smile as I picture Mum in her floral apron that she's had since I was a kid. "My dad is a judge, the fairest man I know, but he forgets he's not in court sometimes. He caught me and my sister Sophie drinking underage at a family party once and turned the living room into a courtroom while he put us on trial. It was mortifying." I put my hand over my eyes as I laugh at the memory. "We were so embarrassed in front of all our cousins; I swear neither of us touched another drop for years!"

Jay laughs, his eyes twinkling in amusement. "Your dad sounds like a character!"

"How about you?" I ask Jay, turning the spotlight onto him as I take another sip of my drink.

"Well," he says, leaning back in his chair, "I grew up in a small town close to here. My mom likes to fuss over me and my brother Blake whenever we go visit, and my dad runs his own home maintenance business. They met when they were sixteen and have been in love ever since. Dad told me she was the prettiest girl he'd ever seen."

"That's so sweet." I lean my chin into my hands as he lights up, talking about his family.

"Blake runs his own outdoor pursuits company. Takes people on these wilderness survival experiences. He's done well for himself, although never tell him you think that. He'll get an enormous ego!" Jay laughs, shaking his head as he looks at the table.

I smile. It's obvious that family means a lot to him.

"Did you dream of being an actor as a kid?"

"Hell no!" He laughs. "After being scouted for modeling, I went on to commercials, then got my first film role. It just kind of snowballed from there, but I wanted to work in conservation and study animals."

I snort some of my drink up my nose and cough. "I'm sorry." I smile, patting my mouth with my napkin. "I just can't believe how you went from wanting to be Dr. Doolittle to what you're doing now."

He laughs and his eyes crinkle in that way I love. "I guess I wasn't meant to talk to animals after all. We don't all have a magic tongue for words." He smiles, his eyes holding mine, and I can just tell he's thinking about us in bed together and how I have a desire to talk dirty with him.

I smile down at my drink as Jack appears with our food.

"This looks delicious," I say, taking in the steaming plates of pad Thai, and the delicately arranged sharing platter, decorated with frangipani flowers.

"Here," Jay says, picking up one of the miniature tofu wraps.

It looks too delicate and cute to eat. He holds it up to my lips and I open my mouth as he feeds me. My lips slip over his finger and thumb before he moves them away.

He sucks in his breath. "God, Holly, you've no idea how much I like your lips, what goes in them and what comes out." He raises an eyebrow and smirks.

"You're a bad boy. I don't know what you're talking about." I smile.

"Perhaps you need reminding later." He smirks back and my stomach flutters at the thought.

We don't stop chatting as we eat the rest of our meal. Jay's so easy to talk to and the conversation just seems to flow. I tell Jay about Rachel and Matt, and what I do at home between trips. It must all sound so mundane, but Jay listens without taking his eyes off me. He tells me more about the small town he grew up in and stories about his family, but he doesn't mention Rob again.

When it's time to leave, we make our way back through the main restaurant to the exit, Jay keeping his hand low on my back.

"I'm just going to use the ladies' room," I say, gesturing to the restroom sign.

"Okay, I'll wait here for you," says Jay, perching on a stool at the bar.

I float off on a cloud of, I don't know what, happiness, excitement? I just know that I've had a wonderful evening. I've gotten to know Jay a lot better and I don't know where this is going, but I hope it doesn't end with tonight. I find the restroom and look at my reflection in the mirror. My eyes sparkle back at me. Maybe he has always dated models before, but I don't look too bad. I admire the job the Macy's makeup girl did and the outfit Matt helped me pick out.

I'm smiling as I come out of the restroom. I must look like a lovesick teenager.

Jay is sitting at the bar where I left him, but he's no longer alone. There's a woman talking to him. My step falters. It's Anya Katiss, the model he was rumored to have dated once. She's not just talking either. She has one hand draped across Jay's shoulder, the other playing with her hair. She's talking animatedly about something. I swallow down the sick feeling in my stomach and walk over to them.

"Holly." Jay stands as he sees me, his face looking puzzled when he sees my expression. "This is Anya," he says as she turns to me.

She's even more beautiful up close. She makes no attempt to hide the fact she's studying me, as her eyes sweep over me from head to toe. She's taken her arm off Jay's shoulder now and reaches her hand out to me, leaning in to kiss me on both cheeks as I take her hand. She smells amazing; I recognize it as her new perfume we got samples for at the show last night.

"Holly, it's a pleasure to meet you," she says in a sexy accent—is it Argentinian?

"You too," I reply, remembering my manners as I take in her long, sleek hair and beautiful, exotic features.

"Well, I won't keep you," she says as she turns her attention back to Jay. She lowers her voice, but I can still hear her. "Think about it, Jay," she purrs, and then she turns and walks away, her long, perfect legs on full display in her short red dress.

"Are you okay?" Jay asks me.

"Absolutely!" I lie.

He pauses, his beautiful blue eyes looking at me quizzically for a moment. When I don't say anything else, he takes my hand and leads me out of the restaurant.

We drive back to my hotel and I try not to obsess over Anya Katiss and what she meant.

What does he need to think about? Does she want to get back together again? It must be that. I mean, who can blame her?

I look across at Jay driving. He *is* the sexiest man alive. He expertly maneuvers the car, the muscles in his arms visible as he holds the wheel. We pull up to the hotel and Jay hands the keys to Cooper, who looks like Christmas just arrived early as he realizes he gets to drive Jay's Ferrari again.

Jay guides me into the lobby and toward the elevator, his hand resting on the small of my back.

"You've got an incredible ass," he whispers, leaning down toward my ear. His breath tickles my neck and a jolt of electricity shoots through me.

When the elevator doors open, we step in together. The minute they close, Jay pushes me up against the wall inside, his hands moving down to squeeze the cheeks of my ass hard.

"I've wanted to touch you all night, Holly," he breathes against my neck as he kisses it up and down roughly, sucking and nipping with his teeth. It's so good, all I can do is stand there with my hands on his hips, pinned to the wall, enjoying his every move against my body. "You smell incredible. I can't wait to get you naked," he says, his deep voice speaking directly to my pussy as it grows slick with arousal.

I will the elevator to hurry so we can get to my room.

When we reach my floor, the elevator doors open in slow motion. I stumble out, followed by Jay, one hand still on my ass. Luckily, the corridor is empty.

What must we look like?

We get to the door of my room and I fumble about in my bag, trying to find the key card.

"Come on, Berry," he groans in my ear as he presses into me from behind. He slides one hand up my dress and straight inside my soaking wet panties. "Oh, fuck yeah, you're so ready for me," he says, the same moment the door swings open.

We tumble inside the room, Jay behind me with his hand still buried inside my underwear, and his lips on my neck. Another rush of my wetness covers Jay's hands as he leads me over to the desk and sinks two fingers deep inside me.

"Ahh," I cry out at his blatant claiming of me. It burns but feels so good.

"I was gentle with you last night," he growls in my ear from behind as he uses his free hand to pull my dress up around my waist. "But I don't want to be tonight. Not now that I know just what that pretty little mouth of yours is capable of." He pushes his hips forward so his rock-hard cock presses against my ass. "You can trust me, Holly. I'll look after you." His voice softens as he kisses my neck again. He removes his fingers from inside me and unzips his fly.

It's followed by the sound of a condom packet ripping.

"Do you trust me, Holly?"

"Yes," I whimper, placing my hands flat on the desk and leaning forward.

I can't wait to see what he has in mind for me. He roughly pulls my panties to the side before he plunges his cock deep inside me in one quick move. I gasp as the force of it throws me forward onto the desk and my muscles clench around him.

Fuck.

"Does that feel good, Holly?" Jay asks, sucking his breath in.

"Yes!" I cry. "Oh God, yes!" My orgasm is already building. He turns me on that much.

"Then tell me baby," he growls through gritted teeth as he grabs my hair with one hand and pulls my head back toward him.

"You feel so good. I love the feel of your cock inside me. I want to feel every inch of you. I will never get enough," I cry as he pounds into me, our skin slapping together.

"Oh God, Holly, keep talking," Jay moans.

"Slam into me; give me your beautiful cock," I scream as he thrusts deeper and deeper. The hand pulling my hair yanks harder and his other hand goes to my ass. One cheek stings as he slaps me with his hand and drives down harder.

"Oh, fucking hell, Holly, you feel so good," he groans as he keeps slamming into me.

All I can do is drop my mouth open and moan as I try to stay standing. It feels so good. No one has ever fucked me so roughly before. Yet somehow it feels intimate.

"Jay, I'm going to come."

"Not yet, Holly, hold on to it," he fires back as he continues driving his body into mine with force.

"I can't," I cry, my legs shaking beneath me. "Please," I whimper.

"Okay, baby, let me feel you," Jay moans, giving me the permission I crave.

"Fuck!" I cry as I come undone and orgasm with a giant shudder around him.

My legs collapse under me as Jay lets go of my hair and brings one arm around my waist to hold me up.

"Holly!" I hear him moan as he plows into me hard one more time as his cock jerks deep inside me, emptying all he's got inside me.

My legs are like jelly and my ears are ringing. I can't even hear properly. I'm lost in the incredible calm that comes after a huge release. Jay gently pulls out of me, steadies my feet on the floor, and turns me around to face him. We are sweaty and panting and still fully dressed. His blue eyes hold mine as he breaks into a huge grin. I can't help it; I grin back as I catch my breath.

"That was incredible, Holly," he pants as he leans in and kisses me softly on my lips.

"I can think of worse standby callouts I've had," I say and we both laugh and kiss as we catch our breath.

Jay stays the night with me, and I lose count of how many times we have sex. We just can't get enough of each other. When I wake up in the morning, I'm sore, but satisfied. My aching muscles are a sign of what an incredible night I've had. I've never come so much in my life.

I discovered that Jay gets really turned on going down on me, especially if I pull his hair as he does it. It seems to be his thing. One hair pull and he's fired up even more. He would have spent all night with his head between my legs and my hands in his hair if he could.

"Hey, gorgeous." He smiles at me across the pillow, one arm slung up above his head, the other casually resting on top of the sheets.

"Hey to you too," I say, stifling a yawn. "I hope you know this is cruelty to a flight attendant. Keeping me up all night with your magic cock when I now have to operate a flight back to London. I won't make it to my bed for another twenty-four hours."

"Well, on behalf of my magic cock, I apologize." Jay smirks. "He's very hard to control when he's around you—seems to have a mind of his own." He stretches his muscular arm up behind his head. "So, when are you next back in LA?" he asks casually, not looking at me.

Oh, here it is. What do I say?

Do I be honest and tell him I've got a trip rostered in just over a week? Or would that make it awkward if he's just trying to be polite, and this was just a fun, short-lived hook-up for him?

"Um, I'm not sure."

"Can I see you next time you're here, Holly?" he asks, turning to me, his eyes fixed on mine.

"Oh, sure, if you want to."

"I want to," Jay says as he draws me into a kiss. "Give me your phone."

"Okay, why?" I ask as I hand it to him.

"So I can put my number in it, and you can text me to let me know when you'll next be in town."

I smile.

Maybe he really does want to see me again.

He holds the phone up and it clicks as he takes a photo of the two of us lying together.

"What did you do that for?" I cry. "I've just woken up; I must look terrible." I throw an arm across my face.

"No, you look amazing and like I've just fucked you all night. And the photo is so you can look at it and think of me," he says sweetly. "You know, when you're touching yourself back home."

"You just ruined the sweet thing you said." I laugh.

He pulls my arm off my face. "But it's true though, isn't it? Please tell me it's true so I can imagine you doing it." He smiles as he kisses me again.

I grab a pillow and hit him with it.

"Stop talking, you fool. I have to go shower and get ready for my flight."

"Aww, come on, Berry, you've got time to say goodbye to me properly," he teases, as his head disappears under the covers, back to his favorite place once more.

Jay's gone home and I'm ready to check out of my room for the flight home.

I sigh as I zip up my suitcase and stand to smooth down my red uniform.

This has got to be the best work trip I have ever had. In the last forty-eight hours, I met an incredible guy, who must have given me fifty orgasms by now, and I discovered dirty talk during sex really turns me on. Even if I never see Jay again, I will always have the memories of the last three days. Especially what he did in the shower at his house, for which I will be forever grateful for. He made me feel beautiful and sexy when I've felt far from it since breaking up with Simon. Since well before that too if I'm honest.

I stand my suitcase up and pull out the handle. After one last look around the room to make sure I have everything, I turn and leave with a heavy heart.

Goodbye LA.

Goodbye Jay Anderson.

Chapter 8

THE FLIGHT HOME TO London is long and boring compared to the trip out to LA. I find myself standing in the galley when most of the passengers are asleep, staring at the seat Jay sat in just three days before. This time the seat is empty as the flight isn't full. It's taunting me, making me feel his absence even more.

"Penny for them?" Matt says as he comes and stands beside me. He pulls me into his side with one arm, resting his chin on my head.

"I'm being stupid, aren't I?" I sigh. "It was just a wonderful, crazy few days that ended too soon."

"I'm sorry, babes," Matt says, kissing my hair. "What did he say when he left?"

"What do you mean?"

"Was it, this has been nice, blah blah? You're a great girl, but? It was nice meeting you, yada yada?" Matt says, tipping his head to each side as he speaks.

"Oh, he didn't say anything like that. He wants me to text him to tell him when I'm next in LA," I say, moving out of Matt's hug so I can make a cup of peppermint tea. "You want a cup?"

"Hang on." Matt ignores my question and looks at me with narrowed eyes. "He wants to see you again next time you're in LA?"

"Yeah." I shrug. "But maybe he was just being polite, you know? It's the sort of thing you'd say, isn't it?"

"No!" Matt scoffs. "Here I am thinking you're moping about with a face like a slapped arse looking at that empty seat because he found a nice way of saying thanks for the mind-blowing sex. Now I'm off back to my mansion never to think of you again, see-ya!"

I look at Matt as I take a gulp of my tea; it's too hot and I wince. "You don't think he was just being polite?"

"Holly, did you or did you not have the most incredible sex of your life with this man?"

"I did." The corners of my lips curl in a tiny smile.

"And did you or did you not get to know him and like what you found out?"

"I did." My smile grows.

"And did he or did he not ask to see you when you're next in LA?"

"He did." I'm properly smiling now, mulling over Matt's words.

"Well then, case closed," Matt says, snapping his hands together as though he's slamming a book shut. "He totally wants to see you and shag your brains out again. What exactly did you do to the boy? I need to know! Maybe some of your lucky charm can rub off on me!"

I look over at Matt's eager face. He is so into Jay's manager.

"How did you leave things with Stefan?" I ask.

"Oh, Holly, he's so great. We get on so well and have some great discussions and debates. Deep, intellectual stuff. But even though I fancy the pants off him, I can't read him at all." Matt sighs, his head flopping toward his chest. "I've no idea whether he likes me in the way you'd like an old lady next door that brings scones around to feed you. Or whether he likes me in the 'I'm desperate to get into your pants but I'm playing it cool and won't show it' way." Matt leans his back against the galley side dejectedly. "I've got another LA at the end of next week, so we've said we will meet up. There's a photography exhibition or something on that he's going to."

"Well, there you go," I say, drinking my tea, which has cooled down now. "He obviously values your company and brain. See where it leads. Maybe he just likes to take things slow."

"You're right, Holls. I will just wait and see where it goes. You know, you need to listen to your own advice," Matt says gently. "If you ask me, Mr. Jay Anderson is rather taken with you. I know Simon was a shit to you and nuked your confidence, but give yourself a chance to see where this goes. Even if it's just a fun time for a while. We both know you need it."

"As always, Matt, you are the voice of reason." I smile at him.

"I know, babes, that's me. Mr. All-knowing. You may call me Your Highness," he says as he bows his head.

I curtsy in response and we joke around for the rest of the flight as I call him Your Highness. I make him a crown out of some tinfoil, which he wears in the galley to cook the breakfasts.

Fifteen hours after leaving my hotel room in LA, I finally roll my suitcase in through the front door of the house I share with Rachel in a small town near Heathrow Airport.

I am beyond shattered.

"You're home!" I hear Rachel shout as she runs into the hallway wearing a pair of black leggings and an oversized rugby sweatshirt she stole off a guy she brought home one night. She wraps her arms around me in a hug and her glossy dark-brown bob is like silk against my neck. She is gorgeous and petite, but she makes up for it in feistiness. I've seen grown men retreat if she's angry about something. She looks up at me with her large dark-brown baby doll eyes. "You have exactly fifteen minutes to get showered and get your ass back down here on the sofa with me. I want a full debrief as to what happened in LA." She heads off toward the kitchen. "I'll put the kettle on; get moving!" she yells over her shoulder.

"Alright, alright." I smile. I texted her the entire trip and even video called her to tell her about what was going on, but she's my best friend, so I was expecting this. She will want to know every single detail.

I carry my suitcase upstairs. I love our little house. It's cozy and perfect for the two of us. Just a small kitchen and a living room downstairs, and two bedrooms and a bathroom upstairs. It's smaller than some two-bed apartments we could have rented together, but we wanted a garden so we could sit out in the sun and have friends over for barbecues.

I open the door to my room. The walls are a super-pale-gray and I have white ruffled bedding on my velvet upholstered bed. It was a present to myself when I moved in here. The room has built in mirrored wardrobes and some white drawers doubling as a dressing table with photographs on top. My favorite is one of me, Mum, Dad, and Sophie at my wings ceremony when I passed my initial cabin crew training. There's another one of me and Rachel as teenagers grinning at the camera, arms wrapped around each other the day she got her braces off. We've been friends since we were eleven and she lived on the same street. When I started flying, she decided she didn't want to miss out on all the amazing places I told her about visiting, so she applied and got a job too. Then we found this house to rent together.

"Ten minutes!" I hear Rachel shriek up the stairs.

She will come and pull me naked out of the shower if I don't hurry. I would not put it past her. I quickly shower and put on some sweatpants and a matching cropped hoodie before making my way back downstairs.

"Sit," commands Rachel as I walk through the door to the living room. She's made tea and has the good cookies out in preparation to dissect my trip. I flop down next to her on our squishy cream sofa. "I need to know everything!" she says, her eyes trained on me like a hawk. She should be a police interrogator; she'd have them all confessing.

"Argh, where do I start?" I put my hands up against my cheeks. "Okay, so I didn't make the pre-flight briefing because I was called off standby. I had no clue if we had any high-profile passengers traveling." Rachel nods in understanding. "So, I get on and Matt's the flight manager."

"Love Matt," Rachel says without breaking my train of thought.

"Yeah, me too," I say, but Rachel's spinning her hand in front of her to urge me to keep going.

"Anyway, turns out Jay Anderson is onboard; I wasn't even sure who he was. Had to google him when we landed." Rachel looks shocked at my lack of celebrity knowledge.

"I made the stupid bird comment I told you about in my text and he gave us the show tickets. You know all this already."

"Okay, okay, skip to after the show," she says, curling her feet up underneath her on the sofa.

"Okay. We go to this amazing bar, with sparkly walls. Like some cool underground cave, you'd love it," I say, looking at Rachel as I take a bite of cookie. "Then we chat for a while and he's actually a really nice guy. Then he kisses me." I pause, remembering how his lips felt that first time against mine. "Then we had a dance, and that's when I ended up going back to his place."

"How was the sex?" asks Rachel, her eyes wide.

"Incredible!" I laugh. "Out of this world, mind-blowing, earth-shattering, orgasmic!"

"Oh my God, Holls," she says, reaching out to grip my arm.

"He dropped me back at the hotel the next morning and asked to take me to dinner that night. We went to this beautiful Thai restaurant in Hollywood and had such a great evening, just chatting, you know?" I smile, thinking back.

"Has he asked when you're going back to LA next?"

"Yeah, I thought maybe he was just being polite. Matt thinks he's genuine, but a weird thing happened."

"What?" asks Rachel, leaning forward.

"I saw him chatting to a model after dinner. It looked like she was flirting with him; she had her arm draped over him and according to the papers they used to date."

"Bitch, okay, we hate her," Rachel shoots back. "What did Jay say about it?"

"Nothing, I didn't ask him," I confess. "Who am I to ask about other women he talks to?"

"He was there with you, Holly, not her, so that should tell you something. So then what happened?"

I sigh. Maybe she's right. There may have been nothing to it.

"We go back to the hotel and he stays the night. More incredible sex. And then he leaves, and I fly home. Back to the real world." I lean back on the sofa, blowing out a breath.

"Wow, Holls, just wow. I mean of course he fancies you; you're a fox," Rachel says matter-of-factly, gesturing her hand up and down my body as I laugh. "He wants to see you again to give you more toe-curling orgasms, no doubt. I am super jealous!" she says and we both laugh.

"This feels so surreal though, Rach, especially now that I'm back here."

"Of course it does. You're back in your sweats having tea with me when for the last three days you've been getting serviced by an Adonis!"

This is one of the many reasons I love Rachel. We are so different, but that's what makes us get on so well. She's a funny, kick-ass chick and so loyal to her loved ones.

"What's meant to be will be, I guess." I reach for another cookie.

"You can make it be. Whatever you want, Holls, you can make it happen, I believe in you. You should too." She takes a sip of her tea. "Besides, this needs to work as I bet he's got fit friends and I need me some of that," she says as we erupt into giggles again.

We spend the next hour having a good catch-up. Sometimes we're lucky and get to fly together, and other times we can be like passing ships on opposite rosters and not see each other for two weeks.

"Do you think you can do me some more photos, please?" Rach asks me.

"Sure, they want more already?" I ask in surprise.

"Can't get enough of these girls," Rach sings as she lifts a leg into the air. She goes off to her room and comes back wearing glossy nude tights and her red work heels, the oversized sweatshirt still on her top half. "Okay, so maybe some of my legs crossed sitting in the chair. and then if I bend over and wrap a hand back around my calf, can you get that?"

"Sure." I snap some photos of her legs and feet using her phone. She comes over to look.

"Oh yeah, cool. They'll work, thanks."

"No problem," I say as I sit back down on the sofa. "So how many are you sending those to?"

"Mmm, five this time," Rach says as she pulls her leggings back on. "Then the panties are going to Mr. X."

I grin. "You're a shrewd businesswoman."

"I can't help it if these guys want to give me money for photos just of my feet and legs in uniform." Rach shrugs, stretching out next to me. "I told Mr. X he has to pay extra this time as the flight time is over ten hours."

I tip my head back on the sofa and look at the ceiling. "You mean, he'll not only pay for you to post him your stinky-ass panties you've worn on a flight, but he will pay extra if you've worn them on a really long one?"

If I didn't already know this from Rachel, I would find it hard to believe. Basically, guys online send her money for pictures of her legs in uniform. Nothing on show. You can't even see her face. Then some will even pay to have the tights or panties she's worn all flight. It's nuts.

"Yeah, Mr. X can't get enough so it seems." Rach smiles.

We call him Mr. X as that's his online name. Rachel has no idea who he is. He asks her to mail them to a PO Box address. Probably doesn't want his wife opening the packets over the family breakfast table with the morning mail.

"Some people have some weird turn-ons. Good money opportunity for you though."

"Mmm, and lucky for you, Holls, you seem to be Jay Anderson's turn-on." She looks at me with one eyebrow raised.

I picture Jay's intense blue eyes, tousled sandy hair, and muscular, tanned body.

I am lucky that someone like Jay Anderson would even notice me.

Incredibly lucky.

I wake up to the sound of my phone beeping. I'm on our sofa with a blanket over me. I must have fallen asleep and Rach covered me up. Ugh, I hate how tired I get after a flight home. I reach over to my phone to read my message.

Magic Cock: How was your flight home? J

Huh? That can't be. I didn't give him my number, did I?

I think back to the hotel room yesterday morning. He put his number in my phone and asked me to text him, but he never took mine; I'm sure of it. Plus, he's saved himself in my phone as Magic Cock! I burst out laughing as I text back.

Me: Not as exciting as the one out. Your text is a pleasant surprise. H

I wait for a reply and within minutes it comes.

Magic Cock: I confess, Stefan got your number from Matt. There's a matter of great importance that has come up I need to discuss with you.

Mental note to self, have words with meddlesome Matt later. What's Jay talking about? Great importance?

Me: Sounds intriguing.

I drum my fingers on the screen of my phone as I wait to see what he's going to say.

Magic Cock: I realized it was rather unfair that you have a photo of me, and I don't have one of you.

I smile. Jay's talking about the photo he took of us in bed the morning I flew home. I bring it up on my phone to look at. My breath catches as Jay's blue eyes stare back at me from the screen. He looks edible. Tanned, muscular shoulders against white bed sheets, his sun-kissed hair scruffy from sleep and his white teeth grinning at the camera. You can just about see the side of my face nestled up against his chest, my eyes looking up at his face. We look good together, relaxed and happy.

I remember the joke he made about me needing the photo of him to look at when I touch myself. This'll show you, Jay Anderson, I smirk as I google a picture of a spiky holly bush and text it to him.

Me: Here you are, stud. Hope it helps get the job done.

My lips spread into a smile as I imagine his face when he opens the text.

Magic Cock: Oh, Berry, that was a mistake. I'm going to punish you extra hard next time I see you now.

Winding him up is fun. Who would have thought that me, Holly Havers, would tease a man like Jay Anderson?

Me: That's if you can even recognize me again, with only the bushy version to remind you.

Ha! See what you can reply to that, Mr. Anderson.

Magic Cock: I could never forget your beautiful face, Holly. It's forever etched into my memory.

Oh. I did not expect that. I grin ear to ear, holding my phone to my chest like an infatuated schoolgirl. It beeps again in my hands.

Magic Cock: As is the sight of your perfect ass bent over the desk for me.

I laugh at how he's managed to lighten the tone. That is a pretty hot memory. Okay, if he wants to see me again, then let's see where this, whatever 'this' is, goes. Jay Anderson thinks I'm the one who is full of surprises, but he keeps surprising me. I didn't know for sure if I would see him again when I left LA, but now I can't help hoping that there was more to our three days than just sex.

My guard is slipping.

Me: I'm flying back to LA in 9 days.

Jay replies almost instantly.

Magic Cock: Can't come soon enough.

I'm already wishing the next nine days away now.

Maybe, just maybe, I can trust Jay Anderson with my heart.

Chapter 9

I LEFT LA FOUR days ago, and time is dragging. All I can think about is going back and seeing Jay in person again. He has texted me every day since I left.

I lie back on my sun lounger and let out a deep breath, putting my book down on the table next to me. It's no use. I can't concentrate on anything except what will happen when I fly back to LA.

"Have you finished, miss?" asks a server.

"Oh yes, thank you," I say as he takes my empty glass.

I'm poolside at the crew hotel in Dubai. It's late afternoon and the other crew have gone up to get ready for drinks in the bar later. I chose to stay behind by myself. I'm trying to distract myself with something, anything other than the fact it's still five days until I see him again. His texts have been flirty and lighthearted, and I'm trying my hardest not to get swept along by it all. I will get a better grasp of this whole crazy situation when I can see Jay in person again.

My phone buzzes and my stomach clenches, as it has every time I've had a text, in case it's one from Jay. This time it's from Matt; I can breathe again.

Matt: OMG Holls! Check out Celeb Central's website.

What is he going on about now? I load up *Celeb Central*'s site on my phone. We get *Celeb Central* onboard the aircraft. It's the highest selling celebrity gossip magazine available. The crew love reading it in the galley to see what's happening.

The site finishes loading.

What the hell?

I bolt upright into a sitting position and push my sunglasses up onto my forehead.

Oh my God.

The main image on their headline page is of me and Jay the night he took me to dinner. It's a clear side shot of the two of us holding hands outside the restaurant. Jay looks gorgeous as always, ever the American jock, all muscles, eyes, and smile. I must give it to the photographer; I don't look too bad as far as photos of myself go. I look curvy and sun-kissed and dare I say it, sexy? That dress was a great buy; I will have to thank Matt again for all the hours spent shopping to find it. I scour down the page and see there's a short written piece accompanying the photo.

Pictured above: Jay Anderson, 31, with a mystery beauty.

Jay, one of Hollywood's most in-demand actors—known for his smash hit show Steel Force, *and numerous film roles and advertising campaigns—was spotted out at Fusion restaurant in Hollywood with an unknown date. Sources suggest she could be an English flight attendant he met on a recent flight from London.*

The actor has been linked to Victoria's Secret model Anya Katiss, and other models and actresses, but has never confirmed being in a relationship with anyone.

This is crazy! Maybe I shouldn't have been so naïve. I mean, Jay is well known. Of course the press is going to be interested in who he's out with. Luckily, they didn't name me, although anyone who knows me could recognize me from that photo.

I text Matt back.

Me: I've just seen it! OMG.

Seeing myself online like this is weird. I glance around the pool. I'm not expecting a photographer to be hiding in a bush watching me, but sunbathing alone doesn't seem appealing anymore. I pack my book and phone into my bag and throw the caftan I packed for the trip over my head before making my way back up to my room. I've just about made it through the door when my phone rings. I fish it out of my bag. The screen's lit up with the name *Magic Cock*.

"Hello?"

"Hi, Holly," the voice as smooth as velvet says.

Warmth spreads inside me just from the sound of his voice saying my name.

"Listen, I wanted to call and warn you that the magazine *Celeb Central* is running a story with a photo of us together." Jay sighs. "Stefan held it off as long as he could, but they ran it anyway. I'm sorry to drag you into this. I know it's a lot to take in."

"It's okay," I say, trying to reassure him he doesn't need to worry about me. "They don't even know who I am. My name's not in it or anything."

"I know, but I know how they can be, like a dog with a bone. They'll be wanting to find out who you are."

"Well, it'll be a bit disappointing for them if they find out. I'm just me." I drop my bag onto the floor and sit down on the bed.

"I happen to think that *just you* will excite them tremendously." I can hear the smile in his voice. "But not as much as you excite me," he adds.

I laugh down the phone. That's better. The cheeky Jay is back, all trace of seriousness now gone from his voice.

"Oh? Maybe you can show me in five days? If you can last that long," I tease.

"Ugh," he grumbles. "That's such a long time, Berry. Where are you now?"

I sink back against the plush pillows. "I just got back to my room. I didn't feel like staying at the pool any longer."

There's a pause, and it sounds like a door closes.

"What are you wearing?" he whispers.

I smile as I pick up on the aroused tone in his voice. He wants to play, does he?

"Just my bikini. My tiny string bikini," I say, biting my bottom lip with a gentle sigh.

"If I was there, I would undo that with my teeth."

"I can take it off." I pretend to sound all innocent. "I mean, it is still wet. I shouldn't wear it on the bed."

"That sounds like it's for the best. Take it off and tell me what you see," he says.

I sit up to remove my caftan and bikini and lie back naked against the pillows, the phone glued to my ear. "I see my body...naked; it's all warm from the sun."

"Yeah?" Jay sucks in a breath. "What else?"

"I see my breasts; my nipples are hard wishing you were here to suck them."

"God, Holly," Jay groans. "Touch them for me, tell me how it feels."

I put my phone on speaker and place it on the pillow next to me.

"Mmm, it feels so good, Jay," I murmur as I run my hands down and over each breast, cupping them underneath. Then I roll each nipple between my finger and thumb. "I'm touching my nipples and imagining it's your mouth there. All hot and wet, sucking them hard."

Jay lets out a low growl. "I'm so hard for you, Holly. What I would give to be there right now."

"I wish you were."

"Open your legs for me, put your hand there and tell me what it feels like."

I do as he says and snake one hand lower between my legs, keeping the other on my breast, tugging my nipple. "It feels smooth."

"Yes?" Jay's voice sounds strained.

"It feels hot."

"Yes?"

"And it feels so wet."

"Aargh, fuck, Holly," he groans. It sounds like a belt buckle and zipper is being undone.

"I want you to touch yourself for me, baby," Jay says. "I want to listen to you do it and I want you to tell me exactly what you're doing."

"Okay," I whisper. "Are you touching yourself too?"

"You bet I am. I can't listen to you, knowing you're naked and ready for me, without my cock feeling like it might explode."

I grin at the picture my mind conjures up. I know just what that looks like. Jay all hot and aroused, his eyes intense and his hand on his huge erection. A rush of wet arousal floods my pussy at the image.

"Oh, I feel so wet, Jay. So wet and ready for you to fill me up with your big, hard cock."

"Fuck," he hisses.

"Mmm, I'm stroking myself in circles, Jay, and imagining it's your tongue," I gasp, arching my back off the bed as another wave of arousal washes over me.

"Just wait until I see you, baby. I'm going to suck that pretty little pussy of yours dry."

"I can't wait. I love you going down on me, your head between my legs and my hands in your hair, pulling you closer."

"Oh God," Jay moans through gritted teeth. "Put your fingers inside yourself for me, Berry; imagine it's my cock filling you up."

I do as I'm told and slide two fingers deep inside myself and let out a loud gasp.

Jay clears his throat. "Oh yeah, that's it. Tell me how it feels."

"It feels so hot and wet, Jay. My body is grabbing onto my fingers, wishing it was your cock," I moan.

"Fuck yourself with them," he demands.

I bury my fingers deep inside myself and slide them in and out, moaning and writhing on the bed. It's so good and the sound of Jay's heavy, aroused breathing on the phone turns me on even more. I know I'm getting to him.

"Oh, it feels so good, Jay!" I groan.

"That's it, Holly, don't stop; do it faster for me. Faster and harder."

I pick up my pace and slide my fingers in and out of my dripping wet sex.

"Touch your clit with your other hand," Jay orders.

I take my other hand off my breast and do as he says, rubbing in circles as my other hand continues to thrust in and out.

"Oh, Jay," I moan.

"That's it, Holly. Let me hear you when you come. I need to know just how you sound when you do it for yourself."

My orgasm is building deep inside me, my entire body rigid as I climb higher.

"Oh, oh, it's coming. It's coming!" I pant as my muscles clench hard.

"That's it, baby," Jay growls.

My fingers move faster and faster, imagining that it's him inside me. The sound of my wet arousal is loud in the room and he must be able to hear it on the phone.

"Oh, Jay! I'm going to come! Jay!" I scream as a huge orgasm hits me and lifts my back off the bed as my muscles contract around my fingers. I'm shuddering as each wave crashes over me, stealing my breath.

I collapse back on the bed, panting.

"Oh, Holly." Jay's breathing gets faster and faster until he lets out a loud, deep groan. "Fuck! Oh fuck, Holly." He moans as his orgasm rises and reaches its peak. It's got to be one of the hottest things I have ever heard.

We are both out of breath, just listening to each other's breathing return to normal.

Not being able to help myself, I giggle.

"What's so funny?" comes Jay's warm voice through the phone.

"I've never done that before," I confess. "You have this knack for bringing out all these new naughty streaks in me."

"Ooh, naughty streaks. I look forward to seeing more of those when you're here."

I bite my lip as I look across to my hotel room window. Thank goodness I'm up high and there's no way anyone could have seen me.

"Seriously, though. I don't know what it is."

"Holly, it's nothing I do. It's all you. You are so fucking hot."

Heat flushes my cheeks, hearing him talk about me like that.

"Did I hear you shut the door earlier?"

"Yeah, I'm at home, but we were having a work meeting. I stepped out into the bathroom downstairs."

"*W-we* were having a meeting?" I stutter.

"Yeah, me, Stefan, and a couple of other people. They're out on the deck," he states.

"You mean to tell me we just did that," I whisper, "and there are other people in your house?"

He laughs. "Relax, Holly, no one could hear. I wouldn't let anyone else share you. Your sexy little mouth is all mine."

I let out the breath I was holding. "Okay." I pause as I smile. "I better let you get back to work." I sigh. I could chat with Jay all day.

"Yeah, they may start to miss me soon. I'll see you soon, Berry."

"Bye, Magic Cock," I say, and hang up to the sound of Jay laughing.

I lie back on the bed until my heightened senses have all calmed down. Then I decide to order room service and have a hot bath. I have time to go to the hotel gym in the morning and do some yoga before checking out for the flight home. I'm looking forward to it. I always find it helps put me in a good mood when I make the time to do it. Although, after earlier this evening on the phone with Jay, I would say I'm in a great mood. I keep telling myself not to get carried away; this might just be a brief fling, but I can't help feeling that it's more.

My phone beeps with a text from Matt. He's in Boston now on a one-night layover.

Matt: Hey Holls, I'm just about to get onboard to fly home. I need to come and see you tomorrow night when you get home.

I'm looking forward to it already; it'll be great to see Matt. We haven't seen each other in person since landing back from LA.

Me: Rachel is home too. Come to our place and we can get takeout. 7 pm?

Matt: It's a date! See you then.

He said he needs to see me. Sounds urgent. Or maybe not, knowing Matt. That's just the way he talks. He could have found a new favorite flavor of coffee at Starbucks and *need* to see you, desperate to share his discovery.

I curl up in the big plush bed. This hotel outranks the LA crew hotel for having the best beds. They're so cozy and luxurious.

My thoughts move to LA and what Jay is doing as I drift off.

"This is lovely," Matt says, sitting back on our sofa with a glass of wine.

We've ordered Chinese and have it all set out on the coffee table for the three of us to share.

"Isn't it?" agrees Rach, clinking her glass against Matt's and then mine.

"So, I was meaning to talk to you about something, Holly," Matt says.

I look at him, puzzled. "Okay?"

"Simon was the first officer on the Boston flight I just did."

"Wanker," Rach throws in as she takes a bite of her spring roll.

"Massive wanker," continues Matt. "So, one of the crew had the latest issue of *Celeb Central* on the crew bus to the hotel and they recognized you."

"Mmm, I worried that might happen," I say, taking a sip of my wine.

"Only, they got rather excited about it and were talking about it pretty loud. Simon heard and wanted to see the photo."

"Oh." My face falls at the mention of Simon.

"Yeah, it was so funny, Holly! You should have seen his face. He looked like a bulldog chewing a wasp!" Matt claps his hands together gleefully. "I reckon he swallowed a bit of his own vomit back down when he realized it was you looking all smoking hot in the photo!"

"Ugh! Hello, I'm eating." Rachel gestures at the takeaway.

"Sorry, babes," Matt says.

"Anyway, he was seething. Could practically see the steam coming out of his ears." Matt laughs. "I just had to tell you, Holly. I think he's realized what a fool he was to be such a prick to you. Now you've moved on to new pastures. Much, much greener, sexier pastures." Matt grins.

"Huh," I mumble, letting Matt's words sink in. "Well, I hope he never treats anyone else the way he treated me. But I don't wish him any bad."

Matt and Rachel both look at me open-mouthed.

"You're a much better person than me, Holly," Rach says. "I would want to feed him his balls. Shove them down his slimy, lying throat." She demonstrates by jabbing two fingers in the air.

"Me too, Holly. All those hurtful things he said and did to you and the rumors about the other women." Matt shakes his head in disgust.

"I love you guys." I smile at them both getting worked up. "You've always got my back and I love how much you want to fight for me. But I want to leave him in the past. It was almost ten months ago now. I need to build a bridge and get over it," I declare.

"Or you could get a Jay, and get under him," Matt says with a cheeky wink as we all laugh.

"You're so naughty." I raise an eyebrow at him over the rim of my wineglass.

"Don't give me the innocent butter-wouldn't-melt face, Holly. We both know you've been loving your newfound naughty behavior since meeting Mr. Anderson."

He's got me there. I can't deny I have been enjoying every minute.

"I don't know what you're talking about," I say, trying to hide my smirk.

"Oh, really? Rach, do you hear this? She doesn't know what we're talking about."

"Bullshit," Rach fires back.

"Well, it's a good thing that Rach and I swapped onto your next LA flight then, isn't it?" Matt says with a poker straight face, as I turn to him with my eyes wide.

"Absolutely," says Rach. "There will be witnesses to your behavior."

"You guys are both on the same LA as me?" I beam, leaning forward on the sofa.

"Looks that way." Rach shrugs with a wink.

"This is going to be so much fun!" I squeal. The three of us hardly ever get to all work the same flight.

"LA, here we come again, baby!" Matt announces with a grin and we all clink our glasses together.

I take a big gulp of my wine.

LA, here we come again, or more accurately, Jay Anderson, here I come.

Chapter 10

The wheels of the Boeing 747 touch down on the runway into LAX international airport. It's a beautiful day and the sun shines through the window by my jump seat.

"Ladies and gentlemen, welcome to Los Angeles International Airport. For your safety, please remain seated with your seat belt fastened until the aircraft comes to a complete stop and the captain has switched off the fasten seat belt signs. The local time here is three o'clock in the afternoon."

I switch off as Matt continues his announcement over the PA system. The last nine days have felt so long, but now that we are back in LA, it doesn't feel like I've been away.

I say goodbye to all the passengers as they disembark and do my post-flight landing checks to make sure nothing has been left behind. All the crew gather around the disembarkation door and wait for the pilots to join us.

When they do, we all begin the trek through the terminal to immigration and baggage reclaim.

"Ugh, why does the west coast have to be so far away?" Rach grumbles as she pulls her carry-on alongside me.

"Forgotten what it's like, little Miss. East Coast?" Matt teases.

"Hey, I love the East Coast," Rach fires back. "Shorter flight times, New York, Boston, hot men in suits. What's not to love?"

Me and Matt smile sideways at each other; Rach is a sucker for a hot guy in a great suit.

"I know what you two will be setting your trip preferences as. You'll be bribing crewing to roster you as many LA flights as possible to see Jay and Steven," she says, rolling her eyes.

"Stefan," Matt corrects her, "and yes, you're right." He laughs. "At least if I get my way and Stefan realizes the sun shines brighter when I am around." He looks up to the ceiling theatrically with one arm raised above his head.

"Oh God," Rach groans. "You've got it bad."

"Not yet, darling, but I will be getting it bad soon. Watch this space," Matt says.

I smile as the three of us carry on teasing each other and chatting all the way to the crew hotel. It's such fun being able to fly together like this.

After we pull up at the crew hotel, we stand and talk with the other crew as our suitcases get unloaded from the back of the van.

"Hey, guys, we're off to a bar around the corner tonight if you fancy it?" says Chris, one of our pilots. "The captain from yesterday's crew texted me and said they'll meet us there."

"Oh, okay, thanks," I say. "Sounds fun."

"Aren't you desperate to meet lover boy?" Rach says, checking out Chris' ass as he walks off to collect his suitcase.

"I wish." I sigh. "Jay texted me to tell me him and Stefan are going to be busy at work until late tonight. The show needs to shoot some promotional material for season three. We're going to meet them tomorrow. You coming?"

"Yeah. I guess someone has to come and make sure this guy isn't a total tool," Rach says. "It's not like we can trust him." She jabs her thumb toward Matt. "One flex of a bicep and a pretty face, and he'd sell his own grandmother," Rach jokes.

"Hey! I heard that!" calls Matt in mock outrage. "It would take much more than just biceps and a pretty face, Rach. I'd need the chiseled jaw, strong pecs, weakness for kittens, the entire package! My grandmother would expect nothing less."

I laugh. These two crack me up.

I spy Cooper, the valet, at his desk.

"You two go on inside and get checked in. I'll be there in a moment," I call to Matt and Rach as I go over to say hi.

His eyes light up when he sees me.

"Hi, Holly. I was wondering when you might be back."

"Hi, Cooper. Couldn't keep away," I joke.

"I can't blame you. Are you going to be seeing Mr. Anderson while you're here?"

"That's the plan."

"He's a good man," Cooper smiles. "You know, last week he came by, took me for a ride to visit my brother at work. Let Eric drive his Ferrari, man!" Cooper's whole face glows. "Should have seen his face. Made his year!"

"Really?"

"Yeah, it was so cool of him to do that, man. Eric loves cars; he's a talented mechanic and wants to run his own garage one day. Me and him are saving up to go into business together." He smiles proudly.

"Oh, that's amazing! I'm sure you'll get there. It sounds like you both have the passion for it to work."

"We do. The rate it's going I might be sixty by the time we've saved enough, but we'll get there."

"Well, I'll be rooting for you," I say as I wheel my cases toward the lobby door.

"Thanks, Holly," Cooper calls. "Have a great trip; maybe see you later."

It's evening and Matt, Rach, and I are all having a drink in Matt's room before we head out to the bar around the corner to meet the rest of the crew.

"I love that dress, Holly" says Rach, eyeing me up.

I'm wearing a casual black sleeveless dress that fits close on the top half and then has a short flippy skirt that swishes as I walk.

"Thanks, hun. I wish I could look sexy like you. I could never pull your outfit off," I say as I admire Rach in her skin-tight black shiny trousers and spiky heels. On her top half she's got a white ripped T-shirt and cropped denim jacket.

"Ahem." Matt clears his throat.

"You look great too, Matt." I laugh, as I look over at him in his black skinny jeans and V-neck T-shirt.

"Why, thank you, darling." He smiles, satisfied.

We head off to the nearby bar where the crew are meeting. It's a sports bar, with a nice laid-back atmosphere. There's often crew from another day's flight here, so we get to catch up.

We open the door to the bar and head inside. It's busy already and there are a lot of people standing around, drinking and talking. There's sporting memorabilia on the walls, a couple of big TVs behind the bar showing a baseball game, and two guys sitting at the bar cheer and shout every now again. You can just about make out music playing in the background, disguised by the loud hum of animated chatter.

"First round's on me," Matt calls as we head to the bar.

We order two house cocktails and a whiskey for Rachel, clinking the glasses together when they arrive.

"To flying with friends," Matt says.

"Flying with friends," Rach and I echo.

We have a great time talking and laughing together and have had a couple more drinks when my phone buzzes in my pocket. It's a text from Jay.

Magic Cock: Hey, Holly. Filming has wrapped up for the night. If it's not too late, do you fancy a drink?

I would love to see him, but I can't ditch Matt and Rach.

Me: I'm at a bar around the corner from the hotel with Matt and Rachel at the moment.

Magic Cock: What's it called? Stefan and I will come meet you.

I text him the name of the bar and the street it's on before putting my phone back into my pocket and picking up my cocktail, downing the rest in one go.

"What's got into you?" Rach eyes me suspiciously.

"That was Jay. Him and Stefan are coming here to meet us." I take a deep breath and blow it out.

Matt's eyes widen. "That's amazing! Why do you look like you've swallowed a fly?" he says, studying my face.

"This is the first time I've seen Jay since the last time." I gulp. "What if it's awkward, or he remembers me differently and sees me tonight and runs for the hills?" I drag my hands down over my face.

"Then good riddance to the silly bastard," Rach pipes up. "I'm sure he won't though, Holls; as I've told you, you are a fox. Besides, haven't you been like sexting each other and shit nonstop since you left last time?"

I chew on my lip. "Well, yeah. But that's different. He's going to be here in person soon."

"Just think of all that pent-up sexual energy he will have stored up for you," Matt exclaims in delight. "You lucky bitch. I bet he's going to give it to you good tonight!"

"Matt!" I gasp, hitting him on the chest with the back of my hand.

"What? Don't pretend you aren't secretly hoping for the same thing." He winks.

I smile as he's right. I've missed the feel of Jay Anderson's body pressed against mine. It's been all I can think of for the last nine days.

"Okay. But I'm going to need another drink to calm my nerves," I announce.

"Bartender!" Matt calls to the friendly barman, handing him some money. "My friend needs a drink and make it a strong one, please!"

I'm a lot more relaxed after the whiskey Matt got us all, although God, it was strong. My throat is still on fire. Rach knocked hers back like it was water.

The hairs on my neck stand up and my body goes on high alert, like it senses something. I turn my head toward the door. Jay has just walked in with Stefan. He looks incredible, even better than I remember. He seems taller, bigger, stronger. His sun-kissed hair is screaming at me to run my hands through it. He's wearing tan boots over faded jeans and a white T-shirt. His intense blue eyes lock on to me as they make their way over to us. All I can do is stand rooted to the spot and watch. My legs won't work now even if I wanted them to.

Jay stops in front of me and just studies me to begin with, a smile spreading across his face. God, that jaw and stubble. Heat radiates from his body and my heart races in response to him. Stefan and Matt are greeting each other to the side of me and Matt's introducing Rachel, but I can't tear my eyes off Jay's face.

"Holly," his deep dreamy voice purrs, and I swear I flutter in places I didn't know existed.

"Hi, Jay," I squeak, staring up at him.

He cups my face between his large warm hands and leans in, kissing me on the lips. I suck my breath in as his soft lips touch mine. Then he presses harder and I sink into him, reaching up to wrap my arms around his neck, my lips parting to allow his tongue full access to my mouth. He kisses me deeply, taking my breath away before pulling back and grinning.

"It's good to see you, Berry," he says, his eyes glinting. "You're even more edible than I remember and not as spiky as the picture you sent."

I laugh as he refers to the holly bush photo I sent him.

"I reserve my spikes for special occasions," I tease, relaxing in his company once again.

I'd forgotten this feeling, how right it feels to be near him, how easy he is to talk to.

"Do I get a hello now that you two have finished?" Stefan interrupts, leaning in to give me a hug.

I giggle. "Sorry, Stefan, how are you doing?"

"Better now," he says, as I catch him sneak a quick glance at Matt. "That was a long day though. We've been on the go since six a.m."

"Why so early?" Rach asks after she says hello to Jay and introduces herself.

"We have to be first to the makeup trailer," Stefan says. "It takes hours to make this one's ugly face presentable." He points a finger at Jay. "I'm surprised the makeup girls haven't gone on strike!"

Jay laughs and grabs Stefan in a headlock, ruffling his hair.

"Stop! Not the quiff! Anything but the hair!" Stefan cries as Jay lets him go and we all laugh.

"See what I have to put up with?" Stefan says, straightening himself up. "I work with a psycho."

We all grab another drink from the bar and stand, laughing and chatting. Stefan regales us with stories about a mystery practical joker on set, whose latest prank today was to swap Jay's costumes for identical ones two sizes too small. He came out of the dressing trailer looking like he'd turned into the hulk. The crew thought it was hilarious.

I look up at Jay, who's smiling as Stefan finishes the story. He's holding my hand in his, rubbing his thumb back and forth across my knuckles. I can't believe I'm standing here with him. It's like a dream. I don't want to let go of his hand, but I'm aware that I really need the bathroom after all the drinks I've had.

"I'm going to the restroom." I stand up on my tiptoes to kiss Jay on the cheek. He smiles at me and I let go of his hand reluctantly. "Back in a minute."

I weave my way through people on my way to the restroom and see our pilot Chris across the room. I give him a smile and wave and then stop dead. I can only see the back of the man he's talking to, and it's been ten months, but there's no mistaking that it's my ex, Simon.

I rush to the restroom.

Please say he didn't see me!

I might have gotten away with it. He *was* facing the other way. I haven't seen him in all this time. I thought I was over the things he said and did to me, but seeing him again and knowing he's here just brings it all back to the surface again.

I stand by the mirror and use a tissue to dab at the sweat along my hairline and back of my neck. I'm not the same girl I was back then. I can't let him control me and make me feel worthless again just by being in the same room as me. *I can do this.* I need to walk out there and past him, back to my friends. Then if I want to leave, I can. Okay, here goes.

I open the restroom door and go back out into the bar. I glance across at Chris, who's talking to a girl now. No sign of Simon. *Shit.* I look around. With any luck, he's already left.

"Looking for me?" a voice sneers behind me.

I turn around and am face-to-face with Simon. He's attractive, or at least I used to think so, but since finding out about the real him, I can't stomach looking at him.

"No, I was just—"

"You were just what, Holly?" He cuts me off. "Just off back to your friends? Don't think I haven't seen who you're with," he says, his eyes flashing with something. "It's pathetic. What do you think he'd want with you? He will soon realize he's wasting his time," Simon spits. "Unless you've already opened your legs for him?" He sneers and I recoil in disgust. "Ha, you have, haven't you? You've let him pork you and now the poor fucker is planning his escape."

My cheeks burn and my eyes sting. I can't stand to be anywhere near him. I try to push past to get away from him, but he grabs my wrist.

"What's going on, Holly?" Jay's deep voice asks as he appears beside me.

"N-nothing, I was just coming to find you," I stammer, rubbing my wrist that Simon has let go of. A red mark is forming on it. Jay looks at it and then back at Simon.

"Who are you?" Jay says, his eyes are on fire and boring into Simon.

"Jay, leave it," I whisper, trying to take his arm.

"This is him, isn't it? Your ex?" he says, looking at me. Oh God, he's furious.

"Talked about me, has she?" Simon pipes up.

Shut up, you idiot! He's obviously had a few drinks and is feeling cocky.

"Cries out my name when you fuck her, I bet," he slurs.

A roar unlike anything I've ever heard before explodes next to me. It sounds like an animal going in for the kill. Before I know what's happening, Jay has Simon up against the wall by his throat. There's a loud gasp around the bar before it falls silent as everyone stops to watch what's going on.

"What did you just say?" Jay says through gritted teeth.

His eyes look wild and the veins are visible in the arm he's holding Simon with. I can see the vein in his neck pulsating and his breathing is fast, drawing his huge chest up and down. Simon's trying to say something but can't get his breath enough to get it out. Jay puts his face right up against Simon's, his eyes locked on him.

"If you ever," he hisses, "talk about Holly like that again, or even look in her direction, I will *finish* you. Do you understand?" Simon's eyes widen as he grasps at Jay's arm with his hands. "Do you understand me?" Jay growls. Simon nods weakly and Jay lets him go. Simon drops to the floor, coughing and clutching at his throat.

"Come on, Holly, we're leaving," Jay says as he grabs my hand and pulls me past astonished faces with mouths hanging wide open.

I catch sight of Stefan, Matt, and Rach. Matt's eyes are wide open; Rachel's smirking over at Simon, and Stefan doesn't look flustered in the slightest.

I might be sick after what just happened. I can't believe Simon was here and said those awful things. I thought I was past him being able to hurt me.

Jay marches me back to the hotel without saying a word. We pass Cooper on the way in, who takes one look at Jay's face and averts his eyes back to his desk and away from us. I press the elevator button for my floor, and we ride up in silence. I glance over at Jay, who still looks furious. Not as wild as before, but his jaw is clenched, and his eyes focus straight ahead.

"Jay?" I whisper.

"Give me a minute, Holly, please." His voice sounds strained.

Tears prick at my eyes as I swallow the lump in my throat.

Is this it? Is all this over?

I've never seen Jay so angry before. The first time I ever mentioned Simon to him, he flew into a rage, but nothing like this. He doesn't even want to speak to me. I'm out of my depth. What am I doing here with someone like Jay? Simon's right. Maybe he's realized I'm not worth the trouble and is about to end things.

The elevator doors open, and we walk down to my room. Jay stays one step behind, his hand still holding mine.

We get to my door and I turn around to face Jay, my eyes blurry.

"I understand if you don't want to come in," I say, not able to look at his face.

If this is going to be goodbye, then I can't bring myself to look in his eyes when he tells me.

"What are you talking about?" Jay says as he puts the fingers from his spare hand under my chin and lifts my face until my eyes meet his. His brows are pulled together.

"I thought after meeting Simon that you might, you might…" I trail off, not sure what I was going to say.

Jay looks deep into my eyes. "You thought I might agree with him and think you're not worth it?"

I gulp and nod as a tear betrays me and slides down my cheek.

"Holly, don't," Jay says with concern as he brushes it away with his thumb. "The only thing on my mind right now is taking you inside your room and making love to you, the way I should have the last time you were here."

"That sounds better than what I imagined," I say, and he smiles at me, the corners of his eyes crinkling.

"Then open the damn door, Berry!" he says impatiently.

I open it and look back over my shoulder at Jay as I lead him inside by his hand. The door closes and Jay takes a step toward me, resting my back against the wall. He reaches down to my wrist, still red from where Simon grabbed it, and lifts it up to meet his lips. His eyes never leave mine as he kisses it. My breath catches in my throat as he holds me under his gaze, his beautiful blue eyes watching me intently.

Somehow this feels even more intimate than being naked in front of him.

He places my wrist against his chest as he leans in to kiss my mouth. One hand cups the side of my face, his thumb stroking my cheek as he kisses me, his tongue rolling against mine, then his lips softly sucking mine. I let out a soft sigh and melt into his touch as his kisses trail down my neck and onto my shoulder.

"You are so beautiful, Holly. I won't ever get enough of feeling your skin against mine," he whispers as he reaches around my back to unzip my dress, slipping it down over one shoulder.

His kisses change direction and trail across my collarbone to my other shoulder as he pushes my dress down over that one too, returning his mouth to my neck as my dress falls into a puddle around my feet.

"Jay," I whisper.

"Yes?"

"Don't stop, will you?" I whisper.

"I've no intention to," he replies as he continues kissing and caressing my neck.

It's not what I mean, but his answer will do, for now.

"I need you naked," he says as he moves to unhook my bra.

"That's not fair." I smile.

He smiles back at me as he kicks his boots off and reaches down to pull off his socks. He raises an eyebrow at me as he lifts his T-shirt over his head, his abs rippling as he stretches up. Then he unzips his jeans and with one swift move pulls both them and his boxer shorts down, throwing them to the side. His hard cock hangs heavy between his legs as he stands again.

"Better?" he asks.

"Much."

"Now, where was I?" he says as he returns his attention to my bra.

With one quick flick between finger and thumb, he's unhooked it, and it's on the floor with my dress.

He pulls back, his eyes resting on my breasts. "Holly, I've missed these," he says as he strokes them with his hands, rolling my nipples between his thumb and forefinger, watching in awe as they harden under his touch. "God, you're beautiful." He dips his head down to suck and pull on each of my nipples.

I moan in ecstasy and arch my back off the wall to meet his mouth.

"So beautiful," he murmurs again with his lips around my nipple.

Oh God, that is so good. My body remembers his touch so well and melts further into it. His kisses move down my stomach, his hands caressing my waist.

"These have got to go too," he says as he kneels in front of me and slides my panties down my legs, helping me to step out of them when they reach the floor. He draws in his breath and raises his eyes to look up at me. "You are incredible, Holly." He leans forward and kisses me between the legs. "So wonderful," he murmurs as his tongue licks me, coaxing my lips apart so he can taste deep inside my pussy.

"Jay," I moan as I lean back against the wall and my hands find their way into his hair.

He groans and dives deeper, licking and sucking, my arousal flowing to him. He drinks it up, a deep groan vibrating his throat. My legs tremble as his tongue licks me harder before he presses his lips against my clitoris and sucks.

I come with a cry and almost collapse on top of him.

"Oh, Holly," Jay moans as he sucks one more time before standing up, catching me in his strong arms and lifting my legs up around his waist. He leans back against the wall. I'm breathing heavily, surprised by my sudden orgasm.

"Holly, you taste so sweet." His eyes are sparkling and alive, my wetness evident on his lips.

I lean forward and lick his bottom lip, tasting myself on him. He moans and looks into my eyes before kissing me, sucking on my bottom lip.

"I want to feel you, Jay," I whisper. "All of you."

He looks at me.

"Have you always used condoms?" I ask him.

"Yes, every time," he says, his eyes intent on mine. "And you?"

"Always," I say, "and I'm on the pill."

Jay looks at me again and seems unsure of what to say or do next.

"Please, Jay. I need to feel all of you tonight. I need to be closer than before."

He studies my face and I know he still sees the earlier hurt that was in my eyes.

"If you're sure, Berry?"

"I am." I nod.

He takes my face in his hand again and kisses me deeply as his other hand holds me up around my waist. He pulls back and I loosen the grip of my legs around his waist.

Then he's there. The warm, slick tip of his cock against my entrance.

He draws back from kissing to look at me again and without taking his eyes off mine, he slowly slides into me, inch by thick, magical inch.

I gasp. I'm so full. I will never get enough of feeling him inside me like this. Jay moans as he draws back and then sinks back deep inside me.

"Holly," he says, looking deep into my eyes. "You take my breath away."

I tighten my legs around his waist as he carries me over to the bed and lays me down, never breaking contact, his body over mine. I run my hands up to the back of his head and stroke his hair.

"You are incredible," Jay breathes as he supports himself on his elbows above me, his arms wrapped underneath my shoulders and his hands holding the sides of my face. He slides in and out of me, deep and slow, as I keep my legs wrapped around his waist to pull him deeper.

"Jay, you feel so good," I cry as he touches places deep inside me.

He moves faster as my wetness rushes between us.

"Holly," he breathes, dipping his head down to my shoulder.

"Kiss me, Jay."

He moves his lips to mine and kisses me hungrily, his movements getting faster and faster. I can't get enough of him. I want to pull him deeper and hold him close to me. Another orgasm is already building deep inside me, preparing to take over my body. The sensation of Jay's body moving against mine, the heat of his body over me, and his scent, are all too much.

"Jay, I'm going to come," I moan.

"Holly," he groans against my lips.

The wave builds to its peak inside me, until it's too much and I crash underneath him, my body tightening around his, my moans muffled against his lips as he kisses me harder.

"Holly," he moans against my lips. "Oh God, Holly," he groans as he comes undone.

There's an unmistakable swell of his cock, followed by heat as he releases himself. His hands are still in my hair and his lips murmur my name as he presses his face to mine.

We lie like that for a long time, kissing each other, Jay stroking my cheek with his thumb.

"That was incredible," he says as he pulls back to look into my eyes.

"Your magic cock strikes again." I sigh.

Jay smiles before kissing me again. "You're the magic one, Holly. I want you to see what everyone else sees and understand how special you are."

"You're very deep tonight, Mr. Anderson."

"Yes, I am." He smirks, flexing his cock, our bodies still connected.

"Not what I meant." I roll my eyes.

Jay kisses me again as he gently pulls out of me, leaving an emptiness that has my body screaming in protest.

"Come take a shower with me." He grins, taking my hand and lifting me up off the bed.

I shake my head with a smile at his cheeky tone.

"I thought you'd never ask, dirty boy," I tease as he leads me into the bathroom and starts the shower.

"I'll show you what dirty is." He winks as he pulls me into his arms under the warm water.

I laugh as I press up against his hot, muscular body and prepare myself for Jay Anderson to take command of my body and senses all over again.

Chapter 11

JAY'S ARMS WRAP TIGHTLY around my waist from behind as I snuggle back into him. I wish I woke up like this every day. Last night was incredible, so tender. I've never experienced that before or felt so close to anyone.

Jay stirs behind me. "Good morning, beautiful." He yawns.

"Good morning." I turn my face toward him and he kisses the corner of my mouth.

I take a deep breath. I don't want to bring Simon up again and ruin a perfect morning, but there are things left unsaid. I need to clear the air, so I can move on.

"Thank you for what you did last night, standing up for me like you did."

Jay's gaze grows serious. "Holly, that guy is a jerk. The way he spoke about you. I wanted to rip his head off. He's lucky I didn't."

"He wasn't always that bad. He was nice in the beginning."

"He's an abusive moron. The thought of you with him..." Jay frowns and takes a deep breath, his forehead furrowing.

"I'm glad you didn't," I say.

"Didn't what?"

"Rip his head off. I don't fancy visiting prison when I fly over." I give him a small smile.

Jay raises his eyebrows, his expression softening. "You'd visit me then?"

"Well." I shrug. "I would be obliged to if you committed murder defending my honor." I look up and Jay's smiling to himself. "So, you've met one of my exes now," I begin, not sure where I'm going with this.

"Holly?"

I look over at Jay who is propped up on one elbow, studying me. "What? I just wondered what, you know, what yours are like?"

"My what? My exes?" Jay asks.

"Yeah," I say, avoiding eye contact. "Are they all actresses and models like Anya Katiss?" I'm trying to sound casual, but it's not working.

"My exes are all in the past, Holly. I've dated for a few months here and there, but that's all."

"So, did you..." I swallow. "Did you date Anya Katiss once like the papers said?"

"Holly." Jay sighs. "Do we have to talk about this?" He looks over at me, before blowing out a breath. "Yes, briefly. It was a while ago now, but it wasn't going anywhere."

My stomach cramps imagining them together. Him and Anya. Beautiful, exotic Anya, with her perfect hair and long legs up to her ears. Her long legs wrapped around Jay.

Oh God, why did I ask?

"Honestly, I've found it hard to open up to anyone since losing Rob," Jay says, his voice heavy.

I look up into his beautiful eyes and all their hidden sadness.

"So yeah," he continues, "there's been women, but nothing serious."

I wait, willing him to say, *'until now.' Please say it, Jay.* Tell me I'm special and not like the others. But he doesn't.

He's turned onto his back and is looking at the ceiling.

Why did I have to sound so needy? I swallow down an uneasy tightness in my chest. What if I am just one in a line of many? But then, that doesn't make sense. The way we laugh together, how he was last night, so tender. There must be more to it for him. I hope there is; otherwise, I'm in it up to my neck.

The hotel phone next to the bed rings and cuts into my thoughts. I lean across Jay to answer it, but he gets there first, putting it to his ear.

"Holly's room." He smirks at me as I try to grab the phone off him. "No, I'm afraid she can't come to the phone right now." He's nodding and listening.

Who is he talking to? I try to grab the phone again and he leans out of reach, grinning at me like it's a game.

"Jay!" I whisper. "Who is it?"

He puts his finger to my lips, indicating me to hush. "Yeah, she was participating in a magic show last night; it finished late," he says with a straight face. "Oh? Okay, I will tell her. Bye."

I stare at Jay as he hangs up the phone. "Who was that?"

"Oh, that? You know, I didn't ask," he says with a smirk.

"Jay!" I push him in his chest, and he laughs and grabs my hands, holding them above my head as he rolls me onto my back and lies over the top of me.

"Oh, you're so cute when you're getting mad," he jokes, his eyes crinkling at the corners.

I can't help it, and I grin back. It's all I can do when he looks at me like that. He kisses me and I melt underneath him.

"It was Rachel," he says, kissing me again. "She says you've got half an hour to get yourself off my cock and get your ass dressed and ready for breakfast."

I laugh. "Okay, I believe you; that sounds exactly like what Rach would say."

"See, Holly, I would never lie to you." His blue eyes are bright as they look at me, before he kisses me once more.

I hope not, Jay Anderson. I'm not sure my heart could take it.

"There you two are!" Rach says. "You're late! You know what, never mind. I do not want to know the reason."

"I do!" Matt announces. "At least someone is getting laid around here."

Jay has his arm slung over my shoulders. He looks incredible. Even in last night's T-shirt and jeans, he looks like he's stepped off a photo shoot. His hair looks extra tousled this morning. Probably because five minutes ago I was grabbing handfuls of it as he went down on me. We were just about to leave the room when he pushed me against the door and dropped to his knees. He said I looked so sweet in the flowery dress I'm wearing that he had to taste me. My body heats just remembering it.

"I know a place we can go for breakfast," Jay says. "I'll drive us. I left my car here last night."

"Did you guys pack your swim stuff like I said in my text?" I ask Rach and Matt.

"Yes, Mum." Rach rolls her eyes with a smile.

"Absolutely!" says Matt, waving his bag in the air to show me. "Packed the eagle smugglers."

"The what?" Rach scoffs.

"Darling, budgie smugglers are just too misleading for what's in mine," he says, pursing his lips at her.

"Ugh, please, that's not an image I want before breakfast." Rach curls her lips in disgust.

Jay and I laugh, listening to the pair of them. "Come on, you two, let's get going," I say.

"Stefan said he'll meet us there," Jay adds.

Matt's eyes light up. "Come on, Rach, stop holding us up!"

"Oh yeah, because I'm the one talking about my eagle smugglers and stopping us from leaving," she shoots back.

They continue bickering with each other as we head out of the hotel's main entrance and into the warm sun. Cooper sees us immediately.

"Good morning, Mr. Anderson, Holly," he says, smiling and nodding at Matt and Rach too.

"Cooper, call me Jay, please. You make me sound so old."

Cooper smiles. "I've already brought your car around, Jay. I heard you guys in the lobby."

Rach pokes Matt in the ribs. "See, now Cooper's been put off his breakfast by your oversharing too."

Cooper laughs. "Not at all. Where you guys headed?"

"We're going to get some breakfast at the coast, and then I want to show these guys around my neighborhood," Jay says.

"Well, have a great day," Cooper calls.

"Thanks! Say hi to Eric," Jay calls back as we get into his Ferrari.

"Well, it'll do, I suppose." Rach shrugs as she slips into the back seat next to Matt.

"Oh, come on, ice queen," Matt teases, "you can admit this is pretty cool."

"Okay, Matt, I will agree with you on this occasion, but don't get used to it," Rach murmurs.

"Wouldn't dream of it," Matt says with his hands up in front of him.

"Nice car, Jay," she says with a smile.

He looks at her in the rear-view mirror. "I'm glad it meets your approval. I wouldn't want you thinking I drive Holly around in an old death trap." He smiles.

"Okay, you get one point," Rach jokes. "And two points for almost strangling Simon last night. That's the best thing I've seen in ages." She laughs. "I would give you three points if you'd finished the job."

Jay catches my eye at the mention of Simon. I reach over and squeeze his thigh in reassurance that I'm okay, before he starts the engine and drives off.

"Are we almost there yet?" Matt asks from the back seat. We've been driving for just over twenty minutes, chatting and listening to the radio.

"Yeah, any minute now," Jay says as he turns the car off the main road and pulls over to park. We are right by the beach and I can see sand and sea stretching off into the distance.

"Where are we?" asks Rach.

"This," Jay says, extending his arms toward what looks like a large wooden shack on stilts, "is Malibu's best breakfast spot. The views are amazing."

We all climb out of the car and make our way over to the white painted structure.

"Ladies first," Matt says as Rach and I climb up the wooden steps to the deck at the top.

Once up there, I can see what Jay means. "Wow." I smile over at him as he gets to the top behind us. He smiles back and wraps his arm around my waist. The view up here is incredible. You can see right across the white sand beach. The coastline curves around and off in the distance and there's a large arched rock formation that reaches out into the sea from the beach.

"Brides and grooms travel across the county to have their picture taken there under that archway," Jay says as he sees me looking.

"I can see why." I sigh. "It looks so romantic. I wonder how many couples have stood there together, feeling the sand beneath their feet."

He smiles at me, his blue eyes bright and clear.

"Hey, guys!" Stefan's waving at us from a table on the outer deck, which runs the length of the building, out over the sandy beach. Next to the deck is the roofed part of the restaurant. It's all whitewashed wood, rattan chairs against driftwood tables, and comfy-looking deck sofas you can imagine sinking into.

We make our way over to him and say hello, before sitting down into the plush blue cushions of the sofas. Jay and I on one, Matt and Stefan on another, and Rach with one to herself.

"This place is stunning," Matt says. "What other surprises do you have up your sleeve?" He looks at Jay and Stefan.

"Wait until you taste the food," Stefan says, rolling his eyes back in his head as he touches Matt on the knee.

Matt beams back at him like the Cheshire cat.

"I hope they do a strong Bloody Mary. I'm going to need it playing gooseberry with you lot," Rach says, leaning back into her sofa. "What the hell was I thinking? I could be in New York hooking up with a hottie in a suit," she says, tilting her face up toward the sun.

"Come on, Rach, you know having wild sex with a stranger is nowhere near as fun as hanging out with us," Matt teases, "no matter how big his cock is."

She looks over at Matt with narrowed eyes.

"We love you, Rach. I appreciate that you're here with us and missing out on having sex with some random guy." I smile, reaching over to squeeze her leg.

"That's what friends do"—she sighs—"sacrifice for the good of the team."

We all smile at her dry sense of humor.

"So, you hook up with random guys on your layovers, Rach?" asks Stefan, fascinated by the mechanics of it all.

"Yeah, if I feel like it." Rach shrugs. "Why don't you, if you get the chance?" she redirects back at Stefan, who looks flustered.

"Well, I, um, no. I've never had a one-night stand, only long-term partners."

"Really?" says Matt, his smile wide.

Oh hell, here we go. Matt's going to be even more into Stefan now that he knows he follows his heart first and not his dick.

"Your loss, I guess." Rach shrugs.

A server comes over to take our orders. Rach orders a Bloody Mary and the rest of us go for various breakfast smoothies from the menu. We decide to order a breakfast sharing platter to have between us all.

"Oh, could I please have a peppermint tea as well?" I ask before he leaves.

"You like peppermint tea?" Jay says.

"Yeah, I do. I find it calming." I smile back at him. He studies me for a moment and then pulls me back into the sofa so I'm nestled under his arm, against his chest. I inhale. Just the natural smell of him is such a turn-on; he couldn't get any sexier.

I look up at him. This is where he belongs, by the coast, under the sun. He seems relaxed and free, smiling and chatting with everyone. There's a tug at my heart. I don't want to admit it, but I know I'm dangerously close to falling for him.

How could I not? I never stood a chance.

We chat and laugh, enjoying the warmth of the sun as we have our drinks and breakfast. Stefan is right. The food here is amazing. We have fresh tropical fruit platters, mini granolas and yogurt, small pastries, and warm egg fritters. It is all so delicious and now I'm stuffed. We settle the bill; Jay insists on getting it.

"Shall we head back to my place?" Jay asks. "The sun will be on the pool for the rest of the day now; it'll be perfect for swimming." He leans down to whisper in my ear, "Plus, I want to see you in that sexy little bikini I heard so much about when you were in Dubai."

I chuckle and go to swat him on the chest, but he catches my hand and brings my fingertips to his lips instead where he kisses them, keeping his eyes focused on me.

"Sounds like a plan," says Matt, stretching his arms over his head as he gets up.

"You can ride in my car," Stefan says to him.

"Oh, sure," says Matt casually.

I know in his head he's high-fiving himself.

"I'm coming with you guys," Rach says to me. "If I must watch someone flirt and make sexy eyes, it is definitely not going to be Matt. I'm still preparing myself for what we have in store when his peanut smugglers come out at the pool. I don't think I can take much more."

"I know it's just because you're jealous, darling," coos Matt. "How someone as charming and funny as me can also have the body of a God, is too much to take in for some people."

Rach snorts and we all laugh as we make our way back to Stefan and Jay's cars.

Jay slings his arm around my shoulders again as though it's the most natural thing in the world.

We drive back to Jay's house with the windows down and the radio blaring. Rach and I sing along to some of our favorite songs as they play. Jay laughs at us to begin with until we persuade him to join us. My mouth drops open when I hear his singing voice. It's deep and sexy and if he weren't an actor, he could be a chart-topping country singer. I shouldn't be surprised. I guess it goes with the territory, having multiple performing talents.

I gaze over at him.

"What?" He catches me looking.

"Nothing." I turn back to look out the window, a smile glued to my face. I can see him from the corner of my eye and he's smiling to himself too.

We get back to Jay's house before Stefan and Matt, and we head inside.

"This is some place you've got here," Rach says, looking around as we walk through from the entry hall into the large open-plan living and kitchen area.

"Thanks." Jay smiles, leaning back against the kitchen counter. "Why don't you two get ready to swim and I'll get some drinks ready for us all. Stefan and Matt can't be far away."

"Okay," Rach says. "Holls, you can give me a tour of upstairs."

"You head up. I'll be right behind you," I say, but Rach is already going up one staircase.

I turn back to Jay and wrap my arms around his neck, standing on my tiptoes so my lips almost meet his. His eyes sparkle at me as I rise and dust my lips against his, kissing him.

"I will be back soon," I whisper, "in my string bikini."

"Then you'd better go now, before I have you right here on the counter," Jay says, mirroring my smirk.

"Feeling naughty, Mr. Anderson?" I murmur against his lips, kissing him once more before I pull myself away.

"Always with you, Berry." He winks at me as I head off to find Rach.

"I love that swimsuit," I say to Rach, taking in her abstract print one-piece with sexy cut-out sides.

"Thanks! It's new. It was a present to myself with the extra money I got from Mr. X last month." She smiles as she looks down at herself.

"Mr. X is turning out to be your most loyal customer." I raise an eyebrow.

"I know, right?" Rach shakes her head in disbelief. "It's crazy. And get this." She leans in closer to me. "He said he wants sole purchasing rights." Her eyes are wide.

"What?" I laugh, amazed at what I'm hearing.

"Of course, I've already told him exclusivity will cost more."

"What did he say?"

"He said the cost was inconsequential."

"Wow, he's really into it, Rach."

"I know," Rach says, delighted. "I'm going to have saved a deposit for a house much sooner than I thought at this rate!"

"You must have some serious pheromones." I giggle. "He just can't get enough of whatever it is you smell of."

"Power," she says. "The power to fulfill his secret sniffing fantasies."

I look across at her and we both giggle more.

"Come on, let's go see if Matt and Stefan are here yet."

We head downstairs and into the kitchen. Jay looks up as he sees me and rubs his hand across his chin as his gaze roams over my body in my white string bikini. Arousal stirs inside me, seeing the effect I'm having on him. His eyes lock on mine and he doesn't need to say anything.

I know that look.

He wants me and he wants it to be rough.

"There you are!" Rach calls out as Stefan and Matt walk in. I catch Matt's eye and he gives me a *tell you later* look, so I know better than to ask where they've been.

Rach and I head out to the pool. It's even more beautiful in the daylight; we can see for miles across LA. The pool itself is so clear and inviting, and around it are sun loungers and one large four-poster cabana bed with sheer white drapes. Jay was right. The sun is hitting the deck and pool right now and its heat warms my skin.

Rach and I lie back next to each other on two sun loungers as the boys come out in their swim trunks. Stefan's are black and Matt's, I'm relieved to see, are a cool tropical print with no eagles visible anywhere. Then Jay comes out. He has on a pair of loose-fitting light-blue trunks. His thighs are large and muscular and his broad, tanned chest, defined abs, and toned *V* are hard to miss. He looks like a billboard advert for *Men's Health* magazine.

"Totally see why you're smiling all the time if you're banging him, Holls," Rach whispers out of the side of her mouth before they get too close. "Fucking hell."

I just reply with a smile. What can I say? She's right. I am smiling all the time because of him.

"I made drinks, guys," Jay says, gesturing to a table of glasses and two large jugs of something fruity.

"I'll pour," offers Matt, handing one around to everyone before settling down on a lounger between Rach and Stefan.

Jay grabs another sun lounger and pulls it along the deck so it's flush up against mine, before he lies down on it. He rests one hand on my thigh and the other behind his head, closing his eyes up toward the sun. He looks so relaxed, so sexy.

"Did you squeeze the fruits for this juice between your thighs too?" I whisper, remembering the first morning I woke up in his house.

His eyes crinkle at the corners as he smiles. "I'm conserving all my energy for you later," he says as he runs his hand up and down my thigh.

"Is that a promise?" I tease as I close my eyes and relax back on my lounger.

For a while we all just lie there, enjoying the sun and peace until Rach's phone vibrates. She picks it up to text whoever it is back, and it buzzes again as she taps out another reply.

"Who are you texting?" asks Matt.

"Well, if you must know, Mr. Nosy, I'm texting a guy I know in Vegas. I'm flying there next week."

"So, you're arranging your booty call then?" Matt teases.

"Hell, yes, I am!" Rach almost shouts. "Do you know how long it's been?"

"Are there cobwebs?" Matt asks with a smirk.

"Ew, gross." Rach wrinkles up her nose. "Of course not. But it's been long enough that last night I had another of the sexy dreams I get. This time about Boris Johnson. My body is screaming out for it," Rach groans, crossing her arms, her glossy dark hair shining in the sun.

"Oh, Rach." I laugh.

It's her weird thing that when she's sexually frustrated, she dreams about some rather unusual partners. They're almost always politicians.

"You're having sexy dreams about your prime minister?" Stefan laughs in delight.

Rach eyes him darkly. "Don't laugh too hard. It could be you next. Maybe you'll get Joe Biden, or Donald Trump!"

Stefan's face is a picture. He's horrified. I can't stop myself; I laugh out loud, almost spilling my drink. Jay takes it from me and puts it on the floor next to him.

"Thank you," I manage through my laugh.

Just when it seems over and I take a breath, it starts all over again, and I'm in hysterics once more. Soon everyone else is laughing just as much, and each time we think we've stopped, one of us will smirk and it all starts over. I look around. I'm so lucky to be here with everyone.

"Hey, Holls, can you help me get some more drinks?" Jay asks, picking up the tray of empties and heading toward the kitchen.

We've been enjoying the sun for the last couple of hours and I'm so relaxed.

"Sure. Back in a sec, guys," I call, but the others don't reply. Rach is listening to music with her earbuds in, and Matt and Stefan are in the pool talking.

I follow Jay into the kitchen. The sudden change in temperature from the air conditioning makes my nipples harden. It hasn't gone unnoticed by Jay, who is leaning against the kitchen counter with one hand inside his trunks, stroking his cock.

"Starting without me?"

"Get over here," he says, his eyes dark.

I do as I'm told and walk over to him, stopping in front of him and sliding my hand down to join his on his cock.

"Save some for me." I smile, biting my bottom lip.

"God, Holly, you're so fucking sexy," he says as his other hand grabs my breast and pulls my hard nipple through my bikini top.

I moan and arch into his hand. Then his lips are on mine, hot and urgent, his tongue finding mine and stroking and sucking so perfectly that my legs tremble.

"Jay, they'll see us," I say between kisses.

"So?" he says, kissing me harder. "Okay, get in here," he growls, pulling me into the laundry room and shutting the door.

He backs me up against the counter, his kisses growing deeper and more dominant, claiming my mouth as his. My body is hot and wet with arousal, my pussy throbbing for him.

"Jay," I pant against his lips. "I need you."

"Holly, I fucking need you too." His voice is deep and fierce, and I can tell he wants to play dirty.

He lifts me up onto the counter and I wrap my legs around his waist, drawing him in closer to me. I run my hands up over his chest and around the back of his neck, up into his hair. He kisses me harder, pulling back to bite and suck my bottom lip, his hands gripping my ass and pulling me against his body.

"Jay?"

"Yes, Berry," he growls, turning his attention to kissing and biting behind my ear and down the side of my neck.

"Fill me up with your cock," I moan as I grab fistfuls of his hair between my hands and tug.

It has the effect I knew it would. Jay groans and grabs at the ties for my bikini, lifting me up to remove it. He reaches down and slides his trunks off. I lift my legs over the top of his arms and wiggle my bottom forward to the edge of the counter.

He looks at me with his piercing blue eyes, dark with desire, before slowly sliding his cock deep inside my pussy, inch by thick inch.

"Yes, just like that," I moan, taking my hands from his hair and placing them on the counter behind me so he can pull my hips even closer for deeper access.

"Fuck, you're tight," Jay hisses through his teeth as he pulls out and slides back in deeper, his hands holding my hips, his eyes watching where our bodies meet.

"I need you to fuck me hard, Jay, so hard, baby. I need to know how much you want me," I moan as another rush of wetness flows over us.

"You need to know how much I want you?" Jay asks darkly as he slides out and rams back into me so hard it makes me gasp.

I nod.

"Oh, I want you, Holly," he growls, pulling out again and slamming back into me harder. "I've never wanted anything more." His hands dig into my skin and he starts to really give it to me, his hard, deep thrusts growing faster and faster.

"Oh God, Jay!" I call out. "Your cock feels so good fucking me like that. Please don't stop."

Every inch of him is sliding in and out of my body, and it's incredible. I look up into his eyes as he fills me.

"Fuck, Holly, I don't want to come before you," he groans as he struggles to keep control. "Touch yourself for me," he orders.

I place two of my fingers up to Jay's lips and he takes them into his mouth, rolling his tongue over them and sucking them. I pull them out and place them against my clit while he watches.

"Oh yeah," he groans. "Do it, baby."

I rub circles against myself, throwing my head back to moan at how good it feels combined with the fast pounding he's giving me.

"That's it, baby, tell me how it feels," Jay growls.

"It feels so good. I'm so wet for you. I can't ever get enough of having you inside me," I cry as his thrusts grow even faster. "Oh, Jay! I'm going to come," I cry out as the pressure becomes too much.

"Yeah, baby, come on my cock for me. Wrap your tight little pussy around me and squeeze," Jay hisses.

I explode with a scream, my body convulsing around him. My legs shudder in his arms as wave upon wave of pleasure rolls through my body.

"Oh God, I can feel you," Jay groans. "You feel so good, so fucking good!"

His cock swells inside me before he moans my name and comes in a rush. He keeps thrusting as he empties, and I sigh at how good it still feels. His movements slow down to a stop as he reaches forward and pulls me to him. His hands go to either side of my face as his mouth finds mine.

"It just keeps getting better with you, Holly," he says as he rests his forehead against mine.

"I could say the same thing," I say, looking into his eyes.

He smiles and gently pulls out of me.

"I'll check the others haven't missed us too much. You take your time," he says, leaning in to kiss me once more before putting his trunks back on.

He goes back out to the kitchen, closing the door behind him.

I slide off the counter and put my bikini back on before heading down the hall to use the downstairs bathroom. When I come back into the kitchen, the others are still outside. They're all in the pool, laughing and splashing each other. It doesn't look like they missed us at all. I smile as Jay gets soaked by a perfectly timed splash from Stefan and laughs out loud.

Jay's phone lights up on the counter with a message. I pick it up, about to take it to him.

Anya: You were incredible the other day. I can't wait to do it again! Anya

My stomach churns as I process the words. It must be from Anya Katiss.

What the hell?

Jay's laugh echoes in my ears. He sounds like he's having fun out in the pool. Has he been having fun with Anya too? I swallow the lump that's forming in my throat.

Just what the hell has he been doing with her?

Chapter 12

The rest of the afternoon rushes by. I push the thought of Anya's text to the back of my mind. I shouldn't have been looking at Jay's phone, even if it was just left on the side. The nausea I've had all afternoon is my own fault. I can't ask him about it, as he might think I was snooping. I replay her words in my head for the millionth time.

You were incredible.

What the hell could that mean? My chest tightens at the most obvious meaning. What if Jay is seeing Anya too? It's only been two weeks. How well do I actually know him? Plus, I'm not even in the same country most of the time. He could do whatever, or whoever, he wants, and I would have no idea. Maybe this is what he does? Sees more than one woman at a time. But I don't want to believe that. The way we are together, the way he looks at me sometimes. Surely you couldn't be like that with more than one person. He's an actor though, a great one. What if it's all an act for him?

"You alright, gorgeous? You look deep in thought?" Matt asks, swimming over to me. It's late, and we were all talking about where to go for dinner tonight.

The others are all out of the pool now and drying off.

"Me? Yeah, I'm good." I sigh.

"You can't lie to Uncle Matt, you know?" He smiles, leaning up against the side of the pool next to me.

He's right. Matt knows me too well and can see when something's troubling me.

"I saw a text on Jay's phone," I say, keeping my voice low.

"And?" Matt leans closer.

"It was from Anya Katiss. She said he was incredible, and she couldn't wait to do it again." The hurt creeps into my voice.

Matt frowns. "I'm sure it's not what you're thinking, Holls. The guy is so into you, anyone can see that. I just don't think he would see her too. There's got to be another explanation."

"I hope so. I don't think I'm cut out for this dating game, Matt."

"Look, I'll talk to Stefan, see what he knows. Those guys are together all the time. He will know if anything's going on."

"Thanks, Matt." I smile.

At least if the worst is happening, I will know about it and can walk away now before I get hurt.

"So, where did you and Stefan get to after breakfast? We were back way before you two."

Matt smiles and looks up at the sky. "Oh, Holly, it was great. Stefan said he wanted to take me to a viewpoint on the way back. It was pretty, but I wasn't looking at that view, you know?" Matt winks at me. "We had a deep chat, about what we're looking for in a partner and where we see ourselves in the future."

"And?" I say, encouraging Matt to continue.

"And we kissed!" Matt squeals, clamping his hand over his mouth and glancing to the side of the pool.

"That's brilliant!" I beam at him.

"I know! Oh, Holly. He's a dream. He really is. I've never met anyone quite like him. I'm enjoying getting to know him. I usually just jump into bed and realize they're all wrong for me afterward." Matt pauses. "This feels different."

"I'm thrilled for you both, Matt," I say as I put my arm around him. "You deserve someone who makes you happy."

"So do you, Holly." His voice turns serious. "Don't write Jay off until you know what's going on."

"I know. I hope it's nothing," I say as Jay smiles and beckons to us both from the poolside.

"Come on, you two," he shouts. "Let's get something to eat."

"Yeah! I'm getting hangry over here," Rach adds.

"Alright, alright!" Matt shouts back. "Don't get your panties in a twist! You'll have to discount them if they're creased!"

Rach glares back at him and sticks up her middle finger. Despite feeling uneasy about what's going on with Jay and Anya, I can't help but smile at my two friends. They're enough to lift anyone out of a slump.

We head out for dinner at a Mexican restaurant Stefan recommended and have a great time eating tacos and drinking too many frozen margaritas.

Jay spends the entire night with his arm around me, kissing me as much as he can without making the others feel awkward. The times I look into his eyes throughout the evening, all I can see is openness, not a hint of him hiding anything from me, anything like Anya anyway. My heart's telling me I can trust him. I've never felt a connection with someone before that's telling me I can let my guard down. But I have it with Jay. I must have gotten the text all wrong and there's an innocent explanation.

As we are finishing dinner, Rach gets a text from a friend, so she says goodbye to us and heads off to have a drink with them. This is only a two-night stopover, so we fly home tomorrow.

"We're going to go for a drive, then Stefan will drop me back at the hotel," Matt announces to me and Jay.

"Okay, have fun. I'll see you at checkout tomorrow," I say to Matt and go to give Stefan a big hug goodbye. "It's been so great to hang out with you this trip, Stefan," I say. "I hope I see you again soon."

"Me too, Holly." He squeezes me. "I can see how much happier Jay has been recently, and all I can think is it's down to you," he says discreetly in my ear as Jay and Matt are saying goodbye.

We wave as they leave, Stefan's words repeating in my head. Is it down to me? Surely Stefan would know if it was actually someone else. Jay's staring off into the distance, distracted suddenly.

"You okay?" I ask, squeezing his thigh underneath the table.

"Oh, yeah, I'm brilliant when you're here," he says, winking at me.

"Alright, Mr. Cheese." I giggle.

"What, can't a guy tell the truth without it sounding cheesy?" he says, putting his hands up in protest.

"Okay, okay, fine. How about you show me instead?" I say, reaching up to put my hand in his hair and drawing him to me for a kiss.

He kisses me back, his fingers caressing my cheek. I can't put my finger on it, but he seems different since the others left. Less light and carefree.

"Am I coming back to your place, or are you coming to the hotel?" I ask him as I pick up my bag and get ready to leave.

Jay rubs his hands across his eyes. "I'm sorry, Holly. I can't tonight. I need to go home and make a work call that could take a while, and then I've got an early breakfast meeting tomorrow." His eyes meet mine, but he seems miles away.

"Oh, er, okay, sure!" I force my voice to sound light.

This is the last night I have in LA until I come back again in another week. I swapped onto another LA flight by giving up some days off, but I still have a one-night New York trip to do in between first.

"I'll drop you back at the hotel," he says, getting up and taking my hand, and although we chat on the journey, it seems like there is something hanging unsaid in the air between us.

We pull up to the hotel and Cooper smiles and waves from his valet desk. I wave back and then turn to Jay.

"So, I'm back in a week," I say, looking at him, searching his face for a clue of how he's really feeling. He smiles at me and I'm still just as clueless.

"I know, and I will count down the days, believe me, Berry."

He leans over, dusting my bottom lip with his thumb before taking it between his lips and sucking. I close my eyes and melt into him as he gives me a slow, deep kiss that feels heavy with emotion.

"See you in a week," he whispers, pulling back and staring into my eyes before he jumps out and opens my door for me.

"A week." I nod as I climb out of the car.

As Jay drives off I feel like I'm missing something. It's like he wanted to say more but decided not to. Cooper is talking to another hotel guest as I pass, so I give him a small smile and wave as I head into the hotel and up to my room, alone.

I have one day off when I get home before my flight to New York, so I go for a run and do some yoga. Then I get all my washing sorted and phone my mum to catch up.

"Hi, darling. It's so nice to hear your voice."

"You too, Mum." I smile as I settle down on the sofa with a mug of peppermint tea. It's always such a comfort hearing her voice.

"How are you?"

"I'm good, Mum. I've just flown with Rach and Matt, so that was fun."

"Oh, how are they both? You must all come and visit me and your father again. That was such a fun weekend when you all made it down," she says.

I remember the weekend that she means. We were lucky with the weather and had a great time at the beach, having barbecues and taking Mum and Dad's dog, Muffin, for long walks. Mum loved having us all there. She must enjoy the activity of having guests when it's just her and Dad now that me and Sophie have moved out.

"They're good, Mum. How are you and Dad?"

"We're okay, love. Your father's helping Ted next door put up a new fence, the other one blew down in all those gales we've been having." I smile as Mum chats, and I imagine her sitting at the kitchen table in the house me and Sophie grew up in.

"I'm going to go in a minute, Holly love. I've got a pistachio cake in the oven. It's a new recipe I'm trying."

"Okay, Mum. Speak soon. I love you." I smile. That's just like Mum, always baking.

"Love you too, darling."

I hang up and think about how much I miss home as I sip my tea. I will have to go back soon and visit.

I pick my phone back up to check the time. It's just after two in the afternoon, six in the morning in LA. Jay will just be waking up. After we said goodbye in LA Thursday night, I didn't hear from him again until I landed back home Saturday. He said he had a work call that night to make and an early meeting Friday morning, so I didn't expect to, but it's the first day since we met we haven't texted each other or spoken. I swallow down the growing, uneasy feeling. I'm just being stupid. He was busy with work and he was texting me yesterday, just like usual. Nothing else is going on.

I decide to send him a text to wake up to.

Me: Morning, handsome. How did you sleep?

I sit back and finish my mug of tea before my phone beeps with a message. My stomach leaps, as it does every time I receive a message from Jay.

Magic Cock: Not as good as if you'd been in my bed with me. Can't wait to kiss those gorgeous lips of yours... both pairs.

I smile. That's more like the Jay I know. Cheeky and flirty. Maybe he was just having a bad day before and had a lot on his mind. He works a lot, and Stefan said he's constantly getting offers of new contracts and ad campaigns. They go to a lot of meetings. It must get quite busy sometimes.

My stomach unclenches. I didn't read the text properly and got the wrong idea. That's all there is to it, I'm convinced. Well, ninety percent convinced. Okay, eighty-five percent convinced. I run my hands down over my face. I'm going to give myself an ulcer at this rate.

I go and pack for my New York flight in the morning to keep myself occupied.

The flight is turbulent. Coming into JFK airport, we have to circle for over an hour to get a landing slot on the runway. We just keep flying around and getting bumped about by the weather. I've never handed out so many paper sickness bags. Even some crew needed them. I've held on to my stomach somehow, and for that I'm grateful.

After we land, the passengers' faces look as relived as I am to be on stable ground.

We are fortunate that we stay in the center of Manhattan for this trip, right near the Empire State Building. It's still mid-afternoon in New York when we get to the hotel, so I have a quick shower and head out for a walk around the shops, calling in a Starbucks order to grab a peppermint tea to take with me. It's still only around midday in LA. I pull out my phone and reread the last message Matt sent me after I landed a few hours ago.

Matt: Hey, gorgeous! How was your flight? I can't wait to catch up after you're back from your next LA. Sucks that we won't have a day off together until then. Love you.

I smile. I'm so lucky that I have such a good friend. Matt told me he brought Anya up in conversation with Stefan. All Stefan said was that he didn't think Anya was dating anyone and that he wouldn't know if she was anyway, as he only knows her in a work capacity. Matt couldn't dig any further or bring up Jay as it might have looked suspicious.

I sigh and take another sip of my tea. I'm no closer to understanding what her text was all about. Jay hasn't mentioned her to me at all. Maybe the text wasn't even meant for him and she sent it in error, but how likely is that? I look up.

Wow.

I've walked farther than I thought. I'm near the Rockefeller Center now, where the Magnolia Bakery is. It's one of mine and Rachel's favorite places to get cupcakes. Just the smell of it is incredible. I swear you can taste the sugar in the air. Looking in the window probably consumes calories. Their cupcakes are just so pretty. They come in lots of pastel colors and they have a big dollop of icing on top, no scrimping.

I head inside and buy one for now, and two to take home for Rach and me. It's become a bit of a tradition for us to do this if one of us is in New York. I pick three different colors and pay the cashier before leaving and heading back to the hotel, devouring my cupcake far too fast on the way.

It's early when I wake up and after trying, and failing, to get back to sleep, I decide to get up early and try to nap later, before the flight home.

I pull on my running gear and get ready to head out to Central Park for a run. I love going out around six or seven in the morning in New York. It's when the city is waking up, with steam rising out of the road drains, just like in the movies.

I can call Jay for a chat later when I get back. He's three hours behind in LA, so it's far too early to try now; he'll be asleep. I imagine his toned, tanned body stretched out underneath his white sheets. It's been four days since I saw him, and three more days until I fly back there. How my nerves are handling it is beyond me. It's like torture having to go so long in between seeing him. When I'm with him, everything feels so intense. Everything is intense! We talk and laugh, and the sex is just insane. I don't know what it is about him, but I don't feel embarrassed to let go when we are together.

I finish tying the laces on my trainers and put some money, my room key card, and my phone into my armband. I grab my headphones off the side and walk out the door, ready to burn off yesterday's cupcake, and a whole load of unused sexual energy from thinking about Jay.

It's a bright, crisp morning, and the three miles to Central Park whizz by. I'm panting, sweat beading on my brow by the time I get there. My mouth is dry, so I head across to one of the street vendors at the edge of the park. He's just setting up for the day, unpacking the papers and magazines.

"Just a water please." I hand him some money in return for the cool bottle. I stand and drink half of it in one go.

"Hard start to the day, eh?" He grins at me as he continues cutting the string holding the bundles of magazines together.

"You could say that." I laugh. "It's all good for us though."

"I'll take your word for it." He chuckles.

"Thanks again," I say, holding up the water bottle.

He gives me a nod and I look down at the magazines he has in his hand. I freeze as I recognize the person and place on the front cover.

"Sorry, can I just see that for a moment, please?" I ask, my eyes glued to the picture.

"Sure, here you go. This week's new *Celeb Central*, that is. Was only released this morning."

"Thanks," I croak out as I hand him some more money for the magazine.

"You alright? You look like you've seen a ghost." I hear him ask.

I fake a smile and nod. "Oh yeah, I'm fine. Thanks," I say, walking off.

I can't tear my eyes away from the picture in front of me. I recognize it as the outside of Jay's house.

The caption reads, *"She was seen leaving Jay Anderson's house early Friday morning."*

There in the picture, walking out the front door and looking every inch the stunning supermodel, is Anya Katiss.

Chapter 13

DIZZINESS HITS ME AS heat burns through my body. I rush over to a bench to sit before I fall.

There's no denying that's Anya coming out of Jay's front door. She's smiling and wearing a tight red sundress with heeled sandals and large black sunglasses. She looks incredible. Is it because she spent the night having passionate sex with Jay?

Oh God.

It says this picture was taken at eight thirty Friday morning. Friday was the morning after we went for the Mexican dinner. Jay told me he had to go to a breakfast meeting; that's why he didn't spend the night with me before my flight home.

He lied to me.

The nausea in my stomach builds. He wasn't at a meeting. He was with Anya Katiss. She left his house in the morning. That means she must have been there all night.

I can't get my head around this. I could be sick right here on the floor, probably throw my heart up with it.

People are passing me on their way to work, not even noticing the girl with the breaking heart. They're all going on with their daily commutes and routines and I'm sitting and feeling like I've just been slapped hard in the face. That text message was a clue. It was all there for me, but I was just too stupid and drunk with lust, or whatever it was, to even see it. My head drops into my hands as I suck in a couple of deep breaths.

I'm so stupid.

I need to get back to my hotel room; I need to be alone. I drag myself up off the bench and hail a cab.

I make it back to my hotel room without bumping into any of the crew from my flight in the lobby or elevator. Thank God. I can't face making small talk right now. I let myself into my room and collapse against the door. I sink down to the floor, and the magazine hits the carpet with a *thud*. How could I be so stupid to think that Jay Anderson was interested in me? Plain, boring Holly Havers. I was just another girl who filled some spare time he had.

I look at the picture of Anya again. It makes sense he would be with someone like her. She's from his world. She belongs. I don't. I pull in a deep, shaky breath as tears of shame stream down my cheeks. I can't stop them coming so I admit defeat and sit on the floor and cry.

I stay like this until I've got no tears left. I need to pull myself together. So what if Jay lied to me? I've been lied to before by Simon, and I survived. I don't need an actor with far too much money to know that I deserve better than this. I've got great friends and I'm a good person.

Fuck you, Jay Anderson! Fuck you and your blue eyes and big cock.

I'm better than this. I shouldn't be sitting on the floor in tears over him.

I get up and go in the bathroom, turning the shower on. Peeling off my running clothes, I turn to face myself in the mirror. My face is red, and my eyes are puffy, but there's a new strength in them shining back.

This is the last time I waste my time and heart on a man who lies and cheats.

Never again.

I step under the scorching water of the shower and try my best to scrub all trace of Jay Anderson away.

The flight home is quick and most of the passengers want to sleep, so I sit in the galley with some of the crew, chatting over cups of tea. They moan about their other halves, or lack of dating lives. I'm not the only one who isn't living a fairy tale.

Maybe this is just life.

The movies and stories have a lot to answer for. We are conditioned from a young age to expect too much. We are told we can do anything, be anyone, and the right person will come along, and we can live happily ever after. It's all a big fat lie, a conspiracy made up to give people hope so they can get out of bed each day.

After landing, I run to catch the bus to the staff parking lot. If I miss it, I will have to wait another twenty minutes. My suitcase is in one hand with my carry-on bag strapped to the top, and in the other I'm holding the box of cupcakes from the Magnolia Bakery. It's about the only thing I'm looking forward to today.

"Whoa." I swerve to avoid a little boy running toward me without looking where he's going.

A man rushes past after him, knocking into my arm.

"Sorry!" he calls, but it's too late. The box of cupcakes flies out of my hand and flips upside down, landing on the floor.

Great, just great.

Can it get any worse?

"I don't know what to say, Holls. I didn't peg him as a two-timing rat." Rach looks at the cover of *Celeb central* again.

"Me neither." I sigh, leaning forward with my spoon to scoop up another pile of mashed cupcake. The lid stayed shut when it fell, so although they were flattened, they still taste good.

Small victories, I guess.

"And he's been texting you since this was published?"

"Yeah, he hasn't mentioned it, though. Although now he's started asking if he's done something wrong as I haven't replied to anything from him since I found out."

I sit back into our sofa, so relived to be back home again and for Rach to be here today. I would have hated coming home to an empty house.

"He either has no clue you've seen it, or he's playing ignorant and is going to deny it all," Rach says, licking her spoon as she thinks. "What did Matt say when you told him?"

"He was as shocked as I was. He couldn't believe it. Didn't want to believe it. He's spent almost as much time with Jay as me, and he thought he was a great guy. Plus, Stefan always says how genuine Jay is, and he's worked with a lot of people in the industry who are fake." I shrug, unsure what to make of it all.

"I'm so sorry, Holls. I thought he seemed great too. He was so into you. Fucking snake," Rach spits. "Do you want me to visit his house one night and chop his balls off for you?"

I smile; that is such a Rach thing to say.

"Thanks, but he can keep his wandering balls. I don't want to think about them anymore. At least I won't have to see him again. I'm not likely to bump into him."

"This is true," Rach agrees. "You never have to see the lying bastard again. What about your LA flight tomorrow though? Are you still going to do it?"

"Yeah, it's too late to swap off it now. Anyway, he doesn't own LA. I loved going there before I met him and I will not let thoughts of him put me off," I say, spooning another giant dollop of icing into my mouth.

"You know you're only getting away with eating most of the icing because of the sex-rat circumstances, don't you?" Rach raises an eyebrow at my spoon.

I laugh. "I know. There's no way you'd stand for it usually."

"Hell, I wouldn't, it's the best part!" Rach laughs.

"So, are you all packed for your Shanghai tomorrow?" I ask.

"Yep, all done, got lots of space in my suitcase to bring bits back." She smiles mischievously.

"Why, what are you going to buy?"

"Panties. Sexy little panties, and lots of them!"

I laugh. "What?"

"Yeah, Holls. There's this lady at the fabric market near the hotel who can make you anything in a couple of days. Got all different fabrics you can choose from."

I nod as I listen.

"I'm going to get some *Rachel specials* made up and charge Mr. X extra for the bespoke package," she says, eyes gleaming.

"What's the bespoke package?" I ask, eyes wide. Only Rach would have thought this up.

"I'm not sure yet. I'm probably going to ask her to embroider them with messages, like *scent by Rachel*, or *inhale, Mr. X, you bad boy*," she says, before shrugging her shoulders. "I'm not sure yet. But it'll be something that'll make his balls swell when he opens it and realizes, they're not only worn but also made specially for him."

"Eww, Rach!" I throw my head back and laugh. "You've no idea who this guy is! He could be some creepy old guy with black fingernails or a young lad who's never even had sex before." I wince at all the possibilities.

"You're right, he could. I just don't see it though. The way he writes his messages suggest he's well educated, and he mentions things someone around our age would talk about. Plus, he's spending a shitload on my panties now. I can barely keep up. So he's got money to burn, or sniff." She cackles at her own joke.

"Okay, just so long as you're careful," I say, reaching over to hug her. "You're my best friend and I need to know you're safe."

She hugs me back. I'm one of the few people Rach will hug for over two seconds. She doesn't trust easily, but when she does, she will do anything for you.

"I'm fine. He's never seen my face, and there must be hundreds of crew called Rachel. He doesn't even know that's my actual name. He sends money to my account and I have a special email address set up. You don't need to worry, Holly, although I'm glad you do." She smiles.

We're interrupted by my phone beeping with another text from Jay. I couldn't bring myself to delete his number yet, but I changed his name from Magic Cock. I hated seeing it flash up on my screen.

Lying Cheat: Holly, please talk to me. I've seen the photos. I can explain.

I throw my phone back down on the sofa in disgust.

"Was that Jay?" Rach asks.

"Yeah, he wants a chance to explain," I say as my phone rings. "God, it's him," I groan, putting my hands up against my face.

"We'll see about that," Rach snaps, picking up my phone and hitting answer. "She doesn't want to talk to you, arsehole. Why don't you go back to your supermodel girlfriend and cry on her shoulder?" She stabs at the disconnect button and hangs up. "There. He won't ring again if he thinks he will get me giving him an earful each time," she says, satisfied.

"I can't believe you just said that to him," I say, putting my hands over my mouth.

"Well, it's true, isn't it? You don't want to talk to him, and he is an arsehole."

"You're right, Rach. I would just never have the guts to say that like you just did."

"Well, you're going to start today, Holly! No more men treating you like a fool. Stand up for yourself and tell them where to shove it!" Rach says, holding her fist out so I can bump it.

"Yeah," I agree, not quite feeling as confident as her. "You're right. It's time I started speaking up for myself. It's time I stopped being a pushover."

"You can do it, Holls. I believe in you. You can start by forgetting all about Jay, whatever his name is."

"Yeah, I will."

I will forget all about Jay Anderson.

I can do it.

The next day's flight to LA drags and I'm glad to be on the bus to the hotel. I've decided to catch a cab to the mall after I've showered so that I can get noodles from a place the crew have been raving about. We pull up at some traffic lights and my eyes wander to a giant billboard advertisement on the side of a building. My chest tightens. It's for season three of *Steel Force*. It must be one of the photos they shot the night Jay met me in the bar. The night I saw Simon. Jay's intense blue eyes stare back at me from the poster. He's in full FBI gear and looks mean and sexy as hell.

"Oh, *hello!*" pipes up one of the crew on the bus, pointing to the poster. "I wouldn't kick him out of bed."

"I don't think anyone would," another girl agrees. "You'd need your head tested," she says.

I sink down in my seat. Maybe forgetting about him will not be as easy as I'd hoped. Not when he's here in glorious giant-sized high definition wherever I look.

I put my earbuds in and lean back, closing my eyes for the rest of the journey.

After I've showered and changed into a summery dress and flip-flops, I head outside the hotel entrance to get a cab. A movement on the other side of the street catches my eye and I look up just in time to see a guy in dark glasses and a hoodie turn and walk around the side of a building. My fingers tingle.

Was he watching me?

No, I'm being stupid. He would have no reason to be interested in me.

"Hi, Holly." Cooper looks up from his desk where he's texting on his phone.

"Hi, Cooper, how you doing?" I smile. Cooper is always so upbeat. I enjoy having a chat each time I'm here.

"I'm all good. I've got the day off tomorrow. Me and Eric are heading to a car show down the coast." He beams.

"That sounds fun! Okay, not my kind of fun, I know nothing about cars, but it sounds like your kind of fun." I smile.

"You know us," he chuckles, "can't get enough of a great car. It'll be so good to spend some time with my brother too. How about you? What you got planned for this trip?" His eyes are on my face, waiting for my answer.

"Oh, I don't know. I haven't decided yet. Not too much."

Cooper's brow furrows, and he opens his mouth, then stops, seeming to change his mind about what he was going to say. He opens it again, and says, "You need a taxi?"

"Yes, please, to the mall."

He goes out to the road and hails a cab. He bends down to the window to talk to the driver and hands him something.

"Here you go, Holly, this one's all yours." He smiles, opening the back door for me.

"Thanks, Cooper," I say, climbing in.

As we set off, I pull my phone out to text Matt.

Me: Hey gorgeous. How you doing? How was your flight?

He should have landed in Barbados a few hours ago.

Matt: Busy! Full of honeymooners and holiday makers. Feel like I've been dragged through a hedge backwards. Nothing a cocktail at the beach bar won't fix though! How's LA? Heard any more from Jay?

I would much rather be at the beach bar with Matt right now.

Me: Have a drink for me! Nope, nothing from Jay since Rach answered my phone and gave him an earbashing. He's probably given up now.

I look out the window as I wait for Matt to text back. It's funny, I don't remember ever driving this way to get to the mall before. Maybe there's a road closure or something. My phone beeps in my hand before I can give it much more thought.

Matt: Stefan said he's been a right grumpy git since you left, Holly. Been a nightmare, apparently. He told me not to tell you as it's none of his business, but he thinks you should hear Jay out. Maybe there's more to it??

Huh? What does Stefan mean by that? What could Jay possibly have to say to explain why his ex is leaving his house early in the morning?

I sit back and fold my arms across my chest as I look out the cab's window. We are definitely not on the right road. We aren't even going in the right direction for the mall. The driver must be lost, or misheard Cooper when he told him where to go.

"Excuse me." I lean forward between the two front seats.

The driver raises his eyes to look at me in the rear-view mirror.

"Yes, miss?"

"Are we heading the right way for the mall?"

He looks puzzled. "The mall? No, I'm taking you to where the valet guy said," he says slowly, as though I don't understand.

"What do you mean, where the valet guy said? What's going on?"

"Like I said. The valet guy gave me this address and paid in advance. Gave me a big tip too," he says, his forehead wrinkling. "Hell, this isn't some weird setup, is it? We're almost there now. Look, I don't want any trouble. If there's something fishy going on and you don't feel safe getting out, then just say the word and I'll drive you straight out of here!" he says, turning his head to look at my face. His eyes are wide. "I mean it. I thought the guy was just doing you a favor, you know? Paying upfront like that. I didn't think anything was going on."

"Don't worry. It's fine, I'm not in any danger. But Cooper will be when I get my hands on him," I say, narrowing my eyes as the cab pulls up to a stop outside Jay's house.

"You sure, miss?" he asks, his face relaxing.

"Yes, thank you. Thanks for the ride," I say as I get out and shut the door behind me.

I walk up the driveway, aware I'm being watched.

Standing there on the doorstep in black jeans and T-shirt, his muscular arms folded across his chest and his intense blue eyes burning into mine, is Jay.

Chapter 14

"Adding kidnapping to your list of talents now, are you?" I snap at him as I reach the front door.

"Don't be smart, Holly." He glares at me. "What was I supposed to do? You haven't answered my texts or calls for days."

I shrug and look over at the garages, anything to avoid his glare.

"So that's it? One photo, and you're never going to speak to me again?" he says, his voice low.

He sounds like he's barely containing his anger. Something inside me boils over and I bring my eyes up to him and glare back.

"That's about right, yeah. What do you expect me to do? Keep running back to you whenever I'm in town so I can be your booty call while you carry on your life with your real girlfriend when I'm not here?" I hiss.

Jay's eyes widen and his jaw tenses as he clenches his teeth. "Come inside, Holly."

"What if I don't want to?" I sniff.

"Then God help me, I will lift you over my shoulder and carry you in," Jay says, and I know he isn't joking.

"Fine." I brush past him, trying not to inhale his mouth-watering scent.

I head straight through into the kitchen. It looks just as I remember it, the view out of the open glass doors at the back stunning as always, the sun setting outside, the sky a vivid pinkish red.

"It's not what you think, Holly," he says behind me.

"It never is," I say sarcastically as I turn to face him.

He strides over, stopping inches away from my face.

"Don't you dare! Don't you fucking dare put me in the same category as your ex!" he shouts, his arms shaking by his sides. "I would never lie to you, Holly. I would never cheat on anyone."

I stare up at him. "Like I've never heard that before," I fire back.

"For fuck's sake, Holly!" Jay slams his fist down on the kitchen counter so hard that a glass tips over and rolls off, smashing all over the floor.

I jump, but Jay doesn't even flinch. His eyes are blazing into mine, his chest rising and falling with each breath.

"Go on then, explain," I say.

Heat radiates from his body and the veins in his arms are protruding. He's so close to me I can smell the same earthy citrus scent that I noticed the first time we met. I shake the thought out of my head. Now is not the time to get distracted by him.

So what if he smells incredible? He's lied to me. I can't trust him.

Jay takes a step back from me, running a hand through his hair, his shoulders still tense.

"It was work, Holly."

"Sure it was," I scoff and roll my eyes.

"Are you going to listen to me or not? Because right now, Holly, I'm wondering why I'm even bothering," he says, sounding exasperated.

I clear my throat and avoid making eye contact. "I'm here now, you might as well say it." I shrug.

He looks at me, shaking his head before continuing. "Anya was here Friday morning for a breakfast meeting, like I told you." He gauges my reaction. I don't say anything, so he carries on. "She wasn't here alone. Her agent, Doug, was here too, and so was Stefan. Only, they weren't the ones photographed leaving."

My eyes widen. "Stefan was here?"

"Yes, he was, and I asked him not to say anything to you once I realized you were pissed about it. I was too angry that you would even think she was here for any other reason. I told him I would explain it to you myself when I spoke to you. Only, you ignored all my calls." He glares at me again. "What would make you even think there was anything to it?"

"There was a text on your phone that day. She said you were incredible, and she couldn't wait to do it again," I blurt out, turning my back on Jay so he can't see the heat flaring up in my cheeks.

Even if she was here for a meeting Friday morning that doesn't explain the text message or that time we saw her at dinner when she was flirting with Jay.

"Turn around and look at me please, Holly," he says, his voice strained.

I take a deep breath and turn around, lifting my chin up in defiance as I'm caught in his intense blue stare. He's scowling at me and his pulse is beating hard in his neck.

"We did a test shoot together a couple of weeks ago. She wants me to promote the male version of her new fragrance. The photos came out well, so we had a meeting here Friday to discuss the contract." He lets out a big sigh.

I stand there as my anger slips away and my cheeks cool. I look up at his face. His brow is furrowed, and his eyes are burning with intensity.

He's telling the truth.

I don't know whether to laugh or cry. He really is telling the truth; I can see it in his face. I was so ready to believe the worst in him. It was so easy for me to think so little of him. My heart is heavy in my chest at the thought of what that must have felt like for him.

"Why didn't you just ask me, Holly? Why couldn't you trust me enough to just ask me what was going on, instead of assuming the worst? All this time we've spent together," his eyes bore into mine.

"You seemed different after dinner, distracted. You didn't want to spend my last night in LA together," I say, my voice thick with hurt.

"Holly," he swallows, taking a deep breath. "I *was* distracted. I saw you saying goodbye to Stefan, and I knew I was next. I'm not good at goodbyes," he says, looking down at the floor. I take a step closer to him and he looks up at me. "I knew you were different, but it was that moment that I realized I didn't want you to leave. Ever again." He rubs his hands up through his hair, his face pulled tight in anguish.

As he brings his eyes to meet mine, they are full of hurt. There's more to it.

Rob.

The final goodbye that he never got to say.

"Jay," I whisper, closing the gap between us and reaching up to touch the side of his face.

He grabs my hand and his eyes flash. "Don't, Holly. I'm still livid at you for thinking I would treat you like that," he snaps.

The return of his anger toward me is like a slap in the face. He still has hold of my hand and his eyes fix on mine.

"You punished me for the mistakes that Simon made," he says, pulling me hard up against his chest.

My heart pounds against him. The heat of his body is almost unbearable next to mine.

He dips his head to my ear. "Don't ever do it again," he growls, and then his teeth find my neck and bite, just enough to make me wince.

I let out a small whimper, and then his lips are on mine, rough, commanding, his tongue dominating mine. He pushes me up against the wall, one hand holding my neck, the other reaching between my legs. My body betrays me and wetness rushes to meet his fingers, which are now inside my panties. I've spent days trying not to think about him, being so hurt at what I thought he had done. Now he's said a few things and I'm back here already. My body completely at his mercy.

"Stop!" I shout. Jay freezes and draws back to look at me. "You said you used to date?" I pant.

"Holly," Jay says, a warning tone creeping into his voice.

"So, you have slept with her before?" I continue as he takes his hand back from my soaking wet underwear.

"No, Holly," he says, his lips only inches from mine. "God, you're infuriating." He sighs, reaching to stroke my jaw with the thumb that's holding my neck, his eyes looking down at my lips. "We dated for a couple of months. Her agent thought it would be good publicity. We had a drunken kiss one night after a party, and it just felt *wrong*, for both of us. She told me she was in love with someone else." Jay leans forward so his lips are almost on mine.

"Oh," I whisper.

"Yes, oh," Jay says. "So, if you've finished, then I would like to continue, please?" he whispers against my lips.

I nod.

"Say it, Holly," he growls.

"Yes, Jay."

"Yes, what?" he says, pressing against me harder so his huge erection pushes into my stomach.

"Yes, Jay, I want you to… I need you to fuck me, please," I whisper, all my restraint against him gone.

His lips shoot back to mine, and his tongue presses back inside my mouth, claiming me. He has me pinned against the wall, one hand holding my neck, and it's so fucking arousing knowing that he has complete control. Another rush of wetness soaks my panties as his fingers push back inside them. The fabric pulls against my skin and there's a sound of tearing silk as Jay forces his fingers in and tears them right through. I suck my breath in as he sinks two fingers deep inside me. All I can do is moan against his lips as he fucks me with his fingers, circling my clit with his thumb at the same time.

"You like that, baby?" he murmurs against my lips.

"Uh-huh," I manage as the pleasure takes over my body.

"Tell me properly," he says, giving my neck a gentle squeeze.

"I love it, Jay; you know just how to touch me," I whisper, my legs already growing weak.

"Never forget, Holly. I want you and only you." He plunges his fingers back inside me again.

I cry out and put my hands around his back, digging my nails in.

"I'm going to fuck you," he growls. "And you're going to tell me how sorry you are for doubting the way I feel about you."

"Yes," I moan as he lifts my dress up over my head and unhooks my bra, throwing it onto the back of the sofa.

He leans down to suck my nipples and I press my head back further into the wall as I gasp at how good it feels.

"I've missed your tits, Holly. Don't you ever stay away from me again."

"I'm sorry," I moan as my breathing quickens.

God, he's amazing. No one else has ever made me feel like this. No one else has ever had such an effect on my body.

He straightens up and I help him lift his T-shirt up over his head, kissing his chest and running my hands over it as soon as it's exposed. He grabs a handful of my hair and pulls my neck to one side as he sucks and kisses one side of it roughly. My pussy throbs painfully.

"Please, Jay, I'm sorry."

He must believe me. He must know I mean it. I want him so badly.

He unzips his jeans and pulls them down, kicking them off.

"I'm not done with you yet, Holly. I need to fuck you hard and you've got to be ready for it."

This is torture. I just need to have him inside me now. I want to scream at him to give it to me. I'm panting and sweating, and every nerve ending is waiting to explode under his touch. He drops to his knees and lifts one of my legs over his shoulder.

Oh fuck. Here we go.

He can't get enough of going down on me. I've got no chance of getting him back up here until I've come now.

He will make sure of it. His mouth kisses my burning hot skin, and I cry out in pleasure. He is so good at this. He parts me wider with his fingers before his tongue slides in, tasting me. I can barely stay standing as my legs shake with the intensity of his touch.

"Jay," I pant, reaching down to grab his hair in my hands.

There's a sharp intake of breath as he feels my hands there. He licks me again, deeper, and faster, his tongue sliding up inside me and caressing in long strokes.

"Oh, Jay!" His mouth finds my clitoris and sucks as he sinks three fingers inside me, stretching me wide open.

It's so intense, the pleasure more than I can handle. "Oh fuck!" I cry as I come hard on his face.

He growls and pushes his fingers deeper inside me, his tongue driving in circles over me as I keep coming in hard waves all over him. He laps each one up, licking and sucking until I beg him to stop.

"Please, Jay, I'm sorry!" I cry.

I'm panting as he stands up and kisses me so I can taste myself on his mouth.

"Come on, Berry," he breathes against my lips as he lifts me up with my legs around his waist and carries me out the back door and over to the cabana bed on the deck.

He lays me down on my back and rises over me.

"I need to fuck you hard, baby."

"I need it too. I want you to know I will never doubt you again," I whisper, looking up into his piercing eyes.

He uses one hand to bring my wrists together above my head and holds them there as he slides into me in one deep thrust.

I throw my head back and moan.

"Oh, Holly. You've no idea how much I love your tight little pussy. Especially when it's soaking wet for me," he says, sliding his cock in and out.

All I can do is lie there with my legs spread for him and watch him take complete control. It's a massive turn-on.

His thrusts grow deeper, and I'm forced down into the mattress.

"Yes, Jay!" I cry. "That feels so good!"

He lets go of my hands and grabs on to my hips, rising onto his knees and bringing my legs up, opening them wide. His pace quickens and he drives into me over and over, pulling my hips back onto his thick cock. It feels amazing. My entire body is tense and tingling.

"Oh fuck, Jay, I'm going to come," I cry.

My hands grab on to his, holding my hips as he drags my body back onto his.

"Tell me, Holly," he growls.

"I'm going to come all over your big hard cock, Jay!" I cry. "I'm going to come so hard for you, baby," I say as I shake underneath him.

"Oh, fuck yeah," he groans through his teeth.

My orgasm builds until I can't hold it any longer and it rips through me. I scream out loud underneath him, squeezing my eyes shut and digging my nails into the backs of his hands.

"That's it, baby," he hisses, pushing into me harder as I ride my orgasm out around him.

I fight for a deep breath as I continue shuddering beneath him.

"Oh fuck!" Jay growls as he quickens his pace. "Fuck, fuck, Holly!" He lets out a loud groan as he comes inside me. His cock pumps deep inside me as he lets it out, his body hot and swollen. It feels raw and amazing.

He slows down and stills inside me, panting and sweating.

"Jay." I reach up and cup his face in my hands. His beautiful blue eyes look back at me. "I'm sorry I doubted you," I whisper. "I'm so sorry."

We lie out on the cabana in the warm evening air for a while, just content to be together.

I'm tracing patterns on Jay's chest with my finger as he lies on his back, his arm holding me against his side.

"You know one thing that made me feel better when you weren't here?" he says.

"What?" I ask.

"I knew if you felt so hurt, you must have strong feelings for me. Otherwise, you wouldn't have cared so much." I look up and he's smiling at me.

"Oh, I must have strong feelings then," I tease.

He grins. "I would even say you like me better than peppermint tea."

"Don't go getting carried away. That's not just any old tea, you know." I smirk, kissing his side.

"No, you're right. I mean, that's like you saying that I must like you better than my Ferrari," he says, his eyes crinkling at the sides.

"Preposterous." I giggle.

"Outrageous," he agrees.

He looks into my eyes. "I'm glad you're back, Holly."

"Me too." I smile as he leans down and kisses me.

"Let's get you up to bed. You must be shattered after flying in today."

I am. Not only the flight, but all the emotions of the last few days have just exhausted me.

"That sounds good."

I start to get up, but Jay stops me and wraps his arms underneath me, lifting me up off the mattress.

"Come on, sleeping beauty," he says as he carries me to his bedroom.

He lays me on his bed and covers me up with the duvet before lying down beside me.

"Jay," I murmur.

"Yes, Berry?"

"You're much tastier than tea," I say as I drift off to sleep.

MEETING MR. ANDERSON

Chapter 15

I WAKE ALONE IN Jay's bed. The bedside clock shows it's almost ten a.m.

Wow, I was tired.

I sit up and stretch my arms above my head. There's a familiar ache between my legs, evidence of last night's incredible make-up session. I got it all so wrong. I'm an idiot for putting us both through the last few days. I just thought the worst. After everything with Simon, I was so quick to jump to the wrong conclusion, without even giving Jay a chance to explain. I should have trusted him. My body knew that very first night to trust him. I've done and said things in bed I would never have dreamed of doing before. Jay makes opening up to him seem safe and right. I feel desired and wanted. He deserves so much better than the way I flew off the handle.

My phone is on the bedside table, charging. Jay must have plugged it in for me. He's so thoughtful. I bring up Jay's number in my phone and delete 'Lying cheat,' replacing it with 'Jay' before sending a quick text to Matt and Rach.

Me: Hey, guys, I've seen Jay and we've sorted everything out. I totally got the wrong idea! He's doing Anya's perfume promotion. There's nothing going on. I feel so stupid. You guys have both been there for me this week and I can't thank you enough. I have the most wonderful friends. I love you both.

They'll be wondering what's going on. They both knew I was coming to LA yesterday, and I spoke to them both before I left the hotel last night. They've been so sweet, checking in on me and listening to me rant. My phone beeps.

Matt: That's such amazing news, Holls! I just knew he wouldn't have done that. It's so obvious he only has eyes for you. Can't wait to hear all about it. Love you.

I've just finished reading Matt's message when Rach's arrives.

Rach: I hope you sat on his face and he made it up to you hard! Seriously though, I'm happy for you.

I smirk at Rach's text. Knowing how much Jay loves going down on me, I'm not sure who would be the one making up to whom in her scenario.

I swing my legs out of bed and use the bathroom before pulling on one of Jay's T-shirts. I have to stay naked on the bottom half after he ripped my panties to shreds last night. God, that was hot. I was putty in his hands. I would have done anything for him. The level of arousal he brought out of me was off the scale. I'm not sure I will ever get used to the intensity of his touch on my skin.

I pull his T-shirt down as far as I can and head downstairs.

Jay's voice is drifting up the hallway from his office. It sounds like he's on the phone. I walk into the kitchen and decide to get a glass of juice before going to say good morning. I glance down at the floor as I open the fridge and take out a small bottle of juice. All signs of last night's smashed glass have gone.

"Good morning, dear, you must be Holly?"

I gasp and the juice nearly slips from my hand as the fridge door swings shut and I look at the lady in front of me. She's older, probably in her seventies. She has a kind smile framed by bright-fuchsia lipstick. She's wearing purple trousers and a floral blouse underneath her apron, her feet in a pair of green Crocs. If she were your nana, she'd be a funky one.

"I'm Margaret." She smiles, holding out her hand. I shake it and give her a small smile. "Call me Maggie." She looks at my puzzled face. "I'm the housekeeper." She chuckles.

"Oh." Realization hits me. "You do the beautiful flower arrangements."

She puffs her chest up at my compliment and her face breaks into a wide grin.

"Always loved flowers, I have. You know they have their own language?"

"I, er, didn't know that." I smile, pulling Jay's T-shirt down as far as I can.

"Oh, don't you worry, Holly. If I had legs like yours, I wouldn't hide them away." She chuckles again. "Not around a man like Jay, anyway. He's a good egg, love; he'll look after you." She squeezes my arm before turning around to continue her tidying. She picks up some mail and sorts through it, humming a tune to herself. "Don't mind me. I'm just about finished," she says as she takes her apron off and looks up at me with a bright smile. "Nice to meet you, Holly."

"You too, Maggie." I smile back.

She's warm and friendly. I can see why Jay enjoys having her as a housekeeper. I smile again and wave as she leaves, and the front door clicks shut behind her.

I head down to Jay's office and knock before poking my head around the door. He's sitting in the chair at his desk and looks up when he sees me. His beautiful blue eyes look straight into mine. Inside, my stomach dances in response. He's wearing his faded jeans and a khaki T-shirt. He leans back in the chair, his legs wide as he watches me.

"Good morning, sleepyhead." He stretches his arms behind his head, his tanned biceps flexing as he gives me a slow, sexy smile.

"So... I just met Maggie," I say, biting my lip.

"Ah, great. I wanted you to meet her."

"Yeah, she's lovely. I didn't know she was going to be here though; otherwise, I would have put more on."

I step out from behind the door. Jay's eyes scan down my body and he raises an eyebrow as he takes in my bare legs.

"Now that's a sight." He puts one hand down to his crotch and adjusts himself.

"I just hope she didn't notice what else was missing."

I turn around and look back over my shoulder at Jay, lifting the T-shirt.

He lets out a low whistle and pats his lap.

"Bring that gorgeous ass over here, Berry."

I saunter over to him and he pulls me down into his lap, lifting my legs over one arm of the chair. I sink into his chest as he wraps me in his arms and presses a kiss to my forehead.

"You let me sleep really late," I whisper.

"You looked so beautiful; I didn't want to wake you." He traces a finger across my cheek.

Could this man get any better?

I soak up his attention. I love it when he's like this, tender and attentive. I also love it when he's commanding and dirty. Two pieces of a perfect package.

"Have I interrupted you? Were you hard at work?"

"You'll always be a welcome interruption, and yes, I am hard." He smirks, lifting his hips so his erection presses into me.

"Oh, I can see you've had your clown juice this morning." I shake my head at him.

"I'm always ready to clown around with you, Berry," he says as his hands go to the sensitive area below my bum and dance on my skin.

I shriek and kick my legs.

"Jay, stop!" I laugh as he tickles me.

"Why would I do that?" His hands grow more determined in their attack.

I can barely talk for laughing. "Because." I try to catch my breath between giggles. "Because I might wet myself!"

His eyes light up. "Don't all clowns have one of those flowers that get you wet? Seeing as I am a clown."

"Okay." I pant. "I'm sorry I called you a clown."

"Mmm, you don't seem that sorry," he teases and tickles me harder, delighted that he's torturing me.

"I am! I swear!" I'm almost crying from laughing now.

"Nah, not convinced." He smirks.

"Please! I'll do anything!" Inspiration hits me. "I'll suck your cock!" I shriek.

Jay's hands freeze and I try to catch my breath, my chest heaving up and down. I wipe away the tears from my eyes as my last giggle subsides.

"I think I've discovered your special spot."

"Oh, you found that the first time," I say, my breathing returning to normal.

"Is that right?"

He leans down, his warm lips pressing against mine, his tongue tracing my lips. It's such a sensual kiss, I could get lost in it.

He repositions me in his lap and unzips his jeans, his eyes bright and playful.

"Time to collect my bribe."

I slide myself off his lap and onto my knees between his legs.

"Well then, these will need to go." I tug at his jeans.

Jay lifts himself up off the chair so I can pull them and his boxer shorts off. His cock springs free, a bead of arousal on its tip.

"Now, what should I do with you?" I say as I part Jay's legs wider and lean back onto my heels.

I run my hands up his tanned legs, pausing at his hips. Then I stroke down the inside of his thighs, my thumbs skimming his balls. Jay sucks in a breath as I look up at him from under my eyelashes.

I dip my head without breaking eye contact and part my lips to kiss his inner thighs. I have his full attention as I flick the tip of my tongue over his balls. He moans, his eyes never leaving mine. I curve my tongue around them, one at a time. I love doing this for him. I want to give him everything. With one hand wrapped around the base of his cock, I take one ball into my mouth and suck.

Jay lets out a low groan as I swap to the other side. "Holly..."

Rising onto my knees, I lick all the way up his hard length, every vein pulsing underneath my touch. I pause when I get to the top. Jay's still watching me, his eyes hooded. They widen as I lick my lips and wrap them around the head of his cock, sucking the bead of arousal off.

He tastes so good.

I moan as I suck him, knowing that he'll feel the vibration.

He sucks in his breath. "Fuck."

I love hearing the effect I'm having on him. I sink down, sliding him deep into my throat and look up. He brings his hands to my hair, gathering it off my face into his palm. The action has me soaking wet between the legs as his gaze burns into me. I suck back up him, swirling my tongue, before taking him deep again. The hands in my hair guide my head as I tug on his balls.

"That feels amazing," Jay hisses as his grip on my hair tightens.

He lifts my head up again, drawing his cock almost all the way out of my mouth before pushing me back down, raising his hips at the same time. His cock is so thick, I have to open my throat to stop myself from gagging. I moan again and rise back up, looking up into his eyes as I suck harder.

"Holly." His eyes flash as he pushes my head back down and drags it straight back up.

His hands pull my hair tighter. I rest my hands on his hips and will him with my eyes to fuck my mouth. He looks at me, understanding clear in his eyes.

"Fuck," he groans as he guides my head up and down faster, slamming his hips up to meet my lips.

I'm at his complete mercy now, only able to moan at how good he tastes, deep inside my mouth. The heat of his cock fires through my entire body.

"I'm going to come, Holly."

Jay's jaw tenses as his eyes burn into mine. I hold my breath in anticipation as his thighs tense and his balls pull toward his body.

That's when I taste him, hot, salty, and fucking delicious.

He hisses my name as his cock pumps into my mouth. I suck each fresh release up and swallow it down, not wanting to lose any drop of him. He's just so raw and sexy like this. His grip on my hair loosens, but I keep sucking him, sliding my mouth up and down over his cock until he puts his hands on my face and stops me. Sliding my lips over his tip one more time, I kiss it and tilt my face up.

He's looking at me in wonder, an easy smile spreading across his face.

"Remind me to tickle you more often if that's what happens," he says, pulling me up and into his lap.

He leans forward and dusts his thumb across my tender lips before kissing them.

I love this feeling of him taking care of me. Whatever I did in a previous life to deserve to meet Jay in this one, I am eternally grateful for. Sex with him is so intense, and he's so gentle and caring the rest of the time.

I'm hooked.

"If you've got any energy left, I thought you might like to come and spend the night away with me tonight," he says, between kisses.

"Sounds interesting. Where are you going?" I ask, running my fingers up and down the stubble on his jaw.

"To see my parents. My brother Blake is going to be there too."

"You want me to meet your parents?"

"Yes, Holly, I do." He smiles. "Is that such a crazy thing?"

I swallow and try not to grin. "No, not crazy at all. That sounds lovely."

I can't believe he wants me to meet his parents. Guys don't introduce every girl to their parents, do they? This must be a good thing.

"But I don't have any panties to wear. You ripped them off me," I tease.

"I would happily have you not own any clothes and just stay home with me," he jokes, nipping my bottom lip between his teeth before kissing me again. "We can go back to your hotel to pack some things. You can wear a pair of mine for now."

"Okay." I smile.

I can't believe I'm meeting his family.

Back at my hotel, I leave Jay chatting with Cooper while I go change. I've given him a telling-off for tricking me with the taxi last night. He was so apologetic about it all, and Jay said not to blame him as he had asked for his help. Cooper looked so sorry for himself that I had to forgive him. I even ended up thanking him, as I wouldn't have given Jay the time of day otherwise. I would still be miserable and would have ruined the best thing to happen to me in a long time.

I pack my bag with enough to last me for the night. I go for a slouchy T-shirt that ties around the waist and has a faded beach scene on it and some denim shorts to wear tomorrow, along with my toiletry bag and makeup bag.

I twist my hair up into a messy bun in front of the mirror. All the sex is making my eyes sparkle. Pulling the floral dress I had on last night over my head, I change it for a coral off the shoulder one. I call my flight manager's room and leave a message and contact details, telling her I'm staying out of the city for the night. Then I head back down to the front of the hotel.

Jay and Cooper are standing where I left them, chatting and laughing. As I walk over to them, something dark across the street moves. Then I see him. A man disappearing around the corner again, just like last night.

"You okay, Holls?" Jay asks, concerned when he sees my face.

I look past him, searching the street opposite.

"It's probably nothing." I shrug, not wanting to make a big deal out of it. "It's just, there was a guy standing over there watching me. He went down that side street."

I point to a building. "He was there last night, and he was just there now too."

"I'll check it out."

"No, Jay, it's nothing. Just leave it."

But he's already halfway across the street.

Cooper and I watch as he disappears down the side of the building the man had gone down a few moments ago. A few minutes pass and then Jay reappears, jogging back over.

He's shaking his head. "It runs down to the next street over. No sign of anyone."

"I'll check the CCTV." Cooper taps at the computer at his desk. "I can check last night's too; it picks up quite a large area. Leave it to me and I'll let you know if I find anything."

"Thanks, man." Jay pats him on the shoulder.

"Thanks, Coop, I appreciate it."

"No problem, Holly. If there's someone snooping around, we'll get him. Probably a photographer looking for a story."

"Yeah. I guess I'm just not used to it," I say as Jay wraps his arm around my waist.

"Come on, Berry, we better hit the road."

"See you later, Coop," we both call as we climb into Jay's car and head off for his parents' house.

It's such a gorgeous, sunny day that we drive with the windows down and country music blaring. The car fills with song after song of toe-tapping tales of romance, whiskey, and starry nights.

I sink back in my seat and smile. This feels so right, just driving in the car with Jay behind the wheel. I look across at him. He looks relaxed, his sun-kissed hair blowing in the breeze. He's got one arm resting on the open window the steering wheel between his fingers, and his other hand resting on his leg.

I reach across and slide my fingers between his, the back of my hand lying on the muscles of his thigh.

"You okay, Berry?" He turns the radio down and brings our intertwined hands up to his mouth to kiss my fingers, his eyes bright as he catches my gaze.

"I am now." I smile. "It's almost worth fighting to get the making up afterward."

Jay smirks at me. "I like the making up part too." His face turns serious. "But I never want to fight with you again, Holly. It was a rough few days, wondering what you were doing, and what I could have done differently not to hurt you."

"Jay, it's not your fault. It's mine, my past. Dating someone like Simon ruined my trust in anyone and my confidence in myself." Jay's hand squeezes mine tighter at the mention of Simon, and he's clenching his jaw. "Then I met you and it was different. I feel different. I do things I've never done before. I like things I didn't even know I liked."

Like being a dirty-talking nymphomaniac.

"I want you to be yourself, Holly. You can trust me. I will never intentionally hurt you." He looks over at me, his beautiful blue eyes searching mine.

"I know that now. My body knew a long time ago." I blush. "My head just took time catching up."

Jay is smiling as he looks ahead at the road. "Well, I'm just glad it's all in the same place now."

"It is. It's all here, with you," I say as I lean my head against his shoulder, inhaling his scent.

He kisses the top of my head and I know it's going to be okay. I lift my free arm and turn the radio back up as I snuggle up to him and gaze out at the road ahead.

Chapter 16

WE DRIVE UP THE high street of a small coastal town before turning off into a tree-lined residential street.

"Here we are," Jay says as we pull up on the driveway of a pretty white weatherboard-clad house.

It has a veranda running all around it, manicured flower beds, and a lush green lawn to the front.

"It looks lovely." I smooth down my dress, nerves rising in my stomach. "So, is there anything I should know? I don't want to say the wrong thing."

"Holly." Jay leans across and catches my lips in a tender kiss. "Just be yourself. It's what got my vote." He winks as he climbs out of the car and comes around to open my door.

I take his hand and he leads me up to the large wooden front door. The door flies open before he even knocks.

"Hey, cock-face! You made it!"

A dark-haired guy with a short beard grabs Jay into a hug. He's wearing green cargo trousers and a black T-shirt.

Jay laughs and slaps him on the back.

"Good to see you, bro. You still got those pubes on your face, I see. Holly, this is my little brother, Blake." Jay smiles as he pulls back from their hug.

"Hardly little, man, you've seen it," Blake jokes as he takes my hand and smiles at me.

His green eyes crinkle at the corners, just like Jay's. He's seems cheeky and fun. I like him instantly.

I smile back at him as he lifts my hand to his lips and kisses it.

"It's a pleasure to meet you, Holly. Although, I think you'll soon agree that you're dating the wrong brother," he says, flirting shamelessly.

Jay pulls my hand back from Blake and wraps an arm around my shoulders.

"And you'll soon agree that flirting with my girlfriend may be one of the last stupid things you do."

Blake chuckles and holds his hands up in front of him. I sneak a sideways glance at Jay.

Did he just call me his girlfriend?

We follow Blake into the house and down a light-colored hallway. The house is bright and welcoming, vases of fresh flowers all around and family photos on the walls. One that must be Jay and Blake as kids catches my eye. Piercing blue and warm green eyes shine back from two young, grinning faces on a beach, their hair messy and covered in sand. Jay sees me looking and smiles as we continue down the hallway.

The back of the house opens into a beautiful, bright kitchen with doors leading out onto the rear veranda and garden. The sunshine pours in, making the room cozy and inviting.

A man and woman hurry in from the garden.

"Jay," his mum cries, throwing her arms around him and kissing him on the cheek. "Oh, it's so good to see you. You feel thinner; have you been eating enough?"

"Leave the boy alone, Sheila," says his dad kindly as he gives Jay a hug. "Good to see you, son."

They both see me, and I fiddle with my hands as I smile.

"Mom, Dad, this is—"

"Holly! Oh, it's so lovely to meet you," Sheila cuts Jay off and sweeps me into a hug. She smells beautiful, a mix of lavender and rose.

"Nice to meet you," Jay's dad says, enveloping my hand inside both of his and shaking it. His hands are large and warm, comforting.

"It's lovely to meet you both too," I say. "Thank you for inviting me to your home; it's beautiful."

"Oh, we couldn't wait, could we, Bill? We were so excited that Jay was bringing a girlfriend home," Sheila gushes. "You're the first one, so we knew you were special."

"Alright, love, let the girl breathe," Bill says affectionately.

"Yeah, don't scare her off, Mom," Blake chimes in. "It could be years before another girl will tolerate him."

I grin. it's easy to see what a close, loving family they are.

"Holly, love, would you like a drink? I've got some of that peppermint tea Jay says you like." Sheila fills up the kettle.

"Oh, lovely, please."

I look up at Jay. Warmth spreads through my chest. I can't help feeling thrilled that he's been talking to his mum about me.

"So, Holly, what's a beautiful woman like you doing dating a douche like my brother?" Blake jokes, earning himself a playful punch on the arm from Jay.

"Oh, I—"

"Leave the poor girl alone." Bill chuckles. "Barely through the door and she's under interrogation."

I smile at him gratefully, and his blue eyes twinkle back at me.

"Blake here forgets his manners in company," Jay says, wrapping his arm around my waist. "He spends his days hiding under bushes and yelling at people."

"Oh, that's right. Jay said you run an outdoor survival company?" I look at Blake, who seems more than happy to have the spotlight reflected onto him.

"Sure do. I started off doing personal training and boot camp classes, and it's kind of evolved from there. We do a lot of outdoor survival weekends. Getting back to nature and all that."

"Did you tell Jay your news, Blake?" Sheila calls from across the kitchen where she's setting up a tray of drinks.

"What news?" Jay asks, looking intrigued.

"So, it seems you aren't the only brother who will be in front of the cameras." Blake lifts his chin. "They want us to make a reality TV show. Regular people pushing themselves out of their comfort zone in the name of entertainment."

"That's amazing, bro!" Jay pulls Blake into a hug. "You so deserve this; you've built that company from the ground. I'm so pleased for you."

Blake beams at his big brother. It's obvious how much they love each other, despite enjoying teasing each other.

"Come on, let's sit out back," Sheila says, carrying a tray of drinks and cookies over.

Bill takes it from her, and we follow him out onto the back veranda where there are some wicker chairs, a swing seat, and a low coffee table.

"Holly, why don't you and Jay sit on the swing?" Sheila says. "It's the comfiest."

"Thank you," I say, sitting down and sinking into its soft cushions.

The seat rocks as Jay sits down next to me.

"I've always loved these swings; my nana used to have one. We would sit on it and talk, looking out across her garden." I smile as I remember my lovely nana, who I lost years ago.

"That sounds lovely, Holly." Sheila smiles warmly. "I've done some of my best thinking in that swing. When

I was pregnant with Jay, it's the only place I could get comfortable. Of course, it's been repaired and had new cushions since then. But I could never bring myself to part with it."

"I don't blame you. It's lovely."

Sheila grins at me and passes a plate of cookies around.

"Aww, mint chocolate chip, my favorite," Bill says, taking one and biting into it. "Sheila makes the best cookies. You've got to try one, Holly."

"Thank you." I take a bite. They're sweet and soft, melting in my mouth. "Delicious!" I smile. "My mum loves baking too."

Sheila's eyes light up. "Really? Let me fetch you the recipe. You can give it to her, see what she thinks. I find they always go down well." She motions toward Jay, Blake, and Bill who are all silent, their mouths full of cookies.

"What?" they all mumble.

I catch Sheila's eye and we both laugh.

"Nothing, nothing at all," she says as she disappears back into the kitchen, coming back moments later with a handwritten recipe. She hands it to me, and I thank her.

"Oh, I've forgotten to get the cheese I need for dinner tonight." Her brow wrinkles.

"Don't worry, Mom. Holly and I can pick some up. I wanted to give her a tour of town, anyway."

"Thanks, Jay, love." Sheila smiles.

"That'll take all of ten minutes." Blake laughs. "It's a lot smaller than LA here."

"You eat cheese, don't you, Holly?" Sheila asks, looking worried.

"Oh, man, don't tell us you're a vegan?" Blake shakes his head.

"Yes, I do, thank you, Sheila." I look over and see her shoulders relax.

"Blake doesn't understand vegans," Jay says, turning his face toward me. His breath on my neck sends goosebumps up my arms. "He goes all back to nature in the forest for days on end so has to catch his own dinner."

"Absolutely." Blake nods. "It's nature. The circle of life."

"Before that debate begins, I think now is a good time for me to tidy up." Bill chuckles, collecting the empty glasses and mugs and heading back into the kitchen.

"We'll go get the cheese you need, Mom."

"Mozzarella, please, Jay," she says as we all get up and head inside.

We walk from Jay's parents' house into town. Blake's right, it's not huge. But it's got a charm about it. There's a sense of community. People are stopping to chat with each other. A mother and her two children are talking to an older man walking his dachshund. The children seem delighted to see the little dog again, who's obviously a friend of theirs.

We go in the local store and get the mozzarella for Sheila. The shopkeeper seems pleased to see Jay and asks after his family. On the walk back, Jay points out the high school he went to.

"I bet you were captain of the football team." I lean into the warmth of his arm wrapped around my waist.

"You got me." He smiles. "Blake made captain of the wrestling team though. Much more hard core."

"Yeah, I can see that." I smile.

Blake is rugged and seems like someone who likes to jump into a challenge.

"I bet you dated the head cheerleader, didn't you?" I tease.

Jay doesn't say anything, so I look up and see something—unease?—flash over his face, which he quickly hides. I follow his gaze to a lady approaching us on the path. She looks to be about the same age as my mum and Sheila.

"Jay?"

"Beth," Jay says as she grabs him and pulls him into a hug.

"Oh, Jay! This is such a lovely surprise. I haven't seen you in a long time. How are you? How's your mom and dad, and Blake?" she asks, no longer hugging him but holding on to his arms as she smiles at him.

"They're all great, Beth, and Hank?"

"Oh, he's doing okay. You know how he is." She smiles, and then turns to me. Her eyes widen and she tips her head to one side. Her eyes study me, moving over my face and hair and back again.

"Beth, this is Holly, my girlfriend," Jay says.

My stomach does a little flip at the sound of him saying 'my girlfriend' again.

Beth's mouth drops open, but she closes it quickly.

"Holly, this is Beth, Rob's mom," Jay says, looking at my face.

Oh shit.

Jay hasn't spoken much about Rob. I've always got the impression it's too painful for him to talk about and that he will open up to me when he's ready. Beth seems very fond of Jay though, judging by how pleased she is to see him.

"It's nice to meet you." I smile at Beth, who has stopped studying me and is now looking backwards and forwards between Jay and me.

"You too, Holly." She says my name slowly, as though she's thinking about saying something else.

I wait to see if she'll continue.

She turns her attention back to Jay instead. "I'd better be going. It was so good to see you; don't be a stranger." She squeezes his hand, and Jay smiles at her, his eyes full of emotion.

"Bye, Holly." She smiles at me and continues up the street.

"Are you okay?" I look up at Jay, who seems weary suddenly, his usual easy-going, happy demeanour flattened.

He smiles down at me, but his blue eyes have lost their sparkle.

"I'm fine, Berry." He sighs. "It's hard seeing Beth. Brings back a lot of memories."

"I'm sorry," I whisper as I wrap my arms around him and hold him close. I wish I could take away the pain in his eyes.

His arms tighten around me.

"I'm here for you, Jay." I kiss the side of his face.

"I know, Holly." He brings his hands up to cup my face. "You are the best thing to come into my life in a long time. I'm happy to think about the future for once." He pauses. "You make me happy."

His eyes search mine and he leans forward, catching my lips in a sweet kiss, heavy with meaning. I kiss him back as something hits me. Something, if I'm honest with myself, I've known for a while.

I'm falling in love with Jay Anderson and I couldn't stop it even if I wanted to.

We decide to take a detour on the way home and walk along the sandy beach that runs alongside the main town road. I'm carrying my sandals in my hand and enjoying the sand underneath my feet.

"It suits you." Jay smiles at me.

His eyes have regained some of their sparkle since seeing Beth.

"What does?"

"The beach. Something about it and you seem to go together. You look relaxed."

"I love the beach. Growing up near the coast in Cornwall just put it in my blood, I think. The smell of the sea, the way the wet sand changes color as you walk on it. I love it. I just feel grounded." I shrug, hoping he won't think I sound silly. "I saw a photo of you, taken on the beach in a magazine," I continue.

Jay looks at me, amused. "Been reading up on me, have you?"

"No. One of the crew had it on the flight you were on. I didn't know who you were." Jay pretends to look outraged and I giggle. "You just looked happy in it. You seemed at home."

"Yeah, I love the coast. Probably from growing up near it, like you. I had a happy childhood here," he says.

I think back to the photo of him and Blake at his parents' house, young, smiling, and covered in sand.

"You know those photos in my bedroom in LA? Those are all photos of the beach here. Blake gave them to me as a gift to stop me feeling so homesick."

"Did Blake take them himself?" I ask in surprise.

"Yeah, he did." Jay smiles as he runs his hand through his hair. "He's all tough guy exterior, but he's got a sentimental side, and he's pretty good at photography."

I smile as we keep walking. I love hearing about Jay's family and childhood. I feel even closer to him the more I learn.

"You know, growing up, I used to go down to the beach at sunrise and do yoga, then sneak back in before breakfast," I confess. "Probably one of the naughtiest things I've done."

"Oh, I know that's not true." Jay's eyes glint at me. "I can see you doing that, though. Yoga next to the water, like some kind of ocean goddess." His eyes crinkle at the corners.

"Maybe more beached whale," I say.

"Holly, stop." Jay catches my hands and I stop walking to face him. His eyes hold mine. "Stop putting yourself down. Can't you see what I and everyone else sees? You have a beautiful spirit. You're a loving person who would do anything for your friends. And you always try to see the best in people." He dusts his finger across my bottom lip. "And you're cute and funny, it's one of the things I noticed about you first."

I blush under his intense gaze.

"Thank you," I mumble. "I won't call myself a whale again."

"No, or you'll have me to answer to."

"I wouldn't want to be in your bad book." I raise my eyebrows at him.

"No, baby, you wouldn't," he says as he pulls me in for a kiss.

His lips are warm against mine, his tongue gently finding my own. His hands slide down to my bum and pull me against him. We stay wrapped in each other's arms, as though we are the only two people in the world.

"Come on, Berry," he says, finally releasing me. "Otherwise, I'm going to get you naked right here in the sand."

"You're very sure about yourself," I joke as I take a few steps away from him and into the edges of the waves.

Before he can respond, I draw my leg back and kick the water, sending a shower of shimmering droplets all over him.

Jay looks down at his wet T-shirt and then back up at me.

"Oh, you did not just do that!"

I kick the water again, getting it as high as his face this time.

"Oh, I so did, pretty boy," I shriek as his face takes on a 'this means business' look and he lunges toward me.

"Uh-uh-uh," I tut, sidestepping him and ducking low under his arm.

He goes to turn after me, but trips over my foot as I run. It's like a slow motion shot in a comedy film, where he tries to get his balance, but it's too little too late. I can't do anything but watch as he tumbles down into the edge of the water, soaking himself from head to toe.

I gasp and clasp my hands over my mouth to stop the hysterical giggle that's forming in my stomach from escaping.

"What the...?" Jay stands up, his clothes soaked through. His wet T-shirt is now see through and clinging to his pecs, his nipples visible through the thin fabric.

It's one of the hottest things I've ever seen—as well as being hilarious.

My shoulders are shaking, trying to hold it in, but it's all too much. I erupt into giggles, unable to even speak. Tears run down my cheeks as I look him up and down. His eyes meet mine and narrow, a dangerous glint in them.

"No, Jay," I splutter, backing away from him as he takes a step toward me, eyeing me like a cat eyes its prey. "Jay!" I say as he steps toward me again. "It was an accident!" I squeal as I laugh again.

He's coming toward me again with every intention of soaking me too. I turn and run up the beach, laughing and screaming as he takes chase.

We play the game all the way back up the road to his parents' house. As I'm running up to the house, I see his dad mowing the front lawn.

"Hi, Bill!" I wave as I nip past him toward the safety of the house.

"Holly." He chuckles in greeting. Then he notices Jay behind me. "Alright there, son, got a bit wet, did you?" He laughs as Jay follows me in through the front door.

I head into the kitchen and put the shopping bag down on the side.

"We got the mozzarella," I say brightly to Sheila, who's washing some tomatoes in the sink.

"Oh, thank you, Holly." Then she sees Jay behind me. "Jay! What happened?" Her eyes widen. "You're dripping all over the floor! Take those wet clothes off! I'll put them straight in the wash."

"Sure thing, Mom," Jay says in his deep, sexy voice, a smirk playing on his lips.

She turns her attention back to the tomatoes. "Ah! Basil, I knew I'd forgotten something." She smiles at me as she heads out into the garden.

Jay's eyes hold mine as he pulls his T-shirt up over his head, then unbuttons his jeans and slides them down, before peeling off his boxer shorts, dropping them all on the floor next to him in a soggy heap.

I stand there and my eyes widen as I take in his tanned, toned physique. His biceps look even larger than ever, his abs are rock hard, the perfect *V* down past his hips, and then *oh my God*, his cock. I've never really looked at it when it's not hard before, but it's large and thick, hanging between his legs.

As I'm staring, Blake comes in through the back door and glances at Jay.

"Yep, still only the bigger brother in age," he says casually as he continues into the house.

Jay grabs a tea towel off the side and holds it across his front as Sheila comes back in from the garden and deposits a mound of basil leaves on the kitchen side.

She gathers Jay's wet clothes off the floor, not batting an eyelid.

"Well, don't stand there all day, Jay. Go get in the shower and wash the sand off."

As she turns, she gives me a small wink and I realize she's trying not to laugh.

"Fine." Jay's amused eyes are still on mine. I'm going to pay for this later. "I won't be long."

He turns and walks up the hallway, and I get a glorious view of his tight ass.

"Cup of tea, Holly?" I have to break my ogling stare away from Jay to answer Sheila.

"Yes, please. I'll make it."

We sit together out on the swing seat with our drinks, while Jay has a shower, and Blake helps Bill in the front garden.

"We saw Rob's mum in town," I say to Sheila, not sure whether I should mention it.

Sheila sighs. "That poor woman has been through so much. Losing a child like that. It's a parents' worst nightmare."

"She seemed happy to see Jay." I blow on my tea before taking a sip.

"Oh, she would be. She's always loved Jay. He was a good friend to Rob. They were inseparable, thick as thieves." Sheila smiles at a memory. "Jay took it hard. He's always blamed himself. Thought he could have done more. But he couldn't. No one could," she says sadly. "I'm so pleased he met you, Holly." She turns to me, her eyes sparkling. "It's the happiest I've seen him in a long time. You've brought him back to the present. He's been stuck in the past for so long."

"I haven't done anything," I say, looking into her kind eyes.

"You may not think you have, Holly, but I'm his mother and I can see it." She rests her hand on my knee. "Plus, it's nice to have another female around. You've seen the levels of testosterone I have to put up with in this house!" She laughs.

I laugh too. She's an incredibly special and strong woman to have raised two men like Jay and Blake.

"What are you two laughing at?"

We look up and Jay has appeared, fresh out of the shower. He's wearing a pair of blue shorts that match his eyes and a white sleeveless vest. His hair is still wet. He looks edible. I gulp and stare at him.

"Nothing, dear." Sheila smiles, patting his arm on her way past into the house. "Just girl talk."

Jay looks at me questioningly, but I just smile at him as he sits down next to me. I get a sudden hit of his fresh skin and my nipples harden. It's insane the effect he has on my body, just being near me.

"You know, I'm going to get you back," he says calmly, looking ahead at the garden.

"Oh, I know, I'm looking forward to it." I smile.

He has no idea how much.

We have a great evening. Sheila makes a homemade pasta bake with melted mozzarella, and a salad from things she and Bill have grown in the garden. Jay and Blake take turns trying to tell the most embarrassing story about the other one, and Sheila and Bill trump them every time with stories of them as kids. I'm sad when the evening ends and it's time to say good night.

Jay and I go up to the guest room. It's pretty, painted pale cream with a white wooden bed and floral bedding. Sheila has left us a jug of water and glasses on top of some drawers. Next to that, a small vase of roses picked from the garden.

I use the en suite bathroom and put on a white satin slip with thin straps that Jay hasn't seen before. When I come out, he's lying on the bed and his eyes roam up and down my body, coming back to rest on the curves of my hips and breasts. He swallows and puts his hand to his chin, rubbing his fingers over his stubble as his eyes stay fixed on my body.

Climbing into bed next to him, I cuddle into his side.

"What a shame we're at your parents' house and have to behave ourselves," I tease, tracing my fingers over his chest.

"Like hell we do," Jay says, and in a flash he's over the top of me, his legs between mine, spreading them. His hands hold my wrists down on either side of my head. "You need to make it up to me for your behavior at the beach earlier," he says as his mouth finds my nipples and he sucks and bites them through the fabric.

"Aww." I wriggle underneath him. "And how am I supposed to make it up to you?"

"Give me your body to do as I please," he says as he bites my nipple again and my back arches off the bed toward him.

"I can't be quiet, Jay," I moan as he kisses my neck at the same time as sliding two fingers inside my panties and against my wet skin.

"Yes, you can, and you will," he orders as he pulls my panties to the side and presses his hard, slick tip against me.

So, he wants it dirty and fast.

Okay, baby, I can give you what you want.

"But it feels so good when you fill me up with your big cock, I can't help but scream," I whisper in his ear with mock innocence.

"God, Holly," he groans, "you know what you fucking do to me when you talk like that."

I pretend I don't know what he's talking about.

"When I talk like what?" I bring my hands up into his hair and tug between my fingers, knowing exactly what this does to him too.

"Oh, fuck," Jay groans and pushes his cock inside me.

I bite my lip to stop myself crying out in ecstasy. He's big and rock hard, stretching me deliciously around him.

"You feel so good, so tight," he growls into my ear as he slides out and pushes back in hard.

I throw my head back and am about to moan when Jay clamps his hand over my mouth.

"Quiet, remember, baby."

His blue eyes are dark with desire as he pulls back and then sinks in deeper. His eyes are on fire as he stares back at me, his hand firmly over my mouth.

Fuck, this is so arousing. I'm completely at his mercy and it's so hot. He knows this is doing it for me as he grins and then slams into me again.

My eyes roll back in my head and I pull his hair harder, lifting my hips to meet his.

His face is just inches from mine as he fucks me. I can barely move. All I can do is lie there and take it, my moans muffled against his hand.

"I'm going to fuck you harder now, baby, but remember you need to be quiet," Jay growls.

I nod underneath his hand, my eyes pleading with him to do it. Not being able to scream out in release is torture.

Jay pulls back and drives into me hard. I whimper against his hand as he does it again and again, building up a relentless pace. Thankfully, the bed isn't moving.

All I can hear is our breathing. Our foreheads press against each other as he pumps into me with his hips, circling them each time, his body rubbing against my swollen clit.

Pressure builds inside me. I part my legs wider and Jay seems to know what's about to happen. He slams into me harder and harder, circling against my clit each time, his hand still over my mouth. I can't hold it anymore; I arch up away from the bed as my orgasm rips through me. I moan but Jay tightens his grip over my mouth and fucks me harder.

It's so intense that I have to do something to stop myself moaning loud enough that I'm heard through his hand. I force my mouth open under his fingers and sink my teeth down into his flesh as contraction after contraction from my body tightens around his cock.

Jay sucks his breath in, and then he buries his face between my neck and the pillow, muffling his groans as he comes deep inside me. His cock jerks and pulses inside me, and I clench down on it to squeeze every drop out inside me.

I want all of him.

He brings his face back up to mine and takes his hand off my mouth, leaning down to kiss me. His tongue dives into my mouth, finding mine, sucking and tasting, not able to get enough.

We're both panting as he stops and grins at me.

"I think I almost lost a finger." He brings his hand up and turns it so I can see the deep red teeth marks around it.

"Jay!" I grab his hand and pull it closer to my face to get a better look.

Oh my God, I've hurt him.

"I'm so sorry, are you okay?"

"Holly, I'm better than okay." He beams at me, shaking his head. "I'm fucking amazing!"

I smile back at him, my chest relaxing.

I guess fingers come after mind-blowing sex on his priority list.

Chapter 17

"Damn it, I forgot to charge my phone last night," Jay says, plugging it into a socket in the kitchen.

"Bit distracted, were we?" Blake grins as Jay shoots him a warning look.

We are all downstairs having breakfast together before we head back to LA. My flight home is this afternoon, and I can't help feeling sad we can't stay here another day. It's been wonderful meeting Jay's family.

"Sleep well, did you, Holly?" Blake asks.

"Yes, thank you," I say, eyeing him over the rim of my mug.

He smirks as I narrow my eyes at him. Thankfully, Sheila and Bill aren't paying any attention as they're too busy discussing a news article in the paper.

Jay's phone buzzes, his missed messages coming through.

"Stefan's tried calling me five times." Jay sounds worried as his phone rings in his hand.

"Stefan? What's wrong?"

He nods and his expression turns serious.

We've all stopped eating and are watching him.

"What? When?" His brow furrows and he reaches up to rub his hand over his eyes. "Do they know who? Okay, we'll be back as soon as we can."

He hangs up. Something is very wrong. He looks like he's trying to make sense of what he's just been told.

"The house was broken into last night," he says as he stares at us.

"What?" Sheila gasps.

"Fuck, man," says Blake.

"Language, Blake," Sheila scolds half-heartedly, her face still looking shocked at Jay's news.

I'm at his side in moments, wrapping my arms around his waist.

This is crazy. Of all the houses up in the Hollywood Hills, why choose Jay's? He puts an arm around me and holds me against him.

"Did Stefan say what they took?" Bill asks, standing up and moving across the room to put a reassuring hand on Jay's shoulder.

"Stefan's there now. He said it doesn't look like much is missing, but they have turned the place upside down. Maggie found it like that when she let herself in this morning and rang Stefan when she couldn't get me." Jay sucks in his breath and his body tenses in my arms. "We'd better go, Holly. It's going to take us an hour and a half to get back. Stefan said he's there with the police now."

"Of course. I'll grab our things."

I look up at everyone's worried faces and leave the kitchen, rushing upstairs to pack. I throw my toiletry bag into my bag and lift the satin nightie from on top of the duvet. Last night seems like a distant memory now. Is this actually happening? I zip my bag up and grab the rest of Jay's things before heading back downstairs. Jay is on his phone again, pacing up and down the hallway, his eyes cast downwards.

"It's Stefan again," Sheila says, coming over to me. "He's going to stay there with the police until you get back."

All I can do is nod at her, trying to take it all in. Her lips are pursed, lines visible on her forehead as her worried eyes meet mine.

"Drive safely, won't you?"

"We will." I hug her and can smell lavender and rose again as she rubs my back.

She pulls back and smiles at me. "We'll see you soon, Holly."

"I look forward to it," I say, squeezing her hand.

Bill comes over and goes to take my hand, but then pulls me into a hug. I gladly reciprocate, his warm arms comforting.

"Such a pleasure to meet you, Holly. I just wish you weren't having to rush off under such circumstances."

"Me too." I gulp as my eyes sting with the threat of tears.

"Hey, don't get upset; you'll see me again you know," Blake jokes, lightening the mood as he comes and hugs me too. He smells woody and masculine and I'm grateful for his cheekiness at a time like this.

I laugh in his arms and my body tingles as I sense Jay approach.

"Hey, don't go thinking a crisis is the ideal opportunity to put the moves on my girl," he jokes. But I can see by the way his smile doesn't reach his eyes that his mind is back in LA, and what's happening at the house.

Jay hugs Blake, and then Sheila and Bill, who give him words of encouragement and support. He promises to call them all when we get back to update them on what's going on.

We wave out the car window at the three of them standing out on the front veranda as we pull away. My stomach churns at what are we going to find when we get back.

Jay reaches across the car and takes my hand, his warm fingers interlocking with mine. I look over at him, his jaw is tight and he's staring straight ahead at the road.

"It'll be okay; we can sort it out. The police will find out who's responsible." I try to sound reassuring, not even convincing myself.

"I just keep thinking, what if you'd been there?" Jay turns to me, his blue eyes pained underneath his knotted brows. "I could never forgive myself if they'd broken in and you'd been there. Anything could have happened." He swallows and turns back to stare at the road.

"I wasn't there, Jay. No one was. Maybe that's why they broke in. They saw an opportunity as the house was empty."

"Yeah, maybe. He lifts our joined hands to his lips and kisses the back of mine, leaving my skin warm. "I'm sorry we had to cut the visit short, although maybe it was a welcome escape to get away from my family."

"You're kidding. I love them!"

"Really?" He looks over at me, his eyebrows raised.

"Really." I smile. "They're all lovely. You can tell you're a close family; it's really nice."

"As long as you don't fancy my brother." Jay smirks.

I tip my head back and laugh. "Seriously? You're so different. He is fun though." I raise an eyebrow at Jay, and he eyes me seriously.

"Don't, Holly. We can't afford to be late right now because I've had to pull over and spank you."

"Okay, but just so I know, if I were to mention Blake being fun again when we don't have to be somewhere urgently, then you would spank me for it?" I ask, biting my lip to hide my smile.

"Yes," Jay says darkly. "Then I would fuck you so hard you'd still be feeling me next week, just so you never forget whose girlfriend you are."

"Oh, right, gotcha," I say as I turn to look out the passenger window.

Even under these circumstances he can arouse me so easily. I'm definitely bringing Blake up again in the future if that's what Jay thinks is punishment.

The sound of my phone ringing breaks into my dirty fantasy, and I dig around in my handbag by my feet to fish it out.

"It's Matt," I say to Jay as I hit answer.

"Hi, Matt."

"Holly! Where are you? Stefan called me and told me there's been a break-in at Jay's house!"

"It's okay, we're alright. We were at Jay's parents' last night. We're on our way back to the house now."

Matt lets out a big sigh. "It's good to hear your voice, Holly, and er, parents' house? We're so coming back to that one later."

I smile; he never misses anything.

"It's good to hear yours too. Where are you? I thought you were flying on the Havana; you should be in the air now."

I work out it must be five o'clock in the afternoon UK time, eight hours ahead of LA.

"I swapped it last minute for LA tomorrow. I knew all those bottles of wine I've dropped into crewing over the years would come in handy," he jokes.

"You'll be here tomorrow?" A weight lifts off me knowing that Matt will be here to help Jay and Stefan at the house.

"Yes, I'll be able to help out with whatever needs doing, so don't you worry."

"Thanks, Matt." I look over at Jay and he mouths *hi.*

"Jay says hi by the way."

"Hi back. Tell him I will be at his complete disposal ASAP."

"Thanks, I'm sure he'll appreciate it."

"When are you next back? Haven't you got leave coming up?"

"Yes, I do actually."

I look back across at Jay, who looks at me quizzically. I've got two weeks leave after this trip, but Jay doesn't know that. I've forgotten to mention it since we made up. I don't know what he's going to think about me not being back for at least two weeks, especially now with so much happening.

"I've got to go, Matt; we're not far away now. I'll call you later before you go to bed and let you know what's going on."

"Okay, Holls, love you."

"I love you too," I say to Matt, but I'm looking at Jay. His eyes are focused on mine as I hang up the phone.

I break his gaze, dropping my phone back into my bag and leaning back into the seat.

"Matt's coming out on tomorrow's flight. He said he'll be able to help you and Stefan."

"That's good of him." He pauses. "When are you next here, Holly? We've been so busy you haven't even told me yet."

"I, um…" My hands are clammy as I brace myself for his reaction. "I've actually got leave booked, I had to book it months ago."

"For how long, Holly?" Jay's voice has a hard edge to it.

"Two weeks," I say and hold my breath.

"No way!" he snaps. "Not happening."

"I can't cancel it now, Jay."

"Holly, I've just got you back after you went silent on me. I'm not spending another two weeks without seeing you again." His grip has tightened on my hand and the knuckles on his other hand are turning white. "Spend it here."

"What?"

"Spend your leave here, in LA."

He wants me to spend my leave here? With him? Every day for two whole weeks. We've spent a fair bit of time together but never for more than a few days in a row.

"I guess I could." I don't have any other plans, except a visit to my parents and I can see them afterward... "Okay, if you're sure?"

"Holly, I've never been surer of anything." He keeps his eyes on the road but his grip on my hand softens and he strokes mine with his thumb. "We'll see what state the house is in and if necessary, I will book us into a hotel."

"Okay, I'll ring staff travel later and book a ticket."

"When will it be?"

"I don't know. They're standby tickets so it depends how full the flights are and who else has a higher boarding priority."

"You don't even know if you'll get a seat on the flight?" Jay frowns.

"No, you're never safe on staff travel until the door shuts and you push back from the departure gate," I say.

I've seen many staff get comfy only to be offloaded at the last minute.

Jay's jaw stiffens. "I'm booking you a ticket."

"No, Jay, there's no need."

"There's every need, Holly. I will charter a fucking rocket to get you here if I have to," he snaps.

I'm not going to argue back. He's made up his mind. He must be so stressed about the house and this is something that's in his control that he can fix. I need to let him do it.

"Okay, thank you," I say, running my free hand up his forearm and snaking it around his bicep, before leaning across and resting my head against his arm.

He lets out a big breath and relaxes under my touch.

He needs me right now and hell, I'm going to be there for him.

There's a police car in the driveway as we pull through the gates of Jay's house. Apart from that, nothing looks out of place outside, but it's when we get to the front door that the level of what's happened really hits.

Jay's arm goes around me as I gasp. Everything has been turned upside down. It's like the house was lifted, turned over, and shook hard. The drawers of the hall table are on the floor, their contents scattered. Beyond the foyer in the living area the sofa cushions are all over the floor, and all the kitchen cupboards are open, their contents thrown out.

"Jeez," Jay lets out a low moan.

"Hey, guys." Stefan comes in from the back deck where two police officers are standing and talking. He hugs us both. His eyes are red, faint dark circles underneath them. "They've finished dusting for prints so you're safe to touch things." He sighs. "I'm sorry, man."

"Thanks, bud." Jay pats him on the back. "Thanks for being here and taking care of it all."

Stefan shakes his head. "I wish I could have done more. I sent Maggie home; she was just getting more upset staying here."

I look down. The beautiful flowers she always arranges for the hall table are strewn across the floor, trampled over, their vase smashed into tiny fragments of crystal, glittering in the light.

"You did the right thing," Jay reassures him.

"The police said the alarm was deactivated. They knew what they were doing." Stefan's shoulders drop. "They'll want to talk to you." He gestures to the two officers out back.

"Of course." Jay takes my hand and leads us carefully through all the broken glass and debris, out to the rear deck.

"Hello, Mr. Anderson, Miss. Havers. I'm Detective Hooper and this is Officer Kane."

The female detective doesn't smile. I take in her short dark hair and straight posture. She's confident and commanding. She reaches out to shake Jay's hand and then mine; her younger male colleague does the same.

"We've got some questions to ask if you don't mind," she says as Officer Kane stands next to her and reaches into his pocket, taking out a book and pen, ready to take notes.

"Sure," Jay says, his hand going up to rub his eyes.

I find his other hand and take it in mine, squeezing gently.

"Your friend Stefan tells us you were at your parents' house last night?" She recites the address and Jay nods.

"Yes, we left here about eleven yesterday morning, spent the night there. My phone ran out of battery and I didn't get the messages until this morning."

She nods as Officer Kane writes in his pad.

"We've already spoken to your housekeeper, Maggie, and to Stefan. They don't seem to think there's anything missing, but we'd like you to look around and confirm that."

"Of course," Jay replies.

"Nothing missing? Isn't that a bit weird?" I ask. "Don't people usually break in to steal things?"

Detective Hooper looks at me.

"Yes, that's usually the case, which is why we wanted you both to have a think about whether there's anything you can think of that might explain why someone would break in or what they might have been looking for."

"I have no idea," Jay says blankly.

"Jay," I murmur, "you don't think that guy I saw at my hotel is connected to this, do you?"

"What guy?" the detective asks.

"There was a guy outside my hotel yesterday morning and the night before. I thought he might have been watching me. I just had a weird feeling about it."

"Our friend, Cooper, he's the valet there, he said he was going to check the CCTV," Jay says.

"We'll check it out," she says. "Stefan logged us into yours and they're checking it now. Kane, see how they're getting on, would you?"

Kane disappears inside toward Jay's office and we stand there in silence, waiting for him to return. The detective doesn't seem the least bit uncomfortable about no one speaking. Officer Kane comes back a few minutes later.

"We might have something."

We follow him into Jay's office where Stefan is with another officer on Jay's computer.

"Here," the other male officer says. "We've got him coming in at half past midnight."

My stomach lurches at the footage on Jay's computer. There's a guy, all in black with a black cap on, searching through each of the rooms in the house. He's throwing things about and moving on to the next when he doesn't find whatever it is he's looking for. We watch him disappear into Jay's walk-in closet, where there's no camera. I look up at Jay and he looks murderous. His arms are folded over his chest and he's breathing heavily, his jaw clenched hard. Whatever it is that he thinks the guy is looking for or possibly even found, he's furious about it.

The police leave, taking a copy of the CCTV recording with them. Then it's just me, Jay, and Stefan.

"The press have already got wind of this," Stefan exhales, putting his hands behind his head and stretching his back out. "I'm getting call after call asking for a quote."

"New travels fast," Jay says flatly, looking around at the mess in the open living area.

I go to the utility room and grab a broom and roll of trash bags.

"I'll start in the kitchen," I say and start sweeping up the broken glass, which covers the floor.

"Holly, don't," Jay says. "I'll sort it. I need to take you back to the hotel. You need a rest before your flight this afternoon."

"Like I could sleep now," I huff. "Come on. I've got at least two more hours before I need to even think about going back. We can make a start." I keep sweeping, determined to do something to help, even if it's only this.

"Fine, I know better than to argue with you when your mind's made up." Jay manages a small smile as he leans down and kisses me on my lips.

"Good. You're learning," I wink at him and press the roll of trash bags into his chest. "You start in there." I motion toward the living area where Stefan is on the phone again. By the sounds of it, he's fielding another press call.

We all work quietly alongside each other and before I know it, we've been at it for a couple of hours. The kitchen is almost back to normal. Everything that wasn't broken has been put away. The cupboards are all back in order, and the floor swept and mopped.

Jay's made good progress in the entryway and living area too. The pictures on the walls are all straightened; drawers and their contents are all back in their rightful places, and the sofa has been put back together.

"You know, if you ever feel like retiring from acting, I'm pretty sure you could give Maggie a run for her money," I say as I walk over to him and wrap an arm around his waist.

He pulls me into his side and his soft lips brush against my temple.

"Thank you, Holly." His breath is warm against my skin.

"For what?" I lean into him and close my eyes as the familiar citrus and earthy scent comforts me.

"You, just being here and helping. I really appreciate it."

"Of course I'm going to stay and help. Listen, this is nothing compared to the state of the plane after a full Orlando flight. Excited kids, too many fizzy drinks and sweets do not mix." I smile, looking up at him.

Jay smiles back at me; his eyes hold mine and my heart beats faster in response.

I would do anything to make him feel better right now. I feel his pain like it's my own.

"I think the downstairs is almost sorted," Stefan says, walking up from the office. "It's a good thing you're not a hoarder, Jay, or this would have been a much bigger job."

"We haven't started upstairs yet," Jay jokes, rubbing his hand across his eyes.

"I can do that," Stefan says. "You need to get Holly back."

I look at my watch; he's right. I need to go back and pack for the flight home. I want to stay and help; leaving now couldn't have come at a worse time.

I look up at Jay. "I'm sorry." I swallow down the lump in my throat.

"Hey, it's okay, you'll be coming straight back." Jay presses his nose into my hair.

"Yeah, we got you on the flight the day after tomorrow," Stefan says. I have the urge to hug him, and he laughs as I grab him. "You're welcome, Holly."

"Thank you, Stefan." I look into his tired eyes. "I feel awful leaving you guys now."

"We'll be fine. You'll not even be able to tell anything happened when you come back. I've got the alarm guys booked in later. They're going to upgrade the whole system."

"Great. There's no way this can happen again," Jay says firmly. "If I get my hands on the guy, I'll rip his head off."

"It's weird that nothing was taken. I still can't understand what they were doing here," I say.

Jay clears his throat. "Come on, I'll get you back to the hotel."

I give Stefan another hug goodbye and we head out the door.

When we pull up outside the hotel, Detective Hooper and Officer Kane are talking to Cooper at the valet station.

"Do you think he found anything?" I look across at Jay.

"One way to find out."

Jay opens his door and comes around to open mine. Even when he's stressed out, he's still such a gentleman.

Coop looks up as we reach them, but Detective Hooper talks first.

"We've found something interesting on the CCTV." She gestures to the screen at his station. "Seems you were right, Miss. Havers. Someone was watching you."

"Really?" My hand flies over my mouth. Jay's arm wraps around my waist, supporting me.

"Look here." She points at the screen. "That logo on the sleeve of his sweatshirt? Matches one we saw on the CCTV from Mr. Anderson's house. It's the same guy."

I narrow my eyes at the image on screen. There's some kind of sports logo on the sleeve, barely visible.

"We got a good shot from the house footage. The station is running it through facial recognition as we speak."

"I can't believe this. Who is he?" Nausea churns my stomach as I try to process it. "Why is someone following me?" I look to Jay, wide-eyed as a cold sweat breaks out on my skin.

"It's okay, Holly. I won't let anything happen to you." His voice is deep, reassuring.

I look up into his eyes and they're concerned. I know he's trying to make sense of all this too.

Detective Hooper's phone beeps and we all watch silently as she reads it. She turns the screen toward me and Jay. There's a picture of a middle-aged man on it with shaggy dark-brown hair.

"Does he look familiar?"

I shake my head. "I don't think so. Should he?"

"Hang on, yeah." Jay studies the photo closely. "I'm pretty sure he's a reporter. He was at the restaurant I took you to on our first date."

I'm amazed at Jay's memory, and a tiny sprinkle of joy at him referring to it as our first date warms me.

"His name's Ryan Baker, and yes, you're right; he's a reporter. Known to us for his less than honorable ways of getting a story, shall we say?" Detective Hooper says, her face scowling at his picture.

"We've already got a unit heading to his address to bring him in. See what he's got to say for himself. I'll give you a call when we have an update." She gives me a small smile. It's the first time I've seen her look less than stern.

She nods to Jay and Cooper before she and Officer Kane head back to their car.

"This is crazy, man," Coop says. "At least you know it was probably just some desperate attempt at getting a good story."

"Why break into Jay's house though? What did he think he was going to find?" I shake my head, not understanding any of this.

"Dunno. Who knows how these guys think? Go through your trash and all sorts looking for an exclusive." Coop shrugs.

"We'll get to the bottom of it, Holly." Jay rubs his hand up and down my arm where goosebumps have formed.

"Yeah, okay." I don't feel convinced though. "I need to go pack. The crew pickup is in an hour," I groan, putting my hands over my face. The last thing I feel like doing now is putting on my uniform and working the long night flight home.

"I'll come with you. I can get a ticket for the flight at the airport and fly back with you the day after tomorrow," Jay says.

I shake my head. "No, no, there's no need for that. You've got enough to do back here, at the house...and the police might have more news."

"None of that matters, Holly. I need to know you're okay."

"I am, I promise. I'll be busy on the flight and it'll keep my mind off it. Rach will be home when I get back and I'll be packing and coming straight back more or less."

Jay doesn't look convinced.

"Really, I'll be fine. You'll barely notice I'm gone."

"I doubt that," he says, his eyes catching mine. "Come on, I'll walk you up to your room."

"I'll see you soon, Coop." I lean over and give him a kiss on the cheek. "Thank you for everything you've done for us."

"Hey, don't mention it." He blushes. "What are friends for, eh?"

"Thanks, man, we mean it." Jay shakes his hand, and then we head up to my room.

My heart sinks in my chest.

I can't believe it's time to say goodbye again already.

Chapter 18

"Honey, I'm home!" I call to Rach as I pull my suitcase in through the front door.

I know she's expecting me, as I called her when I landed. She can't believe what's been happening either.

"Holls!" She comes running out of the living room and crushes me into a hug, almost toppling us both over. For someone so petite, she sure is strong.

"This is some weird shit going on." She draws back to look at me, her eyes wide.

"Tell me about it." I sigh. "It feels so surreal," I say as I kick my shoes off.

"You look knackered. Go, shower, get changed, I'll put the kettle on," Rach orders and pushes me toward the stairs.

"I love you," I call over my shoulder as I pick up my case and carry it upstairs.

"I know, I would love me too," her voice sings from the kitchen.

Fifteen minutes later, showered and in clean loungewear, I collapse back onto the sofa. Now that I'm back home in our little living room, LA seems a world away. The whole break-in and being followed feels like a bad dream. Only the sickness that's still in my stomach tells me it's not. I texted Jay as soon as I landed. It was super early there, but he was awake. He probably couldn't sleep. I couldn't either. We got three hours' crew rest on the way home in the bunk beds. Usually I would sleep on a night flight from pure exhaustion, but this time I just lay there listening to the hum of the plane's engines, unable to switch off.

Jay said they'd almost got the house back in order and the security company came and upgraded everything. Stefan stayed over for the night as they'd still been putting the house back in order until late.

"Here you are." Rach hands me a steaming mug of peppermint tea and plonks herself next to me on the sofa.

"Thank you." I smile. "You're the best housemate, you know."

"I know." She sighs, stretching her feet up onto the coffee table, the red polish on her toes shining. "Has Jay heard any more from the police?"

"Not much. They took the guy, Ryan Baker, in for questioning. They've got him on camera breaking and entering. He won't admit to taking anything, though. But he said he was paid to snoop around."

"Paid? By who?"

"No idea. He's not saying any more at the moment. It looks like someone paid him to follow me when I was in LA. Maybe to see when I was with Jay and wait until the house was empty, I guess."

"Creepy, but why?" Rach frowns in confusion.

"I don't know." I shudder. "It's Hollywood. I guess it's not unheard of for actors' houses to be broken into. Maybe he was just looking for a story. Nothing was taken though, so I guess he didn't find what he was looking for."

"Maybe it's just about getting the latest scoop on what Hollywood's golden guy is up to then?" Rach offers.

"Yeah, maybe. Although Jay is pretty open with the press. Stefan said if they get the frequency and content of interviews right, then it tends to stop them digging around so much as he's always feeding out stories himself."

"Smart and tactical, I like it." Rach smiles.

I smile back half-heartedly. "Stefan knows what he's doing when it comes to that. He's been fielding calls about the break-in non-stop since."

"Poor guy, busy day at the office."

"Yeah, bless him; he's working so hard. He's such a nice, normal guy too. I can see why Matt likes him so much," I say before having a sip of my tea.

"Oh God," Rach groans, tipping her head back against the back of the sofa. "He's so into him. It's all I've heard about! The sooner they shag, the better, as far as I'm concerned. Might get him to shut up for a while at least."

"You're kidding? This is Matt." I laugh.

"You're right; he never shuts up." Rach sighs.

"And we wouldn't have him any other way." I smile, looking at her.

"Speak for yourself," Rach says, but the corners of her mouth curl into a smile.

"So, enough about creepy reporters; my head feels like it might pop," I say, rubbing at my temples. "Let's talk about pantie-loving men called Mr. X instead." I elbow Rach and look at her from the corner of my eye as I take another sip of tea.

"Mmm," Rach murmurs, acting unusually coy for her.

"Mmm, mmm?" I ask, "or just mmm?"

"Mmm, mmm, mmm," she says and we both laugh.

"Okay." She lets out a big breath. "So, I sent him the first pair of my special, personally designed panties that I got made in Shanghai."

"Yeah?"

"And he loved it!"

"So, what's the problem?" I ask, confused by the frown on her face.

"He started getting a bit funny. Wanted to know how many I had made and if I was sending them out to anyone else, even though I agreed in the beginning they were only for him."

"Wow, so he's jealous?"

Rach sighs. "Yep, seems so. I had to shoot him right down in my email back to him for not believing me and now I've not heard from him in five days."

"So, he's jealous and pissed?"

"Totally. He's my best customer! I don't want to lose him," Rach moans in frustration. "Plus, and you better not tell Matt this..." She pauses.

"Of course not, you can trust me, Rach; you know that."

"Well..." She fidgets around on the sofa. "His emails were kind of hot, you know? He made me feel like I was the sexiest woman on earth to him. I miss it." She tucks a stray strand of her glossy dark bob behind her ear, her eyes staring off into space, deep in thought.

"I'm sure he'll be back. If he's that jealous he's not going to want to give you up easily. Although, you still don't really know who he is, Rach. Just be careful."

"Oh, I know." She sighs. "It's just the way he writes; I told you before, didn't I? He doesn't sound much older than us. I reckon mid-thirties."

"Maybe you ought to be the one asking him how many other girls' panties and tights he buys to sniff on. Turn the question back on him," I say.

"That's another thing. He says I'm the only one. He was very insistent that there's never been anyone else and he's not been into that kind of thing before."

"Why would he be so bothered about you knowing that? To show you're special to him, do you think?" I frown as I try to make sense of it all.

"I don't know. I just don't know. It's all a bit weird, isn't it?" She turns to me and gives me a lopsided smile. "But weird or not, he's my cash cow, and this baby calf needs some more milk!" she says, catching my eye, and we both erupt into giggles.

"You have such a way of putting things, Rach." I lean over and squeeze her hand.

She smiles back at me, but I can sense this Mr. X stuff is getting to her.

"Hey, you should get packing." She changes the subject. "Two weeks with lover boy coming up." She raises her eyebrows at me.

"I know. He might be sick of me at the end of it. We've only ever had a few days together at a time, and then I've flown back home again."

"As if, Holls. He's totally love drunk when you're around. Can't keep his hands off you."

"I think it's the other way around," I gush. "I'm the one who just can't get enough. It feels so right with him. I trust him and the results are…" I trail off with a stupid grin on my face.

"I know, Holls. Bet he brings out the inner slut you didn't know you had, huh?" Rach eyes me, looking amused.

"Oh my God, yes!" I whisper, even though no one else is here. "Has that ever happened to you?"

"No. I'm always a slut in bed, regardless of the guy," Rach says seriously. "But Jay's special, Holly. If he's the only one who's ever made you feel like that, then he's your one."

"My one?"

"Yeah, your soulmate of fucking."

I laugh as I spit out some of my tea.

"My soulmate of fucking?"

"Yeah." Rach shrugs. "You have no problem doing the dating and nice girlfriend shit, but no other guy has brought out your inner slut. He's special."

She's right. I've had boyfriends before, not all as bad as Simon, thank God. But only Jay has ever made me want to do and say the things I have when we're together.

I turn to Rach. "So, if you're always a slut in bed, then does that mean you have a load of soulmates?"

"No. Mine will be when I find a guy that I actually want to go out on a date with like a normal couple. I'm fine fucking them, but I never want to stick around long. Once the sex is over, I don't really see the point."

"That sounds kind of sad when you say it like that."

The idea of sex without emotion is pretty alien to me. I study Rach's face as she continues.

"I suppose it is a bit sometimes. Nothing another orgasm hasn't been able to fix yet, though." She smirks. "Maybe I'll meet my soulmate of dating one day. Until then, I'll just have to put up with plenty of hot, meaningless sex."

"Sounds so tough when you put it like that," I say, and we smile at each other. I can always rely on Rach to lift my spirits.

"Right, come on." She grabs my hand and I'm hoisted off the sofa. "I'm helping you pack. Two weeks of outfits worthy of being fucked senseless in are needed."

"Okay, okay." I laugh as I follow her up to my room.

Time to pack and get back to LA.

Back to my soulmate of fucking.

My flight lands on schedule and I step off the plane, back in LA once again. It's starting to feel like I've spent more time here in the past couple of months than at home, but I guess I nearly have.

Rach helped me pack like she said she would and if I hadn't snuck in some extra clothes when she wasn't looking, I swear I would be wearing mostly underwear and dresses short enough to be T-shirts for the whole trip.

I glance down at my phone and re-read the text my sister sent me before I left.

Sophie: Enjoy the sunshine for two weeks, sis! Looking forward to seeing you at Mum and Dad's when you get back. S

I called Mum and asked to postpone my visit until I get back from LA and she was more than happy to. There's some local baking competition she wants to prepare for anyway. She sounded so excited about it. I sent her Sheila's cookie recipe, and she was delighted, said they were so delicious that she's going to use them as one her entries to the competition. Dad sounded more than happy to be the taste tester. Sophie managed to get a few days off work so we'll both be there together, which will be lovely as I don't get to see her that often.

My suitcase comes around on the baggage carousel, so I lift it off and make my way through customs, then out into arrivals. Scanning through the sea of faces waiting to collect people, a huge grin spreads across my face as a familiar pair of blue eyes catch mine.

Jay is standing there in a baseball cap, jeans, and T-shirt. The sleeves stretch over his biceps. In his hands is a homemade sign, which I read it as I get closer. The words *'Pick Up for Berry'* are written on it in thick black ink. He sees me looking and turns the sign over so I can read the other side. *'Missed me?'*

I increase my pace and when I'm almost in front of him I drop my bags and jump up on my toes to wrap my arms around his neck, crashing my lips against his. His arms wrap around me and lift my feet off the floor. I kiss him and bring my hands to his jaw so I can run my fingers through his stubble.

"That's a yes?" he says in his deep, sexy voice, his eyes crinkling at the corners underneath his cap.

"It's a maybe. Perhaps if you show me what I've been missing later, then I can give you a fully informed and final answer," I say cheekily.

"Oh, really? It's like that, is it?" He leans forward and bites my bottom lip between his teeth.

A rush of heat fires through my body. I am total putty in his hands and I'm sure he knows it.

"This suits you, I like it," I look up at his baseball cap.

He looks embarrassed. "Yeah, it helps me not get recognized quite so easily somewhere like this, where there's so many people."

I look around. He's right, no one's looking at him at all. I forget what it must be like for him sometimes. He's just Jay to me.

"The only thing is…" I whisper in his ear, "I can't run my hands through your hair when you're wearing it."

He swallows. "I think that's probably a very good thing, Holly. Unless you want to be fucked right here in public," he murmurs, nipping my ear with his teeth.

"I think the press would have a field day."

"Mmm, as if we don't have enough trouble with the press already," Jay says.

His eyes are full of tension. He's so stressed about the break-in.

"Have there been any updates while I was on the flight?"

Jay sighs. "Nothing much. Ryan Baker is still insisting that it was just a digging mission to try and get an exclusive. He was the one who photographed us at Fusion when we went for dinner. He got paid pretty well for those pictures."

I remember the pictures. Stefan tried to stop them being printed. He was worried about my privacy and how I would feel if I got put on the reporters' radars. Turns out he was right to be concerned. Look where we are now.

"But why did he break into your house and make such a mess?"

"Apparently, you being British and us meeting on a flight like we did, makes a good story. He said he was looking for things to add to it, photos of your flying ID, stuff like that."

"That's doesn't make any sense though. He knew where my hotel was. He could have gotten pictures of me in uniform when we got dropped off there or broken into *my* room. Why go to your house?"

"I know," Jay says, pressing his lips together and rubbing his chin with one hand. "It doesn't make sense. He's lying. He was looking for something. I just don't know what. He was in my closet a long time where I keep personal things like family photos and letters, but nothing was missing."

I don't know what to make of what Jay's just told me. Nothing was taken, yet there's more to it than Ryan Baker's letting on.

"The police are charging him with breaking and entering. It's all they can do; there's no other evidence. He was given bail until his hearing."

"He was given bail?" I whisper, my stomach clenching.

Jay looks down at me. "Don't worry. He's got a restraining order issued against him. He won't be coming anywhere near you or me."

Jay's voice is firm, and I'm reassured, slightly. I don't want to think about it anymore right now. I'm back here with Jay and I want to have a nice couple of weeks.

I look up at him and place my hands against his broad chest.

"Take me home, baby." I smile.

"Yes, ma'am," he says, tipping the peak of his cap toward me and picking up my bags.

We head out of the terminal and toward the parking lot. As we pass a trash can, he goes to throw the sign he's made into it.

"No!" I take it from his hand and zip it into the front pocket of my carry-on. "I want to keep it."

His eyes sparkle at me. "Come on, Berry, let's get you home. I want you naked and underneath me."

I throw my head back and laugh.

I've missed LA.

Chapter 19

I'M FLOATING ON A cloud of bliss, a permanent grin plastered to my face. The last few days have been incredible. I've had Jay all to myself. He's had some work to do for the upcoming fragrance launch he's working on with Anya, but most of the preparation is done. And his show, Steel Force, is still taking a break before filming starts for season three.

He kept to his promise of getting me naked and underneath him after getting home from the airport. We were up almost the whole night. If this is how it's going to be when I'm away for just forty-eight hours, then maybe I should go away for longer next time! We met Matt and Stefan the next morning for brunch before Matt had to fly home. He was such a big help getting the house sorted. It's elevated him even more in Stefan's book. I keep catching the two of them touching each other whenever they can and sharing private jokes.

I haven't spoken to Matt since brunch, so I decide to call him to catch up. He answers on the second ring.

"Holls! Taken a break from milking Jay's balls dry, have you?" he jokes.

"Matt!" I laugh in shock, even though after all the years we've been friends, his comment shouldn't surprise me.

"Where's lover boy now?"

"Oh, he's on the phone with Stefan, talking about the fragrance launch. I thought now was a good time to call as I knew you'd not be talking to Stefan," I joke as I rest my head back against the sun lounger by Jay's pool.

"Wonderful powers of deduction," Matt teases.

"Thanks." I laugh.

"So, are you having a great time I will no doubt feel green with envy over?" Matt sighs.

"Sorry, but I am." I smile. "I feel so relaxed, Matt. It's nice not to be rushing away after a couple of nights and working a flight home."

"Ugh. Tell me about it. I can't wait for my leave next month."

"Have you made plans?"

"Well." Matt's voice goes up in excitement. "Stefan and I were thinking of going away together. He's never been to Hong Kong before and fancied it."

"Ooh, sounds great! That'll be amazing having all that time together. So, will you be getting one room or two?"

"One, if I've got anything to do with it," Matt answers quickly. "Stefan hasn't mentioned it yet, so I'm going to drop some subtle hints."

"You and subtle?" I tease.

"I know, I know. I've never waited this long with a guy before, but he's so worth it, Holls!" Matt sighs and I can picture the sappy smile on that's on his face right now.

"He is great, Matt. Definitely a keeper. I've noticed how he lights up every time he has a text from you, and yesterday he said you were, and I quote, 'such a welcome surprise in his life.'"

"Really?" Matt squeals so loud I have to move the phone away from my ear.

"Yes, really," I confirm.

"Oh my God. Holly, I've just passed out on the floor. Send help!"

I laugh at Matt's obvious elation to what I've just told him. "Oh, I love you, Matt."

"I love you too, babe. Now, I'm off to bed to dream about what you just told me."

"Okay, sweet dreams," I say as we hang up.

I lean back, closing my eyes and lifting my face up to the bright sun. It's late in the UK, but it's only mid-afternoon here in LA. We got up late this morning, and I did yoga out on the deck while Jay did a weight session in his gym.

We've gotten into such a lovely routine together. Lying in bed for a long time, making love, followed by a workout, and then going out somewhere, like the beach. Jay's been showing me some of his favorite hidden spots. We grab lunch on the go, and then we come back to the house and I swim and sit by the pool reading while Jay makes work calls, if he has any. Otherwise, he joins me.

In the evenings we either go out or stay in to eat and then have heavy, passionate sex.

I can't believe how happy I am, how much my life has changed since we met. It's been a whirlwind, but I wouldn't change a thing. He's everything I never knew I needed.

Goosebumps scatter up my arms before a familiar voice breaks into my thoughts.

"Hey, beautiful."

I open my eyes straight into Jay's clear blue gaze.

"Hey, yourself." I grin.

He leans down and presses his lips against mine. They're warm and gentle as he kisses me, drawing me in deeply, setting a swirl of butterflies free in my stomach. He sure knows how to kiss.

"You know, you don't need to wear this." Jay runs a finger underneath the side tie of my bikini bottoms. His finger trails along my hip, causing my breath to catch in my throat. "No one can see you here, except me." He grins.

"Maggie or Stefan could."

Jay raises an eyebrow at me. "We always know when they're coming around, so that's no reason."

"Someone might fly past in their private helicopter?" I joke, although it's not out of the question here.

Jay tilts his head back and laughs. "Berry, you're losing this argument," he says as he bends his head down and takes one tie between his teeth and pulls.

"I didn't realize it was an argument. I thought we were having a debate," I tease.

Jay keeps pulling until he's unfastened one side, before moving to the other side and repeating. "Call it what you like; I'm winning." He smirks, looking up at me, his eyes glinting.

I wouldn't count on it. I'm pretty sure I'm the one who's about to get the prize.

"Well, I'm saying argument as that means that we get to make up," I say, biting my lip to hide my smile.

Jay has completely removed my bikini bottoms now and discarded them onto the floor.

"Oh, baby, I'll make it up to you; don't you worry."

He pushes my feet back up onto the sun lounger. Even though I know it's coming, I can't help gasping when his hot mouth touches me. He trails kisses all over the skin of my inner thighs as a rush of arousal courses through me, straight to his tongue.

"Oh, Jay," I moan.

He slides his tongue over me, and I tense in anticipation.

"Mmm, my juicy little Berry," he moans as he tastes me all over with his tongue before moving to my clit and sucking.

I suck my breath in and my back arches off the sun lounger.

"That's it, baby, let me make you feel good," Jay murmurs, his lips never leaving me.

Oh God, he is so incredible at this!

He slides his tongue through my lips and plunges it inside me, lapping up the wetness that greets him. I reach down with both hands and run them through his hair, and he groans in response before delving deeper with his tongue.

I don't know how much more of this I can take. Jay sucks on my clitoris again and I almost come on the spot.

"Jay, I'm close," I pant.

He draws back, kneeling between my legs, watching where our bodies meet as he slides two thick fingers inside me.

A small moan escapes my lips. He looks so sexy, kneeling there like that, completely focusing on my body and giving me pleasure. He adds a third finger and I gasp at the fullness.

"Jay..."

His eyes burn into mine as he pumps me with his fingers, the muscles in his arm flexing. I can't take much more of this, not with him looking at me like that. I wriggle underneath his hand as my moans grow louder.

"Don't you dare come, Holly," he growls at me. "Your orgasm is mine and I want to taste it."

"Jay, you need to stop," I pant.

He does as I say, sliding his fingers out of me, and I immediately regret speaking.

"Get up," Jay orders.

I sit up, my pussy throbbing with a waiting orgasm. Jay lifts his T-shirt over his head and pulls his shorts and boxers down in one swift movement. He takes me by the hand and leads me over to the cabana bed on the deck. Even the insides of my thighs are throbbing with the need to have him inside me. Stretching me, filling me, completing me.

"Sit on me," he commands as he lies back on the bed.

I climb up next to him and lift one leg over his waist to straddle him.

"Not there, Berry. Sit on my face," he growls. "I told you, your orgasm is mine to taste." His hand grips his hard cock, and he gives himself two long pumps. "Now!" he snaps.

I hold back my grin from how bossy he's being and crawl up the bed toward his head. I love it when he takes control. He uses both of his arms to lift me over his face, his hands around my bum supporting me. I lean forward so I can rest both hands on the bed, and then I lower myself down to meet his waiting mouth.

"Fuck yeah," he murmurs as he pulls me down onto his face.

I'm in ecstasy. The sensation of his warm, strong tongue stroking and sucking me is almost too much. I'm panting his name within moments.

"Jay, that feels amazing."

He delves deeper with his tongue before turning his attention to my swollen clitoris again, licking and sucking it hard.

"Jay..." My legs start to shudder underneath me as he keeps sucking harder, then licking again with the flat of his tongue. "Jay!" I gasp more urgently.

"Come for me, baby," he moans.

Relief at hearing him say those words is short-lived as the first wave of my orgasm hits me hard. My body convulses, wetness rushing out of me, as Jay pulls me down harder onto his face, groaning loudly.

"Oh fuck!" I scream as the next wave crashes over me.

Jay digs his fingers into my buttocks and teases my pussy open wider so he can suck even harder.

"Jay! No, it's too sensitive," I cry as another hard wave hits me and my arms almost buckle.

Suddenly, he moves his hands to my waist and lifts me like I weigh nothing, moving me back down his body and onto his waiting cock. He slides straight in deep, and I cry out again as my body contracts around him.

"Fuck me, baby." Jay looks up at me, his eyes dark with desire. "Ride my cock and tell me how good it feels."

Oh God, I can hardly breathe, let alone talk; my orgasm has knocked the air from my lungs.

I look down at him as I slide up on his cock and sink back down. There's no other feeling like it. He just feels so perfect. I slide up and down again, faster this time.

"You feel so good, deep inside me," I whisper, tilting my head back and closing my eyes as my arousal is already growing again.

His fingers dig into my hips. "Keep talking."

"Your cock was made for me, Jay Anderson," I say as I return my gaze to him.

His eyes are dark and stormy, drinking me in. I rise again, sinking back down harder.

Fuck, this feels so good.

I find a rhythm, and with Jay's hands on my hips I ride him hard and deep, moving faster as another orgasm builds inside me.

"I will never have enough of you, of your cock," I cry as I slam down onto him, the sound of our skin hitting just making me want to ride him even harder.

"Holly..." His voice comes out strained and he sucks in a breath.

"Please," I whimper, "I need you to fill me up deep inside."

I sink down onto him again and his hands tighten on my hips before the telling swell and jerk of his cock tells me he's close.

"Oh fuck, Holly," he hisses through his gritted teeth as he screws his eyes shut and fills me with his hot orgasm.

I keep slamming down on top of him and the sounds of his orgasm are enough to bring mine rushing to me.

"Jay!" I cry as I throw my head back and come in waves all over him again.

My legs are shaking so much I can barely keep moving. Jay brings one hand down to me and rubs slow circles against my clitoris with his thumb, helping me ride the wave of my orgasm down with him.

I'm still puffing when I bring my eyes back to his. He looks bright and alive. We're both covered in sweat, smiling. He brings a hand up to my face and rubs his thumb across my bottom lip. I kiss it as I look down at him.

"I'm so glad I met you, Holly Havers. My cock was most definitely made for you." He smiles and pulls me down next to him, gently sliding out of my body.

I curl into his arms, enjoying their warmth as my racing heart slows. I lay my palm over his chest and the drumming of his own heart pushes back.

He leans over and brushes his lips against mine. "I think my heart was too," he whispers, barely loud enough for me to hear.

I search his eyes and they tell me all I need to know. I open my mouth, but he catches me in a kiss before I can speak.

I wrap my arms around him and kiss him back. Pouring myself into him, hoping he knows my heart is right there, alongside his, beating in time.

Chapter 20

"Come on, sleepyhead."

I shiver and groan as cool air blows across my skin, causing goosebumps to form.

"No. Ten more minutes," I moan and roll back over, my hand wildly searching for the comfort of the duvet.

"Holls, you said not to let you sleep too long."

I force one eye open and see Jay, bright-eyed and full of energy. He's like a puppy that's always eager to go for a walk.

"If you didn't keep me up all night with that magic cock of yours"—I yawn—"then I wouldn't need a nap after lunch in the first place." I stretch, my back clicking as it straightens.

"That's more like it, baby." Jay leans down and kisses me, his warm breath welcome against my lips. His arm holds me tight around the waist and I'm pulled up to a sitting position.

"You like to get your own way, don't you?" I smile as my eyes open fully and take in his, crinkled at the corners with amusement.

"When it comes to you, Berry, I like you any way I can get you." He smirks as I push his chest.

"Come on." His hands are in mine, pulling me up. "Go get in the shower. Shona will be here soon."

My feet sink into the carpet as I reluctantly get out of Jay's bed and pass him to go to the bathroom. A soft slap lands across my bum, accompanied by a deep chuckle.

"Don't think you've gotten away with it." I glance back over my shoulder. "Revenge will come when you least expect it." I extend my hand and blow him a kiss as I go into the bathroom and close the door, muffling the sound of his laugh as he goes back downstairs.

I turn the shower on full and step under it, my shoulders relaxing with the heat. Tonight is the launch party for Anya's new fragrance. There's going to be a drinks and canapes party with some onstage presentations and entertainment. It sounds like fun, although judging from the butterflies in my stomach, I know I'm nervous. This is the first public event Jay and I will have been to as a couple. He's cool and calm. This is just another night at work for him, but I don't know what to expect.

Stefan arranged for a stylist he is friends with to come over and do my hair and makeup and bring some outfits. I would be lying if I said I wasn't a little excited at the thought of what magic she might perform on me. I've never had anyone give me a head-to-toe makeover before. Except Matt, when he gets a bee in his bonnet before a night out and goes to town barking out orders about what I must wear. But this is different.

I finish washing with the new shower gel Jay bought for me when he knew I would stay for two weeks. It smells like crushed mango and lime, uplifting and refreshing. He must have known I would need some extra help to wake up in the mornings after he's kept me up half the night.

My mouth breaks into a broad grin. He makes me feel like the only girl in the world that he's ever laid eyes on before. I feel special and adored, like we've got a much longer shared history than just a few months. He looks at me sometimes like he's known me his entire life, which I know would sound silly if I told anyone. I can't quite put my finger on what it is, but there's something familiar.

I turn the shower off and step out onto the bathmat, wrapping myself in a large fluffy towel. I dry off and moisturize from head to toe. The LA summer sun has given me a sun-kissed glow, and since Jay insisted I didn't need to wear my bikini, I haven't got any tan lines. I still feel more comfortable with it on, if I'm honest, but he has a habit of removing it whenever he sees I'm wearing it. I run a brush through my hair, which has turned even lighter gold with all the sun, and then put a robe on and head downstairs to see what Jay's doing.

"Hey, baby." He looks up from the chopping board.

The scent of basil leaves reaches me as I move closer.

"That looks nice," I say, taking in the avocado, tomato, and mozzarella he's made into a restaurant-worthy sandwich.

"You need to eat something. These events always have too much champagne and not enough food. You'll feel much better if you eat now, trust me."

"Thank you, Mr. Expert." I take the plate he's holding out to me and perch on a stool at the kitchen counter.

Jay slides onto the one next to me.

"So, what should I do tonight?" I ask between mouthfuls.

This sandwich is delicious, so full of flavor. *Is there anything he isn't good at?*

"Enjoy yourself." Jay looks at me.

"That's it? No pearls of wisdom for the rookie?" I joke.

"These events can be fun. There's usually a good atmosphere, but they also attract a lot of 'look at me' and fake air-kissing types." Jay's mouth turns down as he chews. "There are some genuinely great people who you'll meet too, Holly. It's just being able to tell who's real, and who's just playing a role."

"How do you know?" I take another bite of my sandwich.

Jay raises an eyebrow at me.

"I mean, how do you know who's only speaking to you because you're 'Jay Anderson, actor and heartthrob'?"—I roll my eyes as I say heartthrob—"and who's genuinely interested in you?"

"Heartthrob?" Jay lights up as he catches my eye. "Do I make you throb, Berry?" His eyes glint.

I smirk back at him. "Don't change the subject; this is serious."

"Okay, sorry." His mouth lifts at the corners as he looks at me out of the corner of his eye. "I guess you just get better at reading people, the more you meet. Sometimes you just get a feeling about someone, and other times they can fool you. But they slip up and show their true selves."

My mind flashes to Simon. He sure fooled me. When we first met I had no idea the sort of person he really was. So ready to put me down to make himself feel big.

"Has it happened to you a lot?" I turn toward Jay.

He sighs and runs a hand through his hair.

"Yes and no. I've met people who are just interested in me for their own agendas, but I don't get close to people easily, Holly." His eyes hold mine as he speaks. "After losing someone, you guard yourself more from getting close to people. Well, I do anyway."

He breaks eye contact and looks down at the kitchen counter, his eyebrows pulling together. "Losing Rob was the worst time of my life. I couldn't let myself feel happy...until I met you." He looks up at me, his eyes watery.

"Jay—" I start, but he cuts me off.

"I want to tell you about it, Holly. I need you to know what happened, who I am." He swallows as though the words are painful to speak out loud.

"Jay, I know who you are." I stand up and move over to him, taking his face between my hands and stroking his cheeks with my thumbs. "You are the warmest, kindest, silliest..." I smile at him, "man I've ever met. You do anything for the people you love."

His expression is pained as he looks at me.

"Holly, I'm not. You don't understand." His eyes search mine and he takes a breath, about to speak.

A loud ringing sounds and my stomach jumps into my mouth as I flinch.

"Relax." Jay gives me a small smile, the moment broken. "It's just the new doorbell."

"Gosh, it's loud; are you going deaf in your old age?" I tease.

"I'm only three years older than you," he says as he slides off his stool and kisses my lips before heading toward the front door.

"You're in a whole different decade, though. I mean, I'm twenty-eight, it's practically mid-twenties and at thirty-one you're almost forty," I call after him, wondering what he was about to say before we were interrupted.

"You're itching for a hard spanking, aren't you?" He shoots back and I smile at the mental image he's conjured up.

Jay checks the security screen and presses a button to let our visitor in. A few moments later he opens the door. There's a woman standing there, two large makeup cases by her feet and a clothes rack on wheels next to her.

"Hey, Shona, it's good to see you." Jay leans in and kisses her cheek.

"You too, Jay," she says, flicking her long dark-brown hair over her shoulder.

I look over at her. She's older than me and wearing a very stylish trouser suit with killer heels. She comes into the house and Jay helps her with her things as I make my way over.

"You must be Holly?" she says, her heels clicking on the floor as she closes the distance between us and embraces me in a friendly hug. Spicy, exotic perfume mists around her. "It's so nice to meet you," she says as she holds my hands between hers. They're cool and soft, and there's an enormous diamond ring on her left hand.

"You too." I smile back.

"Stefan has told me all about you."

My cheeks heat.

"It's all good, Holly, don't worry." Her laugh tinkles like tiny bells and her eyes light up as she smiles at me. "So, where shall I set up?"

Two hours later Shona has worked her magic on me. I look at my reflection in the mirror of the guest bathroom. I still look like me, but the flawless HD version. My makeup is immaculate. Smoky, dark-gold eyeshadow brings out the green of my eyes, and she's used some fake lashes, which are full and soft. My skin is immaculate, a touch of golden highlighter on my cheekbones, and my lips are a lovely warm nude. My hair tumbles down my back in large loose curls. Shona's put a shine spray on it, so all the golden-blond tones are glinting whenever the light catches them.

The overall effect is sexy and sultry.

"You're a miracle worker!" I exclaim, turning my face from side to side.

Shona comes up behind me and places her hands on my shoulders.

"I just worked with what you already have, Holly." She beams at me in the mirror.

She is lovely. We didn't stop chatting the entire time she was doing my hair and makeup. She was telling me that her husband runs a large visual effects company that supplies most of Hollywood with special effects and stunt actors. She met him working as a makeup artist on set, and the rest is history.

"Now is the fun part." She grins at me, squeezing my shoulders. "Let's choose the dress!"

"Okay."

I follow Shona back into the guest bedroom and my stomach dances in excitement or nerves. I'm not sure where one ends and the other starts.

"So, I've brought a selection," she says as she unzips each garment bag on the clothes rack.

Glimpses of fabrics draw my eyes. There's a long red dress, a black velvet one, something silver and covered in sequins, a floral embroidered lace, and then the last one is a shimmery, emerald green. It makes me think of a mermaid.

"Oh, this is beautiful," I say, fingering the heavy green fabric. It changes color as it moves, entwined with fine gold threads that catch the light.

"That's my personal favorite too," Shona says. "I thought it would be perfect for you the moment I saw you downstairs." She pulls it out of the bag. It looks like it's fitted to below the hips and then flows out to the floor in a fishtail shape. "Let's try it on!" She grins.

I take my robe off so I'm just wearing a nude thong and a genius stick on bra that Shona brought with her, so I won't have any straps visible. Shona lifts the fabric over my head, and it slides down over my skin.

"Oh yes!" Her eyes light up and she clasps her hands together in front of her chest.

I turn to look in the full-length mirror next to us. For a moment I think I'm looking at someone else, not myself.

"Shona, it's stunning!"

"No, Holly, you are. The dress is just an accessory." She studies me, her long fingers cupping her chin as she watches my face in the mirror.

My eyes sweep over the dress. It's sexy and figure-hugging at the top, but the heavy fabric and fishtail skirt make it elegant. I turn to look at the back. It plunges all the way to my lower back. I bring my eyes back up to my face. Wow, I don't think I've ever felt so incredible in a dress before.

"This is crazy. I feel like Cinderella." A strange laugh escapes my lips.

"Oh, you'll need your glass slippers then," Shona says as she helps me into a pair of strappy gold heels. "And these." She hands me some long gold crystal earrings and a gold clutch bag.

I reach out and take them, forcing my fingers to remain steady. "Thank you."

"I think you're ready for the ball." She smiles as she stands back and takes in her finished handiwork.

Nerves flutter in my stomach again. I look at my reflection in the mirror one last time before I go to look for Jay. Shona wished us a wonderful evening and packed up her things and left. I couldn't stop thanking her. I heard her say "wait until you see her" to Jay as she left, and now I'm so nervous about him seeing me. I take one last big, deep breath, then I head downstairs.

Jay is leaning back against the kitchen counter, his head turned toward the glass doors by the pool. My heart rate races as I watch him. He's wearing a black suit and crisp white shirt, open at the neck. He looks like the epitome of masculinity. I clear my throat and he turns to me.

His eyes widen first as he drinks me in. Starting at my feet, he traces the curves of my hips and breasts up to my face, where his piercing blue eyes stop and hold mine. He swallows deeply as he holds my gaze. Then he raises his hand to his face and runs his fingers over his chin, the way I've learned he does when he's aroused.

"Holly, you look sensational." He strides over to me and placing his hands on my hips as he looks down and takes me in head to toe again. He leans toward me, his soft lips brushing my ear. "You are the most beautiful woman I've ever known," he whispers, placing a gentle kiss on my neck.

My body clenches in response to the closeness of his body and familiar scent.

"You don't scrub up too badly yourself," I whisper.

Jay chuckles and reaches into his pocket.

"I got you something." He pulls out a long blue velvet box.

"What's this?" I frown. "I didn't get you anything."

"Holly, you're all I want," Jay says, his deep voice making me tingle, as I stare at the box he's placed in my hands.

I open it and inside is a delicate gold watch. Diamonds surround the mother-of-pearl face, but it's the two individual sets of watch hands that draw my attention.

"It's got two time zones—one for here, one for England," Jay says, studying my face. "So even when we aren't together, you'll hopefully think of me when you look at it."

I swallow down the lump in my throat.

"It's perfect, thank you," I whisper, blinking, not wanting to ruin my makeup.

Jay's warm hands take my wrist and fasten it on. It sparkles on my arm. No one has ever given me something so beautiful.

"That sounds like our taxi," Jay says, looking over my shoulder toward the front door. "Are you ready?" He looks back at me.

"I'm so ready," I say, blowing out a big breath and hoping I sound convincing.

We head outside and there's a black limousine in the driveway, the driver holding open the back door.

"Good evening, miss." He nods as I slide in and make wide eyes back at Jay. He smirks back at me, clearly amused at my reaction.

"You didn't say we were going in a limo," I hiss at him after the door closes behind him.

"It's a big event... Besides, they can be fun." He grins as he produces a bottle of champagne and two glasses from a compartment by his seat.

"This is crazy."

I watch as he pops the cork and pours. He hands me a glass and I clink it against his.

"To a night of people looking at giant posters of you in hardly any clothes," I say.

Jay laughs. "To a night of me thinking about getting you home as soon as possible, to look at you in no clothes."

"Cheers." I take a large sip. The bubbles dance against my tongue and a rush goes to my head as I swallow.

I have a feeling this is going to be quite a night.

We pull up at the hotel in Hollywood, which is hosting the launch event in their ballroom. The driver gets out to open our door and Jay looks back at me.

"Take my hand, Holly. I promise I won't let go until you're happy for me to."

God, what am I letting myself in for?

I nod and slip my hand into his.

The door opens and I'm blinded by flashing lights as Jay helps me out of the limo.

"Thank you," he says to the driver, who smiles and nods at me before closing the door.

There's a large red carpet leading to the hotel entrance. On one side is a sea of journalists with microphones and notepads and photographers flashing their cameras. On the other side is a temporary backdrop wall showing the perfume logo. There's the frosted glass heart, and Capture for the female bottle, and a frosted glass crescent moon shape for the men's version, Protect. The two bottles fit together and look like a piece of modern art.

A loud hum of excited chatter is coming from the reporters as they interview the guests walking the carpet, and they pose for photos in front of the backdrop. I'm about to overheat when Jay's fingers stroke my hand inside his, calming me. We walk along the carpet together and his name is called all around us.

"Jay! Jay! Over here. Clara from *Celeb Central* magazine." A young woman in a tight black dress thrusts a microphone toward us.

"Jay, it's a pleasure to see you and looking so handsome tonight," she gushes. Her eyes look to me and a flash of recognition crosses them. "Jay, are we correct in thinking that your lovely date here is the same lady we featured in a recent issue?" Her eyebrows shoot up as she looks at him.

"Yes, you're right, I'm Holly," I say confidently, surprising myself. It must be the champagne courage from the limo.

Clara turns her microphone to me, shocked that I can speak. I look up at Jay and he's smiling at me, his eyes bright and amused.

"So, Holly, did you meet Jay on a flight you were working on, as rumor would lead us to believe?" she asks enthusiastically.

"Yes, that's right," I glance up at Jay.

Clara looks down and notices our hands. "So, tell me, are you two dating?"

"Yes, Holly's my girlfriend," Jay says in his smooth, deep voice.

My stomach flutters at his voice saying those words again. I don't think I will ever tire of hearing them.

Clara looks like she can't believe her luck. "Steve, get a shot of the happy couple," she yells at the photographer with her.

Jay moves in close next to me and we smile as they take a stream of photos.

We spend some more time smiling for pictures, and Jay answers questions about the fragrance and his upcoming season of *Steel Force*. Every reporter asks who I am, and by the amount of times Jay says, 'Holly, my girlfriend,' I'm surprised I haven't orgasmed on the spot.

We finally make it to the main hotel entrance and are directed inside to the ballroom. Enchanting music is playing in the background. The lights are low, and the ceiling is covered in fairy lights, so it looks like a starry sky. Performers in silver leotards are hanging down on large crescent moons suspended from the ceiling. They are swaying to the music and doing elegant stretches and slow twirls. Around the room there are large displays of the fragrance bottles among red and white roses. Men and women are walking around giving out elegant-looking goody bags and samples. The room itself smells just like the female fragrance, an enchanting apple orchard in the moonlight. It's sweet and mysterious at the same time.

"This is incredible," I whisper to Jay.

He squeezes my hand in response as Anya Katiss approaches in a long silver dress, a dark-haired man with her.

"Holly, it's so lovely to see you again; you look stunning," she says, kissing me on both cheeks.

"Thank you, so do you," I smile.

I can't believe that I thought she and Jay were seeing each other after I met him. She's actually nice, and it's obvious that she doesn't fancy Jay. She's one of the few women I've met who doesn't check him out constantly.

"Jay." She turns and kisses him on both cheeks too. "I don't think we would have half the amount of people here if it wasn't for you coming onboard."

"I'm sure you would, Anya; you've done an outstanding job."

"Holly." Anya turns to me, smiling. "This is Doug." Her hand drapes over the arm of the man with her. He's very handsome and clean-shaven but looks rather stern.

He extends his hand to me. "Anya's agent," he says before his mouth returns to a firm line.

"Holly," I say back, shaking his hand with my free hand, the other still entwined with Jay's.

"Right, we will see you later," Anya says as she goes off to greet an incoming guest, her arm linked with Doug's.

He's so different than Anya. She's all smiles and engaging with everybody, and he hangs back, looking grumpy.

"What's Doug's problem?" I ask Jay.

"Doug? Oh, he's alright once you get to know him. He's just very protective of Anya. He relaxes more when he's not in crowds."

"Did Stefan not want to come tonight?" I ask, thinking that Doug is here with Anya, but Stefan didn't come with Jay.

"No, he comes sometimes, but he prefers to pass on the events if he can."

"Do you usually bring a date?"

"I would come with a colleague, or someone Stefan knows who has a mutual need for a plus one as well," Jay smiles and nods a greeting to a passing guest.

"So, not like a proper date then?" I probe.

"Holly." Jay's voice has a warning edge to it. "You are the first date whom I care about. Satisfied?" He eyes me and I nod, tipping my head to one side.

"For now." I smile.

He shakes his head at me, but his eyes look amused.

The next hour passes in a blur as more people arrive. We have a few drinks and Jay chats with what seems like everyone, introducing me as his girlfriend. There are more than a few put out female faces when he says it. The performers do some acrobatics displays, much to the delight of all the guests, and there's a steady stream of drinks and food being served around the room.

"Holly, I have to go up on stage in a moment with Anya to do the presentation," Jay whispers in my ear.

"Okay." I smile and let go of his hand. He studies my face.

"Go." I roll my eyes. "I'll be fine."

He gives me a kiss on the lips before disappearing through the crowd toward the stage at the front of the room. I take a sip of my drink and look around at the décor. This really is incredible; they've done a fantastic job, and it's packed with guests.

"Busy, isn't it?" I look to my side as Doug comes to join me. He stands next to me, looking up at the performers above us as he takes a sip of his drink.

"Yes, it is." I nod. I'm too busy studying him now to look at the performers.

The music is turned down, and the room falls silent as Anya and Jay start the presentation on the stage. I watch Jay captivating the audience as he walks about on the stage, talking about the fragrance and how hard Anya has worked.

"You know the break-in at Jay's house couldn't have come at a better time?" Doug says as he watches Anya speaking.

"Pardon?"

I can't have heard him right.

"It was good publicity for the launch." He shrugs. "Put Jay back on the front page just as we were about to release the fragrances."

My stomach churns and I lower my glass, not able to drink any more.

"It was awful," I mumble, remembering Jay's stressed face at his mum and dad's house when he got the news.

"Oh, I'm sure it was a bit unpleasant," Doug says, "but nothing was taken, and look at all the people who've turned up tonight as a result."

I look at him, disgusted by what I'm hearing. "I can't believe you would say that!" I glare at him, my jaw clenching.

He looks at me. "Oh, don't take it personally, Holly. It's just business, that's all. I want what's best for Anya," he says, then he takes another sip of his drink.

"Excuse me. I think I need some air!" I snap, passing a server with a tray of canapes as I turn to leave.

What nerve!

I can't believe he would say such a thing. Maybe this is what Jay was talking about when he said some people are only interested in their own agendas. A sickness creeps over me and the hairs stand up on my neck. Just how far would Doug go for Anya? Someone paid Ryan Baker to follow me and break in when we were out. Surely, he wouldn't? But Jay said he's very protective of Anya, and Doug himself said he wants what's best for her.

I swallow down my growing nausea and stride across the room. I'm less than halfway across when a panicked voice screams.

"Somebody help! He's choking!"

Chapter 21

I WHIP MY HEAD around in the direction the scream came from. There's a commotion coming from a group of people who have turned away from the main stage.

"He can't breathe!" the same voice shouts.

I crane my neck to look through a small gap in the crowd. There's a man with dark hair clutching at his throat.

Oh my God... It's Doug!

Doug is choking!

"Let me through!" I shout as I push my way through the crowd toward him.

It's like swimming through tar, trying to reach him. So many people are in the way and just not moving. I finally break through to where he is. He's still clutching at his throat silently, his eyes wide and panicked. He looks me in the eye and my insides turn to ice at the fear in his eyes.

I know what I must do. They teach us what to do if someone chokes during flight training every year. My body moves on autopilot.

"Doug, can you cough for me?" I ask, looking straight into his eyes.

He shakes his head, his face growing redder.

"Oh my God, he's going to die," someone cries.

I take a deep breath.

"Okay, Doug, I need you to bend over for me. Right over so your head is by your knees, okay?" I instruct him in the calmest voice I can manage, while my heart hammers so hard in my chest I worry I might pass out.

He listens to me and bends forward. I raise my hand high above my head and bring my palm down hard between his shoulder blades. The loud *thump* echoes in my ears and my hand burns as the blood rushes to it.

Nothing happens, so I raise my hand again and strike him harder. The sickening thump is met with silence again.

His lips are turning blue. I must keep going. *Three, four, five,* I count in my head.

After five back blows, Doug is still choking.

Cold sweat beads in my hairline. It isn't working. I've got to try something else. I don't have long before he will lose consciousness, and I know that means his odds are even worse. I have to get out whatever is blocking his windpipe.

I push my hip into his back and wrap my arms around his waist, pulling him up against me, making a fist with one hand and wrapping it inside the other. With all my strength, I pull inwards and upwards as fast as I can. Doug is getting heavier against me, his arms now hanging by his sides.

No, no, no.

I screw my eyes up and use all my force to do the same movement again. Nothing is working. I'm going to lose him.

"Oh my God, he's dead! Where's the ambulance?" someone wails.

Come on, Doug! Please!

I force my fist up and into his torso again.

There's a loud gasp from the crowd. Doug's stomach contracts underneath my arms as his body is overcome with violent, racking coughs and gasps for air.

"It's out! It's come out!" a voice shouts.

My ears are ringing as I stand with my arms still around his body, my heart throwing itself around inside my chest. Doug's gasps are slowing down to deep breaths as he grows steadier on his feet. I keep one arm around the front of his body and move to his side so I can see his face.

"Doug?"

His face is returning to its normal pink color. His wild eyes lock on mine as he squeezes my hand in his, deep shaky breaths still preventing him from talking.

"It's okay, Doug. Just take some nice deep breaths, okay?" My voice sounds so calm, but inside I'm freaking out.

Al I could see before was Doug, but now as I glance around us, there's a sea of relieved faces staring back.

Then someone claps and the sound of my heartbeat in my ears is drowned out by clapping and cheers.

It's surreal.

I turn my face away, back to Doug, who has straightened himself up. No one else can see it, but his hand is shaking in mine as the magnitude of what just happened to him sets in.

"Doug!" Anya breaks through the crowd and crashes into him, her face streaming with tears as she grips on to him.

His eyes look into mine one last time before he lets go of my hand and wraps it around Anya, who is stroking his face between her fingers and showering his cheeks with kisses.

"Holly!"

I turn blindly toward Jay's voice as he wraps me in his arms and draws me against his chest. I bury my face into him as my body shakes, the adrenaline it created declining.

Jay's warm arms feel like the safest place on earth right now.

"It's okay, baby; I've got you," he whispers into my hair. "I've got you. I've got you."

He keeps whispering to me until I force myself to take a deep breath and open my eyes, searching out Doug. He's still standing in the same spot, looking shell-shocked. Anya is clinging to his arm as the paramedics who have arrived check him over.

"Let's take you to the hospital," the female paramedic says. "Always best to get checked out after something like this. You'll feel sore for a few days, but I would say it's just some bruising from the abdominal thrusts you had performed on you. It doesn't look like anything is broken."

Anya is nodding and focusing on the paramedic. "Yes, of course. Come on, Doug. Let's go get you seen at the hospital."

Doug opens his mouth, his voice coming out hoarse. "Anya, this is your event. You stay here. I'll go. It's fine."

"Douglas Thornhill, you're infuriating!" Anya scowls. "I will not let you go alone. You idiot." She glares at him. "I love you! You could have died. Now let's go," she cries as she steers him behind the paramedics and out of the ballroom.

I swear his face almost looks more shocked now than it did when he was choking.

Anya loves Doug?

"Holly?"

I take my eyes off Anya and Doug and lift them up to Jay's face. He's looking down at me, his eyes full of concern, his beautiful heart shining down in them. His caring arms are still wrapped around me, supporting me.

Anya's declaration of love to Doug has just cemented in me what I already knew.

I am in love with Jay and I have been for a long time.

My eyes search his and I swear it must be so obvious in the way I look at him.

"Come on, Berry." His lips dust over my forehead. "Let me take you home."

The limo comes back to pick us up and we ride back to Jay's house with me curled up on his lap, his arms around me and his lips pressed against my hair. I don't say anything and neither does he.

He carries me in through the front door and straight up to his bedroom, before sitting down on the edge of the bed with me on his lap, still wrapped in his arms.

"Talk to me, Holly." His voice is soft as his fingertips touch my chin, turning my face toward him. His blue eyes burn into mine and I can't hold it in any longer. I shake uncontrollably, sobs escaping my mouth as tears run down my cheeks.

"Hey, hey." He kisses my tear-soaked cheeks. "It's okay, baby; I've got you."

My throat is thick as I try to swallow the lump that's stuck there.

"I thought he was going to die. Nothing was working." I bring my shaking hands up to my face. Jay takes them inside his and steadies them.

"But he didn't. You saved his life, Holly. You did that," Jay says, bringing my hands up to his lips and kissing them.

"Why can't I stop shaking?" I search Jay's eyes for an answer.

"It's the shock, Holly. Your body reacted at the time and now your mind is catching up."

I look at him. He's so in control, his voice so calm, that my tears slow down.

"I feel so silly," I say, looking down at my hands.

"Holly, you are not being silly. You're reacting to something traumatic that just happened." He kisses my forehead and I take a deep breath.

"I bet you wouldn't cry and shake like me if it had been you."

"I'm not as strong as you think I am, Holly." His voice sounds strained, and I look into his eyes, which have clouded over as though he's lost in a memory somewhere.

"What do you mean?" I study his face.

"I could barely hold myself together when I saw Rob." His voice cracks before he composes himself.

"You were the one who…"

"Yes, I was there." His haunted eyes meet mine. "And I will never forget that moment for as long as I live."

"Oh, Jay." I bring my forehead to his and rest them together, hoping he will continue and finally let me in so we can face the ghosts of his past together.

"I'm just saying, Holly, what you're feeling is normal." He clears his throat, the moment gone once again. "Let's get you ready for bed. You must be exhausted."

Jay carries me into the bathroom and turns the shower on. Steam fills the room as I take off the green dress and peel the stick-on bra off while his back is turned.

This isn't how I imagined ending the night.

I slide my panties down my legs and step out of them. Jay's taken his suit off and is standing in front of me. He doesn't look at my body, instead keeping his eyes fixed on my face.

"Come on, Berry." He takes my hand and leads me under the hot spray.

It's hotter than I would ever have it, but I finally feel warmer as my shivers subside. Jay picks up the puff and puts shower gel on it, washing me tenderly, only taking his eyes off mine if he has to.

There are black drip marks on my stomach. I must look like a clown with all the tears, making my makeup run down my face. Jay follows my gaze and reaches for a washcloth, rinsing it under the hot water and squeezing it out.

"You're so beautiful," he says as he wipes the washcloth across my cheeks in long, slow strokes.

I stand there and let him wash my face free of all my makeup. It feels like one of the most intimate moments we've ever shared. I'm unable to take my eyes off him as he locks his with mine.

"I'm in love with you, Holly," he says as his eyes search mine.

Time stops as I stand frozen to the spot with my mouth open, the water running down over both of us.

"Jay…"

He puts a finger to my lips. "You don't have to say it back. I just needed to tell you."

He leans toward me, his body hot against mine as he replaces his finger with his lips and kisses me.

I love this man. How could I not? He's incredible. I never stood a chance. I love this man so much and he just told me he loves me too.

All the emotion of the evening combined with Jay's words peak inside me as I wrap my arms around his neck and kiss him back, my tongue exploring his mouth, desperate to stroke and taste his.

Desperate to feel connected.

"Holly," he murmurs against my lips, shaking his head. "Let's get you to bed. It's been a crazy night."

I press myself further into his body; I need to feel him surround me. I need his touch on my skin. I need to feel alive.

"I need this, Jay, please," I plead against his mouth.

His eyes meet mine and understanding flashes in them as his resolve falls away. His fingers trace across my face as he kisses me again, slow and deep. I raise my hands up and stroke up and down the back of his head.

"Holly," he moans, deepening his kisses, still cradling my face between his hands.

I feel safe here, in his arms. The drama of the evening fades away more with each kiss he gives me. He's like magic, kissing all my pain away. My pulse is beating between my legs. I'm wet and aching for him, the desire to feel close and connected overwhelming.

I lift one leg and slide it up around his waist; Jay's hand goes to it and holds it there. His other snakes around the back of my neck as he looks at me, his eyes questioning. I stroke my hands up into his hair again and hold his gaze. His eyes stay on mine as he slides inside me slowly. My breath leaves my body and I sigh.

"Jay."

"Yes, Berry?" he says as he slides back out and pauses.

"I love you too." My voice cracks with emotion, tears streaming down my cheeks again.

His eyes widen, his gaze sparkling into mine as he slides back inside me, and his lips find mine again. The salt from my tears washes away with our kisses. I moan as our bodies meet again and again, each thrust more delicious than the last.

"You're incredible, Holly," Jay whispers as he sinks into me.

"You're the incredible one!" I cry back as the electricity builds between us.

"You make me so happy," Jay moans into our kiss as he pulls me down to meet him again.

We move together, him sliding into me and me sinking down onto him, our lips pressed together as each thrust grows harder and faster, more urgent than the last. It's not long before a familiar tightening spreads throughout my entire body.

"I'm going to come, Jay!" I pant as the intense pressure takes over my body, past the point of no return.

He quickens his pace in response and my body dives over the edge as I come hard against him, crying out his name against his lips.

"You're amazing, Holly," Jay pants, kissing me as I ride my orgasm out over him. I shudder with each wave as I contract around him. He grows harder inside me as more heat ignites between us. "So incredible," he groans as his body convulses and he comes inside me, the air knocked from his lungs. His chest expands against me as he sucks in a deep breath. "Oh God, Holly," he moans, kissing me harder as he empties inside me.

I clench hard to draw it all out to me, wanting every part of him he's willing to share. He sighs as his breathing slows down and we stay connected, just kissing each other and looking into each other's eyes.

"My Holly, my beautiful Holly," he murmurs against my lips.

I can't help being transported back to that first night we spent together. It was here in the shower that he gave me such a precious gift, adoring my body and rebuilding my trampled self-worth.

Now he's here for me again when I need him most.

His words are soothing different pains tonight, but loving and healing me nonetheless. I have never met anyone who has demonstrated just how incredible love is. How it can transport you from yourself and help you find connection in all the beauty and energy around you.

Not until I met him.

I sink into his kisses under the water again and just hope that soon he'll let me be there for him too.

Chapter 22

We sleep late the next morning. Jay was right. All the events of the previous evening exhausted me. My body was drained. Jay dried me after our shower and carried me to bed. I was asleep within moments of my head hitting the pillow.

"Here." Jay hands me a mug of peppermint tea.

"Thanks." My fingers brush against his and a buzz of energy runs between us.

I sink back into the plush gray cushions of the sofa as Jay sits down next to me, lifting my legs as he does, and resting them over his lap. Before he can say anything, his phone rings and he picks it up off the coffee table.

"Hey, Stefan."

He's already spoken to Stefan this morning and told him about what happened last night.

Why is he calling again so soon?

"Okay, what channel?" Jay leans forward in the seat, reaching for the TV remote and flicking it on. "Yeah, I've got it on," he says, and I follow his gaze to the screen. There's a news reporter talking. Next to her is a picture of Jay and me on the red carpet last night. Jay turns the sound up and I hold my breath as I listen.

"Last night was the launch party for model, Anya Katiss' new fragrance line. Jay Anderson is the face of the male version. However, things took a dramatic turn when her agent, Doug Thornhill, began choking. Eyewitnesses at the event said they feared he would have died if it hadn't been for the quick-thinking actions of Jay's girlfriend, Holly Havers. Miss. Havers performed lifesaving back blows and abdominal thrusts on Mr. Thornhill."

The camera cuts to a recorded video from outside the hotel last night. A female guest is being interviewed, her eyes wide as her hands switch between running through her hair and covering her mouth, shock clear on her face.

"It was awful. He was going blue and floppy. I thought he was going to die right in front of me. Holly saved him. She was incredible. She knew what to do."

The camera returns to the news reporter in the studio.

"Jay and Miss. Havers confirmed they met a few months ago on an Atlantic Airways flight from London Heathrow to LAX, where Miss. Havers works as a long-haul flight attendant. Her training certainly came in handy last night. Mr. Thornhill was taken to hospital

to get checked over, but our sources say he left this morning."

Jay flicks the TV onto mute as our picture disappears and the reporter moves on to the next story. He looks across at me as he talks to Stefan again.

"No, she won't be doing that. If they've got a problem, they can take it up with me." His jaw tenses. "Yeah, okay, talk later." He hangs up and blows out a deep breath as he strokes his palm along my legs.

"What won't *she* be doing?" I ask, looking over at him.

"The press want an exclusive interview with you. They've been calling Stefan all morning."

"Oh." My stomach knots at the idea of going back over every detail.

"I don't want them hounding you, Holly," Jay says, his brow creasing.

"Always trying to protect me." I smile over at him and his face softens.

"I have to, Holly. The idea of anything happening to you..." His voice trails off and he swallows, staring into space.

My heart breaks for him. He's so strong and self-assured on the outside, but inside he's scarred by the loss of someone so close to him, someone he loved. No wonder he wants to protect me and feel in control of the situation.

I lean over and squeeze his thigh through his jeans.

"Nothing's going to happen to me. Besides, there'll be someone far more interesting they will want to talk to soon."

He looks over at me. "They don't give up that easily, Holly. Although, I have to disagree; you're extremely interesting to me." He manages a small smile.

"Charmer." I giggle.

"Is it working?" He raises one eyebrow.

"Oh, you charmed me a long time ago." I smile as he moves toward me and brings his face to within an inch of mine.

"Is that so?" His breath tickles my lips.

"It's so," I whisper.

Jay leans forward and kisses me softly. I will never get enough of him kissing me like this, or any way for that matter. I sigh as our kiss deepens and his hands move to hold me around the waist.

"God!" My heart leaps into my chest.

Jay throws his head back and chuckles.

"You're going to have to get used to the new bell, Berry."

"Your old man bell, you mean?" I tease as he jumps up from the sofa and heads to the front door.

He checks the camera before buzzing whoever it is in. I get up and walk over to the front door, standing next to him as he opens it.

"Anya, Doug?" I stare, not expecting them at all. Anya has her arm entwined with Doug's, and she's smiling.

Jay stands to one side so they can come in, closing the door behind them.

"Hey, Anya." He kisses her on the cheek and then throws his arms around Doug. "Hey, man, I don't think I've ever been so glad to see you."

"Ha, likewise," Doug says as he smiles.

He is very handsome when he's not busy being grumpy. His face looks a lot more relaxed, lighter somehow. He seemed so tense when I first met him yesterday.

"Holly." Anya squeezes me in her arms. Her long dark hair presses against my face and I smell her perfume.

My shoulders relax; it isn't Capture.

I don't want to smell that perfume again anytime soon in case it brings back memories of last night.

I look over her shoulder at Doug. Maybe their visit is just what I needed. Seeing Doug here, alive and healthy and a normal color, helps to make last night seem like a distant memory.

Anya lets me go and I'm left with just Doug to greet. I stand there awkwardly until he extends a hand toward me. I place mine in his, expecting him to shake it. Instead, he pulls me toward him, and I'm wrapped in his embrace. His warm chest rises and falls against mine as he rubs me on the back.

"Holly." He draws back, his eyes watering. "How can I ever thank you?"

I stare back into his eyes. "You just did, Doug."

He studies me. "You've no idea how grateful I am for what you did."

"How grateful we both are," Anya says as she puts her arm around Doug's waist, gazing into his eyes.

"It was nothing," I say, watching them with interest.

Jay slips his hand around my waist. "So, everything was okay at the hospital?" he asks.

"Yes, he just has some bruises that they said will heal." Anya doesn't take her eyes off Doug's as she answers.

"I'm sorry," I mumble.

Doug's eyes snap to mine.

"Don't you dare apologize, Holly. I'm alive because of you." He beams at me.

I can't get over the change in him. I like this alternative version of Doug, even if it took a near-death experience to bring it out of him.

"You not only saved my life, but you gave me a better one," he continues, looking at Anya, who kisses him full on the lips in response.

"I don't think I would have ever declared my love for Doug if he hadn't almost died." Anya laughs.

Doug looks at her.

"Oh, come on, babe, you're always so focused on work and uptight. I never thought you'd feel the same about me. You were all work, work, work," she says, shaking her head.

"I'm so focused on you, Anya." Doug takes her face in his hands. "I've always wanted the best for you because you mean so much to me. I thought it was obvious. I knew I wasn't good enough for you, so I would never have said anything."

Jay's watching them with a smile on his face. They've forgotten we are even here. The way they're looking at each other right now, I'm expecting them to tear each other's clothes off in the entryway.

"We're so happy for you both," Jay says, which brings their eyes back to us.

Anya blushes as she leans her head against Doug's shoulder.

"Sorry." She grins. "We've spent all night talking; you'd think we would have said it all by now."

"I don't think you should ever stop telling someone how much you love them once you find each other," Jay says as he looks down at me.

My stomach flutters in response as his eyes catch mine.

"We just wanted to come and say thank you, Holly," Doug says. "I realize I must have sounded like such a cold-hearted jerk when I talked about the break-in." He looks embarrassed and clears his throat. "Listen, I know they caught the guy who did it and there's still some unanswered questions. I've got some contacts. I'll ask around and see what I can find out for you."

Jay pats him on the shoulder. "Thanks, we appreciate it."

"Anything I can do, Holly," Doug adds, looking at me. "I mean, anything at all, you only have to ask."

"Thank you, Doug." I look him in the eye and smile.

"Right, we better leave you guys to it," Anya says. "I'm taking Doug to have a rest and I have a real estate agent coming to the house this afternoon."

"You moving?" Jay raises his brows.

"Yes!" She beams, looking at Doug. "Today is the start of our new life together. I want to start it in a new home that we choose together."

Doug rolls his eyes at us, but he's smiling. "It seems I'm under strict orders today."

Anya taps him on the nose with a long, elegant finger. "Yes, you are. The doctor put me in charge of you to make sure you rest. So, let's go." She smiles at him.

We say our goodbyes and wave them off. Jay shuts the door, and his eyes catch mine in delight.

"That was crazy!" I put a hand over my mouth as I process what just happened.

"Tell me about it. She's in love with Doug?" Jay shakes his head in disbelief. "I did not see that coming. He's been her agent for years. All this time they've both felt the same, but neither said anything? Nuts." He sighs, running his hand through his hair.

"So, Doug is who Anya was in love with when you dated her?"

"Hardly dated, Holly. More like, accompanied to a few events over a couple of months. It was Doug's idea, actually."

"Doug was happy to watch the woman he loved spend time with another man, because he thought you were better for her career? Or more in her league?" I say in disbelief.

"He loves her, Holly. He was willing to forfeit his own happiness for hers. Or what he thought would lead to hers anyway." Jay shrugs as though it's no big deal.

"Yeah... I guess when you put it like that," I say, looking at Jay.

What would I be willing to do for him?

If I knew I could do something that was best for him, but I would suffer, would I do it?

I would. I know I would.

I would do anything for his happiness, no doubt about it. I understand Doug's motives now and I'm sure he had nothing to do with the break-in, especially now that he's offered his help. The break-in was more personal. Nothing was missing, but something was being searched for. I just wish I knew what.

"Hey, baby, I just need to go call Stefan about work," Jay says as he reads a message on his phone.

"Okay. I'm going to text Rach," I say as I flop back down onto the sofa.

Jay leans down and lifts my chin so his lips can reach mine.

"Won't be long, Berry," he says, kissing me before disappearing down the hallway to his office.

I watch him walk away in his jeans and T-shirt, his feet bare against the floor. I smile to myself; sexy doesn't even come close.

I pick my phone up and type a message to Rach.

Me: Hey babe, how's it going? Are you in Washington now? Lots to catch up on when we both get home!

My phone beeps with her reply.

Rachel: Hey, Holls, Matt just texted me! He's been speaking to Stefan. WTAF!!!?? You stopped a guy choking? You're like Superwoman! Just about to check out for the flight home, so I will call you tomorrow. Can't wait to see you in a few days when you get back. That's if he lets you leave! Lol.

I groan. I've got a few days left in LA before my leave is over and I have to go home and back to work. I've tried not to think about what will happen when that day comes. The thought of saying goodbye to Jay and going back to not seeing him again for days, or even weeks, makes my stomach twist in pain. I slouch back against the sofa, contemplating how hard saying goodbye will be.

My phone rings. 'Matt' lights up on the screen.

"Hey, Matt, your ears must have been burning," I joke.

"What? Oh, tell me Stefan has been talking about me again?" he asks excitedly.

"No, Rach." I smile.

"Oh God," he groans. "What have I done now?"

"Nothing." I chuckle. "She just told me you texted her, that's all."

"Of course I did. I couldn't believe it when Stefan told me! How are you holding up?"

I blow out a breath.

"Okay now, thanks. I was pretty out of sorts last night, but I feel a lot better today. Doug and Anya just came to visit. It helped to see him again, you know, when he's not choking."

"Oh, Holls, you went through something difficult. You might find you're fine, and then out of the blue something will make you think of it. Just know that I'm here for you if you ever need to talk. Just like you were there for me last year."

I smile as Matt comforts me. Memories come back to me about the time he and his crew performed CPR on a passenger who had a heart attack. Unfortunately, he didn't make it. Matt took it hard.

"Thanks, Matt, I appreciate it. You're a good egg, you know."

"Like a Fabergé one from the Queen's royal collection?" He jokes.

"If one of those even exists, then yes." I laugh.

"You know what else this smart egg has done?"

"What?" I can't help suspicion creeping into my voice.

"Swapped another flight so I can come out to LA and work the flight you're going home on."

"Really?" A grin plasters itself across my face.

"Yes. I figured you may need a shoulder to cry on when you leave that gorgeous hunk of yours behind. That's if you can even walk after two weeks of being with him. I may need to carry you onto the plane!"

I laugh out loud. "Matt, you and your filthy mind."

"What? You'd miss me hatching out these thoughts. Get it, hatching... egg." He titters. "Besides, I wouldn't be able to walk after two weeks with a hunk like Jay."

"I'll remember to ask how your walking is after you and Stefan come back from Hong Kong in a couple of weeks then, shall I?" I tease.

"Oh, Holls! I can't wait. We've booked a lush hotel, award-winning spa, the works. If he doesn't feel swept off his feet at the end of it, then I don't know what will work."

"That sounds amazing, Matt. I'm sure you'll have a great time together." I smile as his excitement rubs off on me.

"I guess I will see you in a couple of days then?"

"Yes, I can't wait!"

"Mwah!" Matt blows me a noisy kiss down the phone.

"Mwah, to you too." I smile as I hang up.

The next two days pass by in a blur of lovemaking, swimming, eating out, and walking around small local hidden gems, away from the crowds.

"What's the plan for later today, Berry?" Jay asks as he pours two glasses of a smoothie he's just blended.

I lean across the kitchen counter so I can see him better. He's wearing a pair of jogging bottoms low down on his hips. Every muscle on his bare, tanned torso is visible. And his hair is ruffled from where I've just had my hands in it, as he woke me up in his favorite way. I'm still throbbing from the intense orgasm he gave me. I swear if there was such a thing as a school for oral sex, then Jay must have graduated with full marks. Hell, he probably founded the school.

He smirks as he sees me checking him out. "Ready for round two already, baby?"

"I'm ready for a shower. I must reek of sex."

"I like you smelling of sex," Jay says as he comes up behind me and nips my ear with his teeth, holding my hips and grinding himself against my bum.

I laugh. "You would say that. It means you must have gotten lucky."

"Anytime with you and I'm lucky, Holly." He chuckles.

"Smooth, Jay, real smooth." I turn and stroke his chin with my fingers.

"I am, aren't I?" His eyes dance with delight as he rubs his chin into my hand. He's shaved this morning and the designer stubble is gone, for now anyway.

"Not what I meant." I roll my eyes at him. "I don't see you freshly shaven often; trying to look younger, are you? What with your old man, extra loud doorbell and all?" I tease as I lean forward and lick the smooth skin along his jaw.

"Well, it's keeping up with my girlfriend. You know she's three years younger than me! From an entirely different generation than me, if you believe what she says." Jay opens his eyes wide, pretending to look shocked.

My shoulders shake up and down as I try to hold in my laugh.

Jay's eyes light up.

"Oh, I think she needs a tickle to help get that giggle out!" he says as his hands go to the backs of my knees.

"No!" I screech and dart away from him before he can make my legs give way underneath me. I seek safety on the other side of the sofa as he eyes me with a smirk.

"You can't evade me forever, Berry. You know I'll catch you."

"You wouldn't be able to keep up, old man!" I sing as I run out to the pool deck.

"You're going to regret that!" Jay shouts as he chases after me.

I'm laughing as I skirt around the edge of the pool. I stop on the other side and look back for Jay.

That's funny, he should be there.

I rise onto my tiptoes, searching for him. There's a chuckle behind me. I try to run, but it's too late. Strong arms grab me around the waist and the ground becomes sky as my feet slip from under me.

"Payback time for my parents' house," Jay shouts as we both plunge into the pool.

Water rushes over my head and into my ears before I break the surface and gasp.

"You git!" I splutter as I splash at Jay, who's looking rather smug, and dare I say it? Incredibly sexy, all covered in water.

"Just returning the favor." He grins as he splashes me back.

"Oh, really?" I squeal, splashing him again and getting it in his mouth.

"Alright, alright, truce!" He coughs as he swims closer to me.

I swim backwards, holding his gaze until we are both pressed up against each other at the edge of the pool, the sexual chemistry sizzling between us.

"You know, at least you don't smell of sex anymore." His eyes crinkle at the corners as he smiles at me. "For now, anyway," he adds as he reaches his thumb up and pulls my bottom lip down. He looks at it for a second before leaning forward and taking it between his teeth.

I hold my breath as he pulls it back and then lets it go. Then his mouth is on mine, his tongue stroking, lips sucking.

I kiss him back with all I have.

This man, his humor, his heart, he couldn't be more amazing.

"I love you," I confess between kisses.

Jay pauses and looks at me.

"I love you too, Holly."

His kisses slow down and become tender. I let myself float on a wave of bliss. Right here, in this moment, everything is perfect.

A bang inside the house, followed by the radio being turned on, draws our attention.

"Maggie," Jay groans. "I forgot she was coming this morning."

I gasp. "Jay, we're soaking wet! This is worse than last time I saw her, and I was barely wearing anything."

"At least you've got shorts on this time," Jay says, only just keeping a straight face as he looks down at my pajama top and shorts set I'm wearing.

"It's going to be see-through!"

He chuckles. "We can sneak in when she goes down to the office."

"Okay, that's one of your better ideas," I say as we watch through the glass.

We don't have to wait long before Maggie heads down toward the office, apron on, duster in hand, singing out loud to the song on the radio.

"Okay, let's go!" Jay grabs my hand and we climb out of the pool, peeling off our soaked clothes and throwing them onto a sun bed so we don't drench the floor inside.

I follow him on my tiptoes through the house and upstairs to his room, my heart beating wildly in my chest, worried in case Maggie sees us naked and dripping wet at any moment.

"Oh my God!" I shriek as we reach the safety of Jay's bathroom.

"That was close." Jay's eyes are bright.

"I can't believe we're sneaking around in your own house." I laugh.

Jay turns the shower on and pulls me in with him. "I can't believe how much fun a younger woman can be," he jokes, and I swat him on the chest.

"You are an idiot, Jay Anderson." I laugh, looking into his eyes.

"But I'm your idiot." He grins at me, before leaning in to kiss me and finish what we started.

I spray my perfume and am ready to head downstairs, showered, dressed, and expertly fucked again. Luckily, the shower muffled our voices as I know how much Jay loves it when I talk dirty to him and I was feeling generous.

"Hey, baby, I've got to go on a conference call with Stefan," Jay says, checking his phone. "Shouldn't be more than half an hour. The studio wants to talk filming schedule for next season."

"Oh, okay." I smile at him. "I'll see you soon."

He kisses me, one hand reaching around to squeeze my bum before heading downstairs.

I turn back to the mirror. My eyes are bright. I've never seen myself look so happy. I pick up the watch Jay gave me and go to put it on, but it slips, and I drop it on the carpet. It lands upside down and as I pick it up, there's an inscription I haven't seen before. *How did I not notice?* Jay never said anything about it.

The scripted letters make me draw in a sweet breath. *'Time with you is my happiness.'*

There's a lump in my throat as I read the inscription over and over.

Jay says I make him happy but seeing it like this makes me really believe it. I blink back tears. I am so lucky. I've met the love of my life. How many people can say that? I take a deep breath and compose myself as I fasten the watch on my wrist and head downstairs to the kitchen where Maggie is busy mopping the floor.

"Hello, Holly, love." She smiles up at me.

"Hi, Maggie." I grin back. "How are you doing?"

"Oh, I'm good, love. I'm good. Just had my grandchildren for the weekend. I'm pooped." She laughs, shaking her head.

I like Maggie; she's so warm and easy to talk to. We chat longer and she tells me all about her grandson and granddaughter and what their favorite things are.

"Okay, I'm done now. The floor needed that mop today; there were puddles all over it," Maggie murmurs, taking her apron off and squeezing me on the arm as I bite my lip to hide my laugh.

"See you soon, Holly." She smiles.

"Take care, Maggie."

"Oh, I almost forgot. There was a letter for you this morning. Where did I put it? Ah-ha!" She plucks a brown envelope out from under the vase of flowers in the hallway and hands it to me before heading out through the door.

"Cheerio, love."

"Bye, Maggie," I call as I study the envelope my hand.

This is weird; who would send me mail here? The envelope just has *Holly* printed on the front in thick black marker.

I tear it open and pull out a single sheet of paper. It's a copy of a photograph. It's of Jay. He looks about twenty, but there's no mistaking it's him, with his sun-kissed hair and piercing blue eyes. He has his arms wrapped around someone I don't recognize.

Why would someone send me a photo of Jay from years ago? This must be a mistake. I turn the piece of paper over. There's writing on the back.

No... This can't be right.

A coursing pain constricts my chest, crushing the air out of my lungs as I read the words.

Chapter 23
Jay

10 years Earlier

"WHO'D HAVE THOUGHT IT, *eh, Anderson? People can't get enough of your ugly mug. Hollywood must be blind!" Rob elbows me in the ribs.*

"Ouch." I laugh, pretending to look hurt. "I know I'm not your type, but—" Rob's hand clamps over my mouth.

"Stop talking; you're ruining it."

"What are you going on about?" I ask, pulling the hand away. I follow Rob's gaze across the room to a tall, raven-haired woman with a killer body in a figure-hugging red dress.

We've come to a party for a well-known fashion house. They've just signed me to be the face of their entire new season of menswear. I shoot in a week's time. It's an amazing opportunity and my eyes almost bulged right out of my head when I saw how much they were offering as payment. Rob insisted on coming along as my plus one to play the supportive childhood friend card. We both know it's got far more to do with the number of single women that come to these events.

"Why don't you go talk to her?" I whisper in Rob's ear. Just as I say it, the woman in the red dress looks over in our direction and smiles.

"Maybe after another drink. Don't want to look too keen," Rob says, brushing off my suggestion.

"Fine." I shrug my shoulders, knowing better than to argue. Rob's more stubborn than red wine on a white shirt.

"What you having this time?" I shout over the music as we cut through the crowd to get to the bar.

"Just a Pepsi."

I look at Rob with a raised brow. "There's a free bar, and you want a Pepsi? You remember I said I'd drive home, don't you?"

"I know," Rob shouts back, "but it's your night and you should be celebrating. I'll drive us. If you trust me with your car, that is?" A smirk crosses Rob's face, along with a silent challenge.

I never let anyone drive my car, so I know I'm being tested. My entire family jokes about it, saying I'm too uptight. It's not that at all; I'm just a bad passenger. I like to be the one in control. I think it stems from sitting in the back seat when my dad gave my aunt a driving lesson once. I swear my knuckles were so white. I thought they may drop off from lack of circulation at the end of the half-hour ride of terror. There's no way Rob will expect me to agree to it.

I narrow my eyes. "You're on!" I grin, throwing my keys at Rob's chest.

"Seriously?"

I nod and Rob pockets the keys before I can change my mind.

It's time I started loosening up a bit.

"Oh God," I groan, squeezing my eyes shut. My head feels like someone's crushing it in a vise. I run a hand up in my hair and it's met with wetness, warm and sticky.

What the hell?

I force my eyes open and stare through slitted lids at my fingers. They're red, covered in... blood? Is that blood? I try to sit forward but a crippling pain shoots across my chest, winding me, and I slump back, gasping air into my lungs.

Sirens blare in the distance. The smell of gas and something metallic makes my stomach lurch and I gulp hard, not wanting to throw up all over myself.

I wrench my eyes fully open; the searing pain in my head turns into a relentless pounding. It's the only part of my body I can feel; the rest is numb. I look down. My white shirt is covered in blood, as is the seat belt.

I'm in my car.

My head grows heavy and I slump in the seat.

The sirens are louder now. Help is coming. There must have been an accident, but I'm okay, I'm alive.

I'm...

I lurch forward in the seat as adrenaline floods my body.

Rob! I was in the car with Rob!

A sense of dread claws its way inside my body, taking over my soul.

There's only the sound of one set of rasping breaths in the car.

Mine.

I look across to the driver's seat.

"Rob?"

Silence.

"Rob...?"

Dark-blond hair matted with blood clumps around Rob's face.

"Rob...?" I lean over and shake my best friend.

My friend I've known since I was a kid. My friend I traded snacks with at break time. My friend I fell off my bike with, copied math homework from, went to my first underage club with, had my first drink with. My friend I don't know how to live without.

"Rob...!" I scream.

This can't be happening.
This can't be real.
Empty green eyes stare into space, all light from them gone.
No, no, no. Please God, not Rob. Why not me? Take me instead!
Fucking take me!
Strong hands surround me.
"We're here to help; can you tell me your name?" a faceless voice probes.
"He's in shock," they call out.
"We've got to get him out now. The tanks split. It's leaking everywhere," another voice shouts.
People are grabbing me now, pulling me away.
Away from Rob.
I fight back. I scream at them to stop.
They don't listen. They pull me away. Farther and farther away until I can't see Rob anymore.
A police officer asks something about a name as I'm strapped down onto a board.
My eyes dart back to the crumpled metal that used to be my car.
Emergency personnel are surrounding it, talking in hushed voices. One looks at another and drops their head to their chest with a defeated shake.
No.
This can't be real.
This is a nightmare. I'm going to wake up in a minute.
"What's her name?" a policeman asks.
Why is he talking to me? Why isn't he helping Rob?

"What's your girlfriend's name?" the same police officer says.

My lips move and words come out, but I have no idea who's saying them. It doesn't sound like me.

"She's not my girlfriend," the voice whispers. "She's my best friend."

"Her name's Robyn, Robyn Cooper."

Chapter 24
Holly

Present Day

OH, MY GOD.

My heart is beating hard, the sound of my blood rushing in my ears.

I read the words again.

Jay and Robyn, age 21.

I turn the photograph back over. The girl is smiling at the camera, her green eyes sparkling. Jay's eyes are full of love, gazing at her face. Her long golden-blond hair falls past her shoulders and glints in the sunshine.

It's like looking at a photo of myself at that age.

I swallow down the bubble of acid rising from my stomach as I put the photograph down onto the kitchen counter. My hands are shaking as they hover over it.

Rob's a girl? Jay always said Rob, and I just assumed Rob was a guy. But the face in the photo proves just how wrong I've been. The face with the shining green eyes. The face Jay is gazing at with an enormous smile.

Why didn't he tell me? All the times he's mentioned her but called her Rob, he must have known that I would think she was a guy. Why would he lie to me about it?

A cold dagger of realization stabs at my heart as the sickening truth becomes obvious. She wasn't just his best friend. She was his first true love. It's written all over his face by the way he's looking at her.

I take a deep breath, wiping my palms on my top. My head is spinning. Frantically searching for another plausible explanation. But there isn't one.

I look exactly like her.

Jay may be the love of my life, but I'm not his and I never will be.

It will always be Robyn.

My chest burns as I look at the photo. He must be with me because I look like her. She's his first love, the one he's never recovered from losing all those years ago. He doesn't love me, not really. He's in love with a memory of a girl that's not me, will never be me. He's in love with a ghost.

It makes sense, really. I thought he just needed time to talk about it. I never suspected there was more to it. Not like this. I swipe the heel of my hand against my wet cheeks.

It was too good to be true.

My legs are like jelly as I let out the breath I've been holding. A sound like an injured animal pushes its way from my body, from my heart.

I can't stay here. I need to think. I need to be on my own.

I dart my eyes over to the hallway that leads to Jay's office. It sounds like he's still on the phone with Stefan.

I stuff the picture back into the envelope and grip it in one hand.

Jay's car keys are sitting on the counter. My vision is blurred as I snatch them up and run out the door.

The thing about having your heart ripped from your chest is the initial shock of it can send you into denial. Your mind flails around looking for an explanation. Looking for any other reason, like you've got it wrong, that it can't be happening. Only it is happening, and there's not a thing you can do about it. Denial isn't your friend for long before you come crashing back down and your heart breaks all over again.

I push the gas pedal and the Ferrari's engine revs as I drive down a patch of straight road. Where I'm even going is anyone's guess. I just knew I couldn't stay there a second longer. I couldn't stay in Jay's house knowing that he lied to me. Knowing that all this time I've just been some kind of stand-in.

I glance at the envelope resting on top of the dashboard. My stomach lurches again, threatening to make me pull over and throw up at the side of the road.

A tapping noise gets on my nerves. It takes a minute to work out it's my own fingers on the steering wheel. *How can I not even know that I'm doing that?* I must be losing it. I don't even know what my body's doing anymore.

The road ahead of me is scrubland on one side and a rocky hillside on the other. At least I don't seem to have driven toward downtown LA. If I were stuck in traffic now, I would have a nervous breakdown and be screaming behind the wheel.

I glance at the speedometer. I'm going way faster than I thought, probably because the car drives so smoothly. Don't people always use that excuse when they get caught speeding? *'Sorry, Officer, I didn't realize how fast I was going.'*

I ease off the gas pedal and cruise along at a more respectable pace. It's beautiful here. It's a shame I can never think of, or even visit LA again. Not without it feeling like my heart has been fed to a pack of wild wolves, tearing chunks out of it while it still beats.

Fresh tears sting my eyes and I wipe at them angrily with one hand.

How did I end up here?

I was so stupid to think that Jay loved me for who I am. Maybe Simon was right to treat me the way he did and cheat on me. I mean, there must be something wrong with me. I'm never enough as I am. I'm always lacking something. Sexual confidence for Simon, and my entire soul for Jay.

My entire soul is wrong!

A crazy laugh escapes my lips. The only thing I have going for me is that I look like someone else.

I swipe at my tears again. I should have known this was too good to be true. Movie style romances don't happen to girls like me. I was an idiot to believe any different.

No matter what I do, hot tears keep burning my cheeks.

"For God's sake, just stop!" I shout and take both hands off the wheel to wipe my eyes.

A flash of something brown appears through the windshield.

I grab the steering wheel and pull it to the side, swerving to avoid an animal of some sort that's run into the road. The Ferrari's steering is sensitive, and I'm thrown hard to the side as the car spins out of control, the back of it twisting right around. The overwhelming sound of crunching metal is almost deafening as my hands grip onto the wheel.

My brain is spinning; I don't know which way is up. Dust and rocks fly up across the windshield before the glass shatters and my head flies into the side window. A dull *thud* sends shock waves through me.

Then everything goes black and there's only silence.

"She's waking up! Get the doctor, quick!"

My head is pounding. Where the hell am I? Was that Matt?

I try to open my eyes, but a jolt of pain shoots through my skull.

"Errrgg."

"What's that? Say it again, baby. I'm here," a gentle voice says.

A warm hand is holding mine. Whose is it? Jay's? Then there's another, warm and soft across my forehead. It's soothing and I sigh gently.

"I'm here, Holly. You're in the hospital. You had an accident, but you're going to be okay. I love you so much."

My eyelids feel like someone has glued them shut. I peel them open. It takes so much effort and I wince as a hammer attacks my head. This is like the world's worst hangover and then some. My eyes are so dry. I blink twice, trying to focus.

Beautiful, clear-blue eyes are staring at me. They're full of worry.

"Berry?" Fingertips belonging to the voice dust my cheek.

Jay.

My stomach twists.

Just seeing him, his familiar scent invading my senses, my body aching for his touch, it's all too much for my heart to bear. I love him. I love him more than anything. Knowing that he doesn't, and never will feel the same about me, is what being in hell must feel like.

"I can't do this," I whisper. The words come out gravelly and strained.

"Holly?" Confused blue eyes search mine.

This is awful. Knowing what is about to happen makes me wish I were somewhere else right now.

Anywhere else.

"Matt?" I say, trying to sit up to see him.

"I'm here, Holls, I'm here." Matt leaps to my side and stops me from sitting up. "You gave us all such a scare," he says as he smiles at me.

"I'm sorry." My eyes glance over at Jay, who is watching me intently, still stroking my hand in his.

"What were you doing, Holly? Where were you going?" Jay asks, his blue eyes wide as they search my face.

"Matt, could you give us a minute?" I ask.

"Of course, I'll wait outside." Matt squeezes my hand and gets up to leave the room.

I wait until the door closes behind him before taking a deep breath.

"Jay?" My voice shakes, but he speaks before I can continue.

"I'm so glad you're okay, Holly. God, I thought..." Jay runs his hand through his hair as he stops mid-sentence. His face is pale as he drops his head.

"Wait, Jay. I need to say something." I swallow the thick lump in my throat and blink, tears pricking my eyes.

This is it.

This is the moment I set him free. Give him a chance to heal.

I know I'm doing the right thing, but my hands are still shaking. Once I say this to him, there is no going back. He's looking at me, waiting, his hands wrapped around mine.

"This isn't what I want," I croak.

"What do you mean, baby? What isn't?"

I take a deep breath and look away. "Us." My voice cracks on the word, just like my heart does inside my chest.

"Holly?" Jay's desperate eyes plead with me. "I don't understand."

"Please, Jay," I sob. "I don't want this. I don't want us. I thought I did, but I don't. I'm sorry. I can't be with you anymore."

"Holly, what are you saying?" He stares at me, his forehead creased in confusion.

My voice sounds like a stranger's as I utter the words, "I'm saying it's over, Jay. We don't belong together. I'm not the right person for you. I'm so sorry."

"Holly, you can't mean that. After all this time we've spent together? I love you; you love me too. I know you do!" Jay says, grabbing on to my other hand and bringing both up to his lips to kiss them.

I slide them out of his grip and drop them back onto the bed.

He sits there for a moment, staring at me wide-eyed. His eyes fill up with tears and he pulls his eyebrows together and raises his hand, rubbing it over his forehead.

"You hit your head, Holly. You're confused."

"No, Jay. I'm not. It's never been clearer to me," I whisper.

I'm letting you go, Jay. I'm letting you go because I love you.

"You can't mean this, Berry."

"Don't call me that," I say. It comes out harsher than I intended, the pain in my heart pushing out inside my words.

Jay's eyes widen and he moves back as though I've slapped him.

I need him out of here. The sooner he goes and forgets about me, the better.

"I'm so sorry, Jay. You're going to be better off without me; please trust me," I say as my voice wavers. "Listen to me. We can't be together."

"This is honestly what you want?" he asks, the pain on his face more than I can bear.

I can't speak. I know my voice could betray me and tell him I've made a terrible mistake. Tell him I love him more than anything and I will be here with him, even though I'm not who he loves in his heart. I can't let that happen. He must have a chance at genuine happiness. He will never have that with me.

I'm just a painful reminder of what he lost.

It takes my last shred of strength to look him in his beautiful blue eyes, the eyes I will miss for eternity, and nod.

Jay sucks in a deep breath and his eyes drop to the floor, unable to look at me anymore. He gets up slowly from his chair next to the bed and turns to leave.

"I'll be outside," he says, his voice flat.

I turn my head to stare at the wall, even though doing so feels like someone is stamping on it, and wait until I hear the door close behind him. I lie in silence, listening to the rhythmic beat of my heart. I'm surprised it's still going. If someone told me it had stopped and I was in some parallel universe on my way to hell, I wouldn't question it.

A few minutes pass and the door opens again.

"Holly?" Matt says, walking toward the chair Jay just left moments ago. He reaches me and sits down. His eyes are bloodshot and watery. "What the hell's going on, Holly? Did you and Jay have a fight?" he asks, taking my hand in his and squeezing it. He looks at me with so much worry in his eyes that I crack.

"Matt," I whisper, tears falling. "Oh, Matt."

"Hey, hey, it's okay. You're going to be okay. Now talk to me." Matt's voice is full of concern.

"I told him we were over, Matt... I had to." My shoulders shake as my sobs take over.

"What's going on, Holly?" Matt asks again. "You have had a fight, haven't you?"

"No." I shake my head. "It's not that, it's..." I gasp as I try to catch my breath between sobs. "It's so much worse, Matt. He's in love with someone else."

"He's what?" There's disbelief in Matt's voice.

"He only wanted me because I look like her."

"Holly, I don't understand. You look like who?"

"Swear to me you won't tell a soul, Matt, not even Stefan."

"I won't."

"Swear it, Matt! He can't know that I know." I know my shrill voice is making me sound like a crazy woman.

"Okay. Okay, I swear," Matt says, his face serious.

I take a deep, shaky breath.

"Jay lost his best friend in an accident when he was twenty-one."

"Oh my God." Matt's hand flies over his mouth.

"All this time I thought he was a boy, but I found out that she was a girl."

"Okay?" Matt says, looking confused.

"I look just like her, Matt!" I cry. "She wasn't just his friend; she was the love of his life. He's never gotten over her. He's got her initials tattooed on his shoulder."

"What? Holly, that can't be right. Jay loves you. It's so obvious to anyone who sees the two of you together."

I shake my head sadly. "He doesn't Matt. He sees her when he looks at me."

"How can you know that?" Matt's eyes search mine. He looks like he's struggling to make sense of it all.

"I just do. Why else would he keep her being a girl secret if he didn't have something to hide? He didn't like to talk about it; he would change the subject. He didn't want me to know the truth. It was never me he loved, Matt."

"Oh, Holls. I don't believe it." Matt's eyes fill with tears.

"It's true. You promised you wouldn't tell Stefan," I say, grabbing Matt's arm.

"I know, I know." Matt lowers his head, letting out a sigh.

"Jay can't know that I found out about her. It will be too much for him, Matt. I've seen how he can't move on. He has to think I'm leaving for my own reasons, that I don't love him enough to want to be with him."

"What do you mean, leaving?" Matt's eyes search mine.

"I have to go, Matt. I can't be with him anymore. I can't see him again."

"Holly, are you sure that's what you want?" Matt stares at me.

"I have to, Matt. If I don't leave him, he can never heal. It will be like looking at a ghost every day. How can he ever be truly happy when he sees my face, so much like hers?" Fresh tears run down my face. "I'm a constant reminder of his pain. I have to do this for him."

"But, Holly, you love him," Matt whispers.

"I know I do, Matt. I love him so much that doing this breaks my heart. But if it means that his might heal, then I have no choice. I would rather live without him than stay and know I am the reason his soul stays tortured." I look into Matt's eyes.

"You love him that much that you're willing to throw yourself under a bus for the chance to save him?" Sadness fills Matt's eyes as understanding sinks in.

"There's no other way, Matt. It has to be like this. He must think I'm leaving because I don't want this life with him. He has to think I don't love him so he can let me go. I know him. He won't give up if he thinks I still love him."

"I can't believe this is happening," Matt murmurs and shakes his head. "I'll be here for you, Holly. You know that, don't you? Rachel, too. She's been going frantic at home since I called her and told her about the accident." Matt squeezes my hand, tears filling his eyes.

I manage a weak smile back at him.

"I know you will, Matt. You and Rach are like family to me."

We stare at each other for a moment, the air around us thick with emotion.

I'm still staring into Matt's eyes as the door opens. An older male doctor walks in, followed by Stefan, who rushes over and puts his hand on my arm.

"Holly, I'm Doctor Wilson." He lifts his head and smiles at me as he takes the chart off the bottom of the bed. "You were very lucky, gave your friends quite the scare." He looks through the chart, reading my notes.

"Holly, why is Jay outside?" Stefan whispers, too quiet for the doctor to hear. I look at him, not sure how to answer.

The bang from the chart as it's hung back on the bed makes us all look up.

"Everything looks wonderful, just a few bruises. You'll ache for a while, but nothing was broken. You hit your head quite hard, enough to knock you unconscious. We'll keep you overnight for observation, and you should be fine to go home in the morning."

"Can I fly?"

"Sorry?" Doctor Wilson's eyebrows shoot up. He looks baffled by my question.

"I'm flying back home to England tomorrow night."

"Ah, well, I wouldn't advise it so soon after a head injury." He smiles at me.

I fix my eyes on him. "Please! I need to go home."

He looks at me. Desperation must be written all over my face.

"Well, let's see how tonight goes first and as long as there's nothing to be concerned about, then we can discuss it again," he says with another smile.

"Thank you, Doctor, thank you so much." I sigh in relief, sinking into the pillows.

He heads to the door. "You get some rest, Holly. I will check in on you again later."

Once he's gone, Stefan turns his attention to me again, studying my face.

"Holly, I just saw Jay sitting outside. What's he doing out there? He looked distraught. I asked him what was going on and he said he has no idea."

My mouth is dry as the image of Jay out there, alone and upset, comes into my head.

"I told him to go," I tell Stefan.

"What? Why?" Stefan's eyes dart between me and Matt.

"It all gotten to be too much, Stefan. I don't belong here, with him. The break-in, being followed, the news reporters wanting to interview me. I'm not cut out for Jay's world, Stefan. I don't want that life. It's not who I am." The lie rolls smoothly off my tongue. So smooth that I could even believe it. I wouldn't ever choose a life in the spotlight given the choice, but I would have done it if it meant being with Jay. I would do anything if it meant I could stay with him.

Anything except keeping his broken heart from having the chance to mend.

Stefan looks at me, his eyes wide with shock.

"Holly, you can do it. The press aren't that bad if you know how to handle them. I can help you. We can do it together."

"I'm sorry, Stefan. I can't. It's not what I want." I raise my eyes to his even though I can barely look at him, lying to his face like this when he's done nothing but welcome me with open arms.

"But Jay loves you, Holly; he told me," Stefan whispers.

I take a deep breath, knowing what I need to say.

"Then he needs to let me go, Stefan. He needs to give up his own happiness for mine and let me go. If he loves me, then he will do it."

"You've told him all this?" Stefan's face grows pale.

"I have, Stefan. I need him to just respect that this is how I feel, and nothing will change my mind."

Stefan stares at me before closing his mouth and nodding.

"Fine." He frowns.

He looks at Matt and they hold each other's gaze for a moment before he turns to leave the room.

"Stefan!" I call. He looks around hopefully. "Please tell Jay I'm sorry about the car. I know how much he loved it."

Stefan's frown returns and he says nothing. Instead, he turns and leaves, shutting the door behind him.

As it closes, my heart shatters again, and Matt wraps his arms around me as I weep.

I talk Dr. Wilson into letting me fly home. He agreed after Matt insisted he would look after me on the flight and not let me overdo it. So far, I've not lifted a finger. When Jay booked my tickets for me, he booked me into upper class. I've got a seat that turns into a bed and I've slept most of the flight. Exhaustion won against my racing mind in the end. Matt's been flapping around me like a mother hen, plumping my cushions and instructing me to drink another glass of water each time he passes. It's sweet, but I know it isn't just my bruised head that he's worried about. He's trying to nurse my broken heart. I wish it were as easy as just taking a pill to fix it.

Jay packed my things at his house and Stefan brought them over to Matt at the crew hotel. Jay respected my wishes and stayed away from the hospital, but I know he was calling and texting Matt the entire time trying to get answers. I can't blame him. One minute everything's fine, and the next I've taken off in his car, and say that I don't belong with him. I just hope he believes my story. He has to. He must forget about me and move on. The thought of him being reminded of his heartbreak at losing Robyn every time he looks at me is too painful to consider. Maybe he's angry at me for running away. That's good, though. Let him channel his anger toward me. Let him get it all out and then start the healing process.

Stefan said they took the car into the garage and the mechanic cleared any items of Jay's out of it and returned them. He didn't mention the envelope or photograph. I can only hope that they got lost at the scene of the accident when the windshield smashed. Matt's been talking to Stefan a lot, and I know he's furious with me for leaving Jay like this. But I would rather him be angry at me than risk him finding out the truth and telling Jay.

I can't believe everything that's happened these last few months. It feels like a dream. A beautiful, life-changing dream that turned into a nightmare. I don't think I will ever be the same Holly I was before Jay Anderson. Would I even want to be? What is it they say? It's better to have loved and lost than never to have loved at all? Is that still true if the love is only one-sided? I know Jay may think he loves me now, but in time he will realize that I was only ever a distraction from dealing with his grief and moving on with his life. I hope when that day comes, whoever she is, loves him with everything she has. Just like I do. He deserves that. He deserves happiness. I'm just not the one to give it to him.

I look out the window as we approach Heathrow Airport. The familiar mechanical *whirr* of the landing gear being lowered rumbles. London looks gray and miserable, concealed under a blanket of fog. Perfect weather to match my mood and welcome me back to the real world.

Back to my old life.

Where I'm hundreds of miles away from the love of my life.

Chapter 25

THE NEXT WEEK PASSES with me running on autopilot. I operate a flight to Japan and back, welcoming the way the change in time zones throws my body out of whack. At least being physically exhausted means I've been able to get some sleep. Otherwise, I know I would lie awake and think about Jay. I spend my waking hours hiding in bed, crying, or walking around the house like a zombie with red puffy eyes. Rachel's been great, but she's struggling to know what to do with me now. I can see it in her eyes. She's so worried. Matt has been here every day that he's not at work. Between the two of them, I've been under constant watch.

I zip up my bag, everything I need for my stay with Mum and Dad inside. I can't wait to see them and my sister Sophie. I spot my phone charger lying on the bed. I don't want to forget that. I unzip the outer pocket of my bag and shove it in, but my hand scrapes against something. I pull it out and drop it on the floor like it burned me. My eyes fill with tears as I bend down and pick up the piece of card.

The thick black letters, *pick up for Berry,* stare back at me.

I turn the card over. *Missed me?*

"Like you wouldn't believe, Jay," I say out loud to the walls of my bedroom. "I miss you like you wouldn't believe."

I glance down at my watch. Even though I know I should take it off, as it's serving as a constant reminder, I just can't bring myself to do it. I look at it throughout the day, seeing what time it is in LA and wondering what Jay is up to. Matt has been speaking to Stefan constantly, as is normal for them. I know Jay was asking about me to start with, but these last three days Matt hasn't mentioned anything. Stefan is still upset with me. I can't blame him. I hurt his friend. If he knew the real reason why I had to do it, then I'm sure he would understand, but he can't.

No one can ever know.

I open my bottom drawer and tuck the cardboard sign down next to a pink sweater and head downstairs.

"You got everything?" Rach asks as she appears from the living room.

"Yeah, think so." I give her a brief smile.

"This'll be good for you, babe. Having some time with your family. Say hi to them from me." She comes to give me a hug.

"I will, I promise. What are you going to do while I'm gone?"

Rach shrugs. "Clean the house from top to bottom, do some watercolor painting, join a choir."

I raise an eyebrow at her.

She rolls her eyes. "As if I'm going to do any of those things." She smirks. "I've actually got some more post to send out to Mr. X."

I stare at her. "You never mentioned he was back in touch."

She shrugs. "You had enough on your plate. It didn't seem the right time to talk about men."

"Rach," I cry, grabbing her back into my arms. "I always want to know what's going on in your life. No matter what crap mine is turning into, I always want to know what's new with you!"

"I know, I'm sorry, Holly. I just didn't want to seem insensitive."

"You? Insensitive? Blunt maybe!"

"Hey! My *honesty* is one of my best qualities." She smiles.

"So, going back to Mr. X?" I probe.

"Well, he apologized for going all quiet and jealous on me." Rach studies her nails. "Now he wants to, you know, pick up where we left off."

I look at her. "You're sure about starting this all up again?"

"Yes, Holly. It's fine. I've made it so he can't track me online, and besides, I'm getting much-needed deposits made into the Rachel house fund." Her eyes light up.

"It'll be a mansion at this rate. This guy is obsessed with you!"

"I know. Fucking awesome, isn't it!" She claps her hands together and bounces on the spot.

"Oh, Rach. I love you." I smile properly for the first time since leaving LA a week ago.

"I love you too, Holly," she says, serious again. "I'm going to miss you, chick." She hugs me again.

"I'll see you in a few days," I say, hugging her one last time before I head out the door and to my car.

"Oh, Holly, it was awesome. You'd have loved it," Sophie says, telling me about her latest weekend away to Rome. "The history and architecture are incredible. It's such a stunning place."

We're all in the living room, curled up with freshly made cups of tea. It feels so nice to be back in my childhood home with my parents and sister. There's something safe and comforting about knowing the door is always open. It's the perfect place to come when nursing a broken heart. I almost feel like a little girl again, safe in the belief that Mum and Dad know the answer to everything. Although, as I've grown up, I've realized that parents are just winging it some days, like the rest of us.

Muffin, my mum and dad's scruffy little terrier, whines and looks up from his place next to me on the sofa. His big brown eyes gaze at me.

"Oh, I'm sorry, boy; did I stop too soon?" I ask as I rub his tummy again. He sighs and lays his head back down, his tail patting the cushion as it wags, satisfied that he has my attention again.

"We went to all the tourist spots and even went on a tour of the Vatican," Sophie keeps talking.

"I'm glad you had a good time," Dad says from his armchair across the room.

"Did the others enjoy it?" Mum asks.

"Yeah, they did, Mum."

Sophie went with a couple of school friends. They have a twice-yearly weekend away together to catch up as they all work such a lot and don't live close to each other.

"I tell you what we need, June," Dad pipes up. "Some of those biscuits you made, lovely they were. You know your mum won first prize at the contest for those," Dad says proudly.

"Tim!" Mum scolds as she and Sophie both throw him a *shut up!* look.

"Oh right, sorry, Holly," he says, looking at me with concern.

"It's okay, Dad." I know he's talking about Sheila's cookie recipe she gave me to share with Mum.

I told Mum and Sophie what had happened with Jay, about Robyn, the photo, everything. They knew something wasn't right when I came home from LA, but I told them I was just feeling a bit shaken from the car accident. I waited until I got here to tell them the entire story. Mum's filled Dad in on the details.

"How are Rachel and Matt doing?" Sophie asks.

"They're good. Matt's doing all the LA flights he can to see Stefan, and Rach is great too. She's saving for her own place."

I move my hand to Muffin's ears and start stroking behind them. He groans in pleasure.

"Oh, that daft dog will have you doing that all night, Holly," Mum says as she shakes her head at Muffin, who is now lying on his back with his legs wide open.

"Typical man." Sophie glances over. "Thinks we all want to see his bits."

I can't help but smile at Muffin's blissful expression. If happiness was as easy for humans as a tummy rub and an ear scratch, then the world would be a much better place.

The next couple of days pass as I bake with Mum and listen to Dad and Sophie discuss big legal cases in the news. In the mornings I go out to the beach, getting up early when I can't sleep and take Muffin for a run. He loves to take his ball and I throw it for him as far as I can, his little legs tripping over each other to race after it.

As much as I love the beach, being here just makes me think of Jay. He loves the coast as much as I do, growing up near it, the same as me. My mind goes back to when we visited his parents, Sheila and Bill, and his brother, Blake. They were so nice to me. I felt like I belonged there with them all. Now I know why Robyn's mum, Beth, seemed so surprised to meet me, why she studied me so much. It probably shocked her to see Jay with a woman. Sheila said he's never brought a girl home before. Then for Beth to see how much of a resemblance I have to her daughter must have been awful for her.

At least she won't have to bump into me again; it's not like I will go back.

Muffin bounds over to me, his ball in his mouth, covered in sand, and looking like this is the best day of his life.

"Ready, boy?" I say as I hold his ball up.

"Go!" I shout, pretending to throw it, but keeping it in my hand. He looks around and sniffs at the air, not easily fooled.

"Okay, this time it's for real." I launch his ball across the beach. He tears after it at high speed, kicking up wet sand as he goes.

My phone beeps with a voicemail. I must have lost signal farther up the beach.

"Holly, it's Kate in crewing. Just to let you know your swap went through. You are no longer on the AV77 flight to LA tomorrow. You're on the Hong Kong and Sydney now. Log in when you can and confirm the roster change. Thanks."

Well, that's a relief.

I had another LA rostered, which I would have been over the moon about before, but it's the last place on earth I want to go right now. I asked crewing to swap me onto the Hong Kong flight if they needed extra crew. It stops in Hong Kong on route to Sydney and then stops there again on the way back to London. In total, the trip takes nine days. It's perfect as it will keep me busy. The crew always go out together in Hong Kong. It's just what I need.

I look up and see Muffin running back toward me again.

"Well done; you're such a good boy," I praise him as he drops his ball for me and we repeat his favorite game.

I say goodbye to Mum, Dad, and Sophie after lunch. Muffin looks put out his playmate is about to leave and lies with his head resting on my shoes in the hallway so I can't put them on without lifting him up for a big cuddle first.

Sophie and I drive together for a bit, me following behind her until she gets closer to Bath and pulls off the motorway. I carry on, giving her a beep and a wave.

The radio plays a country song and I'm transported back to the car with Jay on the drive to his parents' house. I remember looking over at him while it was playing. He had the perfect amount of stubble that day; he looked so gorgeous, so carefree driving along with the windows down.

My chest tightens as I picture him.

I was so happy that day.

The song cuts out as a call rings through the car speakers from my phone. I hit the button on the steering wheel to answer.

"Hello?"

"Hi, Holly, it's Doug." His American accent seems so out of place in my little car in the middle of a gray English motorway.

"Hi, Doug," I say in surprise. "How are you? How's Anya?"

"We're great, Holly. Just great! We've just signed the paperwork on our new house."

"Wow, that's amazing news, congratulations."

"Thanks, Holly. Listen, I wanted to call you as I've found out something about the break-in."

"Oh?" My breath catches in my throat.

"I've been asking around and I kept hearing the same name. Apparently, there was a guy talking with some reporters, digging for information, that sort of thing. He was seen handing an envelope to that reporter, Ryan Baker. I can only assume it contained cash."

"Oh my God." I concentrate on the road ahead, pulling into the slowest lane so other cars can overtake me as I listen to Doug.

"Yeah, it's an English guy, Holly. I think you might know him." Doug clears his throat.

"His name's Simon Green."

Chapter 26

"Holly? Holly? Are you still there?"

"Yes, Doug! Sorry I was just... Simon Green. Are you sure?"

"That's the name I kept getting. He works for the same airline as you, doesn't he?"

I flex my hands on the steering wheel, loosening the painful grip I have on it.

"Yes, he's a pilot. Not just that though, we used to date."

"Ah. Well, that could explain it then. Jealous with a grudge? Maybe he wanted to scare you off LA, or discredit Jay. I've heard of stranger motives, let me tell you."

I know Simon was angry after we broke up. Another pilot told management about him showing the videos of us around. They hauled him into the head office over it. He somehow got off with just a warning, but he could have lost his career over it. I never thought he would do something like this, though.

My mind flashes back to Matt telling me of Simon's reaction to the photos of me and Jay in *Celeb Central*, then seeing him in that bar. Simon was so vile to me, and Jay had him up against the wall by his neck in front of lots of our colleagues. That would have pissed Simon off. Knowing that he hired someone to follow me, break into Jay's house, and... Oh God. Acid rises from my stomach.

I swallow and find my voice. "Thank you so much, Doug. You've helped so much. It's a relief to know who was behind it."

"Holly, after what you did for me, anything I can do for you, you only have to ask."

"Thank you."

Doug stays silent for a moment, as though he wants to say something else.

"Doug? What is it?"

"Holly, I hope I'm not out of line here but, well, I saw Jay the other day. He looked terrible. He said you guys weren't..." Doug pauses as though thinking of the right words. "He said you'd gone back to England. It's not because of this break-in, is it? Now you know it was just your ex being a jerk..." Doug trails off.

I sigh before answering him.

"It's complicated. It would never work between us, Doug. I just hope he finds true happiness soon."

"Hey, only you know in your heart what the right path is, Holly. If this last couple of weeks has taught me anything, it's that you should never ignore your heart."

I smile sadly. My heart will always belong to Jay but letting him go was the most loving thing I could do.

"Thanks again, Doug. I appreciate it."

"No problem, Holly. Hey, when you're next back in LA, give me a call. Me and Anya would love to have you over for dinner."

"Oh, in the new house? I look forward to it," I say, knowing full well I have no intention of going anywhere near LA if I can help it.

"Great, that's settled then. Take care, Holly."

"Bye, Doug."

I hit end call and stare out at the road ahead. The earlier acid rising from my stomach threatens to come back. Simon paid for the break-in and we thought nothing was taken. However, I know that's not true. Nothing may have been taken from the house, but the photo they sent me of Jay and Robyn must have been a copy. The fact it only had my name on it means that someone, most likely Ryan Baker, had to have been back to the house to put it in the mailbox. I shudder at the thought of him being so near to the house again.

To think that Simon was behind all of this. I clench my teeth. That selfish, cheating bastard! He couldn't bear to see me happy, so he tried to find something, anything, to ruin it. Only he hit the jackpot. I swallow back the horrible taste that's in my mouth. He found out all about Robyn. I bet he couldn't believe his luck. Maybe I should thank him I found out now. Otherwise, I would have carried on unaware, continuing Jay's suffering, preventing him from moving on.

"This is all such shit!" I shout.

A man in a car coming up in the lane beside me gives me a funny look. There's no way he can hear me, but I must look odd shouting to myself in the car. I need to concentrate on driving back. I can fly to Hong Kong tomorrow and drink so much I'll forget about it for a while.

Bliss.

'Ladies and gentlemen, welcome to Hong Kong, where the local time is three o'clock in the afternoon. Please remain seated with your seat belt fastened until the aircraft comes to a complete stop and the captain has turned off the seat belt sign. Thank you for choosing Atlantic Airways.'

I tune out as the announcement is repeated in Mandarin. Three o'clock, so by the time we disembark and get through the airport and to the hotel, it's going to be five o'clock at the earliest. The crew have already decided we'd meet at the hotel bar for some food, then head straight out for drinks after. There will be five of us and three pilots. The rest of the crew are Chinese and live in Hong Kong, so they'll go home now, and the new crew will join us for the Sydney sector in two days.

I stand at my door as the passengers leave the aircraft, smiling and dipping my head as I say goodbye and thank you. I can't wait to get to my hotel room and take a hot shower before going out. Having a few drinks is just what I need right now. I need to be numbed by cocktails. Maybe then I won't feel this pain, the never-ending sickness in my stomach and ache in my chest.

I doze on the bus to the hotel and am grateful to make it into my room. I wheel my bag in and it falls straight over, narrowly missing my foot.

"Ugh." I flop back onto the bed.

I have to get in the shower now or I risk falling asleep right here and missing the entire evening. I drag myself back up to a seated position and flick the TV on. I'll put something on in the background while I get ready.

I hop through the channels until an American one playing commercials comes on. I take my uniform off as they discuss a 'revolutionary new weight loss drug.' I unzip my skirt, which has gaped at the waist since I came back from LA.

Try breaking up with the love of your life. That should help.

I'm heading into the bathroom when a familiar voice makes the hairs on my neck stand on end. I turn around and there on the TV is Jay. I stare at the screen showing a rerun of his show *Steel Force*. He's dressed in his FBI stab vest, his gun drawn, just about to bust down a door.

He's so goddamned sexy.

I stand mesmerized as he fights with the perpetrator before overpowering him and pushing him to the floor, the muscles in his arms straining underneath his shirt.

This is a bad idea.

I force my eyes away and flip to another channel. I can't sit here and watch him. I can't look at what I'm missing, what I had once, or thought I had. It's just too raw still. I groan as I drag my hands down my face. I'm going to need a hell of a lot of cocktails tonight.

Three hours and four cocktails later, I'm dancing to the music in a bar the crew always comes to. The bar owner knows all the airline crew come here; we must keep him in business as there's crew here every day of the year. He even lets us write our names on the peeling painted walls. Somewhere near the back there's a heart with *Holly, Rach & Matt* in it from a trip we all did together a couple of years ago.

"Holly, you want another drink?" our captain, Pete, asks me.

"Yes, please!" I call over the music. "It's my round though."

We make our way to the bar.

"Eight shots of tequila please!" I call, slapping some money down on the counter.

The bar man smiles at me and starts pouring our drinks.

"Tequila? Looking for a wild night are you, Holly?" Pete says with a smile as he subtly looks me up and down, checking me out in my skin-tight black dress and heels.

"Just looking to forget," I say as I pick up half the drinks. Pete grabs the rest, and we take them back over to the rest of the team.

"Yay! Shots!" One girl shouts when she sees us coming.

"Everyone on the count of three!" I say. "One, two, three!"

We all down our shots and I wince as the burn spreads down my throat.

"Whoa, that's some strong forgetting you need to do, Holly," Pete says, smiling at me as he finishes his shot.

He's handsome, in his late forties, with salt-and-pepper hair and a friendly smile. He was telling me on the flight out about how he's just had his divorce finalized. Maybe under different circumstances I would be flattered by his attention, but there's a sinking feeling in my gut that's growing.

I can never have another man touch me again and not wish that it were Jay.

He's ruined me forever.

My phone vibrates with a text.

Matt: Hey, Holls, we've just finished dinner, we're heading to the bar now. See you soon!

I smile. Matt and Stefan are here on their holiday together and wanted to come and have a drink together tonight. They're on some long day trip tomorrow so they won't get a chance to meet up with me otherwise. I'm nervous about seeing Stefan again, if I'm honest. That's why I've moved on to shots. The last time I saw him was in LA, when I left Jay. That he's happy to meet up with me tonight must be a good sign. Maybe he's not forgiven me for hurting Jay yet, but he's not cutting me off completely, for Matt's sake, anyway.

One girl, a pretty brunette called Lauren from the crew, grabs my hands and dances. I hold her hands and lift them up in the air as we sway our hips in time to the music. We dance together for a couple of songs, laughing and twirling each other round. I sense Pete's eyes on both of us. The song changes and I give her a hug as we have a rest.

"Hey, guys, it's my round!" she calls. "Holly, what you having?"

I look at her to answer but can see over her shoulder that Matt and Stefan have just walked in.

"Not for me this time. Thank you, though. I'm just going to go say hi to some friends I've seen."

"I'll give you a hand with the drinks," Pete says to her.

"Okay." Lauren grins at him. "See you in a bit, Holly."

I smile as Lauren and Pete head off to the bar together, his eyes checking out her bum as he walks behind.

"Hey!" I call, waving to Matt so he can spot me.

I head toward him and Stefan and when we meet Matt pulls me into a hug. I wobble on my feet, my head rushing from all the drinks.

"Hey, babe. Look at you!" he says, eyeing me up and down. "Holls, you look hot as always, but seriously, we need to get some more food into you. I can get my hands around your waist."

"Don't exaggerate, Matt." I kiss him on the cheek, missing the spot I was aiming for.

I step back and look over at Stefan who is watching me, his lips in a firm, straight line.

"Stefan, it's good to see you," I say, swallowing the lump in my throat.

"You too, Holly," he says politely. "Doug told me it was Simon who paid that reporter. I'm sorry, Holly."

"Yeah, total arsehole," Matt mutters. "You should report him to the police, Holly. You've got grounds to."

"I'm just glad we know who was behind it now," I murmur as I watch Stefan.

He may know that Simon was behind the break-in, but there's no way he would know about the photograph. Judging from his face, he's still mad at me, which is a good sign. If he knew about the photograph, then he would work out the real reason for me leaving Jay. He wouldn't be angry with me if he knew I did what I had to do out of love for Jay.

"Let's get a drink," Matt says.

I get the impression Stefan is as relieved as me as we order a cocktail each.

"So, are you guys having a good holiday?" I ask once we've found a quieter table to sit at away from the bar.

"Aww, the best!" Matt gushes with delight. "Tell her, babe." He nudges Stefan in the ribs.

Babe? This must be going well. I smile at them.

Stefan rolls his eyes good-naturedly and smiles at Matt.

"It's been fantastic. We've done sightseeing, eaten out at incredible restaurants, done some fun day trips." He glances at Matt. "Our hotel is amazing, Holly. The spa is incredible. We're working our way through all the treatments on the menu!" He laughs.

I laugh too, happy that Stefan is talking to me like he used to, even if it's only for a moment.

"The pool is better than Jay's!" Matt says before catching my eye and stopping abruptly.

"It's okay, Matt." I squeeze his hand.

"How's Jay doing, Stefan?" I ask, avoiding eye contact.

"He's been better, Holly," Stefan says, his mouth returning to its earlier firm, straight line.

My stomach knots at the thought of Jay hurting. "No one will ever come close to him for me," I say, tears threatening my eyes.

"Then why did you run out on him like that, Holly?" Stefan snaps.

He is still pissed.

"I can't explain it." I blink. "I had my reasons, Stefan. Good reasons. Please believe me. I never wanted to hurt him. I only want him to be happy."

"He was happy, Holly. He was the happiest I've ever seen him."

"Maybe he thought he was," I whisper.

Stefan lets out a big breath, his shoulders sagging. "Holly, you've no idea, have you?"

I look at him.

"What do you mean?"

"You leaving the way you did. It hurt him."

"I'm not the one for him, Stefan."

"Holly, listen to me for a minute," Stefan says. "You don't know how Rob died, do you?"

Why is he talking about this?

"No, just that it was an accident of some sort, a terrible accident." I look at him as he seems to choose his next words carefully.

"It was a car accident, Holly. Rob died in a car accident. Jay was in the passenger seat. He was the last one to see Rob alive."

My hand flies to my forehead as I try to make sense of Stefan's words through my alcohol-induced fog.

"So, when you took off and Jay got a call saying you'd been in a car accident, he almost lost it! I've never seen him like that before. It frightened the hell out of me."

I look up at Stefan, unable to hide the tears in my eyes.

"Oh God, Jay," I whisper as I put my hands to my mouth.

My beautiful Jay.

It was hard enough for him losing his love in a car accident all those years ago without me having one too. Instead of staying and helping him deal with all the memories he had resurfacing as a result, I ran away and left him.

"I didn't know, Stefan." My voice cracks as Matt puts his arm around me.

"Of course you didn't, Holly. This isn't your fault," Matt says, pulling me into him.

"Holly, I know there's a lot you don't know, that Jay hasn't shared with you yet. That was a painful part of his life. He doesn't talk to anyone about it." Stefan's voice softens. "I just want you to understand why I'm finding it hard as his friend to see him going through this. He loves you, Holly. You leaving has hit him hard. He never wants to see his car again," Stefan says.

"He loves that car," I whisper.

"No, Holly. He loves *you*. That car just makes him think of you almost being killed. He's given it to Cooper and Eric. Told them if they can fix it up, then they can sell it and keep the money to start up their garage business."

Despite my tears, a smile forms on my face.

"He gave them his Ferrari? So they could start their business like they wanted?"

"Yeah, he's an incredibly kind guy, Holly. But you already know that," Stefan says sadly.

I reach across the table and put my hand on top of his.

"He is, Stefan, and he deserves to be truly happy. I know it doesn't seem to make sense, but trust me, being with me will not make him happy in the long term, not really. Jay will realize that himself too one day."

Stefan squeezes my hand as he looks back at me.

MEETING MR. ANDERSON

"You're right, Holly. I don't understand." He sighs. "What I can see, though, is that you love him. And I can see Matt trusts you and knows the genuine reasons behind your decisions. And I trust Matt's judgment."

Matt smiles at Stefan.

"So, I guess I will just have to live with not understanding for now, and just be the best friend I can be to Jay."

"Thank you," I say. "He's so lucky to have a friend like you."

We all sit in companionable silence for a moment before Matt speaks.

"Fuck me! I need another drink. It's like an episode of a drama show."

"Me too." I smile across at Stefan and raise an eyebrow.

"Go on then. After that, we better head off. We've got an early day tomorrow, haven't we?" He smiles across at Matt, who glows under his attention.

"Right. I'll get them. Back in a moment." I rise off my chair and head to the bar. I'm tipsy. I better make this my last one too and then head back to the hotel.

I'm standing, waiting at the bar when hands slide over my hips and someone presses into me from behind. Warm beery breath on my cheek forces me to hold my breath.

"Looking rather sexy in this little dress, Holly."

My blood boils.

"Simon, get your hands off me," I snap as I turn and glare at him.

"Oh, come on, Holly," he slurs, his breath hitting me in the face. "Don't you want to fuck for old times' sake?" He laughs as he sways toward me.

"What the hell did I ever see in you?" I spit.

"Aw, come on, darling." His glassy eyes look me up and down.

"They should lock you up for what you did!" I glare at him.

Simon's head rolls back and he laughs.

"What I did?" he says, prodding at his chest with his finger. "All I did was unearth a few hidden secrets that Mr. Perfect hadn't shared with you. You should thank me. You didn't belong there with him, Holly. Who are you kidding?" He smirks as he looks at me, before reaching forward and groping my bum with his hand and pulling me against him.

"Come on, Holly. Let me fuck you properly tonight. I can do it better than that pretty boy."

Blood rushes to my ears as I shove Simon hard in the chest and he staggers backwards. People turn to look, but I don't care.

"Don't you dare talk about him!"

"Come on, Holly. You're delusional. You were just some easy stand-in for his long-lost childhood love," Simon sneers.

Crack!

There's a loud gasp from the people around us as Simon staggers backward before losing his balance and toppling over onto the floor.

MEETING MR. ANDERSON

My hand throbs at my side. Giant painful throbs from where I just punched Simon square in the face.

"Holly!" Matt and Stefan run over.

"Are you okay?" Stefan asks, lifting my hand and calling to the bartender to pass some ice.

"That was awesome!" Matt squeals with delight, his eyes bright. "I have waited so long to see you stand up to that arsehole, Holly! This is the best day ever!"

I, however, can't move. My feet are stuck to the same spot as I stare at Simon. He gets himself up and gives me one last dirty look, holding on to his nose, which is dripping with blood, as he staggers off and out of the bar.

"And good riddance!" Matt calls as the door shuts.

"I heard what he said, love," says a man standing by the bar. "He deserved that, he did."

"Me too," pipes up another. "Good for you."

I glance at Stefan, who's studying my hand, holding some ice against my knuckles.

If people at the bar could hear what he said to me, then just how much did Stefan hear? What did Simon say? I'm racking my brain to think if he said anything that would give away just how much I know about Robyn. It's all just a blur but I'm pretty sure, no, I'm certain, he never said anything about the photograph.

I should be fine, I hope.

It will all be fine.

The rest of the trip is great. Punching Simon seems to have been therapeutic for me. I've felt calmer and more positive since. I got my hand checked out the next day. Luckily, it was just bruised. The swelling wasn't too bad, as Stefan had got the ice on it fast.

Lauren and I spend a fair bit of the trip together during the daytime, going to a hot yoga class in Sydney and shopping at the markets in Hong Kong. We meet the rest of the crew in the evenings for dinner and drinks. She has me giggling at the antics her and Pete get up to each night. It seems they both enjoy each other's company a lot when the rest of us go back to our own rooms.

I am so glad to land back into Heathrow. Day nine away and I just can't wait to get back into my own bed.

I collect my suitcase from the baggage carousel and say goodbye to the rest of the crew, giving Lauren a hug before leaving her standing and talking to Pete. I smile. They're probably wondering whether to swap numbers.

I pull my bags through customs and head out through the automatic double doors into the arrivals terminal. A crowd of people are waiting to collect loved ones, their eager faces looking up each time a new person comes through the doors.

I keep walking and am almost at the end of the line of people waiting when I stop dead. Someone behind tuts, sidestepping me.

The air leaves my lungs as I stand frozen to the spot. I never expected to see him again. Not in the flesh. Not here in front of me, his chest rising and falling, his eyes fixed on me.

My mouth falls open and I stare back into the intense blue eyes, which are burning right through me.

Jay.

Chapter 27

Jay.

What's he doing here?

I stare back at him, my heart beating wildly in my chest. Nothing could have prepared me for this overwhelming pain in my chest at seeing him again. He's wearing faded jeans and a long-sleeved, muscle fit T-shirt. His sun-kissed hair looks ruffled and so sexy. The memory of its softness between my fingers rushes into my mind as my breath catches in my throat.

I can't just stand here all day staring. I force my legs to move and walk toward him. His eyes never leave mine. Now that I'm closer, the pain in them is obvious, as are the faint dark circles underneath. If I didn't know how hard these last three weeks have been on Jay from Stefan, then it's glaring me in the face right now. Gone is the mischievous glint in his eyes that I love so much.

In its place is a sadness greater than any I've ever seen in them before.

What have I done?

I stop in front of him. "Jay?"

His eyebrows pull together and he lifts a hand toward my face, dropping it back down by his side before it makes contact. My eyes fall to his Adam's apple as he swallows, seeming to need a moment to compose himself before he speaks.

"Holly."

I suck in a breath, unprepared for my heart breaking as he says my name. I have missed that voice so much.

I have missed *him* so much.

"What are you doing here, Jay?" I whisper.

He clears his throat. His eyes are searching mine, drawing me in. My breath hitches, the same way it did when I first looked into his eyes all those months ago. Something inside me knew then.

Jay Anderson is special.

He will always be the only man I can ever love. The only man I want.

The man I can never have.

"I had to see you, Holly. There are things I need you to know."

"Jay." My voice threatens to crack. "You shouldn't be here." I shift uncomfortably and look at all the people around us. I'm a dam that could burst any minute. I'd rather not do it in a packed part of Heathrow Airport.

Jay seems to sense my hesitance, and he glances around.

"Holly, I'm staying in a hotel nearby. Will you come back with me so we can talk?"

I shake my head and take a step back, away from him and his familiar scent. A scent that calls to me like no other, that makes me feel like I'm home.

"Why, Jay? Nothing's changed."

I can't be near him like this. I'm not strong enough to do what I know is right when he's standing in front of me. When he's close enough that I could reach out and touch him. I know he would pull me straight into his arms if I let him. I can't do that to him. I have to be strong. I take another step back, shaking my head.

"Please, Holly." He looks deep into my eyes, searching my soul.

Flutters rise from my stomach all the way to my throat. Every nerve ending feels on high alert with him so close. I'm losing control. I can feel it slipping away, like sand through my fingers.

"Jay..." My eyes are filling with tears now.

"Holly." He grabs my hand and I jump back as a jolt of electricity runs up my arm. "Just give me half an hour, please." His eyes search mine. He looks like he's holding back tears himself. Like he's just holding on to a last shred of hope before he spirals.

I can't leave him here. Not like this.

Not alone.

Even though I fear it will be even harder to say goodbye a second time, I whisper, "Okay."

Jay's shoulders relax as the faintest of smiles passes across his lips.

This is a terrible idea. I'm playing with fire and my heart is already burned. My stomach is in knots as Jay takes my case from me and I walk beside him out of the terminal.

We head to the short-term parking lot and Jay unlocks a white Range Rover, lifting my bags into the trunk as though they weigh nothing. I tear my eyes away from his biceps and look at the car. Jay's eyes follow mine.

"Something wrong, Holly?"

I avoid his gaze, keeping my eyes fixed on the shiny axels of the Range Rover. "I'm sorry about your Ferrari."

"I never want to hear about that car again," Jay snaps.

The power behind his voice draws my eyes back up to his face. He's rubbing his forehead with one hand, his jaw tense.

"Sorry." I manage to choke out, my throat burning.

"Holly." Jay's voice is pained. "I couldn't care less about the damn car."

I stand there in silence, not sure what else to say.

"Come on," he says, steering me around to the passenger door with his hand on the small of my back. He opens the door for me and I slide into the seat. He shuts the door and goes around to the driver's side, pausing outside before he opens the door and climbs in.

We drive the short distance to the hotel in silence.

Jay parks in the hotel parking lot and opens my door for me before going back to the trunk and getting my bags out.

"Why are you bringing those?"

His eyes are dark as he shoots me a look that makes me regret asking. Instead, I fall into step beside him and we head inside and into the elevator, which already has two young women in it, glued to their cell phones. They don't even look up as they move to one side so I can get in, followed by Jay. He hits a button and the elevator climbs. He's staring straight ahead, his expression unreadable. One of the girls prods the other with her elbow. She looks up at her friend, who gestures toward Jay. The girl's eyes widen as she looks him up and down, turning back to her friend with a smile. I know what they're thinking. He's a sex god. He looks so sultry right now, with no hint of a smile on his face. The girls realize I've seen them checking him out and avert their eyes back to their phones. Jay's still staring straight ahead with his jaw set, unaware he's being eye-fucked.

The elevator stops and I follow Jay as he steps out and walks down the hallway. We pass two other doors before reaching a set of double doors, with a sign saying 'Langdon Suite'. Jay scans a key card and pushes the door open, holding it for me to go in first.

I walk into a modern, open-plan living space. There's a granite kitchen area with a breakfast bar to one side. It's all decorated in cream, black, and white. Some large cream sofas are positioned so you can either face the wall-mounted TV or sit with a great view of the aircraft landing and taking off from Heathrow in the distance. There's a door to the side, which I assume must lead to the bedroom and en suite. Large potted plants and vases of fresh flowers are spread about the surfaces.

I reach up to stroke a giant orchid's petal with my fingers and am surprised it's real and not silk.

"Maggie would be jealous," I mutter, wanting to break the silence.

Jay gives me a small smile. "Yeah, I think you're right."

He heads over to the kitchen and opens the fridge, passing me a bottle of fresh juice across the top of the breakfast bar.

"Thank you," I say, my fingers brushing his as I take it. The same buzz of electricity as in the airport terminal is there. My cheeks flush. I open the bottle and take a sip, more as a distraction to stop me from looking at him.

"You know it's funny you mentioned Maggie." Jay frowns.

"Why?" I look at him.

His eyes narrow as he studies my face, and then he fires his words straight at me.

"She said you had an envelope delivered the day of the crash. She forgot about it until recently."

I stiffen. Cold sweat is forming on my skin, underneath my uniform, and on my palms. I wipe them against my skirt.

"Oh, Yeah, that was..." I trail off as Jay's eyes blaze into mine.

Shit.

He's glaring at me and all I can do is stand like a rabbit in headlights. Frozen in fear.

"So, then it got me thinking. Were the contents of that envelope the reason you took off? Because you running away sure as hell made no sense to me, Holly," he says, his voice thick with hurt.

I grip the kitchen counter to steady myself as my legs go weak.

"There was no envelope at the house, so I asked Cooper and Eric to check the car while they were working on it." Jay goes over to a folder on a nearby table and comes back with a piece of paper in his hand.

Bile rises in my throat. I already know what it is.

He puts the paper down on the counter and slides it toward me.

I'm shaking my head, my eyes stinging as I look into Jay's eyes. I don't want to see it again. That picture is burned into my memory forever. Her face, green eyes, golden-blond hair, and his blue eyes bursting with love. I put my hand over my mouth as my tears fall.

"Holly." Jay's voice is soft as he comes around the kitchen counter and he wraps me inside his strong arms.

The past three weeks come crashing down and all I can do is sob, great big heaving sobs. I'm transported back to the moment I first saw the photograph in LA. Back to when my heart first shattered as I realized that the man I loved could never be with me.

I lean into Jay's solid chest and my heart pounds against him. He doesn't say anything, just holds me in his arms until my sobs slow. I take a deep breath and allow myself a moment to inhale his scent, his earthy, citrus scent. My favorite smell in the world. If only I could burn this into my memory too. But no, why torture myself? After I leave this room, it's best if there are no reminders of him. It's my only hope of surviving this racking pain and hopelessness that's threatening to consume me.

"Holly." Jay's voice breaks as he holds me tighter. "I'm so sorry. I'm so sorry, baby."

"It's okay, Jay." My voice shakes. "I understand. I left because I understand. It's what I needed to do. You don't need to be sorry." I squeeze my eyes shut as I say the words.

"Holly." Jay draws back, his hands moving up to my shoulders so he can hold on to me as he looks at me. "There's so much I need to explain."

"You don't have to, Jay. It's okay," I whisper.

"You don't understand, Holly. This is all my fault. If I had told you earlier, none of this would have happened. You wouldn't have left; you wouldn't have had the accident. God, you could have been killed!" Jay's voice breaks as he looks at me. His eyes are wide, his face pale.

"I'm fine, Jay. I wasn't hurt."

He drops his arms and squeezes his eyes shut as his lips tremble.

I reach my hand up to his cheek and he leans into it, breathing in deeply. "You don't need to explain, Jay. You don't choose who you love."

He opens his eyes. "I love you, Holly," he says, his voice strong and steady.

"Jay—"

"No, Holly!" He stops me, grabbing my hand in his. "You need to hear this. I should have told you about Robyn. All about her. I just find it so..." He looks to the ceiling as his eyes fill with tears. He lets go of my hand, sinking down onto a bar stool. I pull the one out next to him and sit down, waiting for him to continue. Jay takes a deep breath, running his hand through his hair.

"We were twenty-one when she died in the accident. There was oil on the road and she lost control."

I swallow as Jay tells me what Stefan had let slip in Hong Kong. I nod at him, encouraging him to go on.

"It's my fault she's dead. I was supposed to be driving that night. She swapped with me. A stupid bet that I wouldn't let her drive my car. That one decision changed everything. It should have been me that died, Holly. Not her. She was never supposed to be in the driver's seat." His voice cracks as grief flows to the surface.

"Stop, Jay." I reach over to take his hand. He grabs on to it and holds it tight. How many times have his hands touched mine? "You can't think like that. You couldn't have known what would happen."

"It should have been me, Holly," he whispers. "Why should I get to live when she doesn't?"

"Jay, it was never your fault. It was just an awful, awful tragedy."

I will him to believe me and let go of his guilt. My heart aches, wishing I could take away the pain it's causing him.

He squeezes my hand and looks down at the counter.

"She was so full of life, Holly, so much fun. She insisted on being called Rob and would punch me and give me a dead arm if I called her Robyn." Jay smiles. "You would have loved her."

Sickness churns in my stomach, making me dizzy.

"You still do, don't you?" I say, looking at Jay. "You still love her."

His eyes meet mine. "I'll never stop."

My heart feels like it has a knife twisted into it hearing him admit it. I tear my eyes away from his as I my pulse races and my hands shake. I knew I shouldn't have come here with him. What good is it doing? It's just making this harder on both of us.

"It's not like you think though, Holly. I wish I had told you sooner. I tried; I really did. I tried at Mom and Dad's, but we bumped into Beth, and then another time Anya and Doug arrived." Jay runs his thumb over the back of my hand. "I should have tried harder. I've caused you so much pain. I've caused both of us so much pain. I'm so sorry." He screws his face up.

"Jay, I don't understand. What didn't you tell me?" I bring my eyes back up to search his face.

"I loved Robyn, Holly. She meant so much to me. I know now from seeing that photograph what you must have thought, but she wasn't my girlfriend."

Jay sees my frown and shakes his head.

"I loved her like a sister." He sighs. "When I realized I was in love with you, it was too late. I knew I'd been calling her Rob all the time and you would think she was a guy. I was worried you'd think I had kept it a secret on purpose, but I swear I didn't. And you look so similar. I thought you'd think it was weird and I would lose you." Jay swallows as he looks up at me, his eyes shining with tears.

"So, what? You're saying us looking alike is just a coincidence?"

"Yes," Jay says straightaway.

He sees the look of disbelief on my face and pauses before continuing.

"Okay. Honestly, when we first met, it's what made me notice you, made me want to speak to you. But as soon as I did, you just made me smile, Holly. You were you, and that's who I wanted to get to know."

Jay's face is tense, waiting for my reaction. His eyes dart between mine as his words sink in. A glimmer of hope ignites deep in my stomach.

What if I got it wrong? Could I have got it so wrong?

"Jay, I don't know what to think." My mind is racing. I desperately want to believe him.

"Holly, please." His eyes blaze into mine. "You have to believe me. I know why you left. The photo, what Stefan overheard Simon say about you being a stand-in? You thought you had to leave so I could move on, didn't you?"

I stare at him as realization hits. My secret is out. I needed him to never find out, because I knew he would come here and try to talk me around. Only I wasn't expecting him to deny Robyn being his girlfriend. Could he be lying about that?

My voice shakes. "I couldn't stay knowing that you would hurt more each time you looked at me. Like seeing a ghost of Robyn. Knowing that I was holding you back from healing."

"Holly, I've screwed this up so much. Robyn really was just my friend. We weren't in love."

"I want to believe that, Jay, I do, it's just—"

"Holly. I swear to you, it's the truth. I swear to you on my life. Robyn was into girls. We were never anything other than friends." His eyes are frantic, darting between mine.

Robyn was gay?

I study his face. His tears have stopped, and he looks exhausted. I stare at him for a long time, tears running down my cheeks.

He's telling the truth.

I can see it in his eyes, hear it in his voice. I'm pretty sure if I kissed him right now, I would taste it in his tears too. My entire body senses it. He's telling the truth.

My tears fall thicker and faster. I've spent three weeks heartbroken, thinking I made the right decision for Jay. I was wrong all along. I move my other hand to join the tight ball where our other hands grip together.

"You know Beth called me after we saw her," Jay says, his voice full of emotion.

"She did?"

"Yeah, she said she was pleased to see me happy again, that it was time I forgave myself. She thinks Rob sent you for me and she wants me to live my life." His chest heaves as he screws his eyes shut.

"Hey, hey, it's okay," I say as I slide off my stool and wrap my arms around his broad shoulders. I lean my cheek against his hair and hold him as his arms snake around my waist and grip on to me.

"I should have said something earlier, Holly. I could have stopped all of this from happening."

"It's okay. It's not your fault." I stroke his back. "I should have asked you when I saw the photo. I shouldn't have just run away. I'm so sorry." I squeeze him as a fresh round of tears escape my eyes. "I thought I was doing the right thing. I thought I had to leave so you could heal." I take a shaky breath in and Jay tightens his arms around me.

"You were willing to give up your happiness for me," Jay says as he loosens his arms and rises to his feet, reaching up to hold my face between his hands. They're warm against my tear-stained cheeks.

"And you were willing to give up yours by letting me go, even though you knew my reasons for leaving didn't make sense," I say as I look up into his eyes.

Jay stares back at me and all the love in his eyes pours down, washing over me.

All the love he has for *me*.

If only we had talked to each other more, we wouldn't have had to suffer so much. We almost lost each other forever.

"We are the biggest pair of idiots" I blurt out.

Jay's eyes crinkle at the corners and he laughs. The sound makes my heart fill. I've missed it so much. I swear my heart is piecing back together inside my chest.

"You can always make me smile, Berry."

My heart leaps into my throat. "Call me that again."

Jay raises an eyebrow before speaking slowly, purposefully. "I love you, my juicy little Berry." His blue eyes sparkle at me.

"I love you too, Jay," I sob, my tears turning to happy ones. "I love you so much."

Jay's hands are still holding my cheeks as he leans in and brings his lips to meet mine. I gasp at the delicious familiarity as I welcome them. He kisses me tenderly, brushing my tears away with his thumbs.

"Jay," I whisper against his lips. He opens his eyes and gazes into mine. His lips pause millimeters from mine. "I've missed you so much," I confess.

"I've missed you too, Berry."

Then he's on me again. Only this time his kisses are deeper, more forceful, full of passion and longing. His tongue slides inside my mouth to taste me. My heart races in my chest as my hands reach up to run through the stubble on the sides of his jaw. I press in closer and kiss him back with all I have, my tongue seeking out his.

This is where we belong, in each other's arms like this. There's no denying the love between us when we are close to one other like this.

Jay turns so my back is pressed into the kitchen counter and his erection presses against my body through his jeans. I have to be close to him. I need to be close to him. I take my hands off his face and drop them to his jeans, unfastening them quickly so there's room to slide my hand inside.

"Holly," Jay groans, his hands still on either side of my face as I wrap my fingers around him and stroke his smooth shaft up and down. I run my other hand back up his body to the back of his head and pause. Jay's kisses stop and his eyes burn into mine as he senses what I'm about to do next.

I grab a fistful of his hair between my fingers, my breath coming out in shallow pants as I hover my lips over his. Jay moans and bites his lip, his eyes lighting up. I want to show him I'm never letting him go again.

"I love you, Jay Anderson, so, so much." I reach up to kiss him again.

We're a tangled ball of limbs, kissing and pulling each other's clothes off as we make our way into the bedroom and fall onto the bed.

"Show me how much this beautiful cock of yours has missed me," I say as I stroke him again.

"God, Holly," Jay hisses, "I've missed that dirty mouth of yours."

His hands leave my face and I gasp as he slides two fingers deep inside me. My body sucks them in, and I throw my head back to moan.

"Holly, I've missed you so much. I've missed this," he says, his eyes dropping to watch our bodies in wonder.

"I need you, Jay," I pant, pulling his eyes back to mine and gazing into them.

He looks back at me with such intensity, it steals my breath.

"I've only ever needed you, Holly."

He slides his fingers out and lifts my legs, wrapping them around his waist as he lowers his hot body down over mine. His eyes never leave mine as he pushes deep inside me. My mouth drops open. Wet arousal rushes to meet him as my heart hammers against my ribs.

"Holly," Jay moans, gritting his teeth. He looks at me and I nod before he draws back and sinks in again, our bodies bucking against each other, finding their own rhythm.

"Don't you ever leave me again." Jay's eyes blaze as he looks at me. "Tell me."

"I won't, Jay," I pant, cupping his face between my hands and pulling his forehead against mine. "I promise I won't."

God, this man, how could I ever think about leaving him again?

"I love you too much, Holly." Jay's voice is tender, our faces wet against each other as I realize we are both crying. "I can't live without you, Holly. You are everything to me."

He wipes my tears away, before kissing me like I'm the only person in the world. Any doubts I have vanish. I see it in Jay's eyes as he looks at me, feel it in every kiss, every touch.

I have never felt so loved.

"I love you too," I whisper, pulling Jay even closer as he slides inside me again. "I'm here for you. I will always be here for you."

Jay's face is only inches from mine as he makes love to me, moving in and out of my body, each stroke more intense than the last, our love for one another deepening with each connection.

I cry out as my legs quiver and the pressure grows inside. I know I'm about to lose control.

"Jay..." I whimper. The pressure is so intense my eyes roll back in my head.

"Oh God, Holly. Come for me," he whispers as he lets go of my face and slides his thumb down onto my swollen clitoris.

It's all too much, more than I can bear. I tingle all over and explode around him.

"Jay! Oh!" I cry as I come in intense, heavy waves, my vision blurring, stars exploding beneath my eyelids.

The strength of it so consuming that all I can do is grip on to Jay to stop myself from collapsing. His eyes never leave my face as I moan over and over again, completely at his mercy.

"Holly..." Jay says in awe. His voice is deep and smooth, full of pure love.

He thrusts deeper and his cock swells deep inside me, his heat emptying into me as his lips murmur my name repeatedly.

I'm not ready to let him go. I don't want this beautiful moment of finding each other again to be over.

Not yet. Please. Not just yet.

I tense around him, holding his body inside mine with everything I have as my hands find his hair. Jay sucks his breath in, and his stomach goes rock hard against me as he spasms inside me, a whole new wave of heat rushing between us as he comes again.

"Fuck!" Jay groans, the unexpectedness of it catching us both by surprise.

He looks at me, a grin spreading over his face as he catches his breath. I smile back at him, wrapping my arms around the back of his neck.

I'm blessed with the love of such a beautiful man. Being here, with him, just shows me how strong our love is. It's taken him years to open up to someone and let them in. He chose me.

There's no greater honor than knowing he chose me to share his heart with.

The way he treats me, the way I feel when I'm with him. I feel worthy of love again because I'm enough for him. He loves me; he loves all of me.

Jay's eyes are on mine, our bodies still connected, our hearts beating in time with each other. We couldn't be any closer. As if reading my thoughts, he lifts my chin, tilting it up toward him.

"I love you, Holly Havers," he murmurs, dusting his thumb over my bottom lip before leaning forward to kiss it.

I kiss him back, allowing my heart rate to slow as I hold him tight.

"I love you too, Mr. Anderson." I smile.

I look into his eyes, clear and bright, and I know beyond a doubt that here, with him is where I belong.

Together is where we've always belonged.

Being here, with Jay, loving each other, I finally understand. I'm exactly where I should be.

Here in his arms, I know... I'm home.

Epilogue

6 Months Later

"Matt, calm down." I shake my head as he flaps around the room.

"Calm down? This is not the time for being calm, Holly. Where the hell is it?" he cries as he upturns cushions on the sofa, before picking up his shoe and shaking it upside down, peering inside with narrowed eyes.

"Yeah, like you'd have put your speech inside your shoe." Rach snorts as she rolls her eyes.

"Don't you start," Matt warns, pointing his shoe at her. "I suppose you've thought of the perfect place to keep yours?"

"Hell, yeah, always prepared," Rach says as she lifts her long gold dress up, exposing a lace garter with a piece of paper carefully folded and tied around it.

"Well, I can hardly pull my trousers down at the reception to untie mine, can I?" he grumbles, unimpressed.

Rach screws up her nose in disgust. "Ewww, I do not want to think about what you would have to tie yours around!"

I giggle at my two best friends.

"There, Holly, I think we're done." Shona smiles over my shoulder at me in the dressing table mirror.

"Oh, Holly!" My mum clasps her hands together. "You look beautiful, doesn't she, Tim?"

"Stunning." My dad smiles over at me, his eyes misty.

"Oh, Dad." Sophie passes him a handkerchief, and he dabs at his eyes.

Shona has outdone herself again. I'm dewy and golden and glowing! My makeup is flawless. I wanted a 'natural, but glam' look, and Shona has nailed it. My lashes are thick, soft, and fluttery, and my green eyes are sparkling with excitement. My hair is curled in soft waves, the front pinned back from my face. It reminds me of a mermaid, perfect for a beach wedding.

"Thank you so much, Shona." I grin at her.

"No problem, Holly." She winks. "I'll see you out there, and don't worry about later; it's all set."

"Thank you!" I beam, pressing my palms together and taking a deep breath.

In less than half an hour, I'm going to become Mrs. Holly Anderson. I can't quite believe it. One year ago, I could never have imagined that this is where I would be today. Mum, Dad, Sophie, Rach, and Matt are all here, in our house, getting ready with me. I couldn't just have one maid of honor, so I've got three! Sophie, Matt, and Rach all wanted to speak at the reception dinner, so I said yes. Who am I to complain? I have a sister and two of the best friends in the world. All here to love and support me and Jay as we start this new adventure together.

I couldn't be more blessed.

"Okay, it's time to put on the dress!" Sophie announces.

There are squeals of excitement, the loudest come from Matt who has given up looking for his lost speech. The girls help me step into my dress and zip the back up for me before I walk over to the full-length mirror. The dress is incredible. Shona helped point me in the right places for where to look for it. She's become a good friend since I left the airline and moved over to LA five months ago. I twirl and the dress shimmers in the mirror. It's got thin straps and a low V-neck front. The material itself is sheer and covered with sewn-on organza flowers. The skirt flows out, and a split runs up one thigh. It's sexy, yet elegant. I didn't want shoes for the ceremony, so instead I've got delicate floral cuffs around each ankle.

"Wow, Holly." Rach's eyes widen. "Never mind Jay; marry me instead!"

We all laugh as we take in the final look now that my dress is on.

"It's almost perfect," Mum says, squeezing my hands. "It just needs this." She hands me an ivory box with a cream silk ribbon on.

"What's this, Mum?"

"Open it and see." She smiles at me.

I lift the lid off and fold back the tissue paper inside. "Oh, Mum!" I whisper as I take out the long, delicate veil she wore when she married my dad. "It's perfect, thank you." My eyes fill with tears as she fixes it into my hair at the back.

She stands back to admire her handiwork. "There, now you look like a bride."

I grin at her. Now I've got the veil as my something old and borrowed, my dress as the something new, and a lace garter as something blue.

There's a knock at the door and Sophie goes to answer it, her long gold dress that matches Rachel's swishing as she walks.

"Hey, Stefan."

I turn and catch his eye as he walks into the room. He looks so smart in his black suit and bow tie, the same as Matt's.

"Oh my! Holly!" he exclaims as he takes me in head to toe, his mouth hanging open.

I grin and kiss him on the cheek. "Thanks, Stefan."

"Wait until he sees you. Speaking of which, I can't be long as I have best man duties with Blake to attend to. But I just thought you might have been looking for this, babe?" He raises an eyebrow at Matt as he holds up a piece of folded paper between his fingers.

"Yes!" Matt cries, grabbing it. "I love you!" he says as he kisses Stefan right on the lips. Stefan clears his throat and straightens his glasses, aware that we are all watching them.

"Right, I better be off; it's almost time, Holly." He smiles at me and nods to the others before his eyes go to Matt's and he shoots him a dreamy look as he leaves.

"I better take my seat too," Mum says. She gives me a hug and kiss, and I'm wrapped in the scent of lilies from her perfume.

"See you soon, Mum." I beam.

"You ready, sweetheart?" Dad asks.

The giant heart-shaped diamond ring sparkles back at me as I look down at my hands. Jay gave it to me when he asked me to marry him, one month after we got back together. So much has happened since then.

I pick up my hand-tied bouquet, a beautiful, fragrant selection of yellow, pink, and white flowers that Maggie grew in her garden. I glance at my wrist; the watch Jay gave me all those months ago signaling it's time.

"Yes." I beam. "I'm so ready."

We walk out through the new house Jay and I bought. It's a beautiful ocean-front house that opens onto a large decked area and pool, much like his house in the hills. Only, behind the pool at this one there are steps that lead down onto the beautiful soft sand of the beach, and behind that the shimmering ocean. Every day I wake up here, next to him, is a dream.

Jay is still acting, but we've also opened a health and wellness retreat. I teach yoga there, and work with a great team who offer holistic approaches to living a happier, more fulfilled life. It's an incredible place. Jay wanted to focus on supporting those who have lost loved ones, so we have trained therapists running group and individual sessions. It's only been open two months, but we've already won an award for 'best service to the community' for our free well-being workshops.

Dad and I follow Sophie, Matt, and Rach over the sand toward where ceremony will take place. I don't know how Jay did it, but he got permission to have our ceremony on the beach this evening. Not just any part of the beach. We are going to say our vows underneath the giant rock archway I saw all those months ago when we had breakfast nearby. He arranged it as a surprise. He remembered the comments I made about all the couples who have stood under there, madly in love with the sand between their toes. It just confirms to me how much he loves me and how lucky I am.

I loop my arm through Dad's as we walk down the beach until the archway comes into view. I hold my breath as I take it all in. There's a band playing a beautiful country love song. The male singer's voice carries over to me on the breeze. We wanted a small, intimate ceremony. There are only a handful of wooden chairs on either side of the aisle, filled with our family and closest friends. The sand is covered in white, pink, and yellow petals that match the flowers tied to the backs of each chair. Maggie insisted on doing it as a wedding gift.

Dad places his hand over mine as we reach the aisle. My stomach flutters with excitement. I can't see Jay yet as the others are in front of me. Stefan was under strict instructions not to let him look around until I walk up the aisle. I take a deep, steadying breath as the band begins a new song, one we've chosen for this moment.

"You're everything I ever wanted, everything I need..."

As they sing the words, I know this is it. This is the moment I see Jay. We spent last night apart, as is tradition. It's the first night we've been apart since getting back together, and I hardly slept a wink.

Sophie turns to smile at me before she walks down the aisle on one side of Matt. Rach is on his other.

I take a step forward and the soft petals surround my foot. I can't help beaming like an idiot as I take each step, holding on to Dad's arm as I look around.

Eric and Cooper are with their girlfriends. Doug is sitting next to Anya, who's glowing with her round, pregnant belly. To my other side, Maggie and her husband are smiling. She doesn't have her purple crocks on today; instead, she has an unusual hair comb with a purple bird of paradise. Sitting in front of them are Shona and her husband, who give me a small wave.

As we near the top of the aisle, there's Mum on one side, and Sheila, Bill, Blake, and Stefan on the other. I draw my eyes to the seats behind Sheila and Bill, to Beth and her husband. Both have tears in their eyes but are smiling at me. We've been up to visit them a couple of times. They really are happy to see Jay and I together, even though we can't deny someone very important is missing today. She's here though, somewhere, making the sun shine down.

Finally, I know the person who I've been aching to see the most is only steps away. A tingle runs up my spine as my body senses him. I grip on to Dad's arm harder and raise my eyes.

There, standing and waiting to marry me, his intense blue eyes focused on mine, is Jay.

He's wearing a black suit and bow tie, his chiseled jaw covered in the perfect amount of stubble, his hair calling to me to grab it between my fingers. We stop in front of him, and he shakes Dad's hand. Dad turns to me, kissing my cheek before he takes my hand from his arm and places it on Jay's. His warm fingers close around mine. His eyes crinkle at the corners as he leans down to whisper in my ear.

"You are breathtaking."

Heat flushes my cheeks as I gaze back at him. I can't even speak, I'm a ball of excited nerves. Jay looks amused as our minister begins to speak. I don't hear any of the words he says. All I can do is look at Jay's face and try to control the hammering in my chest. He speaks his vows to me, sliding my wedding band onto my finger without taking his eyes off mine.

"Holly?" the minister says.

"Huh? Sorry?" I say as I tear my eyes away from Jay. Our friends and family laugh at my total lack of attention.

The minister smiles at me. "Holly, are you ready to say your vows to Jay?"

I nod as I take a deep breath and pledge my promises to him.

Pledge my heart to him.

He watches me, his eyes never leaving mine for a second. I look down to slip the wedding ring down over his knuckle and stop, my eyes widening.

What the...?

I look back into Jay's eyes and they're creased in amusement as he bites his lip to hide his smile. I can't quite believe what I'm seeing. I glance back down and there, around his wedding finger, freshly tattooed, is a tiny wreath of holly.

I shake my head as I struggle to hold in my giggle.

"I now pronounce you husband and wife. You may kiss the bride!" the minister announces.

We grin at each other as Jay reaches to cup my face between his hands. He dusts his thumb across my bottom lip as I wrap my arms around his neck. Then his warm, soft lips take mine as he kisses me.

His love for me speaks to me in that kiss. It takes my breath away.

Applause and cheers erupt around us, and I squeal as Jay dips me back and deepens his kiss. I'm pretty sure it's Blake who calls out "get a room!" before everyone laughs.

Jay lifts me back up and I open my eyes. "Mrs. Anderson." His eyes twinkle. "Any first words for your husband?"

"Mr. Anderson," I murmur, "you're such an idiot." I break into a smile and look back down at his hand, the edges of the Holly tattoo just visible underneath his wedding ring.

Jay throws his head back and laughs. "I love the things you say, Holly." He leans down to kiss me again.

"Oh, I know you do," I whisper. "Just you wait until later... husband."

Jay's eyes light up as he grins at me.

The rest of the evening is incredible. We have an amazing buffet set up out on the deck, all lit up with fairy lights. There are large glass vases with candles flickering inside dotted around the beach, and a dance floor has been placed down over the sand. The band plays one great song after another and we all eat, dance, and sing out loud.

"Now, ladies and gentlemen, if I could have your attention for a moment please," the band's singer says into the microphone. "It's time for the bouquet toss!"

A cheer erupts and I'm bustled to one edge of the dance floor as everyone piles behind me on the opposite side.

"Mrs. Anderson, on the count of three! *One, two, three!*"

I laugh as I throw my bouquet high into the air and over my head, spinning around before it comes down. There's no mistaking Matt's hand as it shoots up in the air, heading straight for it. The look of pure determination on his face is a picture. His fingers skim it, but they knock it off course toward the side of the group and it lands in Rach's arms as she's about to take a drink.

"Hey! What?" she splutters, looking around in shock.

"Not fair!" Matt cries out. "You didn't even want to catch it," he grumbles like a sulking child, crossing his arms over his chest.

His moaning is soon cut short by a loud crackle and pop as the sky lights up in a rainbow of colors. I smile over at Shona, who gives me a thumbs-up. What's the use of having a friend whose husband is the biggest special effects guy in Hollywood if you can't have the best display at your wedding?

Jay's warm arm snakes around my waist. He's ditched his jacket and bow tie and rolled his sleeves up. He looks so edible right now.

My sexy husband.

"Did you do this, Holly?" he asks, his eyebrows raised.

"You aren't the only one full of surprises, you know." I smile at him as he pulls me in to his side.

We all stand and watch the fireworks and lights show. There are plenty of 'ooohhhs' and 'aaahhhs' as images are projected across the night sky. The first being an aircraft flying. The next a heart and two people kissing. The band plays throughout, which just adds to the theatrics of it all. When it ends, there's an enormous cheer and some people dance again, while others go to get a drink.

"Looks like you're next then, Rach?" I say as she comes over with my bouquet in one hand. Jay gives me a kiss and gestures that he's going to talk to Blake.

"Yeah, we'll see about that." She raises an eyebrow, her face unimpressed.

"No one will marry you if you keep your face like that, looking like a slapped arse," Matt quips as he dances past us.

"Takes one to know one!" Rach fires back, but she's smiling as she looks back at me.

"Can you believe two years ago you dated that sleazeball Simon, and now you've married Mr. Perfect God?" Rach asks as she puts an arm around me.

"God, no," I scoff at the mention of Simon. Not long after Hong Kong he was sacked for sexual harassment. He'd had multiple complaints made against him. I've no idea what he's doing now.

"You deserve it, Holls," Rach says as she leans her head against me. "I miss you though!"

"I miss you too. How's it going living with Megan?"

"Really good." Rach sighs. "She's been helping me house hunt."

I can't help my voice rising in excitement. "You've saved the deposit up?"

Rach's eyes glitter. "Almost. Thanks to Mr. X."

"Wow." I blow out a breath. "Do you still hear from him?"

"Oh yeah, he's still my best, and only, customer." She smiles. "I know it's got to stop soon though. I've nearly got the deposit, which is the only reason I was doing it."

"But?" I ask, searching Rach's face.

"But nothing." She shrugs. "I just feel like so much is changing, you know? My best friend has moved across the Atlantic. My other friend has found his soulmate." She gestures to Matt who is now dancing with Stefan, each of them whispering into each other's ears and laughing together.

"You know you're welcome here whenever you like, Rach. I will always be just a phone call or flight away." I wrap an arm around her.

"I know, Holls, I know."

We stand and sway together to the music and watch my dad do some kind of dance move I don't think I've ever seen anyone perform before, and there's a good reason for that. My mum moves back, giving him a wide berth as he swings his elbows around.

"He's got some moves," Rach says with a straight face.

"I'll say." I giggle.

"Do you mind if I steal my wife back for a moment?" Jay asks.

"Not at all. I needed a refill anyway," Rach says, tilting her glass and giving me a squeeze before heading off toward the bar.

"Mrs. Anderson, may I have this dance?"

"You may, Mr. Anderson." I beam.

He pulls me up against him and my breath hitches as his strong body presses against mine. Even after a year, he still has this effect on me. It's only getting stronger. I breathe in his scent and let out a small, contented sigh.

"Are you happy, Berry?" His bright eyes are trained on mine.

"Deliriously. You?"

"Immensely," he says, pulling his eyebrows together so he looks serious, before breaking into a smile. "I've got a surprise for you, Mrs. Anderson," he whispers in my ear as he kisses my neck and a tingle spreads through my body.

"What could be better than this?" I whisper.

"I've booked us a honeymoon."

I pull back to look at him. His eyes are mischievous.

"Really?" I can't conceal my excitement. "Where are we going?"

"I'm taking you somewhere very, very special," he says as I nod eagerly. "Somewhere we have to be on the lookout for something very, very special." I nod again. "Somewhere incredible things happen that someone once told me about."

"Spit it out, Jay!" I laugh.

His eyes crinkle in the corners as he looks at me. "Somewhere that if we are very, very lucky, we may see a male bird, pole dancing for his lady."

I look into his eyes before I howl with laughter. "What?" I gasp.

"As soon as you told me about it, Holly, I knew I would take you there one day."

I look at him, my eyes wide.

"We're going to Indonesia. West Papua to be exact," Jay says. "I'm telling you though, if we don't see one of these damn birds I've heard so much about, then you're going to be the one dancing on my pole to make it up to me." His eyes roam down over my body.

"How about I practice now?" I reach one hand up and tug at his hair.

Jay groans and pulls me against him. "You're a naughty girl, Mrs. Anderson. You want to sneak off and leave our guests?"

I smile up at him. "Don't you?"

"Fuck, yes!" Jay shoots straight back as he pulls me by the hand back toward the house. We get to the door before he wraps me in his arms. "Did I tell you how much I love you?" His blue eyes search mine.

"You did. But tell me again," I murmur as I pull his lips against mine.

"I love you, Mrs. Anderson."

I smile back at him, at the way his voice sounds as he calls me that.

"I love you too, Mr. Anderson."

He wraps me in his arms, and I sink into them, knowing this is where I belong.

This is where my heart will always be.

Here, with my Mr. Anderson.

(The Almost End)

Extended Honeymoon Epilogue

Chapter 1

Jay - Now

"Can I get your autograph, please?"

I turn around to greet the lady behind me with a smile. She has a magazine clutched tightly in one hand and a pen in the other.

"Sure. Who shall I make it out to?"

Her gaze travels past me and her eyes light up as she shuffles closer. Despite her being of similar age to my grandma, I still stiffen and wrap an arm around Holly's waist on instinct, drawing her into my side.

"I'd love yours too, Jay. But actually, this first one's for your wife." The lady thrusts the magazine toward Holly.

It's the interview Holly did before we were married. It's the only one she would agree, providing that the magazine donated a sizeable amount to an animal charity instead of paying her for it.

"This one's for you, Berry," I say into Holly's ear, squeezing her waist.

Her green eyes sparkle, and her lips curl into a shy smile. She tucks a lock of golden blonde hair behind her ear and takes the pen. I watch the easy way she chats and laughs with the lady, who is completely captivated by her. I sign another page in the magazine the lady finds for me, and then she leaves.

"What did she have you sign?" Holly asks as I take her suitcase and stack it on top of mine.

"A lawn mower ad."

She bursts into giggles as she takes my free hand, linking our fingers. "First time for everything, huh?"

The sun has brought out a few freckles on her nose, spinning lighter threads of gold into her hair. My heart squeezes at the thought that I almost didn't have all of this. I almost lost her.

"I love you, Mrs. Anderson."

"I'm still getting used to hearing you call me that."

I stop walking a few meters in front of the airline check-in desk and pull her into my arms, ignoring the fact that someone is bound to catch this on their phone, and it'll be on some online celebrity gossip column before we even take off for our honeymoon.

"Well, you've got a lifetime to get used to it, Mrs. Anderson." I capture her lips in a kiss and groan as she submits and lets me slide my hands up to cup her face.

"Jay," she whispers. Where Holly's concerned, I'm unable to hide the stirrings of my dick in my pants from pressing into her. "People are looking."

"Let them look. I want to kiss my wife."

She indulges me in another kiss and then pulls back, placing her hands on my chest.

"When we get there..." Her eyes drop to my lips as she smiles innocently. But I know my wife; she isn't innocent, not with me. And I fucking love it. "When we get there and it's just us, then..."

She trails off, blinking up at me, and the fire in her eyes has my dick throbbing. It doesn't matter that I woke her up with my head between her thighs this morning. Or that I made her come twice, wrapped around me in the shower before we left for the airport.

All I want is her.

My wife.

I grab her hand in mine and turn, striding purposefully toward the first-class check-in desk.

"Don't *dawdle*, Wife," I say, chuckling as she swats me for putting on a British accent like hers.

But she knows I love everything that comes out of her mouth.

I love everything that is Holly Anderson, and how she came into my life.

Chapter 2

Jay - Then

I LIFT MY HEAD as the flight's safety demonstration begins.

The air is punched from my lungs as vibrant green eyes framed by golden strands of hair fill my vision. The female flight attendant looks down the aisle as she begins to go through the safety instructions.

I don't listen to a damn word. The only thing I can hear is my heartbeat as I watch her. Her eyes flit to mine, then away again. I'm assaulted by a rush of familiar memories all at once. But where they're often painful, these ones are bright, filled with laughter, with hope... with love.

The subtle blush creeping up her neck indicates that she's aware of my intense pull to her. But it's not enough to make me stop. Nothing could make me turn my attention away from her. I've heard of these moments where people say your gut is telling you something. And I'd never have believed them if it wasn't for this undeniable draw I have building in my core.

Maybe this is purely a moment to help me remember something good for a change.

To let go of that self-blame that cursed every breath, every smile, every piece of good news and fortune that came my way.

All those moments have felt stolen, or like I've cheated my way into them.

But right now, I only feel pure calm.

And peace.

"Sir, do you have your seatbelt fastened?"

I stare up at the blonde flight attendant, only managing to say a single word, "Yes." I lift my T-shirt to show her.

"Thank you."

She talks to an older lady sitting on the opposite side of the aisle to me, and then walks off, returning with a glass of water for her.

Damn, why didn't I think of that?

They chat for a moment, and the older lady asks the flight attendant if she's ever been in love. The flight attendant smiles as she says 'no', then introduces herself as Holly.

Holly.

The name circles in my head on repeat; the sound of her sweet voice as she said her name in that British accent like a melody to my tarnished soul.

Holly.

We have eleven and a half hours of flying time before we reach LA from London.

And I intend to know a lot more about Holly by the end of it.

Chapter 3

Holly - Now

"Did you know about this?"

Jay raises his brows in mock innocence. "About what?"

I place my finger on the first-class lounge's menu, tapping the scripted font advertising today's cocktail, 'The Berry Special'.

Jay smirks. "Ah... sounds tasty. Let's order two." He wraps an arm around me and squeezes my hip as he signals to a server.

"Well?" I jab him in the ribs, but he just winks at me as the server reaches us, then orders.

"It might share the nickname I gave you, Mrs. Anderson. But I bet it won't taste as sweet when it comes."

My eyes dart to the server's retreating back. They're far enough away to miss what Jay said. But only just.

I jab him again, making him snicker. "What? It's the truth." He slides his hand up my thigh and toys with the hem of my dress.

"Stop," I giggle and place my hand over the top of his, but make no attempt to push him away.

"You expect me to control myself when I know what juicy deliciousness is under here?" He squeezes my flesh, making me clamp my thighs together as heat rushes between them.

He grins and then moves his hand higher until his pinky finger grazes the damp lace of my panties.

"Fuck, you're wet," he groans, finding my swollen clit and rubbing it.

"Oh my god." My cheeks heat, and I glance around the lounge at the other passengers waiting for their flight. We're in a quiet corner and hidden by the table, so no one can see Jay with his hand up my dress, but it still makes me anxious.

"I can't wait to get there," he breathes against my neck, sliding his lips over my fluttering pulse as he rubs more determined circles over the lace.

"Jay." I fist his shirt and turn toward him so we look like any other in love couple having a cuddle and whispering sweet words to one another.

"You're going to spend our honeymoon with my cum running down your thighs," he groans, sucking on the tender skin beneath my ear, as he hooks the fabric to one side and presses his fingers back onto my bare flesh.

Yeah, sweet words.

"Oh god," I whimper, wishing I could clamp my eyes shut and truly give in to the building pressure between my thighs. But I'm too busy making sure no one's paying attention to us.

I married Hollywood's most in-demand actor and the man who tops all of the 'world's sexiest men' polls every year. It's unusual for us to go anywhere and for him not to be recognized and looked at. But the lounge is quiet, and thankfully, we're the only two people seated in this area. It's almost like he planned it this way.

"Jay," I moan, getting dangerously close to the point of no return as his fingers continue rubbing my slick skin.

"Come for me, Berry," he grunts. "You know I can't fucking get enough of you coming for me."

My eyes land on the server at the bar. He's loading two cocktail glasses with a deep red liquid onto a silver tray. Jay's thumb slides over me again, and my breathing quickens.

"He's coming back, Jay."

He chuckles against my neck. "Better be quick then, *Wife*."

He slides two fingers inside me, curling them forward, all the while continuing to rub my clit. The server picks up the tray and moves toward us.

"Jay!"

"Do it," he urges.

I sink my teeth into my bottom lip, biting back a cry as I come hard on his fingers. "Oh fuc—"

Jay seals his mouth over mine, swallowing down my whimpered moans. My body sucks his fingers greedily, steadily clamping and releasing on them as he finger-fucks me slow enough that his arm doesn't appear to be moving if anyone were to look.

"That's it, let it go," Jay soothes as I squeeze my eyes shut, burying my face into the crook of his neck.

I wrap my arms around his neck as the final pulses flutter around his fingers.

"Thank you," his deep voice says.

"Thank you," I echo. I don't look up until the server leaves.

Jay's blue eyes glimmer with amusement as he slides his fingers out of me and straightens my panties.

I straighten in my seat, meeting his eyes.

He sucks his fingers into his mouth with a deep, appreciative groan. "So fucking sweet, Berry."

I wet my lips, managing to take the cocktail glass from him.

"Why is no one sitting near us?" I ask.

He just smiles as I take a sip of the cocktail, relishing the cool burst of flavor hitting my tongue. It's perfect. Sweet with a rich tang of berry and a splash of rum. Exactly what I'd pick to drink on honeymoon.

"Good?"

"Yes. But how did you get them to do it?"

"Jet Grant," Jay says as he takes a sip of his drink.

"Seriously?" I scoff, staring at him.

He shrugs like it's no big deal. Sometimes I forget how famous Jay is. He's just Jay to me. But to the world, he's Jay Anderson, Hollywood heartthrob and award-winning actor. Something I'm slowly getting used to.

"How did you get the CEO of the airline I used to work for to make a cocktail just for you? And reserve half of the seats in here?"

"For you," Jay corrects, eyeing me over the rim of his glass. "This is all for you."

He places his glass down and takes both of my hands inside his. "I never told you why I was in London, did I?"

I frown. I met Jay when I was called off standby as a flight attendant to operate from London to LA. He was traveling alone and seated in my section. I assumed he was flying for an audition or something to do with work.

"I came over from LA to attend Jet's mother's funeral."

"I'm so sorry." He hates funerals, with good reason after everything.

No one should have to bury someone so young, like he did.

"It is what it is." He rakes his fingers back through his dirty-blond hair.

"How did you two become friends?"

A soft smile stretches across his lips. "We met when Atlantic Airways cast me for an ad. I remember passing the time between takes talking to him. We got on well and stayed in touch."

"I can't believe you're friends with a billionaire airline owner," I tease.

"He's a really nice guy."

I shake my head with a laugh as I take another sip of my drink. I met Jet once at an airline awards dinner when I was working at Atlantic Airways. He was professional and extremely focused on the presentation he was giving. His mother and father were there. She looked so proud of him.

Jay links his fingers with mine.

"I know that look, Berry," he says softly.

"What look?" I sigh as warmth blankets over me. For him, I'm the most precious thing in his world.

"The one where you're thinking of other people." He arches a brow.

Busted.

"So, what should I be thinking of? Tell me, Husband."

He lifts our joined hands and kisses my fingers. The edges of the holly wreath tattoo peek out from beneath his wedding band as his eyes glint.

"Think about how I'm going to worship every sexy inch of you for the next two weeks."

I bite my lower lip, understanding the intensity that has taken over his eyes, making his pupils flare with desire.

"Really? Every inch?"

"Inside and out." He turns our hands so he can press a kiss to the inside of my wrist. Goosebumps scatter up my spine at his touch.

The server approaches us, breaking the tension that could have resulted in Jay taking me on the table if he'd had his way.

"Mr. and Mrs. Anderson? Your flight to New Guinea will be boarding in ten minutes."

Jay smiles. "You ready?"

Butterflies swarm my stomach. "So ready."

Chapter 4

Holly

"Patrick Howard should be worried for his job on *After Hours*. This guy puts on one hell of a show," Jay whispers.

I giggle and lean back against him. The mention of the talk show host that I went to watch Jay on that first night after we met brings a grin to my face. It's the first time I saw the magnitude of his fame and the life he leads in the spotlight all the time.

It was also the first time I glimpsed the pain in his eyes, hidden behind the dazzling smile.

That pain is different now. He still holds the memory of it in his heart and always will. But it doesn't hold him back from living anymore. It doesn't stop him from loving and accepting he's worthy of love in return.

"Love you," I whisper, wishing I could bottle this moment, knowing what we're about to witness.

"Love you too, Berry. Always."

We're sitting in hushed anticipation on a waterproof sheet on the jungle floor, a few meters away from Tooh, our guide. We've spent the last couple of hours hiking to this spot. Tooh said it's the best place to see New Guinea's birds of paradise getting up to their fully-fledged mating season antics.

The bird that Tooh said is called *The Magnificent*, hops around in the clearing we are sitting next to. It takes it's time picking up small twigs and leaves, clearing them away from the branch in the center.

"You had me at pole-dancing bird," Jay murmurs softly in my ear.

"I can't believe I said that."

His chest vibrates with a silent chuckle. "I'm so glad you did. It's the moment I started falling in love with you."

"Jay..." I incline my face toward his, smiling, as his lips dust my cheek.

Tooh lifts his hand in the air, signaling us to keep watching.

I squeeze Jay's forearm that's wrapped around me as the bird begins his mating call, then begins to dance up and down the branch when a female lands nearby and gives him her attention.

I could have died of embarrassment when Jay asked me for an inflight movie recommendation when we met all those months ago. I blurted out about pole-dancing birds on an episode of *Blue Planet* I had seen and thought for sure he'd think I was weird.

But as we sit here, me inside his strong arms after everything we've been through together, it seems fitting that we're watching this little bird try his hardest to find love. I squeeze Jay's forearm again as I will the little bird not to give up. Not to ever give up.

It's worth the fight.

Jay's lips press into my hair, and I sink into him, with a smile on my face that's probably sickening with how in love and happy I am. But it wasn't easy getting here. And that's what makes it all that much better.

It's worth the fight, little bird, I chant inside my head as I watch the female bird tilt her head side to side, enraptured by his efforts.

So worth it.

"Hurry up before I break down the damn door, Mrs. Anderson."

I rest my head back onto Jay's shoulder and laugh as I struggle to pull the honeymoon suite key card from my purse.

"Not helping," he growls, peppering kisses up and down my neck as I keep rummaging in my purse.

"Oh, I don't know. I'm kind of enjoying myself out here."

He clasps my throat in one hand, using his thumb to turn my chin so my eyes meet his.

"Open the door before I fuck you against it and the whole world hears you scream my name."

His pupils dilate with barely contained lust as I bite my bottom lip, playing with him.

"I love when you make me scream."

"Fuck, Holly." He slams his other hand against the door of our suite, pinning me between the wood and his solid frame. "You want me to punish you once we get inside, is that it? You want me to rip these tiny little things you call panties off you so I can plunge my cock into you so hard you'll feel me for days?"

I huff out a strangled moan that's dripping with desire. He's right. I did pack the most delicate, tiny panties I could find. This is our honeymoon. It seemed right that I pack for the occasion.

I love that he noticed.

"I don't think you'll want to rip the ones I'm wearing." I bat my eyelashes. "They're special."

I push my ass back against him, and his eyes flutter closed with a deep groan as I grind against the erection in his pants.

"Don't push me, Berry," he utters. "I'm so close to spanking your ass." His thumb traces a path along my jawline as he pulls my lips to his for a searing kiss.

I melt into him, whimpering, when he nips my lower lip.

"I thought you enjoyed bird watching," I say with mock innocence, pressing my ass harder against him.

"I did," he groans against my lips before kissing me again. "But all I want now is to take my wife inside our suite and spend the rest of the night inside her."

Jay loosens his grip on my neck at the exact moment my fingers curl around the key card in my purse. I pull it out, and the second I press it to the door's sensor, Jay spins me inside his arms and kisses me as we stumble backward.

We're a tangle of groping hands and hungry mouths.

"Shut the door," I gasp as Jay whips my sundress up and over my head before we're fully over the threshold.

He kicks it closed with his foot.

"Feeling shy?" He smirks, his eyes dropping to where I've tried to cover up my bra and panties with my hands.

I drop my arms. The heat in his stare makes slickness gather between my thighs.

"Come here."

He pulls me in and angles my face where he needs it, drawing me into a deep kiss that has every nerve ending tingling with energy. I kiss him back with everything I have, sliding my hands up into his hair and tugging.

"Jesus," he hisses.

Heat fires through my veins as he looks at me with heavy lust-filled eyes. He loves it when I pull his hair.

"Sorry, was I too rough?" I yank his hair again. My pulse pounds at the sinful smile that creeps over his face as his head is jerked back.

"You had to do that, didn't you, Mrs. Anderson?"

For a moment, we stare at each other, hearts pounding, chests rising and falling with labored breaths. Desire thrums in the air between us, making my pulse soar.

Then I smirk. "You can handle it."

Jay chuckles, and it's the only sound I hear as my feet leave the floor and I'm thrown into the air and over his shoulder. His large palm plants a firm smack on my ass, leaving the skin tingling with heat.

"Jay," I squeal.

"Don't act like you don't love it. We both know you've already soaked through these little panties you're wearing." He hooks a finger beneath the silk, sliding it through my wetness to prove his point.

"Do you like them?"

"I'll like them better when they're on the floor."

I giggle, listening to the way his breathing halts as he runs his hand over my ass and the embroidery on the fabric. He strides across the room, stopping in front of the full-length mirror on the wall.

"Holly," he murmurs, positioning the silk across my ass cheeks so he can read what they have stitched onto them.

"They were a gift from Rachel."

"I see." He traces a fingertip over the light blue lettering, over the words my best friend chose. "And is it true?"

"You know it is," I breathe, wriggling on his shoulder as I try to create some friction between my thighs.

"Property of Jay Anderson," he muses, kneading my ass cheek with his strong fingers until I moan. "Does that mean I can do whatever I like with what's inside?"

"Please," I whimper, wriggling some more. "Just touch me, Jay."

He walks us to the bed and tosses me onto it.

"Anything you say, Wife."

He reaches around, finding my bra strap and flicking it undone with ease.

"Jay." I tip my head back with a moan as he throws my bra to one side and his warm lips latch straight onto my nipple and suck.

"Talk to me, Berry. Tell me what you want. You know I love it when you let go."

I arch into his mouth as he towers over me, one muscular arm planted either side of my ribs.

"I want..." My eyes roll in my head as he switches side and sucks my other nipple. "Oh god." A rush of arousal seeps between my legs.

"Talk," Jay barks, pulling back far enough to land a light slap across my nipple before he sucks it into his mouth again.

"Fuck." I push my breast further into his mouth. The feel of his teeth grating over my skin has me grabbing at his hair and pulling his head up.

His gaze blazes with dark encouragement.

"Holly," he grits.

I know what he wants. I know what he likes.

"Jay," I purr, tugging his hair and enjoying the way his eyes narrow as I guide his head lower. "Shut up and lick me. Then fill me with your perfect cock."

A sinful smile overtakes his lips. It steals my breath as he moves down the bed. He hooks a thumb into each side of my panties and slowly slides them down my legs, never taking his eyes from mine. Then he brings the tiny scrap of material up to his nose and inhales.

"Smells like mine," he growls, keeping my panties in his hand as he yanks his T-shirt up and over the back of his head with his free hand.

He stands and pushes his shorts down, freeing his cock. Every muscle beneath his bronzed skin tightens and ripples as he moves. I never knew a man could be so beautiful. So mesmerizing. But that's what he is.

So beautiful that sometimes it hurts looking at him.

He stands at the foot of the bed, his gaze roaming over my naked body, spread wide open for him.

"You want me to lick you?" His eyes take in my pussy, and my cheeks heat at the blatant want in his gaze.

"Please." I wriggle with impatience.

He tuts, his teeth sinking into his lower lip, as he wraps my panties around his cock and fists himself in slow strokes.

He looks like sex. Raw, uninhibited dirty sex. Sex that's going to devour me in the most spine-tingling way.

"Show me where. Show me exactly how you like it."

I rush to do as he says, dropping my hands between my thighs. The deep grunt in his throat as I part my pussy lips wide and show him how wet I am for him makes my clit throb.

"Right here." I slide a finger inside myself. When I draw it back it's coated in wetness.

"Fuck." Jay kneels on the bottom of the bed, his attention glued to my fingers as I push two inside my pussy.

"Lick me here," I pant as I pull them back out.

Jay grabs my hand, holding my eyes as he takes my fingers past his lips and sucks the shining wetness off them with a low hum of appreciation.

Then he guides my wet fingers to his hair and pushes them through it.

"Hold on."

He lowers his head and the second his mouth settles over my clit and sucks; I sink my other hand into his hair and tug.

"God, Jay!"

He smiles against me as he pushes deeper, licking, sucking, and tasting every part of me. The moment his tongue pushes inside me, I come hard on his face.

"Stop! I can't..." I wriggle, trying to break the overwhelming feeling as he moves his tongue back to my clit, flattening over it, and circling with deliberate, unrelenting pressure.

"You will," he growls, holding my thighs apart with his hands as he eats me out without mercy.

I shudder and thrash beneath him, but he keeps licking and sucking at my clit until I'm screaming his name and coming for him again.

"Good girl, Holly. That's my good fucking *wife*."

I'm a hot, trembling mess. He rises from between my thighs, the lower half of his face shining with the evidence of my orgasms.

"Now tell me what you want next."

My eyes drop to his hand, still gripping onto my panties. He starts fisting his cock again, pre-cum gathering in fat drops on the thick, smooth head.

"I want your cock," I breathe, staring at the pre-cum as Jay swipes his finger through it.

"You sure?"

He arches a brow as he brings his cum-coated finger to my lips and pushes it inside my mouth. I groan around it, sucking his taste off greedily until it's all gone.

"I'm sure. Hurry up. I need you inside me, filling me up, *please*."

I'm panting with need as he lowers himself over me until his broad shoulders have me trapped inside his arms.

"Get your legs wider."

"Wider," he hisses, his jaw clenching. "I'm going to fuck you so damn hard. Get them wide."

I stretch as far as I can and cry out as he thrusts inside me with one determined drive of his hips.

"Tell me how it feels." He holds my eyes as he rails into me, setting his own rhythm.

"So good." My eyes flutter as I moan. "I love your cock."

He pushes inside me again with a smirk.

"What?" I smile.

"I love you." He grins. "You're so damn beautiful, looking like an angel. But with me..."

"With you?" I gasp as he bottoms out inside me, and his balls kiss my skin.

His biceps tense as he repeats the depth again.

"With me, you let go," he hisses and pulls out of me; his cock soaked with my arousal. "With me, you're the perfect mix of sweet and naughty." He plunges back inside, making me ripple around him.

"Naughty, huh?" I arch away from the mattress and force his head down to suck my nipple.

"Fuck, yeah," he groans around a mouthful of my breast. "Naughty just for me."

"For you, only for you," I breathe.

Jay's thrusts grow harder, more determined, as he sucks my other breast hard enough to leave a mark. His tongue slides over the sore skin, leaving a delicious ache.

"Jay, I'm so close."

He lifts his head and bends to kiss me roughly.

"Do it."

I stare into his eyes as pleasure crashes through me.

"Come inside me at the same time. Make it run down my thighs like you promised."

His pupils blow wide as I clench around him.

"*Please.*"

"Fuck, Holly. You're so tight when you clamp down on me like this."

Jay holds my gaze as I shatter, coming in hard, consuming pulses around him.

"Jesus. That's it. Come on my cock. Soak it. Good girl."

Sweat pools along his hairline and on the planes of his solid chest as he pounds me through every wave and tightening.

His lips meet mine in a desperate kiss alongside the telltale swell of his cock inside me.

"Please," I beg.

"Fuck, Holly."

He screws his eyes closed, cursing against my lips as he spills inside me, filling me with stream after stream of liquid heat.

"More." I grab his ass cheeks, digging my nails into the tight flesh.

His eyes pop open, and he continues coming inside me with a force that makes them water.

"Fucking hell." He keeps thrusting into me, his lips seeking mine in a blistering kiss. "I love you, I love you, I love you," he chants, emptying everything he has inside me.

He searches my eyes with an intensity that makes my heart skip a beat.

"I love you, Holly. I knew the first time we met... I just knew."

Chapter 5

Jay

I stroke Holly's cheek as we lie in bed facing one another. It's the last day of our honeymoon and I kept my promise. We've barely left the suite since we came back from watching the birds.

I can't get enough of my *wife*.

A serene smile takes over her face.

"You're staring at me like that again." She giggles.

"Like what?" I dust my thumb over her full lower lip.

"Like you can't believe this is real."

"Sometimes, it's like it isn't. There were days I thought I'd never feel happy again."

"Jay." She rests her palm over my heart.

I place my hand over hers, pushing her palm against my skin so she can feel my heart beating.

"At the risk of sounding soppy, you changed everything for me. That day I met you put my life on a completely different path."

A tear slides down her cheek and falls onto the sheet. "You did the same for me."

I curl my arms around her and pull her across the sheets until she's pressed up against me.

"Don't cry, Berry. I know you're stuck with me, but it's not all bad." I take her hand and touch the diamond wedding band around her fingers.

Her laugh lights up her entire face. "Dork."

I grin, my heart swelling at the way I can put a smile on her face so easily. She's fucking radiant.

"So, what's next?" she muses.

"More sex, of course."

Her laugh has me pressing a kiss to her lips.

"We could call it practice."

"Practice for what?"

"For making Baby Anderson."

She stills and blinks at me with wide eyes.

"Making Baby Anderson?"

Her brow creases and then softens, then creases again.

"Making Baby Anderson," she whispers. "It has a kind of ring to it."

"It does, doesn't it?" I quirk a brow, making her giggle.

"So..." She bites her lower lip.

"We should really warm up first," I say.

"Oh, sure. I mean, you could pull a muscle, you have so many." She giggles as I swat her on the ass. "How do we warm up?"

I roll onto my back, bringing her with me. "We start with you sitting on my face, then my cock."

"Ah, gotcha."

"Come on, then." I purse my lips as I grab her hips and pull her up my body. She shrieks as I get her where I want her.

Her laugh dies as she looks at me and strokes my hair.

"I love you, Jay," she murmurs with a soft smile.

"I love you too, Mrs. Anderson. Now be a good wife and ride my mouth."

The Actual End

Elle's Books

Meeting Mr. Anderson is book 1 in 'The Men Series', a collection of interconnected standalone stories. They can be read in any order, however, for full enjoyment of the overlapping characters, the suggested reading order is:

Meeting Mr. Anderson – Holly and Jay
Discovering Mr. X – Rachel and Tanner
Drawn to Mr. King – Megan and Jaxon
Captured by Mr. Wild – Daisy and Blake
Pleasing Mr. Parker – Maria and Griffin
Trapped with Mr. Walker – Harley and Reed
Time with Mr. Silver – Rose and Dax
Resisting Mr. Rich – Maddy and Logan
Handling Mr. Harper – Sophie and Drew
Playing with Mr. Grant – Ava and Jet

(Also available by Elle, **Forget-me-nots and Fireworks**, Shona and Trent's story, a novella length prequel to The Men Series)

Get all Elle's books here: http://author.to/ellenicoll

About the Author

Elle Nicoll is an ex long-haul flight attendant and mum of two from the UK.

After fourteen years of having her head in the clouds whilst working at 38,000ft, she is now usually found with her head between the pages of a book reading or furiously typing and making notes on another new idea for a book boyfriend who is sweet-talking her.

Elle finds it funny that she's frequently told she looks too sweet and innocent to write a steamy book, but she never wants to stop. Writing stories about people, passion, and love, what better thing is there?

Because,

Love Always Wins

xxx

To keep up to date with the latest news and releases, find Elle in the following places, and sign up for her newsletter below;

https://www.subscribepage.com/ellenicollauthorcom
Facebook Reader Group – Love Always Wins –
https://www.facebook.com/groups/686742179258218
Website – https://www.ellenicollauthor.com

http://author.to/ellenicoll

facebook.com/ellenicollauthor

instagram.com/ellenicollauthor

bookbub.com/authors/elle-nicoll

pinterest.com/ellenicollauthor

tiktok.com/@authorellenicoll

goodreads.com/author/show/21415735.Elle_Nicoll

Acknowledgements

My first thank you must go to the incredible TL Swan, and her equally incredible group of cygnets. What was once merely a dream and nothing more, became something real and fulfilling with the encouragement and support of a group of kick-ass women! I've made some amazing friendships on this journey, and it is a wonderful feeling being part of a group where we all lift each other up and help wherever we can. You ladies are all amazing examples of how when women support each other, incredible things happen.

A huge thank you to my beta readers; Hannah, Christi, Dana and Nicola. You ladies were honest (without holding back) and supported me in bringing this story to life. Thank you for all of your patience, pep-talks and encouragement. I couldn't have done it without you all.

Kitty and Fred, thank you for all your encouragement and knowledge helping me navigate this new, and sometimes overwhelming world. Your time and experience has been very much appreciated.

Kimberly; thank you for all of your hard work and time! You made my words make sense, and I will be forever grateful for all of your expertise, the mum/Mum explanations and the discussions over the word 'arse!'

Thank you to Sherri for your beautiful covers! Thank you to my husband, Dan, and my two daughters. I know writing this book meant many late nights where I was sat typing, and you supported me. Girls, you give me a reason to be a better person and to chase my dreams, because I hope in my heart that you will always chase yours too, and never be afraid to take a leap of faith. But mostly, Dan, thank you for the last thirteen years. I couldn't have written about love and all of its beauty if I wasn't living it with you every day. Your sock fluff will never be okay, but you've shown me that real life fairy tales can happen, and for that I will always be blessed. Finally, my biggest thanks is to you, the reader. Thank you for reading this story. Thank you for your time, and for taking a chance on a newbie writer. You've made this dream come true for me by reading Jay and Holly's story. I hope you enjoyed it. I loved writing it, and there are plenty more stories and hot guys to come! Please consider leaving a review. It is one of the best ways to help an author. I never realised just how helpful they can be until I started on this journey.

Until the next book,

Elle x

Printed in Great Britain
by Amazon